THE BARE ESSENTIALS

"Frankie said you wanted me to stop by, any time. So, I'm here." She slipped the raincoat from her shoulders and let it pool at her feet on the wood floor. He swallowed hard and stumbled backward, hitting the door with a thump.

Nothing like black lace bikini underwear to make an impression.

"So, husband, where do we start?"

"About the marriage thing—"

"Makes me feel a whole lot better about what I'm going to do to you tonight." With great fanfare, she pulled the handcuffs from her purse and dangled them on her index finger. "Where's the bedroom?"

"Uh, it's kind of a mess. Maybe we should talk out here." He didn't move.

"Talk? Funny, I didn't picture you as the talking type."

"And I didn't picture you as the man-eating type."

"Well, then we're both pleasantly surprised."

Got a Hold on You

Pat White

LOVE SPELL NEW YORK CITY

To the professional wrestlers who sacrifice their bodies and personal lives to entertain the masses. I'd especially like to dedicate this book to The Blue Blazer.

LOVE SPELL®

August 2003

Published by

Dorchester Publishing Co., Inc.
276 Fifth Avenue
New York, NY 10001

ISBN 0-505-52549-6

The name "Love Spell" and its logo are trademarks of Dorchester Publishing Co., Inc.

Printed in the United States of America.

Visit us on the web at www.dorchesterpub.com.

ACKNOWLEDGMENTS

I couldn't have written this book without the support of my friends in Chicago-North RWA whose belief in my talent helped me believe in myself. A special thanks to Michelle Hoppe, who was with me from the beginning in Bettendorf, and Karen Galvin, who said her favorite books were those that made her laugh. Thanks to Suzanne Brockmann, who read the book when she was sick and said it cheered her up. The ultimate compliment! Thank you, Suz, for our friendship.

I am very grateful to my agent Evan Fogelman for the pep talks, and editor Alicia Condon for taking a chance on my story.

Finally, thanks to my sons Patrick and Jeffrey, for believing in heroes, and Larry, my soul mate, for believing in our love. I'll love you forever, babe, even without the pink tights.

Got a Hold on You

Chapter One

"I said fringe, not feathers! I can't go out there wearing feathers. I'll look like a freaking ostrich!"

Frankie McGee stared up at the nearly seven-foot-tall pro wrestler and realized God was punishing her. This was her penance for not going to confession, forgetting to floss, and refusing to date the men Nana Cooper picked out for her. Yep, Frankie's hell and damnation would be served sewing seams and sequins for the most outrageous group of men walking the face of the earth. At least it would this week.

"Are you mentally challenged or something?" The Purple Panther howled. His echo bounced off the gray cement walls of the cramped dressing room buried beneath the stands of Chicago's suburban Lancaster Stadium.

"I step into the ring in twenty minutes. I can't go out there looking like this." He spun around, the wisp of lavender taffeta floating in a perfect circle around his bare, muscular torso.

He was right, it wasn't his color.

"Fringe. F-r-i-n-g-e," he said.

1

He could spell. She was impressed.

The Purple Panther ripped the cape from his shoulders and tossed it at her. It landed on her head. If he only knew she had the power to send him packing to the local zoo. But no one could discover her true mission. Not yet, anyway.

"It better be fixed by the time they cue my music, or Sullivan's gonna can you before you can say 'headlock.' "

The sound of giant feet stomping across the hard cement floor was followed by a crash. Then silence.

"Is it safe?" she asked her fellow seamstress, who'd kept silent during the tirade.

"He's gone," sixty-year-old Maxine Parker said.

Frankie snapped the purple cape from her head and glared at the door.

"Overgrown ape," she commented, sifting through the pile of sewing supplies on the worktable. This wasn't supposed to happen. She wasn't supposed to have any contact with the wrestling wackos.

"Men aren't supposed to know the difference between feathers and fringe," she muttered under her breath.

"These ain't no ordinary men, hon. Haven't you figured that out by now?" Maxine adjusted her bifocals.

"No, I guess not." But then, Frankie McGee was still trying to figure out how she'd ended up here in the first place. Then she remembered: good old-fashioned duty. Or was it guilt?

Frankie thumbed her tortoise-rimmed glasses to the bridge of her nose. She snatched the ripper and dug the sharp edge along the feathered seam.

"They get a little nervous before a big match, is all," Maxine said. "It's only normal."

"There is nothing normal about this business."

"Now watch it there, toots. Pro wrestling's been my home for more than forty years."

"Right, sorry."

Real smart. Insult the one semi-normal person in this

crazy business. "Semi" being the key word. After all, how many sixty-year-old women would wear a skin-tight, fuchsia leotard and tights, topped by a black sweatshirt with gold lettering that read "Rock 'em, sock 'em, knock 'em"? Maxine's graying hair was swept back into a French knot highlighted by pink glitter and a silver bow. The woman went to great lengths to gussy herself up to sit in a back room of yet another stadium, waiting for the next prima donna to complain about a crooked seam or missed sequin.

"What do you think?" Maxine held up a pair of faux snake-skin trunks. They looked like they'd fit a ten-year-old.

"You sure you got the right size?"

"Too big?"

"Too small."

"Oh, pshaw. These are just right for the Thundering Tornado to show off his package," Maxine said with a wink of her false eyelashes.

Frankie ground her teeth and continued her rip and pull of the purple threads. The Panther had said twenty minutes, and she had a feeling that if he could spell, he could probably count.

Just for this week, she reminded herself, the most critical week of the year according to Uncle Joe, owner of the ridiculous Wrestling Heroes and Kings. Then Frankie could get back to her real job of figuring out how to save her uncle's company from financial ruin.

Hell, she could do anything for one week.

The metal door flew open, and Uncle Joe scrambled inside, slamming the door with a crash.

"We're ruined, completely ruined! This was our big chance." He plastered his portly, middle-aged body against the cement wall, his wrinkled dress shirt gaping at his belly.

Frankie glanced at Maxine.

"Normal," she said.

"It was the perfect story line! It would break new ground,

3

bring our old viewers back from Steel's Outrageous Wrestling. Fans want drama, drama, drama!"

He paced the eight-by-fifteen-foot room, pulling at his thinning hair until it stuck out on top like a porcupine on a good hair day. Frankie glanced at Maxine, who was busy tightening the Tornado's trunks. She obviously didn't think there was anything to worry about. Then again, she probably didn't know about WHAK's financial problems. No one did.

She studied her uncle, his eyes bulging, his lips quivering. He always was one for the dramatic. Still, it might be serious this time.

"What's the problem?" she asked, pinning a strand of purple fringe to the taffeta.

"The new writers came up with a fantastic story line. Tatianna the Tigress is sultry, sexy, wild, the perfect reason for Black Jack to leave his wife!"

"I still can't believe you're exploiting that man's four-year-old divorce to boost ticket sales," Maxine scolded.

"Jack's career needs help. It's my job to keep these guys in the game as long as possible."

"It's your job to make money off their blood, sweat, and tears, you mean," Maxine retorted.

Uncle Joe paced to the wall and conked his head three times against the cement. Frankie looked for blood.

"Take it easy, Maxine," Frankie said. "It's not like any of this is real and the talent gets hurt."

The older woman pursed her bright pink lips and stabbed the snake-skin trunks with her needle. Uncle Joe moaned and pulled on his hair until Frankie thought it would come out in clumps between his fingers.

"Out with it, Uncle Joe," Frankie demanded. After all, troubleshooting was her specialty.

He whirled around. "Tatianna's escaped!"

"Escaped? She's a woman, not a trained seal."

"No matter. She's gone. Got a lead on a sitcom looking for six-foot women who can bench press five hundred pounds. She high-tailed it to California. It's over. We're ruined." He slid down the wall and buried his face in his age-spotted hands.

"You mean to tell me there isn't another female in this entire company who can fill in until you find another actress?"

"No, no, no." He shook his head. "They've all been seen in one form or another. I can't have Monica Moonbeam or Luscious Leeza come strutting out on Jack's arm. There is no one else. Jezebel's got the night off, Cookie's already going out on Louie the Lawman's arm, and Amazing Amanda is helping in Clyde's grudge match against the Titanic. What am I going to do? This was our chance, Francine, a chance to redeem ourselves. I promised the fans high-stakes drama in the main event, high-stakes drama!"

A knock interrupted his panic attack.

"I'm looking for Mr. Sullivan," Bill Billings, Uncle Joe's assistant, called through the door.

Uncle Joe ran his hands through his hair, smoothing it back into place. He cleared his throat and pulled open the door.

"Just checking on the costumes, Bill. What's up?" His voice was deeper, more authoritative, than a moment before.

"Wanted to know if you'd figured out our Tatianna prob—" Bill stopped in midsentence, and his gray eyes locked onto Frankie. "Perfect!"

The hair rose on the back of her neck.

She looked at Maxine, then at Uncle Joe, then back at Bill. All three smiled the same, devilish smile that made her scan the room for a trap door. Unfortunately, she'd have to get by Bill first, formerly known as Bill "the Bomber" Billings.

"Uh, I have to get this cape to the Panther before he rips my head off." Frankie started for the door.

"This is exactly why you're the number-one guy in the business, Sully," the Bomber said, eyeing Frankie. Why did she feel like he could see all the way through her navy suit jacket, cotton blouse and camisole to her lace bra?

"I'll see that this gets to the Purple Panther." Bill swiped the cape from her hand and grinned, a gold-capped tooth sparkling front and center.

He shut the door, and Frankie readied for battle.

"No," she said, squaring off to face Uncle Joe.

He clasped his hands together and fell to his knees. "Francine, please. Your mother and I—"

"Don't you dare bring her into this. If she knew I was here, I'd be disowned."

"I'd better get this to the Tornado before he throws a hissy." Maxine slipped past them and out the door.

Frankie slapped her hands on her hips and glared at her uncle. "I've jeopardized my job to bail you out of trouble. I told my boss I had to take care of a sick relative. I couldn't tell him what I was really doing. My God, if anyone knew I was associated with this—this *business* I'd be the laughingstock of the industry. And to think that I've lied to Bradley—"

"I did it for you, Francine."

"You did what for me?"

"I built you a legacy."

"A legacy of debt, you mean."

"But I had good intentions."

Frankie made for the door, but Uncle Joe caught her arm.

"You know I'd do anything for you. When things were good, I shared my success, didn't I? I loaned you money for school, bought you your first car."

"A hearse."

"It ran, didn't it?"

"It was pink with blue pinstripes!"

"I've always done my best for you," he said, groveling. "I was there for you when that no-good father of yours was off—"

6

"Enough! It won't work this time, Uncle Joe. I have to draw the line somewhere."

"Think about your honor, your integrity."

"A lot of honor I'd have parading myself in front of twenty thousand people on some idiot's arm!"

She ripped open the steel door. Uncle Joe threw himself, spread-eagled, across the doorway.

"Christmas, 1972!" he cried.

"Out of my way."

"Remember what I got you?"

"No," she lied. How could she ever forget the Ice Skating Barbie he'd given her? Dad had promised to bring it, but she'd learned early not to put too much stock in Dad's promises.

"Your sixteenth birthday! The backstage passes at the U2 concert."

"I don't care."

"Harry the hamster, the autographed Foreigner poster, Cinderella in the school play?"

"Now wait a minute, I earned that part."

Uncle Joe grinned.

"Didn't I?"

"I did everything I could for my favorite niece."

The guilt anchor grew heavier by the minute, pulling her down, down, down. . . .

"All I ask is this one thing. Tonight's show is crucial! It could mean going network, big ratings, big advertisers!"

"I won't do this. I have self-respect."

"Think about your poor, poor uncle."

Clink. Clink. The anchor hit rock bottom.

A knock stayed her spiraling guilt trip.

"Is it safe in there?" Maxine called.

"Come in, Max." Uncle Joe opened the door.

He had Frankie right where he wanted her. And he knew it.

He sandwiched her hand between his weathered fingers. "It would mean a lot to me."

"So does my reputation."

"But"—his eyes darted from the scraps of material on the sewing table to the overhead fluorescent lights, back to Frankie—"you'll be wearing a mask."

Maxine coughed.

"No one will even know who you are. It's perfect. You're perfect." He studied her through framed hands as if considering her for a movie debut.

"I thought Tatianna was six feet tall with flaming red hair." On a good day she stood five-three.

"You're better."

"I'm female."

A nervous giggle escaped his lips. He squeezed her hand, then made for the door. "Max will fix you up, snap, snap. She'll make the costume fit you just right."

"I don't have the costume."

He pulled a plastic bag from the inside of his suit coat and tossed it at Maxine.

"Hey!" Frankie protested, smelling a setup.

"Forty-five minutes." He tapped his watch and shut the door, a victorious whistle escaping his lips.

"Sneaky, manipulative, guilt-tripping uncle!" she cried after him.

"Come on, let's get you sized." Maxine opened the bag and pulled out the contents. "This can't be right."

Frankie caught sight of the five-inch triangle of leopard-skin material dangling from Maxine's fingers.

"Whoever heard of a spotted tiger?" Max said.

"My life is over." Frankie's knees wobbled, and she collapsed into the folding chair. "A mask, Uncle Joe said there was a mask."

Maxine tipped the bag upside down. It was empty.

"No mask." Frankie slouched in her chair.

"Not to worry. I'll whip one up lickity split. Something plain, yet exotic, maybe with two pointed ears." She crooked her fingers on top of her head to demonstrate.

Frankie jumped to her feet. "I can't do this."

"Sure you can. You're a good girl. Good girls do these things because they love their uncles."

Frankie fisted her hands by her sides and paced the small dressing room. Uncle Joe had always been there for her. Always.

"The other Tatianna was bigger than you, so we'll have to make a few nips and tucks here and there. Wouldn't want those bosoms of yours to come tumbling out on national TV."

"Work on the mask first. Work on the mask," Frankie pleaded. Anonymity was her only hope.

"You're gonna have to get rid of those glasses. You can see without them, can't ya?"

"I've got tinted contacts in my purse. I hate them."

Trotting from one end of the room to the other, she imagined herself before the board of directors at Smith and Barnes, her biggest client at present. How on earth would she explain prancing nearly naked in front of half a billion people on national TV? Sure, they'd take her next financial analysis seriously. About as seriously as a two-year-old running for Congress.

"Done," Maxine said.

"So fast?"

"They don't call me Maxine the Miraculous for nothing."

She stared at the costume, which looked like it was tailor made for a pre-pubescent teen.

"Go on, get dressed." Maxine shoved it at her.

"I must be out of my mind." She swiped the costume and ripped off the price tag. "Cheapskate," she muttered, glancing at the $17.95 clearance sticker. She went behind the curtain and stripped off her clothes, her toes chilled by the cement floor. A whole lot more of her was going to be chilled in a minute. She stepped into the panties, clasped the bra in front, then slid it around and adjusted herself. She was no Dolly Parton, but she wasn't a washboard either.

"Maxine, I think you made the top too small." She stepped out from behind the curtain.

"Well, whadda ya know. Never would've guessed you had such a round figure underneath all those clothes of yours. I could probably let out the darts a little. But I gotta finish the skirt."

Hope flared in her chest. "A skirt?"

"Sure. We wouldn't let you go out there all bare-legged."

All wasn't lost. Frankie threw on her navy suit jacket to ward off the chill.

The door burst open with a crash. "Where's my cape?" the Purple Panther demanded.

Frankie jumped to her feet. "Hold your shorts, you overgrown slug of testosterone! The Bomber took off with your bloody cape, so go claw his eyes out!"

"Oh, uh, sure, uh, sorry." The Panther paled and backed quickly out of the dressing room, as if he thought she might brain him with the metal folding chair.

"You're a natural," Maxine said, her gray-blue eyes glowing with admiration.

"Don't look at me like that. I don't belong here. I belong in a boardroom, impressing the directors with plans to consolidate and raise the bottom line."

"Oh, you'll impress them with your bottom all right. Skirt's done." She held up the "skirt," a wisp of sheer black lace trimmed in feathers.

She swallowed hard. "I'm going to be sick."

"Nerves. Got something for that too." Maxine dumped out her silver-studded bag. A dozen kinds of lipstick tumbled onto the table, along with a cylinder of breath spray, two backup sets of false eyelashes and a chartreuse feather boa.

"Here ya go, hon." She handed Frankie a dull tin flask.

"What is it?"

"Homemade brew. Never failed me yet. Swallow down and pick out your shoes."

"Uh, thanks, Max, but I don't really drink."

"How's your tummy feel?"

"Like a swarm of butterflies just took up residence."

"Then drink up. A healthy swig should do it."

Well, if anyone knew how to cure nerves, it was an old showgirl like Max. Frankie closed her eyes, pinched her nose, and took a ladylike nip that turned into a generous gulp, thanks to Max tipping the flask. The concoction scorched her throat. She coughed, hiccuped, and gagged, struggling to breathe.

Max slapped her back. "That a girl. All better."

Sure, if Frankie could get her eyes to stop watering.

"Wouldn't hurt to smell a little sexy, get you in the mood to perform. Here." Maxine aimed a small, red bottle in Frankie's direction and squirted.

Frankie coughed again and waved her hand. "What is it?"

"Pandora's Passion." She shoved the perfume, along with her other treasures, back into her purse and started picking through the box of shoes.

"What size, hon?"

"Seven."

"Got an eight. Close enough." She tossed a pair of gold, three-inch spiked heels at Frankie.

"Take 'em for a spin while I whip up the mask."

Frankie slipped on the shoes and admired her feet, not used to wearing anything other than half-inch business pumps or her Keds. With great effort, she stood, then wobbled and tumbled her way a few steps into the concrete wall.

"Hips, hon! Hips! Swing 'em when you walk!" Maxine coached.

She couldn't remember the last time she'd swung her hips, if ever. Pushing away from the wall, she fought for balance, shuffled a hoppity-skip across the room and fell across the worktable, facedown in a pile of flaming pink feathers. "Max?"

"Yeah, hon?"

"I'm not nervous anymore."

"Good girl."

"I also can't focus."

"I don't need a Goddamn gimmick," Jack said, securing the knee brace with a quick tug of the strap. He figured the joint was good for about another year. Then he'd have to go under the knife.

"Part of the show, Jack. Just wait till you see what we've got planned," Billings said.

"The last time you said that, I ended up strapped to the front of a Zamboni." He pulled the skin-tight black leggings over his brace, then reached for his socks and boots.

"This is better, even better." Billings's eyes gleamed.

That meant trouble. "Don't tell me, another stripper match?"

"Nope," Billings's smile broadened.

"Dancing bears?" Hell that would be tamer than some of the stuff he heard they were planning to boost ratings.

"Not even close. We found you the perfect Tatianna."

He shoved his size twelve foot into the black boot and glared at the former wrestler. "Dammit, Bill! I'm not going out there with some flaky bimbo on my arm just to appease the old man."

"It's about the fans, Jack. Never forget that."

How could he? The same fans who'd once paid to see a good old-fashioned rasslin' match, now expected to see sex and blood for their $30 ticket. At least that was Sullivan's line.

But it would all be over soon. He was nearing the end of his contract, and the light at the end of the tunnel burned brighter than ever. The last five years had been hell. Thank God he would finally be free of the insanity and live a normal life.

"We're trying her out tonight to test the new angle," Bill said, walking toward the locker-room door. "She'll be waiting in the Monkey Tunnel."

"Great. Wonderful. Fantastic." He jerked the boot lace with deadly force, wondering when it all started to go south and why he hadn't seen it coming long before now. The traditional wrestlers were slowly being pushed out by the exhibitionists, the superstars of sports entertainment who didn't know the difference between a pile driver and a screwdriver.

It was time to get out. No doubt about it. His body was cashed and his mind was wandering. Not good when you were waving a three-hundred-pound opponent over your head. It had taken nearly twenty years, but Jack was finally ready to hang up his boots. More than ready.

"Hudson, you want to try something different tonight?"

He glanced at Neurosis, tonight's opponent in the main event. The kid's orange hair was pulled into six short ponytails, like bursts of flame escaping his scalp.

"Different as in you win?" Jack said. At least Sullivan hadn't taken the belt away from him. His reign would make WHAK history tonight—champion for fifteen weeks straight, taking on any and all challengers. It felt good to be champion.

"Very funny, old man." Neurosis drew the word "panic" across his chest in red marker. "Let's try some new stuff. I learned a move from the cruiser weights. I do a back swan dive over you from the turnbuckle, land on your shoulders, dive down between your legs, flip you over into a Carter Crush . . ."

Flipping, flying, twirling. Jack's head started to spin. This wasn't wrestling. Not the wrestling he knew. Not the wrestling Butch taught him some twenty-five years ago when he pulled him off the streets and threw him down to a wrestling mat.

"Keep it simple, kid. I'm still healing." Jack ran an open palm across his rib cage.

"Don't heal as quick as you used to, eh?" the punk taunted.

"Watch it, kid, or you'll end up on the receiving end of

13

a Black Jack Banger that'll scramble your brains."

"Don't get your undies in a bunch, old man. So, is this supposed to end in a pin, submission, or disqualification?"

"It's no DQ match. How about a count out?"

"I'll go over the top rope onto the announcer's table. I can take out that jerk announcer Prince Priceless while I'm at it."

"Not bad." Jack smiled, remembering Prince's below-the-belt remarks on last week's show about Jack needing to be admitted to a nursing home. "I'll start with an Irish whip to the corner followed by a few kicks to your ribs. I'll pull you to your feet and do a suplex from the second rope. I'll cover you for the pin and pass you the next set of moves. Let's end it with me shouldering you out of the ring." Jack adjusted his elbow pads and grabbed his drover-style leather jacket.

"And the girls?" Neurosis asked.

"I don't care what they do as long as they stay out of the ring." He snatched the black Stetson from the overhead rack and fingered the picture of his dream cabin tucked inside the rim, his good luck charm. Soon. He'd be free soon.

Neurosis slipped a torn, black shirt over his marked up chest. "Edible Eve isn't going to be too happy if she can't be part of the action."

Jack glared at the kid.

"Okay, okay. I'll tell her to stay out of the ring."

"Although . . ." Jack ambled toward the door and hesitated. "What happens outside the ring is fair game."

"All right! The cats go at it for the crowd. Who's playing Tatianna?"

"Never met her." He slipped the cowboy hat onto his head. "But I hear she's a hot one."

"So, Eve can let loose on her?"

"I don't see why not." Hell, these actresses got paid pretty well for their twenty minutes of fame.

Neurosis rubbed his hands together. "This is going to be one helluva match."

"You can say that again."

And with any luck, it would be one of Jack's last.

Chapter Two

He was huge. Overpowering. Intimidating as hell. And she wanted her mommy.

Frankie stared into Black Jack Hudson's dark green eyes and tried to swallow. Her mouth was as dry as the Sahara.

"You getting this, lady?" He took a step closer.

She backed up against the cold cement wall, breathing in the scent of leather and sweat. He'd been talking to her, but she hadn't heard a word he'd said.

"Stay out of the ring, got it? I don't care what you and Edible Eve do on the sidelines, but if you put your pretty little ass into the squared circle, I swear I'll toss you over the top rope myself."

All she could do was stare at the enormous monster. He was cloaked in black from his cowboy hat to his boots; a day's growth of beard stubbled his tanned skin; and long, wet curls of rich black hair trailed down past his shoulders.

Wild was a tame word to describe Black Jack Hudson.

She finally swallowed the dry ball in her throat. Nothing to be afraid of, she told herself. He was just a dumb jock.

16

Contrary to the belief of the seventeen thousand screaming fans just outside the tunnel, she knew that wrestling was four parts vaudeville to one part athleticism, if that.

"Does this one even speak English?" Black Jack asked the Bomber.

"She's a little nervous, aren't ya, Tatianna? Here, Mr. Sullivan wanted me to give you this." The Bomber held out a black whip. She stared at the strap of leather. What was she supposed to do with it? Defend herself against Mr. Black Jack?

"You're giving this idiot a weapon? Great thinking, Bill." Black Jack glanced down the tunnel toward the ring.

"Here, like this." The Bomber snapped the whip, and she nearly jumped out of her spiked heels.

"Your turn."

She took the whip and snapped away. It fell limp to the floor.

"Think mean, kid, angry, ferocious, like a tigress." The Bomber growled and bared his teeth. "You try."

She scrunched up her nose, snapped her teeth and growled.

"Sounds like my truck running on three cylinders," Black Jack said.

"You'll get better with practice," the Bomber assured her.

She was pathetic, and she knew it. Okay, so maybe she didn't have the guttural sound of a wild animal, but she could sure as hell learn to use this lethal piece of leather. She wound up for another crack.

"So what's the story?" Black Jack asked the Bomber.

"She's your sex slave."

"What!" Black Jack spun around.

The whip snapped, and the tail sliced the Bomber's thigh.

"Sonofabitch! Watch it with that thing."

"I'm his what?"

"His sex slave." He rubbed at his leg. "Jack caught you in an African desert and dragged you back to civilization.

17

See, you were abandoned twenty-five years ago by your parents while on safari. You roamed the desert for five days before a family of tigers found you and—"

"Enough!" Black Jack put up his hand to silence the Bomber. "I'm glad Butch isn't here to see this."

"Who's Butch?" Frankie asked.

Black Jack clenched his jaw and stared down the tunnel.

"It's a great story line," the Bomber continued. "We've got lots of places to go with it, especially at the next pay-per-view when Tiger Man comes back from the desert to claim his woman. In the meantime, you take her into the ring and parade her around. The announcer will give a quick spiel about her being a wild animal, then you tame her with a kiss."

She jumped back and automatically jerked the whip. It stung her toes. A kiss? Uncle Joe hadn't said anything about having to kiss this beast.

"That's it, we're on." Black Jack motioned to her. She stuck out the whip in defense.

"That's my music, cupcake. It's time for us to go entertain the masses."

"I can't."

"Come again?"

"I just can't."

"Nerves. It'll pass the minute we step out into the arena." He took a step closer.

"Stay back." She tried baring her teeth at him.

"I don't have time for this. That's my music. My fans expect me to come strutting out there any second now."

"Go. Without me."

"Sorry, cupcake. No can do."

He lunged and she snapped, but somehow she ended up over his shoulder like a sack of grain.

"Put me down!" she cried, swinging her feet.

"Knock it off before you stab me with those things."

She kicked harder. He smacked her behind.

"Hey!" she cried at the sting. She pummeled his shoulder blades. He squeezed her bottom tighter.

"You ever been spanked on national television? Because if that's an experience you don't want, I'd suggest you calm your ass down."

She stilled and glanced at the Bomber. "Help," she squeaked as Black Jack marched through the tunnel toward the arena.

"You'll be fine," he called after her. "The fans are hot for you tonight, Hudson!"

"Yeah, yeah." He gripped Tiger Lady's thighs in an arm lock. What would they think of next?

Stepping through the nitrogen-generated fog, he strode down the ramp. Luckily the bimbo had given up on the fight, probably petrified that Jack would make good on his threat to give her a good spanking in front of God and everybody. Good thing she didn't know him very well.

He marched toward the ring and waved at the crowd— the little boy in the front row with his hands plastered over his ears, the pack of grown men raising their beers in salute to their favorite star. He'd normally reach out and slap high fives, but tonight he didn't dare get too close with Tiger Lady over his shoulder. The crazy broad might poke some-body's eye out with those spiked heels. She wasn't the most coordinated actress he'd ever worked with.

A throng of young boys caught his eye as they flagged him down with a homemade sign. "Black Jack Attack" was printed in thick black letters on bright blue poster board. His heart swelled with pride at being a hero for these kids. He took that role seriously, stressing hard work and faith in one's self. After all, he'd been there once, searching, lost and alone. Thank God for Butch. If Jack could offer these kids one ounce of what Butch had given him, Jack's sorry life would be worth something.

He smiled at the kids and tipped his hat, his personal sign of endearment. They screamed even louder. He cringed inside at the thought of tonight's story line: Black

Jack snags a wild woman to be his sex slave.

He suddenly wanted to drop Tiger Lady on her ass.

But a show was a show. Besides, who was he to say what would boost ratings? He wasn't a promoter or a business-man. Hell, he'd never made it through college. No, he was the talent, plain and simple. According to Sullivan, Jack's job was to trust the promoter's vision, follow orders, and fight. Nothing more. Only, the past few years he couldn't help wondering what he fought for.

The roar grew to a fevered pitch as he approached the ring. The fans were hot; Billings wasn't kidding. They were salivating for a good fight. He just hoped his knee didn't give out on him before the twenty-minute mark. He also hoped the punk stepping into the ring didn't go crazy and do one of his whirling dervish routines. Jack simply didn't have the patience for that crap tonight.

With a firm grip on her soft behind, he swung Tiger Lady down from his shoulder onto the edge of the ring.

"Get up there and hold the ropes open for me."

Even through that ridiculous black mask he noticed her cornflower-blue eyes widen to the size of silver dollars as she scanned the crowd. She blinked, but didn't move.

"Where'd they find you, anyway?" Not waiting for an answer, he hoisted himself up and stepped through the ropes. He reached over the top rope and gripped her under her arms, pulling her into the ring beside him. Sully had fallen down on the job this time. Tigresses were supposed to be tall, lanky and seductive. This one reminded him of Allison Waters from the eighth grade, on the short side with curves everywhere. She also had as much coordina-tion as Allison, who broke her nose walking into the flag-pole at school.

"Ladies and gentlemen, boys and girls, please welcome Wrestling Heroes and Kings champion, Black Jack Hudson with special guest, Taaaaaaa-tiannaaaaahhh!"

Jack led Tiger Lady to the center of the squared circle and she stumbled, her scantily clad body slamming into his chest. Well, no time like the present. Bill's exact words were "tame her with a kiss."

His hand to the small of her back, he pulled her against him and covered her mouth with a claiming kiss. She tasted better than he'd expected, kinda like those peppermint candies Aunt Vera used to put out at Christmas. Nah. Don't go there.

The crowed went wild, the cheers buzzing in his head. He broke the kiss and glanced into the captured cat lady's eyes. They'd glazed over, and she'd gone limp in his arms.

"Snap out of it. I'm here to fight, not hold you up."

He didn't see it coming. Hadn't a clue she even had the strength. Tiger Lady threw a tight right cross that resonated in his jaw.

"Looks like she's not so tame after all, Black Jack!" Prince Priceless called over the sound system.

She jerked away, but he gripped her wrist in a firm hold. He knew what Sully would have him do next to beef up the drama. Jack also knew who he really was, somewhere, deep down inside.

Pulling away from him, she glared in defiance, digging those ridiculous heels into the mat. The lunacy of the entire scene struck a chord of melancholy in his gut. Nothing was the way it should be.

He let go of her wrist and she stumbled backwards, swinging her arms to regain balance. Instead she landed flat on her behind. With any luck she'd be PO'd about the kiss and high-tail it outta here. Fine by him. He didn't need a sidekick, especially not out here in the ring.

He shucked the leather coat and passed it and the Stetson over the top rope to the stage assistant. As Neurosis's crazy music blasted in sync with blue and orange flashing lights, Tiger Lady crawled backward to the ring post and gripped the ropes. Snapping her head from side to side, she acted as if she expected an assault. She played terror pretty well. Maybe she wasn't such a bad actress after all.

Wrapping his arms around the top rope, he leaned back

21

to stretch out his shoulders, waiting for Neurosis to make his grand entrance. The kid had a certain style; he had to give him that. The shrill sound of sirens and bells grew to an eardrum-shattering pitch. Tiger Lady plastered her gloved hands over her ears and squinted her eyes. She'd better get out of the damn ring before the punk catapulted himself into the center of the action. Jack knew the kid didn't like to wait until the official ring of the bell to throw the first punch, and Jack didn't want to worry about tripping over Tiger Lady.

Neurosis approached the spring device that would send him flying into the squared circle. Jack stormed over to Tiger Lady.

"Get out of the ring!" he shouted at her, competing with the blare of sirens.

She couldn't hear him. He reached down to pull her to her feet. The second his hands made contact with the bare flesh of her shoulders, she lunged at him with a cry, swinging her arms like a mad woman. He lost his balance, falling backward over the top rope, Tiger Lady in his arms. They hit the outside mat covering the unforgiving cement with a thump. Sure, Jack was used to falling out of the ring, but he wasn't ready for this tumble, and he surely wasn't prepared to cushion a freaked-out Tigress.

Shocked and embarrassed, he lay there for a good minute, listening to the crowd heat up with excitement. His ego wasn't too pleased with this turn of events. Being taken out by a little, eye-gouging cat woman would take months to live down in the locker room.

Opening his eyes, he stared at the overhead fluorescent lights. He was getting too old for this.

"You guys done down there?" Neurosis asked, staring over the top rope. Only then did Jack realize that Tiger Lady covered him like a blanket, straddling his groin with those shapely, yet well-toned legs of hers.

Tiger Lady sighed, her warm breath tickling his neck.

This was definitely not part of the plan. Nor was the stirring below his waist.

With flattened palms, she pushed against his chest and gazed at him.

"You okay?" he asked.

"I think so."

"Good, then you'd better get off me before I embarrass myself."

Those cornflower blue eyes narrowed to slits. He saw it coming this time and caught her right wrist, then her left before those gloved hands of hers could make contact.

"I'm getting real tired of being beat up before the match even starts."

He jackknifed into a sitting position and she squeaked, but couldn't free herself. Their faces nearly touched, and a sharp, bitter scent tickled his nostrils.

"Let me go!" she growled, and this time she sounded like all cylinders had clicked just right.

"No slapping."

She glared.

"Are we having a match here or what?" Neurosis called down to them.

"Hold your ponytail," Jack said, then looked into the woman's eyes. They burned fire.

"I'm letting go now," he said.

He slowly loosened his grip and she scrambled off him. He got to his feet, cursing the day he'd failed to add the words "creative control" to his contract. And he'd thought being a hood ornament for a Zamboni had been bad.

A sharp sting sliced his back.

"What the—"

He spun around and caught the thin edge of the whip just as Tiger Lady let a second snap fly.

"That's it!" He yanked the whip, pulling her flat against his chest. "You're on my side, got it?"

She squirmed against him, squeaking and snarling. What a feisty little thing. With closed fists, she hauled off and

23

swung at him, anywhere, everywhere, nearly catching his jaw a second time with a gloved fist. He didn't get paid enough for this kind of abuse.

"I don't know where Sully found you," he muttered, dragging her by the wrist to the ring post. "But after this match I'm going to make sure he sends you right back where you came from, ratings or no ratings."

He ripped a spare TV cable from the floor and wrapped it around her waist. The crowd roared with delight. Tiger Lady kicked and swung, a few punches making contact. He didn't care. She was a menace. Wrestling was dangerous enough without having to worry about being ambushed by a crazy woman. He knotted the cable firmly at the small of her back, trying to ignore the tingling of his fingers as they brushed against her bare, soft skin. Securing the other end of the cable to the ring post, he stepped just out of range and pointed an index finger at her face. "Behave."

She swiped at him with a gloved paw and let out a shriek that made her sound like a stuck pig. He couldn't figure this one out. One minute she was too nervous to do her job; the next she acted the consummate tigress, poised and ready to rip out his heart.

"Let's go, Hudson!" Neurosis called.

Jack circled the ring, playing up Neurosis's position close to the ropes, waiting to take unfair advantage when he returned to action.

The referee finally chased Neurosis to the corner and Jack climbed through the ropes. The crowd cheered and chanted, eager for the fight to begin. Neurosis charged, and Jack clotheslined him across the chest. The kid went down, and Jack promptly applied a sleeper hold.

"They're wild tonight," the kid said through clenched teeth.

"You're not kidding." He pretended to tighten the hold, and Neurosis pounded at the mat with his fist in mock frustration.

Neurosis outmaneuvered Jack and delivered a few

punches to his ribs. He ground his teeth. Great. The damned ribs again. It seemed like it took forever for those things to heal.

"Sorry, I forgot," the kid said, just before whipping Jack into the turnbuckle. He hit chest first and fell backward to the mat. This was going to be a long match. Neurosis pinned him to the mat, and the crowd cheered with delight. What the hell? Jack was the baby face, the champion. They shouldn't be cheering his abuse.

Neurosis threw five punches to Jack's forehead. Usually the fans would shout the number of blows a wrestler delivered to his opponent. Not this crowd. It was as if they were completely uninterested in the match.

The crowd screamed, quieted, and screamed again. He glanced at the sea of faces. None of them was focused on the ring. Neurosis froze in midswing, and both men glanced at the attraction.

The women were going at it by the announcer's table.

"They're scooping our heat," the kid said. "That's not fair. I had some really cool stuff planned for this match."

Just then Edible Eve tackled Tatianna, and they both went down.

"Dammit," Jack shoved the kid off of him.

"What the hell?"

"We'd better break it up."

He marched to the ropes faster than he'd intended. Something swirled in his gut. The thought of Tiger Lady going one-on-one with Edible Eve didn't sit right.

As he approached the corner, Neurosis drop-kicked him from behind and he went flying into the turnbuckle. Was anything going to go right tonight? At least he had the presence of mind to cushion the blow with his arm.

He spun on his opponent and readied for the attack. The kid charged, and Jack shouldered him out of the ring as planned. Only this was supposed to happen fifteen minutes into the match. The kid took out Prince Priceless, landing right in his lap. At least Jack got the satisfaction of seeing Prince dethroned.

"Jack! Jack, help!" Tiger Lady cried.

Edible Eve clutched a fistful of Tiger Lady's hair in either hand and was banging her head against the perimeter mat. He slipped through the ropes, but before he could get there, Eve started clawing at Tiger Lady's mask. Something must have snapped because Tiger Lady started kicking and punching . . . for real. Eve shrieked, a horrified look spreading across her heavily made-up face.

Must have been a pride thing, but Eve wouldn't let go of her opponent's hair. It was getting dangerous. He bolted from the ring, glancing over his shoulder at Neurosis, who was still sprawled across Prince's lap. He'd promised Eve a wild night, and she was getting one. More than she'd bargained for, no doubt.

Jack grabbed Eve from behind and placed her gently aside.

"She punched me! Did you see that? She really punched me," Eve cried.

"Calm down. Go help your boy over there."

Eve rubbed her jaw with expertly manicured nails and snarled at Tiger Lady. She stormed off, waving to the crowd.

He turned to Tiger Lady, who visibly trembled. Long, gloved fingers held her mask firmly in place. When she saw him approach, she started to scoot backward, under the ring skirt. He knelt down.

"Are you okay?" he asked above the howls of worked-up fans.

"She tried to kill me." Her lower lip quivered.

He reached out and cupped her chin between his forefinger and thumb. This was it. He was going to lose a couple of fingers.

"Look at me. You're okay," he said, suddenly wanting to see more of her face than blue eyes and bloodred lips.

What was happening to him? He was in the middle of a match for God's sake.

A blow across his shoulders reminded him exactly where he was. Another crash sent him tumbling into the metal steps. Could this night get any stranger? He rolled onto his back. Eve stood over him, wielding the damn bell. Then she turned to Tatianna. He got to his feet and ripped the bell from her hands.

"I said, stay away from her!" he shouted for the audience's benefit.

She skulked away to help Neurosis recover, or at least to extract him from Prince's lap.

The pressure of two hands snaked around his waist from behind. He looked down to see Tatianna's gloved fingers interlace firmly around his midsection. Now what?

He turned to face her, or rather look over her. Even with those stilts, she barely came up to his neck. Her head tipped back; she stared up at him, glassy-eyed. She looked loopy or goofy or something. He couldn't put his finger on it.

"Thanks," she whispered. She took off a glove and touched his cheek. His face burned red hot. The crowd roared.

He could have sworn this was real. Real gratitude, real attraction. Whoa. Back up. This was all just part of the angle. It had to be.

"You're welcome." He gently closed his fingers around her wrist and removed her hand. If there was one thing Jack never got confused about it was the real and unreal facets of his life. The wild story lines and comic characters were pretend, even if the wrestling itself and subsequent injuries were all too real.

Suddenly his breath was cut off by a TV cable snaked around his neck. Neurosis must be back in the saddle.

"Be good," Jack croaked to Tatianna as the punk dragged him five feet, whipping him into a metal guardrail.

Okay, now Jack was back in familiar territory. A head

crash into the stairs, a few kicks to the face, flinging a metal chair for good measure, and this match would be back on track. Only Jack's concentration wasn't quite back to normal.

"In the ring! In the ring!" the referee ordered from the top rope.

The crowd was back with them, cheering when Jack out-maneuvered Neurosis and sent him flying into a group of spectators.

"Black Jack Attack! Black Jack Attack!"

They were getting worked up, all right. He threw the kid over his shoulder and started an atomic drop, but Neurosis pushed himself off and shoved Jack shoulder first into the ring post. He bounced off the metal and ended up falling facedown in Tatianna's lap.

At this point nothing would surprise her, Frankie thought, staring down at Black Jack's mane of black waves. He scrambled off her, color flushing his cheeks.

"Sorry." A half smile curled the left side of his mouth. Was that a dimple?

The roar of the crowd made her head spin, her heart race.

"Black Jack Attack! Black Jack Attack!" the crowd chanted. He got to his feet, but kept looking at her, as if he couldn't quite break the spell. His eyes weren't nearly as dark as before. Or were they?

The orange-haired wrestler hit him from behind, and he went down in front of her. The crazy wrestler sat on Jack's back and interlaced his fingers under his chin, pulling back on his neck. She closed her eyes. Uncle Joe said it was a skill to wrestle without getting really hurt. Her neck ached just looking at the men go at it.

The crowd let loose a roar, and she opened her eyes. The bad guy had ripped a TV monitor from the announcer's table. He was going to crush Jack's skull. No, she couldn't let that happen. Jack wasn't such a bad guy, even if he had dragged her out here over his shoulder, kissed her against

28

her will, and tied her to the ring post. After all, he had saved her from that raving lunatic who nearly ripped her hair out and exposed her true identity.

She searched for a weapon, fumbling under the ring skirt for something, anything. They usually shoved all kinds of supplies under the ring after setup. She remembered that from the one time her mother had let Uncle Joe bring her to work when she was a kid.

She glanced over her shoulder. The crazy wrestler was closing in on Jack, TV monitor in hand. She dug deeper. . . .

"Ah!" She pulled a ten-inch wrench from beneath the ring and raced up behind the orange-haired freak. Okay, so she wasn't strong, but she was accurate.

The crowd roared as Black Jack's opponent raised the monitor above his head. Any second now it would come crashing down on a helpless Black Jack. Under normal circumstances she hated violence. She couldn't even kill a mosquito if it was biting her arm.

Tonight was anything but normal.

She wound up, closed her eyes, and swung. Her fingers sprung open at the feel of metal hitting muscle. At least she thought she'd hit the wrestler's back muscles.

The crowd let loose a collective gasp.

Taking a deep breath, she opened her eyes, and her stomach clenched at the sight of Jack, sprawled facedown on the announcer's table. No, it couldn't be. She had perfect aim, precision wind up.

His psycho opponent shot her a puzzled look, then yanked Jack from the table to the floor, where he covered him.

"One, two, three!" the crowd shouted with the referee's count.

The punk jumped to his feet and caught his female just as she leapt into his arms.

"Ladies and gentlemen, the winner and new WHAK champion, Neurosis!"

Sirens and bells burst her eardrums. She stared down at Jack's lifeless body. Oh, God. She'd killed him. All Uncle Joe wanted her to do was step in for the missing Amazon woman. Dress the part and satisfy the fans. Instead, she killed WHAK's biggest attraction.

The crowd's roars turned into boos, then silence as a paramedic team rolled a stretcher up the aisle.

"Oh, God," she muttered, a part of her wanting to go to him, another part wanting to escape to the safety of her real life.

"God, what have I done?"

The paramedics shifted Jack's limp body onto a back-board, then placed him on the stretcher. They wheeled him past, the crowd hushed with worry, her ears ringing with panic. This couldn't be. Black Jack had to be okay; Uncle Joe couldn't lose his company, she couldn't go to jail. It would be awfully hard to share a quiet dinner with her future fiancé from a cell in Joliet.

"No!" She chased after the stretcher, sprinting about ten feet then abruptly snapping back and landing on her fanny. The damn TV cable was still knotted at her waist. She shifted it around front, ripped off her gloves and dug her nails into Black Jack's expertly crafted knot. Panic took hold as the medical crew wheeled Jack through the narrow Monkey Tunnel and out of sight.

"No! No!" She pulled, she tugged. No dice. "Someone cut this thing!"

The crowd stared at her in amazement. The security men restrained fans who, no doubt, wanted to string her up for murdering their hero.

No, he can't die. She'd be locked up for twenty to life and her uncle would end up selling shoelaces on street corners. Besides, Black Jack was kinda cute.

"I'm having a breakdown!" she cried, ripping off her shoe and sticking a spiked heel into the knot. "You can do any-thing if you set your mind to it, you can do anything if you set your mind to it." Where was Maxine when she needed her? The knot finally came free.

Frankie took off toward the stretcher, kicked off her other shoe and caught it in midsprint. She raced through the Monkey Tunnel to the back of the arena and glanced right, then left. The paramedics wheeled the stretcher through Gate Six, and the door slammed behind them.

"Wait!" She chased after him.

A shoe gripped in either hand, she sprinted through the exit just as an EMT closed the ambulance door.

"I'm going with you."

"Frankie! Frankie!" Uncle Joe called from behind her. "It was wonderful! Spectacular! Sensational!"

The paramedic blocked the ambulance door. "We've got it under control, ma'am."

"No, but you don't understand. I . . . I . . ." What? She was the one who'd crushed the victim's skull? "I have to go with him and make sure he's okay."

"Sorry, ma'am."

Uncle Joe put a hand on her shoulder.

"Uncle Joe, I need to ride in the ambulance."

"You're a good girl, Frankie. But your job's done now. Let the professionals take over."

"I have to get in there."

Uncle Joe's face lit up. She didn't care what angle was brewing behind his twinkling gray-blue eyes; she had to make things right, had to make sure Black Jack would live to fight another day.

"Of course you need to ride in the ambulance." He motioned to a cameraman. A light above the camera flashed on, and Frankie squinted against its blinding shine.

"Go on, let her in," Uncle Joe directed the ambulance driver.

The paramedic hesitated.

"Out of my way. I'm . . . I'm his woman," she blurted out.

The camera's round lens widened as the paramedic

31

opened the door and helped her climb into the ambulance. She shifted onto the padded bench next to Jack's lifeless body, afraid to touch him, horrified at what she'd done. The door slammed shut and she glanced up, catching sight of the camera's black lens peering through the window.

She looked at Black Jack. Really looked. A goose egg the size of a baseball swelled above his left eye; his forehead was beaded with sweat.

"He's dying, isn't he?"

"Doubtful." The paramedic checked his vitals. "Probably a concussion. Won't know how bad until he wakes up." Gray foam blocks framed the wrestler's head, which was held steady by a white strap.

She caressed Jack's cheek with her fingertips. "You'll be okay," she whispered. His skin felt so warm, so damp. "Are you sure he's not in a coma?"

"I'm not sure of anything, ma'am."

She stroked his eyebrow with the pad of her thumb. A moan rumbled from deep in his chest, and he turned his head toward her touch.

"Whatever you're doing, it's bringing him around," the paramedic said.

"Shhh, it's okay." She placed her palm to his cheek.

Black Jack's eyes fluttered open, then closed again.

"Come on, wake up," she whispered, stroking his cheek.

"Mmmm," he moaned, turning his lips into her palm.

"Then again, maybe he's just having a good dream." The paramedic smirked.

The ambulance hit a pothole and she lurched forward, her breasts smothering Jack's face.

"Now I know he's having a good dream."

She crossed her arms over her chest and glared at the paramedic.

Jack mumbled something about fur and duct tape.

"Wake up, Black Jack. Everything's okay," she assured him.

"Everything . . . okay," he repeated, opening his dark eyes.

He blinked twice, then went completely pale. "Stop the ambulance!"

Chapter Three

"Calm down, Mr. Hudson," the paramedic said.

"Calm down? I'm here because of her. She clubbed me, knocked me out. I'm lucky I know my own name."

Tiger Lady reached out, sympathy coloring her bright blue eyes. He ripped the restraint from his head and tumbled off the stretcher, landing on the bench beside the paramedic.

"Mr. Hudson, please lie down."

"I don't need to lie down. I'm fine except for this damn headache. Judas Priest, what did you hit me with, a brick?"

She jutted out her chin. "It was a wrench, and I didn't hit you that hard."

"The hell you didn't."

"Sir, you need to get back onto the stretcher."

"I'm fine, as long as she doesn't come near me." God, not only was he taken out by the little tiger wench, but he'd also lost the match thanks to her.

Lost the match. Anger exploded in his chest.

"You cost me the belt!"

He lunged and she dodged back, pinning herself to the corner cabinet of supplies.

The paramedic caught his arm. "Sir, this is completely unacceptable."

"No kidding!"

"You have to lie down so I can do my job."

"With her in the ambulance? Are you crazy?"

She hugged her knees to her chest and looked at them with those innocent blue eyes. Right, like she was that fragile.

"I can't believe you cost me the belt. I swear, if it's the last thing I do, I'll . . ." He hadn't a clue what he'd do. But he had some pretty good ideas. "I'll stuff you and put you above my mantel!"

He lunged across the stretcher to squeeze her pretty little neck, but the paramedic grabbed his shoulders.

"That's it. Ed, stop the ambulance," the paramedic ordered the driver.

"But we're almost there."

"I said stop!"

The ambulance screeched to a halt. Tiger Lady shrieked as she flew forward, although not close enough for Jack to get a good hold of her.

"Out!" the paramedic ordered.

"What?" Her eyes widened with disbelief.

"I said, out. We're only a few blocks from the hospital. I'd like to stabilize this man before we get there. That obviously isn't going to happen with you here."

She ceremoniously slipped on her gloves and smoothed her red-streaked hair, which lay mostly beneath that ridiculous mask.

"I'm sorry you misunderstood my intentions, Mr. Black Jack. I was only trying to help."

With a snap of her wrist, she opened the door and stumbled onto the pavement. It was comical, the sight of her dressed in that furry bikini and black mask, standing in the middle of a moonlit street.

"Here." He tossed her a thin, white blanket. "Cover your-self up for Pete's sake."

She glared at him.

"Hospital's three blocks north." The paramedic pulled the doors closed and Frankie stood there, watching as a relaxed Black Jack climbed back onto the stretcher.

The ambulance sped away, leaving Frankie alone on River Road. She unfolded the white cotton wrap. Why not? Toga's were all the rage . . . about two thousand years ago. Walking along the curb, she analyzed the bed linen to con-sider her fashion options. Truth be told, she was a bit chilled.

And angry.

And hurt.

"Where on earth did that come from?" she muttered, adjusting the sheet around her torso. "I don't care one bit what that creature thinks of me. I certainly don't care if he hates me."

Reality stopped her midstep. Not good to have WHAK's biggest superstar come to the negotiating table hating the chief negotiator. Her job was to persuade him to stay with the company, not drive him into early retirement.

She swung the tail end of the blanket over her shoulder and stumbled up the curb, still mastering her balance on the spiked heels. What a sight she must make. She only hoped a police officer didn't happen by. She hated to think how she'd explain her way out of this one.

"Uncle Joe, when I get my hands on you . . ."

She should have known she'd end up like this, or worse. You just never knew what would happen when Uncle Joe waltzed into your life. Like the time he crashed Thanks-giving dinner with Maxine and four wrestlers in tow. Fran-kie was only nine, but she'd never forget the horrified look on her mother's face. Uncle Joe's line of work was not something Emma McGee approved of, to say the least. After all, it was violent and barbaric, and none of it was real. Nothing like the homey atmosphere her mother struggled to provide Frankie to make up for her deadbeat father's absence.

She ambled down the sidewalk, stabbing a hamburger wrapper with her heel. Her mother had taught her strength and determination. Emma didn't let her husband's irresponsible behavior ruin her life. She just carried on, accepted his failures and raised her daughter to be a proud and classy woman.

"Real classy." She jerked the corner of the blanket from a puddle of cigarette butts.

If his outburst was any indication, Black Jack would recover. Whatever pain he felt certainly wasn't preventing him from getting all worked up. Okay, so she'd miscalculated when she'd swung the wrench. It would have helped if she'd kept her eyes open. But mistakes happen, even to someone as careful and meticulous as Frankie.

The image of his swollen face filled her with regret. She felt bad. Truly, deeply, soulfully bad about bashing the man's brains in. And yet he seemed more upset about losing the make-believe championship than sustaining a serious head injury.

"I'll never make sense of this," she said, slipping the mask from her head. Nor should she have to. Her job was to swoop in, perform a financial miracle, then disappear back to her calm, sensible life. Oh, how she yearned for Bradley's broad shoulder to lean on as they sat together on his couch and watched the stock market numbers float across the television screen.

She missed the scent of Bradley's "Manly Man" aftershave and the feel of his starched white shirt as she rubbed her cheek against his chest. She missed her two-bedroom condo, her imported hot cocoa, her Herb Alpert CDs. She even missed that horrible coffee Stella made every morning at Smith and Barnes.

Frankie missed her normal life.

An ambulance whizzed by, pulling up beneath the blue emergency-room awning. She slowed her step and collapsed on a metal bench some thirty feet from the hospital entrance. Why was she even heading in this direction? She'd only make matters worse. If Black Jack caught sight of her, he'd probably rip the IV from his arm and run screaming from the hospital. Still, she felt responsible. And unlike her dad, Frankie McGee faced up to her responsibilities.

She slapped the mask on the bench beside her, balanced her elbows on her thighs and cradled her chin in her up-turned palms. This was a challenge, like any other challenge. She would identify the goal, meet her objective, and finish the job. Whatever it took. That was her motto. And it had served her well.

She was so consumed by her thoughts, she barely noticed a pair of black, crepe-soled shoes hesitate in front of her. Then she heard a "clink." Someone had just tossed pocket change into her mask. She glanced up into the concerned face of a twenty-ish, blond paramedic.

"Is there someone I can call?" he offered.

She considered Bradley's horrified expression if he found out she'd been moonlighting as a ferocious feline and her mother's disappointed scowl at Frankie's involvement with "Silly Sully."

"Um, no, thank you." She attempted a smile.

He nodded and climbed back into his ambulance.

"A bag lady. He thinks I'm a bag lady," she muttered, burying her face in her hands.

The sound of screeching tires echoed off the pavement, followed by the slam of a door, then another. Busy night at the emergency room.

"Frankie!"

She recognized Uncle Joe's voice but didn't look up. Time for him to taste a little guilt.

"You were marvelous!" His arm slipped around her shoulder.

"Princess, you made your uncle proud."

"Proud?" She glared at him. "Proud? I made a fool of

38

myself and nearly killed the superstar you need to save your stupid company. I tried to apologize, and you know what he did?"

He grinned and shook his head.

"He kicked me out of the ambulance! He threatened to have me stuffed."

"Oh, sweetheart, you're my special princess, you know that?"

She jumped to her feet and paced five steps away, suddenly balancing very well on the spikes.

"I'm going home. I don't belong in this . . . this lunacy. I look so pathetic that someone tossed me money."

"It's not that bad." He went to her, put his arm around her shoulder and guided her back to the bench. "I'm sure if we explain things to Jack, he'll understand."

"He wants to mount my head above his mantel."

Uncle Joe giggled.

"Stop it. It's not funny."

"No, but it's the answer to our prayers."

"I'm an atheist."

"You are not. Now, hear me out."

She crossed her arms over her chest and stared beyond him at the Methodist church across the street.

"Tonight was explosive, emotional, highstakes drama! You did it, Frankie. You got the fans more worked up than I've seen them in months. I guarantee we'll draw an even bigger crowd at tomorrow night's show. By the time the Rompin' Stompin' tour starts next month, we'll be selling tickets like hotcakes!"

"This was a one-day special, remember?"

"And you did a fabulous job." He winked. "Now, let's go talk to Jack."

"He'll strangle me on sight."

"He'll strangle Tatianna. Not Francine McGee, my niece and WHAK contract negotiator."

"In case you haven't noticed, I'm not looking a lot like

myself these days." She flipped the corner of the white blanket over her bare shoulder.

He snapped his fingers and Billings rushed forward with a garment bag.

"We thought you might need your clothes," Uncle Joe said with an apologetic smile.

She snatched the bag from Billings. "I can't do this tonight."

"Strike while the iron's hot, my dear." Uncle Joe led her into the hospital and down the hall to the ladies' bathroom. "Hudson needs money, and we need Hudson. It's a match made in Heaven."

"More like Hell."

"Think positive, Frankie, positive."

"I'm positively never going to forgive you."

"Of course not. Now go change before you get arrested for exposing yourself."

She pushed through the bathroom door and laid the bag on the counter. Ripping open the zipper, she glanced at her reflection in the mirror above the sink. Black mascara made rings around her eyes, and her red-streaked hair stuck out in twenty-five different directions.

With her usual efficiency, she went to work washing the war paint from her face and rinsing the temporary color from her hair. She wound the wet, shoulder-length strands into a conservative bun, brushed her eyelashes with a quick stroke of mascara, and drew a thin line of "Perfect Peach" across her lips. Uncle Joe had brought the navy suit she'd worn earlier, along with her half-inch pumps and tortoise-shell glasses. This felt better, much better. A crisp cotton blouse, wool-blend suit and practical pumps would make everything okay. She removed the uncomfortable contact lenses and placed the glasses on the bridge of her nose. Everything was almost back to normal.

Almost.

She shoved all evidence of tonight's fiasco into the garment bag and zipped it shut. Glancing into the mirror, she studied her pale but passable reflection. She might not be ready for a boardroom, but she looked good enough to get through tonight's challenge. She flung the door open and spotted Uncle Joe hovering a few feet away.

"Afraid I'd sneak off?" She shoved the bag at him. "Burn it."

With her brisk business walk, she headed for the admitting clerk's desk. "Black Jack Hudson, please."

The middle aged woman's forehead creased over her reading glasses. "Black who?"

"Jack Hudson. He was just brought in."

The clerk leafed through a stack of papers. "Oh, here, right. Jack Hudson. Trauma to the head. He was unconscious when they brought him in."

"Unconscious?" Her stomach flipped. "That can't be."

The door to the examining area swung open, and the paramedic who'd attended Jack walked out.

"Excuse me. You attended Jack Hudson?"

"Yes, ma'am." He eyed her with suspicion, not recognizing her as the feline femme fatale they'd thrown out of the ambulance.

"He's okay, right?" she asked.

"Doctors are with him now."

"But it's not serious?"

"Can't say, ma'am. One minute he was lucid, ranting about a crazy woman who tried to smash his skull. The next, he was out cold."

The paramedic pushed past her, leaving her stunned. She stared at the door to the examining area. No, she couldn't have hurt him that badly. She wasn't that strong or willful or malicious.

"Guess you hit him harder than you thought," Uncle Joe said.

A nurse swung open the door and Frankie seized the opportunity to prove them all wrong and ease her conscience. With a deep breath of antiseptic air, she slipped into the examining area unnoticed. The door clicked shut behind her, and she aimed for the nurse's station.

"Jack Hudson?" she said, her voice sounding not at all like her own.

"And you are?" The nurse glanced up from a chart.

"His wife." Great. First assault and battery, now impersonating a wife. She was sure to burn in Hell.

"Number four." The nurse motioned toward a row of examining areas sectioned off by curtains.

Inhaling the scent of rubbing alcohol and injury, she ambled toward number four and touched the coarse white fabric, listening for sounds of a doctor's interrogation. When she heard nothing, she pushed the curtain aside and her breath caught in her throat.

The overbearing giant who'd scared the wits out of her at first sight lay motionless on the stretcher. One arm was folded across his stomach, an IV needle embedded in his hand. He was so still, so helpless. The goose egg on his forehead had swollen to the size of a grapefruit, nearly closing his left eye. God, a little lower and she would have blinded the man.

Her legs wobbled, and she collapsed into a padded gray chair reserved for loved ones. Nibbling her thumbnail, she sat there and watched him breathe. In and out. Slow, steady. She still couldn't believe such a powerful creature could look so vulnerable, so broken.

Long strands of dark hair feathered across the institutional white pillow. His lips moved slightly as if he was dreaming.

A nightmare more like it. Probably hallucinating about the Tiger Lady.

She didn't realize she'd gotten to her feet until she stood over him and brushed a strand of hair from his cheek. Confusion knotted her insides as she ran her fingertips across a deep scar on his forehead. She suddenly wanted to know how it got there.

She shouldn't care. He was a commodity, nothing more. A commodity that would help save Uncle Joe's company.

"Sir, you can't go in there!" a woman's voice cried.

The curtain scraped open on metal rings, and Frankie jerked her hand away. Uncle Joe stepped into the examining area with Billings right beside him.

"Sir!" a young nurse protested. "One visitor at a time. And his wife is with him now."

"His wife?" He lifted a brow and broke into a full-blown grin.

"Don't give me that look."

A doctor side-stepped Uncle Joe and walked over to Jack. "You'll all have to leave."

She gripped the starched sleeve of the doctor's lab coat. "He'll be okay, won't he?"

The doctor glanced at the nurse.

"Wife," she said.

Uncle Joe let loose a hysterical giggle. Oh, he was pleased with himself tonight.

The doctor ignored the audience and went to work, checking Jack's eyes, his pulse, adjusting the IV bag.

It was coming. She could feel it. She'd caused a brain hemorrhage, a blood clot, permanent damage that would prevent Black Jack from stepping into the ring ever again. Uncle Joe could kiss WHAK goodbye. She'd ruined two lives in one night. Make that three. Bradley would be disappointed that their five-year engagement plan would have to be scrapped. After all, Frankie would get at least eight and a third to twenty for attempted manslaughter.

"Doctor?" she urged.

"Looks like a concussion. Won't know how serious until we take some x-rays."

"Is it normal for him to be unconscious like this?"

"That's not from the head injury. He passed out when the paramedic administered the IV. Needle phobic."

"Oh," she said, surprised that a man like Jack Hudson could be daunted by something as small as a needle.

The patient moaned and brought his right hand to his face, as if shielding his eyes. "What the hell?"

She backed up into Uncle Joe, afraid of Jack's reaction when he spotted her. Then she remembered: He'd only recognize her as Tatianna the Terrible. She stood a little straighter.

"Sir? I'm Dr. Carson. Do you know your name?"

"Jack. Jack Hudson."

"Do you know what happened to you, Mr. Hudson?"

"I got clobbered by a seven-hundred-pound gorilla."

The doctor pulled out a pen-sized flashlight and shined it in Jack's right eye.

"Enough already," Jack protested, batting the doctor's hand away. "I was clubbed by a crazy woman."

"How about these people? Do you recognize any of them?"

He squinted and stared at Frankie. Guilt flashed in bold neon letters across her forehead. His gaze drifted to her right and landed on Uncle Joe. He closed his eyes and clenched his jaw.

"Jesus, Sully. You don't let up."

"Just wanted to check up on my biggest star."

Jack grunted.

"Doctor?" a nurse interrupted. "We need you in room two."

"Fine. Mr. Hudson, they'll be taking you for x-rays in a minute."

"I've been hit in the head enough times to know I don't need x-rays."

The doctor pushed aside the curtain and glanced over his shoulder. "I'd have to disagree. After all, you didn't even recognize your own wife."

"My what!" He jackknifed, gripped his head with both hands, then collapsed back onto the stretcher.

Uncle Joe giggled.

"Sully," Jack warned.

"I'm going to have to ask you all to leave," the nurse ordered.

"One minute, nurse, just sixty seconds, okay?" Uncle Joe

winked at Billings, who put his arm around the nurse.

"I don't suppose you have any kids who like wrestling. . . ." Billings guided her out of the examining area.

Uncle Joe closed the curtain.

"Get out," Jack said, his right arm shielding his face.

"We have business to discuss."

"Yeah, like the broad standing next to you? Don't tell me, you had a minister marry us while I was unconscious to beef up next week's ratings. Come on, Sully, you know I like them tall and bone skinny."

Maybe insults would get them to leave, Jack thought.

"This is my niece and WHAK negotiator. We said she was your wife so they'd let us in to talk to you."

"Yeah, catch me when I'm down. I know the drill."

"You were great tonight, Jack. The fans were hot, out of control."

Sully took a step toward him. He had nowhere to go. A familiar feeling.

"Things are turning around for us. Just think, when you turn heel on next week's show—"

"Are you nuts!" Jack shouted, clutching his head to ease the spear of pain slicing through his skull. "You've got to be out of your mind."

"Take 'em by surprise, Jack. That's what tonight taught me. That's why we've been losing fans. They want the unexpected, larger-than-life stories filled with emotion and drama and—"

"I won't turn heel."

The thought of thousands of young fans watching him draw blood from a hero tied his stomach in knots. It had taken years to build his reputation, to become a hero whom impressionable kids could look up to. But it would take only one match to trash that image to hell.

"It's only three more months. Then your contract's up and you're free to go on with your life."

"As what? A complete jerk?"

"Heels have gone on to very successful careers as announcers, actors, heck, even governor."

"I came into this business a hero, and I'm going out the same way."

God, let him be a hero at something.

"I'm sorry, but my advisers feel strongly about this."

"And who the hell are your advisers? Billings? The man was a career jobber. He won five, maybe six matches in fifteen years. Or was it this lady here who suggested you destroy the persona I've worked years to build."

Sully's niece crossed her arms over her chest. "I'm here to negotiate, not make up stories. You all seem quite capable of doing that yourself."

Another hard-ass. Great.

"I won't turn, Sully. Now, get out." He crooked his arm over his face. The dull throb grew to a persistent hammer.

He heard Sully shuffle papers.

"I've got a contract here. If you break it, I'll sue you for everything you're worth."

"You sonofa—" Jack lunged for the promoter, hoping to apply an illegal choke hold of his own. Instead, his knees buckled, and he went down. He groped for the counter to keep from falling flat on his face. The room spun; test patterns of red, yellow, and white flashed across his vision.

Someone gently gripped him by the arm and helped him to his feet. He didn't open his eyes, afraid he'd be sick from the sight of IVs, latex gloves, and blood-pressure cuffs spinning around the room.

"Lie down," a woman's voice said. Thank God the nurse had enough sense to come back and save him from Sully and his evil niece.

Flopping back onto the stretcher, he opened his eyes. The drill sergeant niece stood over him, her hand still gripping his bare arm.

"I don't need your help." He wrenched his arm from her and closed his eyes, but not before he caught her pained expression. Why should he care?

46

The hammering grew into a full-blown demolition of his remaining brain cells.

"There is always an alternative," Sully said.

"Yeah, like I strap you to the hood of that fancy Lincoln town car and drive you into Lake Michigan."

"Jack, believe it or not, I'm looking out for your best interest."

He squinted at Sully, who wore that Cheshire-cat smile, the one that meant major pain and suffering was on the way.

"Spit it out," Jack said.

"I'll reconsider your turning heel if you extend your contract by a year."

"You're dreamin'." His knee ached at the thought.

"It's critical to WHAK, a way to recover our ratings."

"I'd rather recover my health."

"How can you do this to the organization that made you what you are today?"

He glared at the promoter. "Don't even go there. I've been a cash cow for the last ten years and we both know it."

"That's why we need you to stay on for a little while longer."

"No."

"Then heel it is. Unless . . ."

Sully nodded at his niece, and she batted her eyes. Boy, they made a great team.

"Will you consider something else?" Sully smiled again and Jack had the sudden urge to buzz the nurse for a quick shot of morphine.

Sully stepped closer, his eyes twinkling with mischief. "You don't have to turn heel if you agree to take Tatianna as your permanent partner."

Chapter Four

"Are you nuts?" Jack shouted. "This was a one-time gig."

A sudden crash echoed through the room, slicing more pain through his skull.

"Sorry." The niece righted a cart she'd knocked over and glared at Sully. The old man ignored her and paced the room, raising one hand in the air as if giving a State of the Union address.

"This is exactly the type of drama and emotion we need to get back on top. You and Tatianna are perfect together."

"Uncle Joe?" The niece grabbed for his arm as he whisked past.

"Tatianna's fascinating, electrifying—"

"She's a lunatic," Jack interrupted.

"She's spectacular, amazing—"

"She's a klutz."

"But she's got that special something—charisma, magic."

"She's dangerous!"

"She didn't mean to hurt you," the niece defended.

He studied the woman Sully claimed was his niece. Her

48

arms were crossed over her chest, her eyes narrowed with determination. Her colorful eyes—a myriad of blues, greens, and yellows—were hidden behind large-framed glasses. He'd never seen eyes quite like hers before. Hell, he was getting sidetracked by a pair of remarkable eyes. The concussion must be worse than he thought.

Clenching his jaw, Jack refocused on the challenge at hand: getting out while he could still walk.

"Tatianna was only trying to help," the niece said.

"I can do without that crazy woman's help. I'll live a lot longer, that's for sure."

"She's new at this, a last-minute replacement. She thought you were going to have your head smashed with that TV monitor."

"If she didn't know the game, she shouldn't have stepped into the ring."

"But—"

"Listen, lady, you obviously don't know much about this business." He propped himself up on his elbows and stared her down, all five-foot-nothing of her. He never knew women came that small. Short, that is. She obviously wasn't small in other, more important places, which he could tell she tried very hard to conceal.

"That Tiger Lady bimbo is a nut case, a psycho, an idiot who had no business being anywhere near the ring."

She flushed bright red and fisted her right hand by her side. If Jack didn't know better, he'd guess she ached to give him a right cross of her own. And they said he took his job too seriously.

Sully side-stepped his niece and grinned at Jack. God, he hated that grin.

"It's okay, Jack, we'll find you a new Tatianna."

"Forget it. I won't have anything to do with that story line, contract or no contract."

It would be nice to keep some personal integrity, he thought. Then he considered the alternative. Not much integrity in turning heel.

"There's nothing that can change your mind?" Sully brushed a speck of lint from his suit coat.

Jack ground his teeth. Sully had him by the balls and they both knew it. Jack couldn't afford to be wiped out financially, not with most of his money invested in Butch's expanding youth fitness centers. Then there was the balloon payment due next month on the construction loan. They were finally about to break ground on his mountain cabin, the dream that had kept him going for the last five years.

"I'll tell Billings you're turning heel. He'll schedule you on the Milwaukee card against Cowboy Gil," Sully said. "We'll send you out with some brass knuckles, a buckskin knife, maybe even a table saw."

"Get the hell out of here!" His pulse pounded in his ears.

A nurse ripped the curtain aside. "What's all this?"

"We were just leaving," Sully said.

The nurse ambled to Jack and checked his pulse.

"Morphine. Demerol. A kick to the head. Anything, just put me out," Jack said.

"We don't want you out, exactly, Mr. Hudson, but we can probably do something for the pain." She tapped at his IV bag, then grabbed something from the tray.

"Milwaukee, next Monday, you can slice Gil to pieces in front of all his little cowpokes," Sully taunted from the curtain.

"Get out!"

"Reconsider my offer and I'll give you a week off followed by two weeks of light promo appearances with Tatianna."

"Nurse, call security."

"Okay now, Mr. Hudson. Just take a deep breath and everything will be fine."

She turned and Jack caught sight of the ten-foot needle squeezed between her latex-gloved fingers. His heart did a skippity-hop-thump, his breath caught in his throat and the world faded to black.

* * *

The next morning Frankie paced Uncle Joe's office like a woman on caffeine overload. "What do you mean you can't find a replacement?"

Okay, so she was a bit overexcited, but she couldn't help herself. She'd tossed and turned all night, thanks to nightmares about leather-clad cowboys.

"Take it easy, Frankie. There's still time. It's not like Jack's going to be back anytime soon. He'll take a few days to recover."

She paced the office, her stomach churning with dread. Why did she get the feeling that her uncle wasn't putting a lot of effort into finding another Tatianna?

"Have you talked to him today?" she said.

"No, but I doubt I was the first person he wanted to talk to when he woke up."

"Gee, I wonder why." She collapsed in the leather wingback chair opposite his desk. "What can I do to expedite this process?"

"Don't you worry your pretty little head about it." He popped another butterscotch candy. "Everything will work out fine, just like always."

She considered that statement. "Fine" was a relative term when dealing with Uncle Joe. Last night's fiasco had proved anything but fine.

"Why don't I trust you?"

"Me?" He placed an open palm to his chest; his gray-blue eyes widened.

She stared him down. "I won't go out there again. I won't dress up and make a fool out of myself."

"But Frankie, you were wonderful, a natural. You saved us from the gallows."

"I'm not an exhibitionist," she said, ignoring his praises. "I don't belong anywhere near a ring."

"The ring is part of your heritage."

"Mama spent my whole life telling me otherwise."

He glanced at her, crestfallen. "When I think about all

51

the hard work, the blood and angst drained from my soul to create WHAK."

She felt the guilt hammer swing away.

"And when I'm gone, it's over. Kaput. No one to take over. No one to carry on my good work."

"Listen here." She stood, plastered open palms on his desk and leaned forward in her most intimidating pose. "My job is to dig you out of financial debt. That's it. No dressing up and prancing around like a furry fluff ball, no hanging on a wrestler's arm, no taking over the family business. The last place I want to be right now is surrounded by a gang of ignorant, grunting, testosterone-charged gorillas that you generously call athletes!"

Uncle Joe's eyes bugged out of his head as if he'd been stabbed with a fireplace poker. He'd never been speechless before. She straightened and righted her linen suit jacket with a snap to the hem. She kinda liked this.

"I'll be in accounting." With a lift of her chin she spun around and came face to chest with washed-out blue denim.

Uh oh. She swallowed hard. Her gaze drifted up, locking on to a pair of fiery green eyes.

"Ignorant, testosterone-charged gorilla?" Black Jack said, his voice low and threatening.

Her voice caught in her throat.

"You don't consider us athletes?"

She backed up against Uncle Joe's desk and fumbled behind her for a paperweight, picture frame, a pen to poke his eye out. Crimeny, the violence was rubbing off on her.

"I . . . I . . ." She curled her fingers around something firm and pointed.

"Who do you think you are, anyway?" he said in that throaty wrestler's voice she knew they all used when being interviewed by Prince Priceless. "You think a lot of yourself, don't you Niece Sullivan?"

"My name is Frankie."

"That's right. A guy's name. Figures."

Out of the corner of her eye she saw him reach out. On instinct, she snatched the weapon from Uncle Joe's desk and raised it over her shoulder, ready to strike.

He chuckled, a deep, throaty sound that made her skin tingle.

"What, you gonna light my fire, babe?"

She glanced at the object in her hand. A cigarette lighter. In the shape of a naked woman. A well-endowed woman no less. And Frankie was fondling her breasts.

"Ah!" She tossed the lighter to the floor.

"Tsk, tsk. Now that's no way to treat a lady." He picked up the hand-carved lighter and rubbed his thumb across the rock-hard nipples. Her pulse hammered against her throat. What was happening?

As he reached around her to place the lighter on the desk, the inside of his muscular arm brushed against her shoulder. She inhaled the clean scent of male mixed with deodorant soap and closed her eyes. Her heart beat triple time as images invaded her thoughts, images of strong, male hands, touching, exploring, demanding.

The sound of a man clearing his throat shocked her back to her senses. Jack stared her down, a sly grin lighting up his face.

"Sully, where'd you find this one? A convent?"

She ground her teeth and fisted her fingers. What she wouldn't give to be able to plant just one knuckle sandwich right on the corner of this guy's cocky jaw.

He took a step back and glanced at her hand, clenched firmly by her side. "Again with the fist. You sure have a short fuse for a *lady*."

The emphasis on the word "lady" wasn't lost on her. The funny thing was, she didn't have a short fuse. Up to this point in her life, she'd had no fuse at all. Anger was a wasted emotion. It didn't change anything. She and Mama had learned that the hard way.

"You surprised me, that's all," she said. "We didn't expect you to be back today."

"I'll bet you didn't." He eyed her, slowly, methodically, as if analyzing every curve of her body. Thank God she was wearing a loose-fitting vest under her suit jacket.

Abruptly, he paced to the window overlooking the workout area and glanced down at the wrestlers using the machines.

"I thought about your offer, Sully. I've decided you're right. I do owe WHAK for my success."

"I knew you'd come around." Uncle Joe jumped to his feet and extended his hand.

"However . . ."

Uncle Joe snatched his hand back and ran it through his hair.

"I need to cut down on my matches. I don't want to push the knee."

"Will you do more promotional appearances?"

"Sure."

"It's a deal," Uncle Joe's hand went out again.

"About the Tiger Lady . . ."

Uncle Joe shoved his hand into his pants pocket. "Non-negotiable. Judging from last night's performance, this story line will catapult us right up there with Steel's Outrageous Wrestling. But don't worry. We're working on finding you a new Tatianna. Someone with more experience and savvy. Someone who can—"

"I want the girl from last night."

"What?" Uncle Joe said.

Frankie's knees buckled. She planted her fanny on the corner of her uncle's desk for support.

"But, Jack, last night you said—"

"I know what I said. But I also know it worked last night because there was something real about her, innocent. She's not a professional actress, is she?"

"N-N-No," Uncle Joe said, turning his back to Frankie.

"I didn't think so."

"She was a last-minute replacement, a friend of the family."

54

"Great, then she'll have no problem helping out her 'family' again."

A knot of panic twisted in her stomach. "The woman who performed with you last night is no longer available," Frankie said.

"Yeah?" He sauntered over to her, and her heart started that double-time rumba beat again. Why hadn't she just kept her mouth shut? If he got any closer, her circuits were gonna fry.

"And why's that, Frank?" he asked, towering over her.

Intimidation. She didn't put up with it from snotty CEOs, and she sure as hell wasn't going to put up with it from an empty-brained wrestler.

She straightened and stared up into his dark green eyes. Way up. "She has other commitments."

"Then uncommit her. I want her back. She's perfect."

His penetrating green eyes bore down on her. Breathe. In through the nose, out through the mouth. That's it. Just like the meditation tape instructed. The last thing she wanted to do was pass out in front of this arrogant bully.

Arrogant and tall. If he just weren't so damned tall.

And handsome.

And virile.

And . . . gawd. She curled her fingers into her palms to keep from ripping off his shirt and running her hands up and down his rock-solid chest.

Snap. Snap. She lassoed the animal lust back into the cage. What on earth was the matter with her? She needed some one-on-one time with Bradley. That would cure this hormonal disorder.

"We'll find you another woman, Mr. Hudson," she said.

"I want the girl from last night." His eyes pinned her in place. Even with his hair tied back, he looked wild, like a crazed boar poised and ready to sink his teeth into fresh meat.

"Now Jack, Frankie does have a point. Wouldn't it be

nice to work with a professional?" Uncle Joe's voice cracked.

"Compromise, Sully. That's what you've always taught me. I'll extend my contract if you bring back the original Tiger Lady."

Jack's plan clicked away in his head as he kept his gaze glued to Sully's hard-as-nails niece. He was going to have fun messing with this little girl's head.

And if anyone needed a little messing with, it was Sully's niece. Hell, she looked like she'd just stepped off the cover of *Young Executives Magazine*. She wore a tailored gray suit, pearl-buttoned white blouse complete with starched collar, and a conservative pinstriped vest to conceal her generous curves. He detected little makeup with the exception of a very light brush of mascara. No, she didn't do a helluva lot to make herself attractive. But then, Jack guessed, attracting men was not her objective. She liked bossing them around.

Jack Hudson was too old and too cranky to be bossed around by anybody, especially the Franken Niece.

This was going to be fun all right.

He couldn't help wondering if prim and proper boss lady had ever had her feathers ruffled. Really ruffled.

"What's it going to be, Sully?" He snapped his gaze from the Franken Niece and glanced down at the gym. He'd have to get down there today, headache or no headache.

"I'll see what I can do."

"What!" Frankie cried, glaring at her uncle. She actually looked kinda cute when she glared.

"Looks like blood isn't thicker than water," Jack taunted, reaching out to chuck her chin with his thumb and fore-finger. She jerked away.

"Yeah, well . . ." He gave her the once over, taking his jolly good time just to piss her off, then turned to leave.

"Jack, wait!" Sully cried.

"It's Frankie's first week here. I'd like to show her around, but I've got so much paperwork." He motioned toward his desk. Two sheets of paper sat dead center.

56

"Uncle Joe—"

"Sure, I'll give her the five-cent tour." Jack rubbed his chin and narrowed his eyes in his best "I'm-gonna-eat-you-alive" look.

"Really, Mr. Hudson, it's not necessary."

"Call me Jack."

"Thank you, but no."

"Now, Frankie, I told you how swamped I am today, just go off with Jack and figure out where the pencils and light bulbs are and we'll talk later." He gave his niece a shove from behind.

Jack didn't know what the old man was up to, but he could play the game just as well, maybe even better, than the next person. Spending a little time with Frank could keep him one step ahead of Sully. Hell, he might even be able to dig up some dirt on the old man, something dark and seedy that he could use to persuade Sully to cut him loose.

"Come on, Frank. I can show you all the ins and outs of WHAK headquarters." He opened the door and grinned. "After you."

"Uncle Joe," she ground out.

"Go on. Learn about the business. There's no one as savvy as Jack to teach you all you need to know."

"I *will* talk to you later," she said. Was that a threat tinging her voice?

Good. Keep her angry and off balance. This repressed, prudish executive would be very easy to keep off balance.

Frank huffed past him, and Jack shot Sully one last smile. "Oh, and Sully? When you do get Tiger Lady back here, tell her I'll be the one to train her and teach her the moves."

Sully's face paled, and Jack knew he'd hit the mark. Which mark, exactly, he wasn't sure. But the promoter was sweating about something. And that's just how Jack liked it. Make him sweat and suffer, like he was going to make Jack suffer.

He shut the door to Sully's office and glanced down the hall. The niece was halfway to Catalina Island.

"Hold on there, Frank. You don't want to get lost." He caught up to her, his head drumming with a dull throb.

"You weren't supposed to come back today," she said, taking short, determined steps.

"Yeah, well, the hospital isn't my favorite place to be."

She smiled at him, her eyes sparkling. "That wouldn't have anything to do with needles, now would it?"

Whadda ya know? The she-devil was challenging him. She was also heading straight for the men's locker room. Jack followed along.

"I have no idea what you're talking about," he said, eyeing the locker room door. Nick the Nefarious had ripped off the sign last month in a fit of rage. Not an unusual emotion when dealing with a promoter like Sully.

"I suppose you don't remember passing out last night because of an itsy bitsy needle?"

She was having fun. He was going to have more fun in about ten seconds.

"I can't believe a big man like you would be scared of a little thing like that."

"You weren't the one being stabbed by that 'little thing.' "

"Not last night. But when my allergies acted up as a child I had no choice but to give myself a shot in the arm . . . with a *needle*," she said, as if trying to make him pass out by saying the word.

"What a brave girl you are, Frank."

He pushed open the door, and she stepped into the locker room. Upon seeing a handful of men in various states of undress, ferocious Frank turned tail and slammed face first into Jack's chest.

"Hey, nothing to be squeamish about. Not for a strong, tough cookie like you who can jab a needle in her arm without blinking an eye."

Her fingers opened and closed twice. He had a feeling

he was going to feel that sucker punch before the day was out.

"Jack! What's up?" Maynard said, walking toward him.

Jack reached around Frank and gave Maynard a high five.

"You okay, man?" Maynard asked.

"A little punch drunk, but I'll survive."

"Who's the broad?"

Jack placed his hands on Frankie's shoulders and turned her around. "I'd like to introduce Sully's niece, Frankie McGee."

"Frankie? Ain't that a guy's name?"

"I call her Frank for short. Helps her fit in, right kid?"

She pumped her fist again.

"Why'd you bring her in here?" Maynard said.

A small crowd started to gather. The usual guys at this time of day: Luther Rawlings, a six-foot-eight-inch black man; Teddy, also known as the four-hundred-pound Bald Basher; and Marco, the hard-core king who had more body parts pierced than Dennis Rodman.

"Coming in here was her idea. She wants to get to know the talent, don't ya, Frank? A chip off the old uncle."

"Did you say she's Sully's niece?" Teddy said, snapping the waistband of his shorts.

"Yes," she said with a lift of her chin.

Jack had to give her credit. She wasn't trying to run. Not yet, anyway.

"Then we got some talkin' to do. I got a problem with clause B6 in my contract." Teddy got right in her face, his blood-shot eyes gleaming, his jaw working a piece of watermelon-flavored bubble gum, his favorite. The Franken Niece probably thought he jawed on a piece of worn leather, or worse.

She glanced over her shoulder at Jack. Those helpless eyes tugged at his heart. Damn. He had to get out of here before he forgot she was the enemy.

"Well, I'll just leave you to get better acquainted." He

slipped out the door and waited for her to run screaming from the room.

He'd give her five, maybe ten seconds. With her mightier-than-thou attitude, the guys would rip her to pieces, verbally anyway, in a matter of minutes. If she thought she was smarter than all of them, she had another think coming. Two of the guys were college grads, and Marco owned a chain of successful restaurants. It always amazed Jack that people assumed just because professional wrestlers had hard bodies, they had mush for brains.

Luther's hearty laugh boomed from the other side of the door. Hell, they were having a great time at her expense. Teddy probably had her over his shoulder by now, demonstrating the Basher Smasher. He loved showing off.

Jack leaned against the beige wall and remembered the last time Marco brought his niece for a visit. Teddy picked up the little girl with one hand and spun her around. The kid screamed with delight, blond hair flying every which way.

Jack ached inside. His recollection of the playful exchange drove home how much he'd missed: a family, a place to come home to. His failed marriage proved he couldn't have any of that as long as he stayed in this business. Although wrestling wasn't solely to blame for that disaster. He'd wanted a normal life so bad, he'd worn blinders when Sandra waltzed into his life. Never again.

One thing was for sure: He wasn't going to end up like his father, blaming everyone around him because he hated his life. Jack had entrenched himself in this insane business without any help from anyone. And it was high time to jump ship, before he lost any chance of a normal, healthy, and happy life. Before he ended up like his dad—angry, bitter, and dead before his time.

"Jesus," he muttered, surprised at the sudden self-analysis. Must be the blow to the head. He touched the goose egg above his eye. Time to put bad decisions behind him and refuse to be manipulated. Actually it was time he did a little manipulating of his own. His first victim would be the terrible Tiger Lady. He was sure he could finesse the batty woman from last night. He wasn't so sure about a professional actress. No, the inexperienced Tatianna would be the perfect pawn to carry out his plan.

The door to the locker room swung open.

"Never would have guessed you're related to that slave driver, Sullivan," Luther said. "No offense, ma'am."

"None taken, Mr. Rawlings. My uncle's been in this business a long time and has some rather old-fashioned views about things. I hope to change that. Bring wrestling into the mainstream."

Luther's eyes gleamed with admiration. She really had him under her spell.

"I'll look into the contract issues, Mr. Rawlings. It was nice to meet you." They shook hands, her small, pale fingers dwarfed in the giant's burly paw.

She shot Jack a smug look, then proceeded down the hall.

He glanced at Luther.

"Nice lady," Luther said. "Smart, too, not like Sully."

"You're still getting paid, Mr. Hudson, even if you're not in the ring," she called over her shoulder as if ordering him to follow her like a puppy dog.

He ground his teeth. He'd like to get her in the ring for just five minutes. A good, old-fashioned submission hold would clear that arrogant tone from her voice.

"Have fun, Jack." Luther patted him on the back and laughed, obviously reading Jack's mind.

"Yeah, a barrel of laughs."

Jack started after her, afraid of what she'd do next. He didn't like surprises, not one bit. Catching up to her, he studied her face, set in stone, like well-carved marble.

"Let's get one thing clear, Mr. Hudson." She stopped and squared off at him. He still had a hard time taking her seriously when she barely came up to his chest.

"I don't like surprises. You pull any more on me and I swear—"

"Hey, lady, you're the one who walked into the locker room. I thought you wanted, you know, to sample some biceps for yourself." He grinned.

"In case you haven't noticed, Mr. Hudson, brawn doesn't impress me, nor does it intimidate me."

Oh, he noticed all right. He also noticed that whenever he got within six inches of her, her face flushed three shades of pink.

Time for a little *non-intimidation*. He planted his hands on the wall at either side of her head.

"I'm not here to intimidate you, Frank. On the contrary, I just want to live up to my role of tour guide. It's the least I can do for you and that generous uncle of yours."

Her eye color changed from light blue-green to cobalt in a flash. He glanced down to see whether she was making that little fist again. She'd shoved her hands behind her back.

His gaze drifted to her peach-colored lips, the lower lip a little fuller than the top, giving her a natural pout that most women would kill for. For an uptight drill sergeant, she had incredible lips, lips that looked like they needed to be kissed something bad. Hell, where did that come from?

"Since you're being so accommodating, Mr. Hudson, please take me to the press office. We need to schedule your appearances for next week."

"Not next week, babe. I get a week off, remember?" He tapped gently at his head injury.

"That was my uncle's deal, not mine. I've got big plans for you, Mr. Hudson, very big plans."

Chapter Five

The next day at WHAK headquarters, Frankie and Uncle Joe brainstormed angles, ticket sales, and Black Jack Hudson.

"I don't know what else to do. A deal's a deal." Uncle Joe dropped a bag containing the infamous leopard-skin bikini in her lap.

"And since when did you worry about keeping your word?" Guilt snagged her insides. "Sorry, I didn't mean it like that."

"I take it you've met some of the guys." He settled behind his desk in the cracked maroon leather chair.

"A few."

Leaning back, he tapped a pencil eraser on the tip of his chin. "Business can get messy. Sometimes I have to make unpopular decisions."

"I'm not here to judge you. Just dig you out of trouble and be on my way. But that doesn't include parading around like a fruitcake."

"Just like your mom. Always worried about appearances."

"What's that supposed to mean?"

"Never mind. I'm sorry, but it's the only way. You'll have to work with Black Jack Hudson."

"For a year?"

"The story line won't last that long. Even if you go back to your real life and that job of yours, you can always make guest appearances for the television specials."

"Uncle Joe!"

"I would find someone else, but I think Jack's got something up his sleeve. You're the smartest woman I know, princess. If anyone can play hard ball with Black Jack Hudson and figure out what he's up to, it's you." He leaned forward and rubbed at his temples.

This wasn't a ploy, or an act, or anything scripted. Uncle Joe looked tired. Dead tired. His eyelids drooped; his skin was paler than usual.

"The mask stays on," she said.

"Deal."

"Maxine designs a new costume to cover up more of me."

"Fair enough."

"What about the books?"

"You got them in pretty good shape. I'd like you to keep consulting with Bert in accounting, if you have time. But your priority has to be working with Jack. This is it, Frankie. My last chance to save this company."

The desperation in his voice touched her heart. She leaned across his desk. "Why is this so important?"

He reached for her hand, and this time she gave it willingly.

"They said I'd never amount to much. And maybe they're right. But I can't give up. Not yet. I have to prove—"

The door burst open.

"You can't go in there!" Cecilia, the secretary, cried.

Uncle Joe snatched his hands from Frankie's and stood, righting his polyester suit jacket. She glanced over her shoulder and her breath caught at the sight of Jack, naked from the waist up. He wore nothing but skin-tight spandex shorts, socks and athletic shoes, and some kind of partial gloves. His body glistened with sweat, and strands of wet hair that had come loose from his ponytail clung to his shoulders.

"Jack, what can we do for you?" Uncle Joe asked, his voice as slick as a salesman's.

He planted his hands on his hips, defining his well-muscled chest. "Where the hell is she?"

"She, who?"

"Don't play games, Sully. I finished my workout twenty minutes ago. Tiger Lady was supposed to meet me in the ring."

"Well, um, we've had a slight problem." Uncle Joe ambled toward him.

Frankie couldn't have moved if her life depended on it. Between her uncle's uncharacteristic and sincere confession, and Jack's magnificent body, her bearings were shot to hell.

"I've got a little over a week to train her. I'm going back in the ring in ten days, not twenty-one. I need to work off some of this steam I seem to have built up." He eyed Frankie.

She dug her nails into the arms of the chair. Giving him a tight promotional schedule next week was her way of letting him know who was in charge. Instead he'd chosen to jump into the ring sooner than he should.

She'd thought he liked meeting with the fans, signing autographs and playing hero. But no. He wanted back into the action, with her by his side. Could she find a replacement in a week? How about thirty seconds? Because this man looked like he fully expected Tatianna to walk through that door.

"Jack, calm down. We've had some problems," Uncle Joe reiterated, placing his hand on Jack's bare shoulder. Jack glared at his fingers. Uncle Joe snatched his hand back and paced to the picture window overlooking the gym.

She couldn't take her eyes off Jack's incredible chest. His firm pectoral muscles rounded down to a hard stomach that looked like it had been sculpted by God's hands. Not a washboard tummy, she thought, remembering the cover of Bradley's "Ten Minutes to a Tighter Tummy" video. No, Jack's stomach was thick and muscular and lightly dusted with dark hair that disappeared just below his waistline.

"It's always something with you, Sully. An angle, a manipulation. I told you my terms, and you agreed to them. Frank, here, witnessed the discussion. So, what's it going to be?"

She tore her gaze from Jack's sleek, sweaty body and glanced at her uncle. His shoulders sagged with an incredible sigh, as if the world was crumbling before his eyes.

"Tatianna's not coming."

"What are you talking about?"

Uncle Joe glanced at Frankie. Her stomach lurched at the look in his eye. The look of defeat.

"The truth of the matter is—"

"She had car trouble." Frankie jumped to her feet and faced Jack. "She'll be here within the hour."

"What?" Uncle Joe said.

"I forgot to tell you. We were so wrapped up in business."

"But Frankie—"

"She'll be here." She glanced at Uncle Joe. "Everything will be fine."

Grabbing the plastic bag, she marched toward Jack, who was blocking the doorway. She focused on her breathing technique, struggling to quell the heat wave that washed over her whenever she got within ten feet of him. Could she survive being so close to this impossible, sexy man? She had to, for Uncle Joe. Bikini or no bikini.

"I just hope she doesn't come dressed in that ridiculous costume of hers," Jack said, pulling off a glove.

"I'm sure she knows the appropriate way to dress for a

workout." She hadn't a clue. Better flag down Maxine on her way to get her head examined.

She sauntered past him, but he grabbed her arm. Staring at his partially gloved hand, she marveled that his touch didn't pinch or squeeze. How could such a large man be so gentle?

Then she glanced into his devilish green eyes.

"I'll hang around for a half hour," he said. "Oh, and thanks, Frank."

"For what?"

"For giving me such a light promotional schedule next week."

The sarcasm hit her right between the eyes. "It's the least I could do."

"I'm sure Tiger Lady will be real happy to know she's booked for a different town each day for the next week."

"Tiger Lady?"

"Where I go, she goes. Kaneville, Plumtowne, Sterling Falls. After all, Tiger Lady and I are partners."

Heavens! When she'd convinced the PR department to boost Jack's schedule, she'd meant to get him out of her hair and teach him not to mess with her. It seemed in the process she'd messed with herself. Big time.

"I don't know that Tatianna can make all those dates," she said with a nonchalant lift of her chin.

"I'm sure you'll work it out. You have a way with people."

A fantastic grin lit up his face, showing off a slight dimple in his left cheek.

"Send Tiger Lady down to the ring. We've got a lot of catching up to do if I'm to train her by the day after tomorrow."

"Train her to sign autographs? I'm sure she can figure that out."

"Not autographs, sweetheart. She's got to learn some of the moves if we're going to step into the ring together."

"Moves—right." She brushed a speck of lint from her

gray blazer. Next he'd be telling her she had to take a course in grunting.

"Why do I get the feeling you still don't respect this business?"

"I don't know what you mean." She narrowed her eyes in challenge.

"I mean . . ." He took a step toward her and she automatically backed into the wall, knocking Uncle Joe's golf clubs to the floor. A five iron would make a good weapon right about now. She couldn't take her eyes off the man long enough to grab a club. His dark green penetrating gaze pinned her in place.

"You act like we're the scum of the earth and you're the queen of England."

"I happen to take pride in things that are real, genuine, and serve a purpose, Mr. Hudson. Wrestling doesn't fit into any of these categories."

His eyes blazed fire. "Pick me up."

"Excuse me?"

She watched him swallow, and her blood pressure jumped. Goodness, even the man's Adam's apple was a turn on.

"Pick me up," he repeated.

"I . . . I can't."

"Why not?" His voice carried a ragged edge. Was he feeling the same heat that set her nerves askitter?

"I'm not strong enough to pick you up."

"But Frank, wrestling's all fake, remember? Smoke and mirrors. You should be able to pick me up with one finger. Or maybe two."

He placed her hands on his waist. Her fingers burned at the contact of his slick, warm skin.

"Come on, Frank. Give it a shot."

She wanted to take a shot, all right. She wanted to take a shot at tasting those incredible lips, running her fingers across every muscle, every curve of his amazing chest.

"Can't do it, can you?" he taunted.

Had he read her mind?

His smile faded, and he took a step back. She clapped her arms to her sides.

"That's lesson number one," he said. "I really pick up three-hundred-pound men for a living. I really get hit with chairs, fall off fifteen-foot cages onto tables and fly out of the ring onto the cement floor. I'd be happy to demonstrate if you'd like to join me in the ring."

It was all a game, a way to make her look small and foolish. He didn't feel any heat, any desire bubbling just beneath the surface. It was all business to him. A way to make his point.

And she'd been sucked in like a naïve schoolgirl.

"I get the picture," she said.

"Good. I'll be waiting downstairs for Tiger Lady." He pulled off a glove with his teeth, his eyes intent on Frankie. Against her will, heat shot to every fiber, every nerve ending of her body. He might be an empty-brained wrestler, but she had to give him an A-plus in the animal magnetism department. The man knew exactly how to use his power. And she had a feeling he planned to use it on her, or Tatianna, or . . . oh, Lord, she was getting confused.

He shot her one last victorious smile, ambled across the office, and slammed the door behind him. She slid down the wall into a heap on the floor.

"Get Maxine up here."

"You don't have to do it." Uncle Joe sat beside her. "I know how uncomfortable you are with all this."

"You need me, and I refuse to be intimidated by that . . . man. Now get her up here before I come to my senses and abandon you for good."

"Again!" he said, running toward Marco. The kid swung his forearm and Jack fell backward, slamming to the ring mat. He sprung back to his feet.

"Three to the midsection," Jack ordered. The kid delivered three open-fisted punches and Jack's body jerked in response.

"Irish whip to the turnbuckle and pummel me with kicks."

He was asking for it today. He shouldn't even be here and everyone knew it. But that scene with Niece Sullivan had set his gut ablaze with an overwhelming urge to do some serious damage to something. He needed to exorcise his demons.

Jack slid down the corner ropes and Marco nailed him twice with his boot, flattening him to the mat. Jack played possum, trying to gather his thoughts, trying to figure out why he had so much trouble shaking this damn business from his life.

"You okay?" Marco asked.

"Wonderful. Give me a minute."

The fluorescent ceiling lights burned bright, and Jack wished it was the sun shining down on him. What he wouldn't give to be sucking down umbrella drinks on a deserted beach, or riding a playful Appaloosa into the Rockies. He'd give anything to be someplace else. Someplace far away from Ms. Frankie McGee.

With a little luck he'd be out of here, starting his new life sooner rather than later. The inexperienced Tiger Lady would ruin the story line, and he'd go about his merry way without turning heel. All would be right with the world.

Unfortunately, there was something very wrong about that scene he'd just played out in Sully's office. If only the niece hadn't touched him. He closed his eyes and ran his hand across his face. A myriad of blues, greens, and yellows filled his vision. Frankie's eyes. He wondered why she didn't wear contacts, why she wore the protective shield of glasses. Then again, he wouldn't want her to change that incredible color. Iridescent, colorful, amazing eyes. Big and round and burning with need.

"Dammit!" He pounded a closed fist on the ring floor.

"Don't look now, but your woman's comin'," Marco said.

Perfect. Just what he needed when his brain was scrambled like a carton of eggs.

Catcalls announced Tiger Lady's entrance into the gym.

"Come on down, baby," Nick called.

"Wooooeeee!" Luther howled. "Look at them legs."

"I like the set of lungs myself," the Basher said.

He could only guess what Tiger Lady was wearing today. He draped his arm over his face, giving himself another second or two of peace. Who was he kidding? Frankie had shot that all to hell.

"Are you okay?" a soft voice said. He opened his eyes and spied Tiger Lady, mask and all, standing over him.

"What's with the mask?" he asked, taking note of the voluptuous body hugged by a skin-tight black-and-gold leotard.

"I always wear the mask."

"Always?"

"Almost always."

She grinned and he couldn't help smiling back. It would be nice to work with someone who had a sense of humor. Then he remembered last night's assault, losing the belt. In one, swift motion he jackknifed and slid under the bottom rope, out of the ring. She took three steps back. He grabbed her by the shoulders to keep her from tripping over a 200-pound barbell.

"You really messed me up last night," he said.

"I'm sorry." She blinked those cornflower blue eyes, and he found himself believing her.

Remember your goal, Hudson. Teach her to screw up so you can get out of this hellhole.

A great plan if they were alone. Unfortunately, a crowd of wrestlers was gathering. Word must have gotten out that Jack was taking on a partner, something he'd successfully avoided for the past nineteen years.

"We don't have a lot of time. Sullivan's witch niece has scheduled us for a whirlwind tour of the Midwest. We go the day after tomorrow."

"You don't like her very much."

"What's to like?" Other than those incredible eyes, up-tight little attitude, and peaches-and-cream skin that probably tasted even better than it looked.

"Come on." He grabbed her hand and pulled her up the steps to the ring. She stumbled. "Take those spiked heels off."

"I need to practice in them, so I don't keep tripping over my own feet."

"Whatever." He held the ropes open for her, and she stepped inside the squared circle.

"Teach her a Bulldog!" Teddy shouted.

"Teach her to sell!" Luther added.

"Show her a clothesline!" Marco said with a hearty chuckle.

"No one said anything about doing laundry," Tiger Lady said, confusion coloring her eyes.

"Man, you are green, aren't you?" he muttered, almost feeling sorry for her. Talk about being out of her league. He reached for her wrist, and she stepped back.

"Hang on, I'm not going to hurt you." Sheesh, why were the women in his life so jumpy around him? First Frank, then Cat Woman. Had Marco been spreading rumors?

"Here." He got behind her and raised her arm at a right angle. "You swing at my chest like this." He moved it backward, then forward.

She seemed softer today, more normal. Her scent teased his nostrils. Different today. More subtle, although he couldn't quite make it out.

"Keep your arm right there." He stepped in front of her. "Okay, now whack me across the chest."

"But I'll hurt you."

"I doubt it."

Her eyes flared and she swung. He fell flat to the mat, and she stared down at him in wonder.

"Clothesline," he said, getting to his feet.

"I did that?" Her eyes grew wide.

72

"*We* did that. It's a partnership. But don't worry, you won't be doing much inside the ring. I just wanted you to become familiar with some of the moves."

He glanced up and spied Sully watching from his office. Good. He wanted Sully to see him working with Tiger Lady, training her, showing her how to be a superb partner. That way no one could accuse him of self-sabotage when she screwed up and ruined the angle.

"Your real job is to distract the ref when I'm being taken down," he explained to her.

"Distract him how?"

"Use your womanly powers to stop the three count."

She pursed her lips. "Isn't that cheating?"

"All's fair in love and wrestling." If only that were true. "You're also supposed to nail my opponent while I'm keeping the ref occupied."

"More cheating?"

"Fans are very forgiving when the face is doing the cheating."

"The face?"

"Baby face, hero, good guy."

"Oooohhhh."

He rolled out of the ring and reached up for her. She hesitated. "Come on, you're giving me a complex. I'm not going to hurt you."

She stepped through the ropes and lost her footing, falling into his arms. Hesitating before placing her on the floor, his eyes caught on her lips. Such beautiful lips, perfectly shaped and ruby red. He bet they tasted like—

"You can put me down now," she said.

"Right." What the hell was the matter with him?

He steadied her and turned to Marco. "Get over here."

The kid actually looked scared, as if Jack was going to let him have it.

"Get in the ring and hang your head over the side."

The kid did as ordered. Jack turned to Tiger Lady. "If

73

you catch my opponent in this position, you nail him in the neck, got it?"

"Nail him?"

"Here." He reached for her gloved fist, and this time she didn't pull away. "An open fist." He loosely curled her fingers. "Not to be confused with a closed fist." He curled her fingers tight into her palm. "We use open fists and barely make contact. That way nobody gets hurt, got it?"

She nodded.

"Like this." He nailed Marco, and the kid jerked in mock pain.

"You said an open fist doesn't hurt."

"Marco does a good sell, don't ya, Marco?" The kid winked, and she smiled back. Jack had a sudden urge to step between them.

"Okay, you try."

She punched Marco, and he jerked on cue.

"Ah!" she cried, stumbling and falling into Teddy's lap. The Basher let loose a hearty laugh.

"You can't be afraid to hurt the opponent. It's gotta look real," Jack said, reaching for her.

She cocked her head in question, and he smiled to himself. He could smell the mountain air already, picturing himself sitting by the fire in his dream cabin on a cold winter night.

Just as he pulled her from Teddy's lap, a loud bang echoed across the gym. He glanced up at Sullivan's office. The promoter's face was plastered against the glass, his palms flattened, his eyes bugging out of his head.

"What's the matter with Crazy Joey?" Teddy asked.

Sullivan disappeared from view.

"Who knows? Probably got in a fight with that neurotic niece of his," Jack said.

"Neurotic?" Tiger Lady asked.

"Uptight, rigid, anal retentive. Take your pick."

"Frankie always seemed okay to me."

"She's anything but okay."

The gym door flew open. Sullivan navigated through the Nautilus equipment like he was running an obstacle course. He stopped just short of Jack, completely out of breath.

"They eloped. Got drunk in Vegas . . . tried to take over Wayne Newton's show . . . sleeping it off in jail. They can't get to Milwaukee. The show starts in four hours!"

"Slow down, what are you talking about?" Jack said.

"Eve and Neurosis! Come, come! I have a limo waiting. You'll have to fill in. Both of you." He grabbed Tatianna's arm.

"But I can't—"

"I have no one else!" Sully cried, pulling her toward the exit.

"Sullivan, I'm not supposed to get back in the ring for ten days," Jack said.

"No fighting, no fighting. Come, come!"

Sully was desperate. Jack smelled victory. A major screw-up tonight and Sully would see the error of his ways. They'd drop the Tiger-Cowboy story line and chase some other soap-opera theme.

"Billings has the costumes," Sully said, leading Tatianna by the arm. "Maxine will ride with you. Two hours, only two hours away."

Billings shoved a sweatshirt at Jack as they followed Sully and Tiger Lady to the waiting limousine.

"Your gear's already in the limo," Billings said.

"Gee, thanks, Bill."

Tatianna climbed inside, and Jack heard her greet Maxine. He hesitated before climbing in.

"But Sully, Tiger Lady has no experience," he said, laying the groundwork. They'd never know what hit them.

"Don't worry. I've got everything under control. You just get there. We'll be right behind you."

Jack smiled. "Anything for you, boss."

The promoter's jaw dropped.

Jack climbed into the limo, and Sully ducked his head inside. "Maybe I should ride with you."

"We'll be fine," Jack said.

Sully narrowed his eyes at Jack, then glanced at Tatianna. "Be careful."

Jack put his arm around Tiger Lady and pulled her against his chest. "Don't worry, Sullivan. I'll take real good care of her."

Chapter Six

She was going to die. Right here, in the middle of fifteen thousand screaming fans on prime-time television. Frankie was going to drop more than a hundred feet from the Milwaukee City Arena catwalk to the middle of the ring and meet her Maker.

At least it would boost ratings.

The boom of fireworks shot panic through her veins as she gripped the metal rail with trembling, gloved fingers.

"You'll go down slow and easy. Just like in Raleigh," the stunt director explained.

"You launched me into a pool of green Jell-O in Raleigh," Jack growled.

"Yeah, well, good thing we made it kinda stiff." He cleared his throat. "Anyway, I checked the harness. You're all set. You've got three safety hooks."

"What about hers?"

"Her what?"

"Her harness, stupid."

"I only got one. She's going down with you."

"Judas Priest, man! She needs her own gear."

"We were lucky to get your equipment on such short notice. Had to pull some major strings."

He gripped the roadie by his worn Grateful Dead T-shirt. "Pull some more strings and get her some gear."

"Uh, I'd like to, man, I really would. But you're scheduled to drop in fifteen."

He released the kid with such force, he landed a couple of feet away. "Do you have any idea whether the harness will hold both of us?"

"It should." The roadie tentatively reached out and secured the hooks to Jack's harness. "It held the Basher at Melee in the Park and he weighs over four hundred pounds. You weigh in at 250, and this one"—he eyed Frankie—"she can't be more than a hundred forty."

"One hundred twenty-six, thank you very much." Good God, she was arguing about her weight.

"You're all set. The lights will go off in about twenty minutes. Then Prince will do his introduction." The roadie put his hand on the metal gate. "Pop the button like this." The door swung open.

Her stomach plummeted.

"And off you go. You'll float down like a feather, no problem."

"And what's to cushion our fall if there *is* a problem?" Jack asked.

"Don't know, man. My job's done once you take flight. I'm sure they've got cushioning under the ring or something." The kid nodded, shoved a screwdriver into his tool belt and backed away.

"We're going to die," she whispered.

"Stop it." Jack scanned the crowd below.

"Why?" She studied his profile.

"Because it will drive you crazy. These guys are professionals. They know what they're doing."

"No, I mean why do you do this?"

78

He glanced at her, his eyes colored with incredible sadness.

"Oh, God, you know it too, don't you?"

He pulled her against his chest. "Sully won't let anything happen to us. We're too profitable. We're the flavor of the week, kid."

"Then why did you look at me like that?" she muttered into his jacket, comforted by the smell of leather.

"Like what?"

"You looked so . . . sad." She glanced up at him.

"You're imagining things," he said, avoiding eye contact. She knew at that moment that he was as nervous as she was.

"Didn't you know I jumped out of airplanes for a living before I became a wrestler?" he joked.

She couldn't help chuckling. But the moment wore off, and she started to shake again. Everywhere.

"Shhh." With a solid arm around her shoulders, he held her close. She clung to the supple leather, thinking maybe if she held on tight enough she could will away her embarrassing reaction.

"I don't usually shake like this."

"Relax, kid. I had to clock forty hours of stunt training before they'd let me do this trick. Still can't believe they've turned me into a damned stunt man," he muttered.

"How many times have you done it with a partner?"

He shot her a wry smile.

A new wave of tremors wracked her body. Her teeth began to chatter.

"Think about something else," he said. "It'll take your mind off the jitters."

Her mind went completely blank.

"April 15, 1978," he said.

"Wha-what's that?"

"National championships. First trip away from home. I was seventeen, went with the coach to Denver. There was a whole other world outside of Carver, Missouri. I'll never

79

forget seeing the Rocky Mountains for the first time."

Studying his expression, the faraway look in his eyes, she knew his mind was recalling a better time.

He blinked and cleared his throat. "Anyway . . . that's what I think about when I'm trying to stay sane."

They clutched each other in silence for a good minute; her trembling slowed to a steady pulse.

"Your turn," he said.

"My life's pretty boring, actually."

"You call this boring?"

A whimper-laugh escaped her lips. "Stop teasing me."

"Is that what I'm doing?"

He shot her a full-dimpled smile, and she warmed inside.

"All right, then, if this is our last performance, we should bare all," he said, lightheartedly. "I tell you how I stole Samantha Peter's milk money in the third grade to buy a Killer Kowalski comic book, and you tell me what Sully's got on you to make you dress like a feline and do suicide jumps for a living."

"True confessions, is that it?"

"Works for me. Either that or make one up."

Looking into his eyes, she wanted to tell him the truth, that the woman he held in his arms was really his mortal enemy, the Franken Niece. She glanced at the ring below and decided the drop was too far to chance it.

"If I knew you better, I'd say you've got something big brewing behind those baby blues," he said. "Then again, I don't know you at all, do I?"

"I . . . you . . . I'm sorry," she said.

"What are you sorry about?"

Lying. Manipulating. Being an all-around crumb.

"The other night," she said, recovering. "Making you lose the championship belt."

"It's okay. Part of the fun is getting it back."

"But you were so mad. Frankie told me the things you said."

80

He looked away. "The first thing you should learn is never to trust anyone in that family. They're like piranha. They'll eat you alive."

She swallowed hard. No, now was definitely not the time to confess her true identity.

"You didn't answer my question," she said, trying to redirect the conversation.

"Which one was that?"

"About why you do this."

"Why do you do this?"

"Stop avoiding the question."

He glanced across the auditorium and smiled. A smile that didn't quite make it to his eyes.

"Wrestling has been my life for the past twenty-five years. I guess you could say amateur wrestling saved my life. But professional wrestling . . . it's changed. I don't recognize it anymore." He ran his hand back and forth across her shoulders in a comforting motion. "Anyway, it's time to get out, time for a new life."

"What kind of life?"

"Whatever I want, kid. The world's wide open once I get out of this circus. I'm going to do things and try things I've never been able to do because of my tour schedule. And I won't have to answer to anybody, not even Sully."

That familiar knot tightened in her stomach. Another irresponsible male. Just like Dad.

The arena suddenly went black, and she involuntarily dug her fingernails into his leather jacket.

"Calm down, sweetheart. It will be over soon."

Sure it would. She could picture the headlines: FINAN-CIAL ADVISOR LEADS DOUBLE LIFE AS CAT WOMAN: PLUNGES TO DEATH IN THE ARMS OF WRESTLING COWBOY.

Good God, what will Bradley think? And what about her mother?

"That's our cue," he said, standing. She clutched his jacket with white-knuckled fingers.

"You're fine. Just hang on. Wrap your legs around my waist."

"But—"

"No time to be self-conscious, kid. Not if you want to come out of this in one piece."

He cupped her behind with firm hands and pulled her up against his chest. Following his lead, she locked her spiked heels around his waist and gripped his shoulders.

The spotlight blinded her, giving her a sneak preview of the journey to heaven. At least that's where she hoped she'd end up.

"Ready?" he said.

"N-N-No," Frankie mumbled between uncontrollable sobs. Good thing she wore little eye makeup this time. She just hoped her contact lenses didn't fall out. Not that anyone would notice her eye color at the wake.

"Look at me," he said.

She glanced into his powerful green eyes.

And he kissed her. Just like that. Without warning or permission or any of the traditional preludes to such an intimate act. It was an incredible kiss, filled with the sultry male taste of Black Jack Hudson. His soft lips coaxed a response, and she automatically opened to him.

Somewhere in the recesses of her mind she heard blaring music and screaming fans. But they were far away, as if on another planet.

She deepened the kiss, knocking off his hat to run her hands through his long, dark hair. She couldn't get enough as she floated on passion's wings, lightheaded with a kind of drugged desire she'd only read about in books.

Their tongues mated and danced, sending shock waves of awareness all the way down to her toes. She felt like she could fly, but she didn't dare let go. No, she wanted to hold on to this feeling to the bitter end.

What a way to go.

Her head spun, and she shifted her hips to hug Jack's

waist even tighter. She acted wanton and crazed. And it felt good. Damn good.

Jack's hand pressed against the small of her back, then slipped down to cradle her behind. God, he smelled good, a mixture of leather and spice. And he tasted even better, like a rare fruit, sweet but tart.

He broke the kiss, and she moaned in protest.

"The shuttle has landed," he said, his voice hoarse.

"What?" She struggled for breath, her gaze locked on to his swollen lips. Lips she wanted to taste again.

"You can let go now."

She didn't want to let go. She belonged right here in his arms, waiting for another blast of passion from his lips.

"It's over," he said.

"I don't understand." She didn't hear a choir of angels or see the pearly gates open in greeting. She glanced at the catwalk above her. Then she peered over his shoulder. The fans waved signs, screamed, and practically jumped from their seats.

"We're down?" she said, still dazed. "I don't believe it."

"It's for real. We're fine."

"We're fine," she repeated.

But she wasn't fine. Her heart pounded an erratic beat, her brain felt as if it were stuffed with cotton, or passion, or both.

He gently untangled her legs, then kissed her on the forehead.

"You're okay," he murmured, peeling her off him.

"You kissed me," she said, still in shock.

"I had to get you down somehow." He winked and unhooked himself from the harness.

"Ladies and gentlemen," the announcer boomed, walking up beside Jack. "WHAK's very own favorite couple, Black Jack Hudson and Tatianna the Tigress!"

The roar echoed off the ceiling, ricocheted off the seats and vibrated her eardrums. She watched Jack strut to the corner, straddle the bottom and middle ropes and raise his hat in salute to the fans.

He'd kissed her.

With passion and heat she hadn't thought possible.

And all because he'd needed to get her to make the jump. A jump that could have killed them both.

Anger simmered in her belly, eating away the passion of a moment ago. She stormed a wobbly path across the ring, ripped off her right glove and tapped him on the shoulder. He stepped down from the ropes and turned to her, a half grin lighting his eyes. A grin she planned to wipe right off that handsome face of his. She wound up and let him have it with an open palm to his cheek.

"What the hell?" He put up his hand as if expecting her to strike him again.

"You kissed me!"

"Yeah? So?"

"To distract me?"

"It worked didn't it?"

She wound up for another swing. He grabbed her wrist before she could make contact.

"We don't want fans getting the wrong idea about our relationship, babe."

"You stupid, ignorant, overgrown ape! We could have been killed!"

"We would have been killed with you shaking like that. You would have slipped right out of my arms."

He had a point. He had gotten her down in one piece, basically saving her life.

No, this wasn't her life. Her life was back in Boston analyzing financial proposals and investing company funds. Her life revolved around her career, Friday night dinners with Bradley and monthly lunches at the Urban Professional Women's Club. Her life included checking the financial section of the paper every morning and planning out her vacations for the next ten years. Hawaii this year,

Mexico the next. Maybe she'd even fit Australia into her schedule in 2010.

Her life.

And she'd almost lost it helping her uncle in his ridiculous, unreal business.

She spun on her heel and headed for the opposite end of the ring.

"Where the hell are you going?" he called after her.

"Home!"

"But you can't leave now," the referee said, chasing her down and gripping her elbow. "We're about to start. The cameras are rolling."

"News flash. I'm done."

"No, that's not in the script!" He pulled her to center ring. She stumbled alongside him.

"Get your hands off her!" Jack ripped the ref's hand from her arm and she fell backward, landing on her fanny.

"But she can't leave. He's here!" the ref protested.

"Who's here?" Jack said.

Organ pipes blared across the sound system, crying out the Wedding March. A man dressed in black carrying an open Bible in his hands paced slowly toward the ring. The referee helped him through the ropes. Frankie just stared, dumbfounded.

"Come on. Let's get this over with," Jack muttered, offering his hand.

"I should be dead. Instead I'm marrying a complete stranger."

"I wouldn't call us complete strangers." He shot her that charming smile and her heart did a skippity-hop. This man was dangerous. And about to become her husband. Or at least her pretend husband.

"I can't do this," she said.

"You also said you couldn't jump from the catwalk."

"You tricked me."

"I kissed you."

"Same difference."

"Actually, it's not a bad story line if you ask me."

"I didn't."

"On your feet, Cat Woman."

He grabbed her by the arms and lifted her to her feet. Damn. The girl really looked nervous, as if the thought of marrying Black Jack Hudson terrified her.

It wasn't like this was a real marriage. Not that the marriage to Sandra was real. His brain had been too pickled with lust for him to recognize the train wreck headed straight for him. But after three long years, he'd finally figured out that Sandra loved the fame, not the man. And that's when Jack had decided he could never find love or a normal life as long as he was a celebrity pro wrestler.

"I don't like this," Tiger Lady said as the minister stepped toward them.

"There could be worse things."

"Like?"

"Like jumping from a catwalk?"

She swung and he stepped out of the way, enjoying the sight of her tumbling in a puff of black and gold feathers. He had to give her credit. She recovered well. Only five minutes ago she was shivering like a victim of frostbite. He couldn't help comforting her, and not just because he thought she'd vibrate right out of his arms. No, there was something fragile about this one. Something that made him want to hold her, protect her.

He rubbed his cheek. But who was going to protect him?

"Dearly beloved . . ." the minister began.

Jack wrapped his arms around her from behind. She stilled, and he wondered what was going on in that mind of hers. He prepared himself for a kick to the shin from deadly four-inch spikes.

"This man and this . . ." the minister eyed Tiger Lady, ". . . woman . . ." She plucked feathers from her mouth. Boy, when Max beefed up the costume she sure added a lot to cover up the woman's finer points.

". . . in holy matrimony . . ."

"It's all pretend," he whispered in her ear.

And it was, for the most part. The drama, the hype. Everything but the physical punishment he sustained match after match, and the burning in his gut every time Sully snapped the cage door shut.

Would Jack ever be free to start a new, normal life away from the madness? He'd give anything to be anonymous and walk into a 7-Eleven without drawing stares. An impossibility thanks to his size, a by-product of working out for hours each and every day to maintain his body.

". . . to love and honor the rest of your lives . . ." the minister continued.

Jack needed his freedom. To travel, work on the cabin, maybe even help Butch with the youth fitness centers. Jack was proud that his money had gone to something good, helping kids who were at that vulnerable age. He didn't care that he might never see a penny from the business. Some things meant more than the all-mighty dollar.

Like living a normal life. That's all Jack wanted. It didn't seem like a lot to ask. He'd been a devoted WHAK employee for nearly twenty years. But it was never enough. With Dad. With WHAK. Was Jack destined to live by another man's script for the rest of his life?

Tiger Lady wobbled, and he steadied her against his chest. She was the reason for the self-analysis; she'd read the pain in his eyes and called him on it. He hadn't realized he was that transparent; it could be a definite disadvantage if he planned to outwit Sully and jump ship ASAP.

". . . if there are any reasons why this man and this woman should not be married, speak now or forever hold your peace. . . ."

The crowd hushed.

"Now that you mention it—" Tiger Lady started.

Jack grabbed her by the shoulders and kissed her before she could finish her protest. It wouldn't look good to his fans to have his wife-to-be object to marrying their hero.

"Excuse me," the minister said.

Jack broke the kiss and blinked twice to get his bearings. The adrenaline from the jump must not have worn off.

"You don't kiss the bride yet," the minister scolded.

"Right. Sorry." He couldn't tear his gaze from her clear blue eyes and ruby red lips. Not real. None of this was real. He tamped down the burning in his gut. The burn of regret? Of having done this once before only to find out it wasn't real either?

"The ring?" The minister poked Jack in the arm.

"Huh? Yeah, we're in the ring. What?"

"For her finger," the minister said.

"I've got it," Prince Priceless cried into the microphone, as he climbed through the ropes. "Although it will probably turn her finger green!"

The crowd booed and hissed Prince on cue.

"I can't help it if Black Jack is a cheap, no-good, bumble-brained idiot."

"Just hand over the ring," Jack said.

"Come and get it."

"My pleasure." He started toward the jerk. Was this in the script? Who knew? No one had told them what to expect. They probably hadn't thought they'd survive the fall.

"Wait," she said, gripping Jack's arm. "Let me handle this."

He narrowed his eyes.

"Trust me."

He stepped aside. He must be crazy.

Tiger Lady sauntered toward Prince.

"What's this? Change your mind? Hey, kitty cat, I'm all yours," Prince flirted.

Jack clenched his fists by his sides. Not real. None of this was real.

Wrapping her arms around Prince's neck, she gave the middle-aged jerk a squeeze. His eyelashes fluttered as he glanced up to the heavens.

Jack was going to be sick. Was this her way of taking

revenge because he'd tricked her into jumping from the catwalk?

"See, Black Jack, I not only beat you in the ring, but I beat you in love. Come on, kitty. Let's go back to my place," Prince cooed.

She shot Prince a charming smile, stepped away from him and stuck out her hand.

"What? You want this?" Prince pinched the ring between his forefinger and thumb. "Okay, but don't get any ideas. I'm not the marrying kind, not until I get to know you better."

He raised his eyebrows twice and dropped the gold band in her palm.

"Shall we?" Prince scanned the crowd, a smug look on his face. Tiger Lady smiled up at him.

Damn, she was really going to humiliate Jack in front of fifteen thousand people. On the other hand, this could be his ticket out. If she paired up with Prince, that left Jack out in the cold.

"Once again, the best man wins," Prince said to Jack, then extended his hand to lead Tiger Lady from the ring. "I'm so glad you all got to see that I'm the better man. I'm the true hero, the—"

With a lunge and a cry, Tiger Lady attacked Prince, biting his hand. He shrieked and the audience shrieked back. She nailed his foot with her spiked heel, and he cried out like a gutted animal.

"She's crazy! Get her away from me." He made for the ropes with Tiger Lady in hot pursuit. She lunged. He screamed and tumbled out of the ring.

Jack burst out laughing. He couldn't help himself.

"You can have her," Prince cried from the bordering blue mat. He hopped on one foot and rubbed the other with his hands. "You deserve each other!"

The fans roared as Prince limped up the ramp and out of sight, obviously in search of first aid. Tiger Lady sauntered to Jack, stumbling only once.

"Nice," Jack said.

"Who needs to throw a punch when you've got these?" She stuck out her heel and grinned, a twinkle in her eye.

"Yeah, but I don't look so good in gold."

"You'd probably fall over in them anyway. It takes a certain talent to keep your balance." She shifted to the other foot and lost her balance. He steadied her by the elbow.

"A talent you've obviously mastered."

"I've mastered the stabbing part," she warned.

"Excuse me," the minister said. "But I have a marriage to finish."

"Right, sorry," Jack said.

"The ring?" the minister said.

Tiger Lady handed it to the minister.

"Not me, him."

She dropped the ring in Jack's palm, not making eye contact.

"Place it on her finger," the ministered ordered.

He eased it over her gloved finger. "I don't suppose you want to take these off?"

"No, thanks."

He adjusted the ring to the second knuckle. "That's as far as it goes."

"Good enough." The minister cleared his throat. "I now pronounce you . . . Master and Tiger Wife. You may kiss your cat." He snapped the Bible shut.

Jack glanced at Tatianna, who fiddled with the gold band on her finger. He cradled her chin between his thumb and forefinger and guided her gaze to meet his. The minister shoved the microphone between them. Jack snatched it from him and the fans roared, thinking they were going to hear personal, intimate words spoken between Black Jack Hudson and his new bride.

Jack tossed the microphone to the corner of the ring and looked into Tatianna's eyes.

"May I? Kiss you?"

She nodded. At least he thought she nodded. If not, he'd

know real quick when she drilled him with those spikes of hers.

Leaning forward, he brushed his lips against her mouth and closed his eyes, savoring the minty taste of this strange woman. He didn't mind kissing her, not really. She felt warm and soft in his arms. When she leaned into him, with that wisp of a moan purring against his lips, he wished the thousands of fans away, wished for a real moment alone with the woman he held in his arms.

A strange woman he'd never met until two nights ago. A player hired to entertain the audience, just as he did day after day, three hundred shows a year.

He grabbed her by the shoulders and held her a safe distance away, if there was such a thing. Her fingers still clung to his hair, her eyes glazed over with desire. She might not be a professional actress, but she was damn good at making this look real.

"Ladies and gentlemen, let's hear it for Mr. and Mrs. Black Jack Hudson," the referee announced. The crowd went wild, showering the ring with popcorn, beer, and anything else they'd bought at the concession stand and hadn't yet consumed.

"It's here! It's here!" The minister squealed like a child on Christmas morning. For an actor, the guy seemed unusually excited. Maybe he hoped for a repeat performance at next month's Hammer Lock Festival.

"Oh, my God," she said, teetering against Jack.

He glanced toward the Monkey Tunnel. A twenty-foot float rolled down the ramp—pink, green, and purple flowers framing a four-poster bed covered in gold satin sheets.

"I didn't know they made sheets that color," she said.

"I'm a flannel guy myself."

"No kidding?" She glanced up at him.

"Would I kid you at a time like this? When we're about to consummate our marriage in front of fifteen thousand fans?"

"Don't even," she threatened.

91

"Lighten up. It's a family show, remember? At least it used to be."

"Take your places!" the minister said, motioning toward the float. Jack eased out of the ring, then caught his new bride as she stumbled through the ropes. Coordination wasn't her strong suit. But then she had other attributes that were more important than being able to walk straight.

He gave himself a mental slap. Get on the float, sail out of here, and get to the condo. He wanted to lock himself inside and stand under the coldest shower possible. Then, maybe, he could forget this night and the seductive taste of peppermint.

Tatianna, Jack, and the minister climbed aboard the floating monstrosity. The minister took his position front and center, waving his Bible at the screaming fans. Jack leaned back against the headboard and waved his Stetson. His "wife" gripped the bedpost with both hands and smiled. Growled, more like it. He had a feeling she wasn't into being paraded around like a star. She'd get used to it. They all did sooner or later.

The float maneuvered around the corner of the ring, taking out the metal steps, a set of guard rails, and a few folding chairs. Good thing this was the end of the show. Between the tossed refreshments and demolition float, the set was cashed.

They cruised up the ramp backstage, the curtain falling behind them.

"That was wonderful! Wonderful!" The phony minister climbed down from the float.

Jack jumped off and the actor grabbed his hand. "I've been a fan since forever! I was raised on Killer Kowolski and Verne Gagne. You don't know how much it means to me to participate in a real rasslin' match. Maybe next time they'll let me be a guest referee."

The guy pumped Jack's hand.

"Jack! Jack!" Sully raced up to them, giving his hair the once over with both hands. "Great show, fabulous. Henry,

I can't thank you enough for filling in at the last minute."
Sully winked.

"It's a good thing I had the experience." The actor chuckled, and Sully slapped him on the back.

"So, you're local talent, then?" Jack said.

"You two haven't been formally introduced?" Sully said.
"Jack Hudson, please meet my dear friend and minister of
the First Presbyterian Church of East Bridge, Wisconsin,
Harold Gardner."

"A real minister?" Jack's blood ran cold. "You had a real
minister marry us?"

"That means . . ." Tatianna's lips quivered.

"We're really married," Jack finished for her.

She collapsed on the makeshift bed in a puff of golden
feathers.

Chapter Seven

It was all a bad dream. Either that or an afterlife hallucination. Frankie and the cowboy had actually died in the fall and her ascension to heaven included a free fantasy: marrying Black Jack Hudson.

"Wake up, girl. You're scarin' me," an angel said.

She opened her eyes and Maxine's heavily made-up face came into focus. The woman's silver hair was trimmed with a bright yellow headband; her eyeshadow was a blend of kelly green and turquoise.

"What are you doing here?" Frankie asked. Maxine hadn't made the jump with them.

"Your uncle wanted me to take care of you. Said you fainted dead away."

"I didn't know you could faint in heaven."

"Heaven? My land, child, where did you get such an idea?"

"But the fall, then the marriage and then . . . oh, God." She clutched her head to stop the spinning.

"When was the last time you ate?" With two fingers on

Frankie's wrist, Max pursed her lips in concentration.

"What happened?"

"My guess? Low blood sugar. Pulse rate's okay." She placed Frankie's hand on her stomach and gave it a pat.

"I thought I was dead."

"Stop that ridiculous talk. You're fine. Probably just exhausted."

"Am I really . . . married?"

"Minister said the words, sure as sunshine."

Max placed a cool cloth on Frankie's brow. She closed her eyes.

"Everything will be fine," Max said. "That scheming uncle of yours miscalculated, is all."

Her eyes popped open. "Miscalculated? I'm supposed to marry Bradley. We have it all planned, a brunch reception to keep the cost down. He's already booked his cousin's polka band that plays three hours for the price of two."

"Thrilling."

"Bigamy is against the law in this state, isn't it?"

Max shrugged.

"What state are we in, again?"

"Sounds like the state of confusion."

"I'm going to be sick."

"Not on my best sweatshirt you're not."

Frankie eyed her companion. Today's shirt read "High Flyers Drool, Mat Men Rule" in electric yellow. A migraine started to burn behind Frankie's eyes.

"I want to go home."

"Of course you do." Max patted her forehead with the damp cloth. "You've had quite a night. I have to say, that jump was amazing. Ratings are gonna soar for sure."

"Ratings!" She sat up and snatched the cloth from the woman's hand. "What is it with you people? I could have been killed."

"Don't be silly. Jack never would have let anything happen to you."

"Only because he didn't know I was the evil niece of his slave-driving boss. Otherwise, you'd be ordering my coffin right about now. By the way, I'm partial to walnut."

"You really woke up on the pity pot." Max paced across the room and unzipped a garment bag that hung on the back of the door.

"Yeah, well, I have a right to feel a little sorry for myself. I'm lucky I survived that stunt." Not to mention the incendiary kisses from Black Jack Hudson.

"No luck involved. The man holding you is one of the strongest, most talented athletes in the business. Talented in more ways than one." She glanced over her shoulder and winked. "My feathers ruffled just watching the two of you play tongue twister."

"It was a trick," she said, her insides tingling at the memory of that intimate contact.

"He didn't kiss you?"

"Oh, he kissed me, all right. It was a trick to get me to jump."

"I could think of worse ways to make you jump."

"I don't like being tricked."

"Ah, honey, he did what he had to do." She ambled toward Frankie, adjusting the black garment bag over her arm. "Would you rather he'd shoved you from behind?"

"He couldn't. I didn't have any equipment."

"My point exactly."

"Don't try to make sense out of this." Stretching out on the cot, she spread the washcloth over her eyes. She sure as heck couldn't make sense of this terrifying night. Terrifying, horrendous, thrilling night. A part of her had actually enjoyed certain moments of the show. Like when she'd attacked Prince Priceless and sent him screaming from the ring. God, she was losing her mind. And with it a part of her heart.

No, she couldn't be falling for the tall, dark, and handsome cowboy-wrestler whose kisses obliterated all sense, all thought. She was being juvenile. They were just a few kisses. Kisses that obviously had no impact whatsoever on Black Jack Hudson.

This was really about missing her soul mate, her sturdy, dependable pre-fiancé. The animal lust she felt for Jack wasn't real, wasn't a threat to her well-crafted life plan with Bradley.

Too bad Bradley didn't kiss like that.

She jumped to her feet and paced the small room. Bradley was perfect, the right choice, the mature choice. He was nothing like Jack, a man who pretended to beat up other men for a living. A man who planned to dump this career and traipse across the countryside like a tumbleweed in a windstorm, doing whatever he wanted, whenever he wanted.

A man who set her body on fire with a single kiss. She stopped dead in her tracks.

"I'm done, Max. I'm leaving tonight and never coming back."

"Don't say that." The older woman took her hand and coaxed her to the cot.

"I've dressed like a freak, performed a suicide jump, and gotten married to a complete stranger! That's it. I'm done."

"Your uncle needs you." Max squeezed Frankie's hand with trembling fingers.

"Mom was right. Uncle Joe is a lost cause." She snatched a dark green pantsuit from the garment bag and started for the bathroom.

Max grabbed her by the elbow. "How dare you talk like that about Joe Sullivan. All he ever did was love you and take care of you when no one else would."

"Now wait a minute—"

"You owe it to your uncle to do everything you can to help him."

"Like marry a complete stranger?" she challenged. Strange, she never raised her voice to her mother like this. "What's next? Should I have his child?"

97

"The marriage is probably invalid. If not, your uncle will figure out a way to have it anulled."

"I'm anulling this whole damn mess right now." She reached for the bathroom door.

"He's going to die," Max said, a tremor in her voice.

Frankie's hand froze on the doorknob.

"What did you say?" She slowly turned, afraid to see Max's expression. The older woman ambled to the cot and sat down, interlacing her limp fingers in her lap.

"You heard me. Your uncle's going to die."

"Is he sick?"

"No, nothing that minor."

"Then what?" She sat beside Max.

"Always had to prove himself, be a success. Went too far this time," Max mumbled.

"You're not making sense."

"Your uncle borrowed money . . . from bad men. They came to the office late one night when no one was around. Heard one call the other Pugsy. The tall one had a tuba case and a pool cue; the other guy carried a family of boa constrictors in a burlap sack. The thugs trashed the place, shouting and screaming obscenities. When they left, I found your uncle curled into a ball on top of his desk. Seems the men left one of the snakes as a reminder they'd be back. Damn thing must have crawled up into the heating duct. Couldn't find him anywhere. Took me an hour to get your uncle off the desk."

"I don't believe it."

"I'm not too proud to tell you I'm scared. I've seen enough gangster movies to know what they'll do to your uncle. First, he'll lose his left pinky. Then they'll crush his right knee cap. If he doesn't cough up the money in six months they'll probably—"

"Stop." She grabbed Max's hand to comfort her, or comfort herself, she wasn't sure. Everything had seemed so normal a week ago.

"He'll be devastated if he finds out you know," Max said.

"He didn't think I'd notice something was up when he started tooling around in a wheelchair?"

"Don't be mad at him."

"Mad doesn't even describe it."

Max studied Frankie with those bright blue eyes, tinged with specks of silver. "He loves you so much. He always talked about his smart little princess. So clever, so precocious. Anyone listening would have thought you were a genius."

"Why, Max? Why did he do this?"

"To prove himself."

"To me?"

"Not just you."

"Who?"

Max glanced at her fingers. "Doesn't matter."

"How can you say that? His life is in danger because of his pride. Does this other person even care about him?"

"Not really. Not like he needs to be cared for." Max straightened and headed for the door.

Frankie realized that Max had always taken care of Uncle Joe, watched his back, cleaned up his messes, even scolded him when necessary, which was more often than not.

It suddenly dawned on Frankie that Maxine loved her uncle.

"Max?"

"I'll give you privacy to change." She turned and shot Frankie a wavering smile. A touch of sadness colored her eyes. "Don't worry about me. I'm a tough old broad." She closed the door behind her.

Frankie wished she could say the same about herself.

Now she had no choice but to be tough. Her uncle's life depended on it.

"I'll bet you were behind this." Jack closed in on Frankie as she waited for the limo just outside the north entrance to the arena. She held her breath. It had been nearly two hours since their "wedding" and she couldn't wipe the taste of him from her lips. It didn't help that he'd changed into hip-hugging jeans and a black T-shirt that spanned his chest like a second skin.

"You set this up, didn't you?" he accused.

Was that smoke streaming from his nostrils?

She struggled to get her wits about her. No longer the nervous cat bride, she was Francine McGee, business woman, and the only person standing between her uncle and the Grim Reaper.

"I had nothing to do with it, Mr. Hudson. Although considering the audience's reaction, I'd say it seems to be quite a clever story line."

"Clever."

"Yes, clever."

"And you didn't dream it up? I'm surprised."

He crossed his arms over his chest, letting his gaze drift from her mouth to her breasts, down to her legs, then back up again. She lifted her chin and pressed her fingers to the lapels of her suit. There was no way she'd be intimidated by his sexual energy. Time to mark her territory.

"The marriage will fit in well with the promotional dates I've set up. You and Tatianna will be quite a draw as man and wife." She glanced across the parking lot. Where was that car? She needed time alone, time to sit with her thoughts and decide to what lengths she'd go to protect her uncle.

"Where is my . . . *wife*, anyway?" he asked, an edge to his voice.

Great, now he hated Frankie as businesswoman *and* cat wife.

"She's got friends in town and decided to stay over." Lies, lies, and more lies. At this rate she'd be bound to weekly confession for the next ten years.

A black stretch limousine pulled up.

"Here's my ride." She escaped into the car and shut the door, finally able to take a deep breath and calm her nerves.

Then she glanced out the window. Jack stood there, glaring through the tinted glass.

She lowered her window. "Is there a problem?"

"I need a ride."

Before she could hit the automatic locks, Jack was settled on the soft leather seat across from her.

It was going to be the longest two hours of her life.

As they pulled out of the lot, she stared out the window at passing office buildings, resentful that the man's very presence did things to her insides she couldn't describe. She heard him fiddle with the mini-bar. Great, now he was going to get drunk and verbally abuse her.

She crossed her arms over her chest, leaned back against the supple leather, and closed her eyes. As if that could wash away the image of the man sitting across from her: his pecs thick and hard to the touch, his hair floating wild about his shoulders. She found herself fantasizing about running her hands across the hard planes of his chest, down his stomach to other, more private places.

Bradley. She had to think about Bradley. He was the one she should be fantasizing about, not Cro-Magnon man. A smile played about her lips at the memory of Bradley straightening her shirt collar before work one morning when he'd slept over the night before. It was nice waking up to a warm body in bed. She'd even suggested they live together. But Bradley was a proper gentleman and believed in cohabitation only if one was married. He would propose the day he got promoted to partner. That way he'd feel like a success, a true provider for his bride.

Frankie recalled the Saturday morning when they'd analyzed the five-year calendar together, planning when to buy what items for their dream house and how to invest for a perfect future. He didn't mind that they'd have to cover the entire wedding expense when usually the bride's family footed the bill. Mama didn't have that kind of money, and she'd forbidden Frankie to ask Uncle Joe.

In time it would all come together. She and Bradley

would save twenty percent of every paycheck, invest in a combination mutual fund and stock program, and before she reached the age of thirty-five, she'd be walking down the aisle to say "I do" in front of a priest.

A priest. That's it. She wasn't really married to Jack because the Rev. Gardner wasn't a minister of her own faith. What a lame thought.

"You could have at least warned me," Jack's sultry voice whispered into her ear.

She nearly jumped out of her skin. Her eyes popped open and she froze at the sight of his tanned, stubbled jaw a mere inch away. He was too close, way too close. And all she could do was stare at his lips.

"What are you doing here?" She dug her fingernails into the leather seat.

"You offered me a ride, remember?" His eyes twinkled with mischief.

"I mean, why are you sitting next to me?"

"I wanted to make sure you heard me, loud and clear." His licked his lips and her pulse did a double-time rumba.

"I can hear you," she said, struggling to maintain a firm tone.

"Good. Because I want you to know how upset I am right now."

Flattening her palms against the soft leather seat beneath her, she edged away from him, until her back was pressed against the door.

He leaned forward.

She wanted him to come closer.

She wanted him to jump from the car.

"You're upset. I understand," she said.

"I don't think you do. I've done the marriage thing once. That was enough." He downed a shot from a small bottle of scotch and swiped the back of his hand across his mouth. The thought of tasting hard liquor had never crossed her mind until she spied a drop clinging to his upper lip.

102

"And nineteen years in this business is enough."

He scrutinized her cheeks, her eyes. Her skin burned. She needed air; she needed to put space between them.

"I'm sure the marriage is nothing to worry about," she said, her stomach tied in knots. "But your contract, I can't help you there. It's binding."

"Oh, you could help me." He ran his tongue over his lower lip. "If you really wanted to."

What she wanted at the moment had nothing to do with money and everything to do with raw, unbridled sex.

No, don't let him control you like this! Fight back. Don't let him melt you like butter on a frying pan.

Giving her blazer a tug to regain control, she cleared her throat. "A contract's a contract. I don't see what the big rush is about. It's not like you're an award-winning scientist who has to discover a cure for cancer."

A new emotion flashed in his eyes, similar to the sadness she'd seen on the catwalk, only different.

"No, that I'm not."

He edged away, and she breathed a sigh of relief.

"Brains never have been my strong suit," he said, glancing out the window.

She'd hurt him. Intentionally or not, she'd struck a nerve. But she couldn't help herself. Worried sick about her uncle, she simply wasn't thinking straight.

"I'm sorry," she said. "That was unfair."

He tapped a fisted hand against his thigh and continued to study the Wisconsin countryside.

"I'm not usually like that," she continued. "It's just . . . I got some bad news. About my uncle."

He eyed her. "Yeah? The old man got three months to live or something?"

She clenched her fist, wanting to lay one right between his eyes. His gaze drifted to her hand and he grinned.

"No kidding? Don't tell me—he's got a tumor in his brain the size of a football," he said, his voice hopeful.

"He doesn't have a tumor."

"What then? Bad sushi? A parasite's eating away at his intestines?"

"Forget it."

"Ah, come on, Frank. Sully's been like a father to me."

"And I'm Santa Claus." She glared out the opposite window.

Out of the corner of her eye she spied him shift beside her. He touched her hair and goose bumps tickled the back of her neck.

"Come on, kid. It will make you feel better to talk about it."

"I'm not discussing this with you."

"You brought it up."

She turned and stared him down. "And I'm dropping it."

"Maybe I can help." He brushed a bit of lint from her blazer lapel, right above her breast. She glanced down at his hand, then up into his eyes. His smile faded. She couldn't move. He was going to kiss her. Wasn't he?

"Confession is good for the soul," he said, his lips slightly parted.

She jumped to the other side of the limo and crossed her arms over her tingling breasts. "He's in trouble, that's all you need to know."

"Man, it's hot in here." He pulled the T-shirt from the waistband of his jeans, flashing a generous amount of taut, muscled stomach. Her pulse tapped against the base of her throat. How pathetic, getting turned on by a glimpse of the guy's gut.

"What kind of trouble did old Sully step into this time?" He adjusted his shirt to cover his bare flesh.

"He got involved with . . ." Her voice trailed off as she watched him stretch his arms along the back of the seat. His shirt sleeves cut into his biceps, accentuating the rounded muscle.

"What? I didn't hear you. Damn, I'm burning in here. You don't mind if I take this off, do you?" He reached for the back of his shirt with one hand.

"He got in involved with the wrong crowd, okay? Keep your shirt on."

He leaned back and shot her a victorious smile. "Wrong crowd? That's what they said about me when I stole Kurt Porter's bike in the eighth grade."

"Trust me. This is more serious than petty theft."

Before she could blink, he was next to her, crowding her, practically sitting in her lap. She blindly reached for the window controls. Maybe a little air would help. Or maybe she could jump. She had a feeling she'd have better luck with the pavement than in a physical encounter with Black Jack Hudson.

"What do I have to do, kiss it out of you?" he said.

She knew damn well she'd never survive another one of his kisses.

"You do and I'll stop the car and have you dumped in the middle of Interstate 294."

"No, you won't. Now come on. Give, just a little." His lips got closer . . . closer. She could taste them already, spicy, sweet, male.

Good God! What was she doing?

She shoved at his chest and hopped to the opposite seat like a jackrabbit.

"He took money from the mob," she blurted out.

He broke into laughter, the hearty sound filling the limo. Eyes watering, he doubled over, laughing and slapping at his knee.

"I don't see what's so funny," she said, her insides burning.

"It's just . . ." he said, trying to catch his breath, ". . . the thought of Sully a few feet shorter hit a funny bone . . . that's all."

"I see no humor in this."

"Too bad. Seems like you could use a good laugh."

"This is my uncle we're talking about."

"It's Sully. The man's been courting disaster for years. Doesn't surprise me it finally caught up with him."

105

"Of course a professional bully like yourself would find humor in this horrifying predicament."

He burst into a new fit of laughter. "It just seems like sweet justice to me."

"He could die because of this stupid business!"

His laughter stopped short. Apparently the seriousness of her uncle's predicament had finally sunk into that thick skull of his.

"Stupid business?" He squinted and leaned forward.

Guess not.

"If it's so stupid, why did Sully risk his life on a bad loan?" he challenged.

"Only he knows that."

"Not for long. The press is going to love this. They're always looking for a reason to kick us in the teeth." He held out his hands as if displaying a headline. " 'Big-time wrestling promoter uses mob money to boost business.' "

"They'll never find out."

"No?" He grinned and both cheeks dimpled.

"You wouldn't."

"You forget, babe, I want out of this crazy business more than you want me out of this car."

"Yet you defend it so much."

"That's because people like you don't understand how real it is, even if it's time for me to jump ship. That is if there's even a ship to jump from after word gets out about Sully."

"I wouldn't if I were you." Now what? Threaten to break his contract? She couldn't. She needed him too much. For the business, only for the business.

"What are you gonna do to me, sweet cheeks? Fire me?"

She wracked her brain. *Think, Frankie. Think. You've bluffed your way out of worse and with enemies the likes of multi-degreed Fortune 500 CEOs. This should be a piece of cake.*

Cash. The key to every victory.

She smiled and casually crossed one leg over the other.

"No, I won't fire you. But I can hold back that incentive bonus my uncle promised you once your contract's up."

He shot her a death glare. At least he didn't reach for his shirt again.

"I assume you need that little nest egg to move on with your life?" she said.

Jack burned to wipe that smug look off her face. And he knew just how to do it. With a kiss.

"Cat got your tongue?" she taunted.

A haze of red flashed before his eyes. Red, orange, yellow. He was seeing fire. And he wanted to throw her right into the flames.

With an arrogant nod, she closed her eyes and laid her head against the black leather seat. Would she sense his approach if he reached across the limo to squeeze that pretty little neck between his fingers?

He glanced at the mini bottle of booze in his hand and shook his head. The damn woman was driving him to drink. Hell, five minutes ago he'd nearly kissed her. He'd wanted to kiss her, this impossible, uptight, bossy broad. What a chump. Letting his body override his better judgment again. This woman was a barracuda out to torture him. The cold-hearted Franken Niece was incapable of understanding anything beyond bottom lines and marketing angles.

Yet he couldn't help admiring her devotion to Sully. It might be painfully misplaced, but her love for her uncle was touching just the same. Anyone who could love a man like Sullivan, seeing his faults yet forgiving him anyway, couldn't be all bad. Or was she just motivated by the money? Was she in this to get a piece of the action?

No, when she had talked about Sully being marked by the mob, real tears welled in her eyes. A twinge of jealousy tickled his gut. No woman would ever shed tears over Jack Hudson. Not in this lifetime.

Staring out the window, he mentally kicked himself for the self-pity. He'd always been a lone wolf. Even as a member of the high school wrestling team he did his own thing, kept a safe distance from the guys. Jack didn't need anyone or anything.

Which was why the cabin was perfect. With the exception of helping out Butch now and then, Jack would live an isolated life, away from stares and judgments. He could travel, explore—heck, he might even rediscover the colorful magic he'd buried years ago. There were so many things he wanted to do. It was time to live again.

The Franken Niece sighed and tipped her head to one side as if drifting off. If she was sleeping, he'd eat his Stetson. Staring at her pale skin and the curve of her jaw, he found himself swallowing his frustration. He needed that bonus. The money would provide security while he explored his freedom. Maybe he and the Franken Niece could meet halfway.

He cleared his throat, and she opened one eye. Yeah, right, she'd been asleep.

"How about a truce?" he said.

She opened both eyes.

"I'm interested." With a lift of her chin, she unfolded her arms and placed her hands in her lap. A little less defensive. A good sign.

"About Tiger Lady . . ." he said.

"Her name is Tatianna."

"Tatianna, right. My problem is, I usually work alone."

"Learning to adjust is a valuable skill." She sounded like Miss Connors, his fifth-grade teacher, who loved doling out daily lectures.

"Let me finish," he said.

She nodded.

"If I'm going to work with her, pretend to be married to her, we need to get to know each other."

She pursed her lips, obviously not pleased with the direction of this conversation. Why? Could she be jealous? He smiled to himself.

"We'd work better as a team if she trusted me more. The

only way that's going to happen is if we spend time together
. . . alone."

"Alone?"

"It's the best way. I don't exactly blend in when I go out
in public."

"Oh, right." She cleared her throat and looked away.

"Tiger Lady was really nervous on the catwalk. I'd like
to loosen her up a bit."

"I'm sure you would." She narrowed her colorful eyes.

"I didn't mean it like that." Then a thought struck him.
He rubbed his stubbled jaw with his fingertips. "Although,
now that you mention it, I am kinda lonely."

"You're a pig!"

"Why? Because I wouldn't mind having a little fun with
an attractive woman?"

"You *would* find that kind of woman attractive."

"Why, Frank, you sound jealous."

"That's so ridiculous. You can't even imagine how ridiculous that is," she said, the tips of her ears turning bright
red.

"Then you won't mind asking Tiger Lady to swing by
my place tonight. I'll even dress for the occasion. I'm sure
I can dig up a leather loincloth and whip just for her."

Her eyes widened in shock. Then she fisted her hand.
She'd lose her shirt at poker, that's for sure. He ground his
teeth at the image of this woman shirtless. Man, did he
need a long night of slow and easy sex.

"I told you, Tatianna's visiting friends in Milwaukee," she
said.

"All night?"

"How am I supposed to know? She's just an employee."

"I'm just an employee, and you keep me on a pretty tight
leash."

"Enough. I'm not having this conversation." She put up
her hands in a halting gesture.

"So that means you won't ask her to stop by? I'll make
it worth your while."

"And how will you do that?"

"I'll keep my mouth shut about Sully's mob connection."

"It's not a connection!"

"It will be when the tabloids get hold of it."

"You won't do anything of the sort. I'll rescind your incentive bonus," she said.

"And I'll take you to court."

And he was talking nonsense. He couldn't afford a lengthy court battle with most of his funds tied up in the youth centers and construction costs for the cabin. But she didn't know that.

"Fine," she conceded. "I'll ask her. But I won't make any promises."

"I hope for Sully's sake that Tiger Lady is in the mood to follow orders, Boss Lady."

"Stop calling me that."

"You can't stand the thought of me and Tatianna doing a tango between the sheets, can ya, babe?"

"I don't care what you do."

"Good. Because I've got big plans for my 'wife.' She's a sweet kid. Could probably use a few lessons on how to please a man, know what I mean?"

Clenching her jaw, she shoved her right hand beneath her thigh. He'd lay odds that hand was balled tighter than a drum.

He shifted next to her, knowing it would drive her crazy, messing up that perfect, orderly mind of hers.

"I'm going to teach her how to drive a man crazy with a single touch, like this." He traced his index finger along her jawline and she looked away. "Then I'll show her how to get a man all hot and bothered with a stroke of her tongue along his pulse point, right here." He placed her hand to his neck and held it there, enjoying the warmth of her fingertips.

She huffed in disgust and pulled her hand away. Was that sexual frustration he read in her eyes?

"See, Boss Lady, by the time I'm through with my little

kitty cat, she'll know how to please a man better than a Texas call girl."

She crossed her arms over her chest and glared at him, her eyes sparking fire behind the conservative glasses. "You really think you're something, don't you?"

He grinned. She was cute when she was angry.

"Don't get too cocky, Mr. Black Jack Hudson. I wouldn't be surprised if Tatianna teaches you a few things tonight."

Chapter Eight

"Teach me a thing or two? The nerve of that overgrown ape." Frankie stormed up the sidewalk to Jack's suburban condo and fumbled in her purse. Where were those darned peppermints?

She still couldn't believe she was doing this. But anger drove her forward. Anger and a desperate need to save her uncle's kneecaps. She simply couldn't chance Jack blabbing to the press about her uncle's mistake. Not now, not when things were looking up. A few more shows like tonight and ticket sales would skyrocket, merchandise would fly out of the stores, and WHAK would be safely in the black. And maybe, with a little luck, she could prevent Pugsy and the snakes from making a repeat performance.

"Mama, I should have listened to you." She paused at the condo steps and popped a stomach-settling mint.

Her mother had always told Frankie to watch out for her uncle, that he attracted trouble like honey attracted bees.

If you get too close he'll draw you right into the eye of the storm, Mama would say. And if anyone knew storms, it was Emma McGee. She was an expert, having lived with and without Dad for some thirty years.

Men. They either dragged you through the mud, let you down, or just plain didn't respect you. Jack Hudson was no exception. She'd heard the rumors about his fleeting marriage and infamous sexual trysts. Women fell at his feet, stunned by his sexual charisma. And he, no doubt, treated them like toys.

"We'll see who's gonna play with whom tonight, Buster," she muttered, glancing at the dark windows of the condominium on the second floor. Good. She'd purposely planned her visit for well after midnight, hoping he'd be asleep and off guard. Tonight she wanted to take the lead. And when she did, whoa baby, he'd never know what hit him. Wouldn't he be humbled when he woke up handcuffed to the bed, dressed in a ladies' negligee?

Balancing a little better on her spiked heels, she climbed the steps and smiled to herself. Yes, sir, this was going to be one interesting night and an even more interesting morning. She smiled at the thought of being the first person to find him hand-cuffed to his bed. How humiliating for him to be found and rescued by his enemy, the Franken Niece. She planned to get a lot of mileage out of that one. A lot of mileage.

"He deserves it," she muttered, still fuming about his threat to go public with her uncle's connection to the mob. Then again, if she hadn't slipped in the first place, she wouldn't be here right now. What on earth had made her spill the beans to the man, anyway?

Primal lust, that's what. The thought of him undressing had sent her into a blind panic. Her world was one of self-control. A nearly naked Black Jack Hudson would blow that straight to hell.

And now she was willingly walking into the eye of that storm all over again. But this time it would be different. This time she was Tatianna the Tigress, not Frankie the conservative businesswoman. This Tatianna wasn't terrified because she hung from a catwalk. She wasn't shy about strutting out onstage. This was the new and improved Tatianna, wild, ferocious and ready for action. She'd show big, bad Black Jack a thing or two. She'd seduce him, wrap him around her finger and leave him begging for more.

She stabbed the buzzer with her thumb. A few seconds passed, and she gave the black button another poke.

"Yeah," a raspy voice crackled into the intercom.

Good, he'd been asleep.

"Jack, it's Tatianna."

"Who?"

"Tatianna from WHAK."

Silence.

"Tiger Lady? Cat Woman? Your *wife?*" she prompted.

"It's . . . what time is it?"

"Aren't you going to let me in?"

"Uh, yeah, okay."

The door buzzed and she pushed her way through, climbing the stairs to the second floor. He waited for her at the landing. His hair hung in wild waves about his shoulders. His chest looked even broader than before. Could a man grow muscle mass in six hours? A loose-fitting pair of sweat pants clung to his hips. Why did she have a feeling he wore nothing underneath? A ball of panic formed in her belly.

I'm sexy. I'm wild. I'm Tatianna the Temptress . . . the Temptress . . . the Temptress.

"You're wearing your mask." He yawned and rubbed his eye with a closed fist.

"I told you I only take it off for one thing." She sauntered up to him and splayed her hands across his bare chest. "I was hoping to take it off . . . tonight."

She licked her lips slowly, seductively. He blinked. Twice.

When it looked like he wasn't about to move, she pushed past him into the condo. The cathedral ceiling gave it an air of spaciousness. A thick-cushioned couch sat at one end of the room, opposite an oak entertainment center bordered by bookshelves brimming with novels of all shapes and sizes. She wanted to get a closer look, curious as to what a man like Black Jack Hudson chose for bedtime reading. As her eyes scanned the room, a painting of snow-capped mountains took her breath away. Rich in greens, blues, grays, and white, it mesmerized her in a way no other piece of artwork had.

"I thought you were coming earlier," he said.

"I just got back." She tore her gaze from the painting and turned to him. He stood a good five feet away at the door, as if ready to make a run for it.

"Frankie said you wanted me to stop by anytime. So I'm here." She slipped the raincoat from her shoulders and let it pool at her feet on the wooden floor. He swallowed hard and stumbled backward, hitting the door with a thump.

Nothing like black lace bikini underwear to make an impression.

"So, husband, where do we start?"

"About the marriage thing—"

"Makes me feel a whole lot better about what I'm going to do to you tonight." With great fanfare, she pulled the handcuffs from her purse and dangled them on her index finger. "Where's the bedroom?"

"Uh, it's kind of a mess. Maybe we should talk out here." He didn't move.

"Talk? Funny, I didn't picture you as the talking type."

"And I didn't picture you as the man-eating type."

"Well, then we're both pleasantly surprised." She sauntered toward him, ran her hands across his hard chest and over his shoulders. His skin was warm and soft, yet firm to the touch.

Focus. Don't get sidetracked.

"You're not wearing your gloves." He closed his eyes and she thrilled at his reaction, the obvious pleasure she evoked with a single touch.

"I've got all kinds of surprises planned for tonight." Lean-

115

ing forward, she laved his nipple, then blew ever so gently.

"Uh . . . I think . . ." he said, his voice hoarse.

"Don't think." She nuzzled his chest, then took a nipple between her teeth and tugged.

"Hey!" Jerking away, he knocked over a wooden coat-rack. He grabbed it from the floor and held it in front of him like a shield. "Maybe this wasn't such a good idea."

"Don't tell me a little thing like me scares a big tough wrestler like you."

With a hungry purr and a slow and steady gait, she stalked her prey. He backed up into the coffee table, side-stepped it, and retreated behind the leather couch, coatrack in hand.

"You're scared," she said.

"I am not."

"I don't believe it. A man who body slams three-hundred-pound gorillas and gets the stuffing kicked out of him three hundred nights a year is scared of a little kitty cat like me." She licked her lips and crawled across the couch on her knees. "Meow."

"I'm just not awake yet. And I didn't expect—"

"What? You didn't expect a frisky feline to show up on your doorstep?"

"I'd feel better if you took off that silly mask."

"And I'd feel better if you spread out on that bed of yours facedown. I'm going to teach you how to purr, real slow." She arched her back, flashing generous cleavage.

He cleared his throat and gripped the coatrack with such force his knuckles turned white.

"Go on. Go get ready for me, Tiger. I'll be right behind you. Right after I freshen up. Could you point me to the bathroom?"

"Down the hall to the left, but—"

"Go on, unless you're really not as tough as you pretend to be. Frankie said you were probably a lot of talk and no action."

His jaw set.

"Well? Was she right?" She edged closer and walked her fingers up his chest. "Are you just a big scaredy cat?"

"I'm not scared of anything. I'll meet you in the bedroom." Pacing down the hall, he glanced over his shoulder, as if he still couldn't believe she was there, offering to fulfill his kinkiest sexual fantasy. He dragged the coatrack into the bedroom and shut the door. Hmmm. This was going to be an interesting night.

Frankie was pleasantly surprised that the bathroom didn't reek of male sweat or moldy towels. She took a deep breath and stared hard into the mirror. She could do it; she could win this battle hands down.

With a snap of her fingers she removed the mask and splashed her face with cold water as a refresher. This was going to be one night Black Jack Hudson would never forget.

She secured the mask back in place, just in case he didn't follow orders and wasn't sprawled facedown on his bed. The last thing she needed was for Jack to find out her true identity. She hated to think how he'd turn that around to his advantage. He knew that Frankie was easily intimidated by his sexual power. Tatianna on the other hand . . .

Grabbing her bag of tricks, she opened the bathroom door and strutted down the hall. She sucked in one last breath of fortification and flung the bedroom door wide.

The glow of a full moon illuminated his room through wind-blown curtains. Her gaze drifted to the beautiful wooden rocker by the window, the oak dresser piled high with books, settling finally on the four-poster bed. She noticed a candle burning on his nightstand.

"You've still got your mask on," he said from the king-sized bed. His hands were folded behind his head, his long legs stretched out and crossed at the ankles.

"And you're not lying the way I told you."

"I can't see your gorgeous body if I'm facedown."

Uh oh. He's waking up.

"This isn't about seeing. It's about feeling." Slipping a

silk scarf from her bag, she ambled toward him. No going back now.

"Roll over, cowboy." She traced the scarf across his chest and noticed his breath quicken. He reached for her, but she stepped back, keeping her balance on the spiked heels.

"This is my game, remember?" she said. "Let's call it my way of thanking you for saving my life tonight."

He narrowed his eyes.

"Well, if you won't roll over, I'll just have to improvise." She ran the scarf along the curve of her palm.

"Take off your mask."

"Patience, cowboy."

She kicked off her shoes, grabbed a second scarf from her bag and tucked it into her panty waist. In one fluid movement, she climbed on top of him and straddled his hips. She slipped one of the scarves around his eyes and tied it behind his head.

"I didn't know you were that kind of girl," he mumbled, reaching for her.

She grabbed his wrists before he could touch her. He didn't resist, didn't fight to get his advantage back.

"There are a lot of things you don't know about me. But after tonight"—she bound his wrists, securing them to the bedpost—"you'll know it all."

"Uh . . . Tatianna?"

"Shhh. Trust me."

"But—"

"Do I have to gag you, too?"

She traced her hands across his chest down to his ribs, ribs she'd heard had been bruised and broken on more than one occasion. His skin burned her fingertips.

This was more fun than she'd imagined. It had to be the power, she thought, as she slid her hands lower, beneath the waistband of his sweatpants. Her hands met with bare flesh, and she suddenly wanted something she couldn't name. She grasped his firm behind and gave it a squeeze, then trailed feather-light kisses across his abdomen. God, he tasted sinful.

"What's your real name?" he rasped.

"Shhh." Just a few more minutes and she'd have him. She'd make her way down his body, past his muscular thighs and injured knee, down to bind his ankles.

But first she'd squeeze him tight between her legs and press a gentle kiss to his lips. She leaned forward and felt him shift to press his manhood against her. Her heart leapt in her throat. He wanted her. This magnificent specimen of a male wanted Frankie McGee. Or was it Tatianna he wanted?

With desperate fingers she squeezed his pectoral muscles and pushed against him with her hips. A moan was ripped from his chest, but she silenced the remarkable sound with a kiss. A long, moist, needy kiss that made her forget why she'd come here in the first place.

He pulled on his bindings, as if to free himself, then suddenly went still. She broke the kiss and glanced down at him. His chest heaved as if he struggled for breath. His mouth was still partially open. She leaned forward again.

"No," he said, as if he sensed her closing in.

"No, what?"

"I can't."

"Sure you can." She ran her index finger across his lips and tried to ease it inside. God, what was happening to her?

"Please . . . stop."

His plea pierced her heart, dead center. He didn't want to do this. If he didn't want to make love to Tantalizing Tatianna, he sure as hell wouldn't want to make love to Frankie the Fussbudget.

She wanted him to want Tatianna, or Frankie. Hell, she wanted him to want all of her.

No, she didn't. This was a game, a trick to knock him down a peg or two.

"Tatianna?"

Climbing off him, she collected her things. She shoved her spare scarf into the bag and slipped on her shoes, choking back the humiliation, the unfulfilled desire.

"I'm sorry," he said.

"Why?" The word slipped out. She clutched the leather purse to her chest.

"Don't get me wrong—you're a nice girl."

"Sure, all the nice girls tie you up and jump you."

"Don't take it personally. It has nothing to do with you."

"Great. So it's another woman, then?"

"No—Yes—I don't know. I shouldn't have asked you up here. It was a mistake."

"That makes me feel much better." She stumbled toward the door.

The bedpost squeaked as he struggled to pull free. "Listen, wait, it's my fault, okay? I'm sorry. It's just . . . I'm confused right now. You're a nice kid. I didn't mean to hurt your feelings."

Kid. He'd called her a kid.

"Tatianna?"

Standing in the doorway, she studied his glorious body illuminated by a shaft of moonlight. Something hot and cold unfurled in her belly, a kind of wanting she'd only read about in books. A kind of wanting that drove a person crazy, out of her mind.

A kind of wanting she didn't welcome in her well-ordered life.

"Tatianna?" He strained against the headboard as if trying to hear her breathe.

"I'm sorry," he whispered. "I'm really sorry."

He didn't ask her to untie him, and she didn't dare offer. She knew he'd just chase her down and demand they talk this out. The man pitied her.

How pathetic.

"Come on, sweetheart, talk to me," he whispered into the darkness.

She spun on her heel and fled, snatching her raincoat

120

from the living room floor. Escaping the condo, she paused at the landing to kick off her shoes. She raced down the stairs and out the front door.

Only when she was safely behind the wheel of the car heading for her temporary home at the Residence Inn, did she let tonight's disaster sink in.

She'd been crazed with lust, offering herself to a man in the most savage way. And he'd turned her down flat.

Thank God. Her cheeks flushed at the memory of what she'd done and how far the game had spun out of control. She'd only meant to put him in his place. Instead, she was driven by a sexual appetite she didn't think existed, then drowned in humiliation of the worst kind. He found her totally undesirable. Which should make her ecstatic. Now she could get back to her normal life and focus on her future with Bradley.

That is if she could wipe the image of Black Jack Hudson from her mind and the taste of him from her lips.

"Take it easy, man. You're gonna kill yourself," warned Jack's trainer, Mick Edwards.

"Forty more," Jack demanded from his prone position on the bench press.

"You're overdoing it."

Jack glared at him. Mick shook his head and slid a twenty-pound weight onto each side of the barbell.

Jack wrapped his gloved hands two feet apart on the metal and gritted his teeth. One. Two. Three.

By rep ten he was groaning like a branded cow. He was into serious pain today and couldn't trust himself around the guys. No, they didn't deserve the punishment. He did.

For being stupid. For being insensitive. For being a complete jerk.

What the hell is the matter with you? The girl knew why she'd been summoned and was more than willing to fulfill her part of the bargain.

But somewhere between limousine warfare with the

Franken Niece and midnight rendezvous with Cat Woman, Jack had grown an overwhelming conscience.

Sure, he'd worked hard to develop a reputation for being a hard-ass, a womanizer, and a loner. A reputation he used to shield himself from women like his ex-wife. He wouldn't let a seductive, manipulative woman worm her way into his life again. And the best way to protect himself was to make it known that if any female came too close, he'd burn her with passion and leave her smoldering. There was no place in his life for a permanent relationship, not as long as he was with WHAK. Once he cut his ties with the traveling circus, he'd reconsider, maybe even find the perfect mate, one who liked to go with the flow, explore, embrace the uncertainties of life. Yet he knew women liked money and plenty of attention. Carving out his new life, he wouldn't have much of either, or much time for romantic entanglements.

Romantic entanglement? What the hell was his problem? He'd sworn off those for good. Or at least until he started his new life. Fleeting trysts were more his style.

His arms shook as he groaned and pushed the barbell up one last time.

If that were true, why hadn't he enjoyed himself last night? Let the cat lady have her way with him so he could brag about her sharp fangs and pleasuring tongue?

"Free weights," he demanded, setting the barbell in place.

Mick brought him the equipment without protest.

A trickle of sweat beaded down his chest, reminding him of Tiger Lady's tantalizing lips. Jesus, he hadn't felt that kind of want since . . .

Since earlier that afternoon, in the limo with the Franken Niece.

"Come on, Mick."

No, it couldn't be. He couldn't be even remotely interested in Sully's repressed little niece, who loved snapping him around like a dog on choke collar.

He gripped a dumbbell in each hand and started the first set of reps. He struggled to focus on his task. Five. Six. Seven.

Women. They were masters of manipulation. He'd been around too many fawning females not to have learned that lesson. And Sandra was the final exam. An exam he'd failed miserably.

Ten. Eleven. Twelve. He gritted his teeth. Okay, so he wasn't a rocket scientist, but he had enough street smarts not to make the same mistake twice. Street smarts that spelled Frankie McGee's name I-N-S-A-N-I-T-Y.

"Uh-oh. Trouble's comin'," Mick muttered.

Jack figured Tatianna had arrived, dressed in feathers and fluff, probably wanting to deck him for rejecting her last night. Instead, Sully's beady eyes stared down at him.

"What?" Sitting up, Jack placed the dumbbells on the floor.

"Just wanted to check on my best man." He slapped Jack on the shoulder, then rubbed his hand on his suit coat.

"Cut the act. What do you want?" He grabbed a towel and wiped sweat from the back of his neck.

"Oh, nothing, nothing. Just wanted to fill you in on a couple of things. Minor, very minor."

"Which usually means trouble."

Sully giggled and tugged on the knot of his tie. "You'll be happy to know the marriage isn't valid since you never got a license. Though you've got to admit it's a great angle."

Jack clenched his jaw and waited, glaring at the promoter.

Sully cleared his throat. "Yes, well, a car will take you to Sterling Falls today for a signing at the mall. It's a big weekend there, lots of people. Some kind of corn festival or something. We've got a show set up for next week at the Marshall Arena some thirty miles away. Your visit should help sell out the house. Only . . ." Sully chewed at his lower lip.

Jack stood, towering over Sully by a good eight inches. "Spill it."

"You're going alone."

"Without my wife?"

"Um, well . . ."

"Where is she?"

"I don't know." He went for the knot of his tie again, a sure sign he was lying through his teeth.

"We were supposed to go together," Jack said, wanting to patch it up with Cat Woman. Hell, if they were going to pull off this pretend man-and-wife thing for the next six months, they needed to have an understanding between them. Besides, she wasn't such a bad kid. And he still felt like a jerk about last night.

He wanted to make amends.

"You're on your own. I . . . I don't know what happened to Tatianna. She's sick or something. Yes, that's it. She called in sick. A virus, bacterial thing, the flu, I mean the chicken pox. Very contagious. Couldn't have her coming to work."

"My fans expect me to show up with my wife."

"Your wife, right, well—"

"Cut the crap. Where is she?"

"At her place, I suppose, nursing her head cold, I mean flu, chicken pox. Anyway, you're going alone. The car will be waiting for you outside at noon. The signing's at three."

Sully started to back away.

"Freeze," Jack ordered. "What's really going on?"

He shot Jack an ear-to-ear smile. "Nothing, everything's fine. It will be a great signing."

"Ya know, Sully, I've got so much on you, I could bury this organization with one phone call."

Sully chewed on his thumb nail.

"What's the deal with Tatianna?" Jack backed him against the lateral press machine. "See, I've got this soft spot for the girl. She stopped by my place last night. We . . . talked."

"Last night? But Frankie said—"

"Frankie? What the hell does she have to do with this?"

"Um . . . well . . . nothing." His eyes darted frantically around the gym.

"Forget it. I'll find out for myself."

He stormed to the exit, suddenly needing to go one-on-one with the pushy, drill sergeant niece. She was probably up in Sully's office right now, perched in his leather chair like royalty. The thought set off an explosion in his gut. The woman hated the business, loathed it with a kind of arrogance that made his blood boil. She wasn't out there getting the crap kicked out of her or jumping from cat-walks.

What the hell had she done to Tiger Lady, anyway? It must have been a number to make the kid back away from her job responsibilities. Then again, maybe it was the number Jack did on Tatianna that was keeping her away. But he'd said he was sorry, words he rarely uttered.

He took the stairs three at a time, having no patience for the elevator. That creeping feeling pricked the back of his neck again. He was being manipulated. Like one of those puppets with strings attached. First pull this one, and watch Jack raise his right hand. Then pull those strings, and watch him do the jig. Swing the middle ones, and watch him spin around like an idiot.

His chest burning with frustration, he marched down the hallway toward Sully's office, where he spied a partially open door. The sound of a woman's voice stopped him cold. He hesitated in the hallway.

"I'm just surprised, Nipper. I still can't believe you're coming to Chicago. Where? I've never heard of it, but that doesn't mean anything. It's not like I've been getting out much. No, I didn't have a chance to check the Markham stock today. It's been kind of crazy."

Jack peered through the door. Frankie sat on Sully's desk, cradling the phone against her shoulder. She fingered a strand of copper-streaked hair and swung her heels,

125

knocking the desk with a soft, rhythmic thud. She looked like a little girl. A sweet, innocent—

"Longer than I expected, unfortunately," she said. "That relative I told you about is sicker than I thought."

Sick? Sully? The only thing he suffered from was a total lack of morality.

He flung open the door, banging it against the wall. She glanced up and hopped off the desk.

"Gotta go, Nipper. Bye. Miss you." She hung up and straightened her shoulders. She was dressed in a gray suit with a pale green blouse. Plain, simple, unappealing on any other woman. A complete turn-on in Jack's eyes.

Damn, he wanted her out of his life.

"A sick relative? My, aren't you a good liar," he said.

"That was a personal phone call. You had no business eavesdropping." Stepping behind the desk, she shuffled a pile of papers.

"Where's my wife?" he demanded.

"Honestly, Mr. Hudson, you sound like a caveman. And besides, she's not really your wife."

He studied her as she scribbled something on an official-looking document. Cold, remote, totally businesslike. Completely uninterested in his presence.

Only . . . he'd caught a different glimpse of her yesterday in the limo. He'd seen the vulnerable, tender side, a girl who worried about her uncle's welfare.

"I have work to do, Mr. Hudson," she said dismissively. So much for her tender side.

"So do I." In three steps he was towering over the desk, close enough to see the rainbow colors of her eyes sparkle through her glasses. "I hate being jerked around."

"Don't we all." She glanced back at her paperwork.

He slammed a closed fist on the desk, and her shoulders jerked.

"Knock it off, Brutus. I won't tolerate physical intimidation."

"I was trying to get your attention."

"There are better ways."

"They don't seem to work on you."

"Well, you've got it now. What do you want?"

"Where's Tatianna?"

"It's not working out with her. I've decided to replace her with a trained actress."

"I like her."

"That's not what I heard."

Jack stilled. "What?"

"I don't know what you did to her last night, but she's done with WHAK."

"What I did? Hell, it's more like what she did."

"Right."

"You don't believe me."

"I don't care." The tips of her ears turned red, and she scribbled something in Sully's appointment book.

"Ah, but you do. That's the problem."

"Please leave," she said, studying the paperwork in front of her as if it held the secrets to the universe.

She wasn't going to get rid of him that easily. He walked behind her and pinned her between his hips and Sully's desk.

"You care very much, don't you?" he whispered into her ear. He felt her stiffen.

"You're imagining things," she said, breathless.

"You mean, you don't want to hear all the juicy details? How she teased me . . . kissed me . . . wanted me," he said, his lips touching her ear. He felt her shudder against him.

"I am not the least bit interested," she said, her voice cracking midsentence.

"I don't believe you." He gently turned her around and stared into her iridescent eyes. "You care very much. Because . . . you're jealous. Jealous of the things Cat Woman and I did together."

"And you have an overgrown sense of ego. I happen to have a financé—I mean a fiancé."

Something drove him forward, riding the wave of insanity into the center of chaos.

"Yeah? Well, does your fiancé kiss like this?"

He gently gripped her shoulders and pressed his mouth to hers, wanting to make a statement, mark some territory of his own. She was repressed as hell and probably hadn't been kissed real good since the last time her investments yielded twelve percent. He also wanted to prove to himself that she wasn't the reason he'd turned down a crazed night of phenomenal sex with Tiger Lady.

What he didn't expect was the wonderful way she fit against him, the softness of her lips, the slight but familiar taste of . . .

Peppermint.

He broke the kiss and stumbled backward. "Who the hell are you?"

Chapter Nine

The look of betrayal in Jack's eyes shamed Frankie to the core.

"Wait a minute, I can explain." She started toward him.

"Don't touch me." He backed away. "I can't believe this. I have to be the biggest chump walking the face of the earth." Running an open palm across his face, he strode to the opposite end of the office.

"You don't understand," she said.

He whipped around and pinned her with his glare. "You and Sully must have had a lot of laughs over this one. The big, stupid wrestler gets suckered in by the Jeckyl and Hyde twins. One's gentle and naïve but with a wild streak, while the other's a frigid drill sergeant."

"Frigid?" Her heart sank.

"But your eyes, your height, your scent. They're all different, even your voice seemed . . ."

"We weren't trying to trick you. It just happened."

"Like you just happened to nail me with the wrench and keep me out of the ring for a few weeks? That was planned,

129

wasn't it? The whole thing? It's been about the angle from the beginning. A damn soap opera. Sully thought I was losing my heat to the younger, more acrobatic wrestlers, so he dreamed up a better way to make money off me."

"No, wait. Just listen for a minute."

"To what? No one's into truth around here. You people lie as easily as you breathe."

He started for the door. She raced in front of him and blocked his way, her hands pressed firmly against his chest. Her breath caught short at the contact, her fingers burning from the feel of slick, wet skin. Damn, but she had to shelve the lust long enough to explain herself.

"Out of my way, woman."

"I know enough about you to know you're a fair man."

"It didn't take you long to zero in on my biggest weakness."

"Jack—"

"Move."

"Not until you listen."

Gripping her by the shoulders, he lifted her, and placed her aside, then reached for the door. She couldn't let him go. Couldn't let him think she was a lying, manipulative snake.

With a desperate cry she charged him from behind. *Hit low and come up swinging.* She remembered Max bragging about how she'd won the WHAK Women's championship back in '64.

So Frankie did just that. She rammed her shoulder into his lower back and knocked him into the door, slamming it shut.

"What the hell?" He twisted at the waist to grab her, but she ducked to elude his probing hands. The door swung open, hitting Jack in the face and knocking them both off balance. They tumbled to the floor, and she miraculously landed facedown on top of him.

"What's going on in here?" Uncle Joe said from the door.

"Get out of here!" she cried.

130

"Okay, okay, sure honey." He closed the door.

"Lady, you'd better be off me in three seconds, or I'll—"

She slapped her hand to his mouth. "I love him, okay? That's my crime. I love my uncle. He's in trouble, and he called me for help. He was always there for us. How could I say no? I wasn't supposed to dress up and go into the ring. The actress he'd hired quit the night of the show. He needed me to fill in. Don't you understand?" She removed her hand. "Don't you have family you love so much that you'd do anything for them?"

"I have no family," he said.

"Well, that's your loss, isn't it?"

"Think so? It doesn't look like loving your uncle has done a whole lot for you."

"Oh, forget it." She pushed herself off him, leaned against the wall, and brought her knees to her chest. "You'd never understand."

She buried her face in her arms, which were folded across her knees. What a mess. The whole damned thing. A man like Jack Hudson would never understand loyalty, supporting people you loved even if you didn't approve of their actions. There were plenty of times she cringed at Uncle Joe's crazy schemes. But he was always there for her. That counted for a lot in her book.

Jack Hudson, on the other hand, wasn't there for anyone but himself. An all-too-familiar story.

"You manipulated me," he said.

She glanced up. He towered over her, opening and closing his hands by his sides as if he struggled for control.

"He was there for me when my father was gallivanting across the country doing who knows what," she said. "Uncle Joe gave me things and took me places. He loved me. How could I say no when he needed help?"

Rocking back on his heels, Jack jammed his hands onto his hips. "That doesn't change the fact that you lied to me."

"It got out of hand. I'll admit it. It's just . . . you hated

131

me for being Uncle Joe's niece, but you started to be nice to me when I was Tatianna. You were so sweet to me on the catwalk and I found myself liking you . . . kind of. But I couldn't tell you who I was then because you might have let me go and—"

"Let you go?"

"It was a hundred-foot drop. I know how you feel about my uncle. I couldn't chance it."

"What kind of monster do you think I am? You think I would have dropped you? On purpose? You're kidding, right? Tell me you're kidding."

She chewed her lower lip and hugged her knees tighter to her chest.

"You really have no clue what I'm about," he said, his voice a mere hush. "Nor do you care. Your job is to control me, lock me into a contract, threaten to take away my incentive bonus, and mess with my insides for a little fun."

"I didn't mess with anything."

"No? What would you call last night?"

She groaned. "Don't remind me. I got the message."

"What message was that, cupcake?"

"Don't worry. I'm done, out of your life. I keep screwing everything up. I'll hire a replacement and get back to the books, where I belong. Now that you know the truth, I'm sure that's what you want anyway."

She stood and paced to Uncle Joe's desk. "But I can't let you out of your contract, not yet. We have to chase the Tatianna angle for a while. It's our only hope of saving WHAK, not to mention my uncle's life." She flipped through Uncle Joe's Rolodex, searching for the talent agency's phone number. "I probably won't be able to find a replacement for a few days. You'll have to go solo until then."

"That's not good enough."

She glanced at him. "What's that supposed to mean?"

"The car leaves at noon for Sterling Falls. Be ready."

"Me? No, I can't go with you. I have a date."

"Cancel it."

"But it's with my fiancé. He's flying in from Boston."

"This is more important."

"Now hang on. My life is pretty important."

"I thought your life was about saving Sully's skin."

"It is, but you don't need me for an autograph session."

"The fans expect you. You're my wife. I need you with me . . . everywhere."

The tone of his voice melted her insides. She swallowed hard. *Not real. None of this is real.*

"I'll be back at noon." He paced to the door and hesitated, but he didn't turn around. "By the way, not a bad move before."

"It's Maxine's. She calls it the Ground Hog Grunt."

"I'll have to remember that." He disappeared into the hallway.

Collapsing into Uncle Joe's chair, she blew out a breath. Now what? She couldn't go with him. Yet he was already so incensed, she didn't want to rile him any more. From a business standpoint, he was right. The fans could make or break an organization like WHAK. And the fans expected Jack to show up with his new bride.

How she wished she could call Mama. But then she'd have to tell her where she was and what she was doing. She needed help, not a well-deserved lecture.

Running her fingers over the black plastic telephone, she considered what she'd tell Bradley. He was so excited about coming to Chicago and working with his new client. She'd panicked at first, thinking he'd find out what she was really doing. Then she remembered Bradley's work ethic. When enthralled in an audit, he crunched numbers from dawn until dusk, even on weekends. He said the only time he could carve out a few hours was tonight. He'd be so disappointed.

That was the least of her concerns. He'd flip if he found out she was moonlighting as a half-naked feline. There was no way he'd understand her devotion to her crazy uncle.

Bradley was a man of common sense and practicality. Emotions and obligation rarely entered into his thought process. She wondered what he'd think about her strutting out on Jack's arm, prancing around in the ring wearing nearly nothing.

"I can kiss my engagement goodbye," she muttered.

And she had the ring all picked out, too. They'd put the half-carat pear-shaped diamond on layaway during a recent close-out sale at Smith and Wesson Jewelers.

But this wasn't about rings. This was about Bradley, her perfect mate. Practical, smart, honorable. You wouldn't find Bradley hopping from city to city, pretending to beat up other men for fun, while jumping in and out of bed with one bimbo after another. Nor would you find him tumbling across the countryside trying to find himself, abandoning his family, his children.

No, Bradley was dependable, stable, the cornerstone of her life.

And she'd lose him for sure if he caught her in this lie.

"Time to come clean." She dialed his number.

"Bradley Dunsmore's office," his secretary Ruth answered.

"Hi Ruth, it's Francine. May I speak to Bradley?"

"Oh, again?"

"I forgot to tell him something."

"Sure, hold on," she said, surprise in her voice. It wasn't like Frankie to call twice in one day.

A moment later Bradley came on the line. "Frankie? Everything okay?"

"Sure, I just needed to talk to you about something. You got a minute?"

"What's happened, sweetums? Did the annuity report come in from Harper?"

"No, it's—"

"Your feet aren't cracked, are they? You know how important it is to continue the cod liver oil massage."

"My feet are fine."

134

"Reservations are all set for tonight. Leo's Fish House. The Thursday special is all-you-can-eat calamari with a side of hash browns."

"Nipper, I'm sorry. I can't make it."

A disappointed hush filled the line.

"You still there?" she said.

"I'm here."

"I've been lying to you, Bradley. I'm sorry, but I didn't think you'd understand, so I made up the story about a sick relative."

Silence.

She took a deep breath. "I'm actually helping my uncle with his business. I've taken the extended leave from work because it's going to be a while, maybe two months before I feel confident the company is back on its feet."

"Your uncle? You never talked about an uncle."

"He's kind of . . . well . . . different. His business isn't exactly mainstream."

"Is he a criminal?"

"No, nothing like that." Not yet anyway.

"Pornography?"

"Bradley, stop. Listen, I can't tell you over the phone."

"I don't like this."

"I know. I'm sorry."

"And dinner? You're breaking our date because . . . ?"

"I have to help my uncle with a promotion."

"What kind of promotion?"

"We can talk about it when I see you. How about Friday night or Saturday?"

"Can't. Working all weekend."

"Sunday night? You'll still be in town, won't you?"

"Let me check my flight."

The sound of rustling papers scratched over the line, and she wondered whether he was making her wait on purpose. After all, she thought, he was staying through Monday, and rarely made plans on Sunday evenings, his designated reading night. Then again, it might be tough to choose between reading *Money Magic* for the fifth time and dining with your future fiancee.

"I can schedule you for Sunday, although the company booked my return flight first thing Monday morning. It'll have to be early."

"Six o'clock early enough?"

"Fine."

"Leo's Fish House?"

"They won't be running the calamari special."

"We'll splurge. I'll buy, okay? I really am sorry about all this."

"Well, you're a sharp girl. I'm sure you have your reasons."

If he only knew.

"And Francine?"

"Yes?"

"Check your e-mail when you get a chance. I sent you a surprise."

"That was sweet. Thanks."

"Bye."

Hanging up, she smiled to herself. Everything would be okay. Bradley would forgive her for not being up front with him once he found out what she was really doing. Well, maybe not *everything* she was doing. Would she ever be able to confess to parading half naked in front of thousands of people? Maybe she wouldn't have to. No one besides Uncle Joe and Jack knew who she really was under the black mask and feathers. And no one ever would.

She logged on to her uncle's computer and checked her e-mail. Bradley's message topped the list. It was entitled, "For my girl."

"How romantic." She clicked it open. A scanned newspaper article popped onto the screen listing growing stock funds. Circled in bold ink were stock figures for Daisy's Diapers. Good old Bradley, always keeping track of things for her. What would she do without him?

*   *   *

Four hours later Frankie scanned the crowd of fans lined up at the Sterling Falls Mall. "I can't believe all these people are here for me."

"Us, sweetheart, not you." Jack nodded to the security guard, who led them down a back hallway.

Jack hadn't spoken a word during the three-hour drive to the capital of the cornfields. She hated silence. Especially when it was directed at her. Mama used to give her the same treatment when she'd bring home a B instead of an A, or if she forgot to stop by Nana Cooper's on the way home from Girl Scouts.

She tagged behind Jack, barely able to keep up with his determined stride. He was determined to get away from her, no doubt. Her temper flared. It was his idea to bring her along. He could have made this appearance alone, without his woman.

You're my wife. I need you with me . . . everywhere.

Her heart skipped at the memory of the primal command in his voice; it made her cringe and thrill simultaneously. How could that be?

"Come on, move it," he said, approaching the entrance to the stage.

"Hold your horses. The fans aren't going anywhere."

It was going to take him a long time to get over her big black lie. Tough. Her loyalty was to Uncle Joe, not Black Jack Hudson.

A voice boomed across the PA system. "Black Jack Hudson and his tiger wife, Tatianna."

He clasped her hand and pulled her to his side. "Smile and wave."

She searched his eyes. Hoping for what? Understanding? Forgiveness? *Dream on, McGee.*

They pushed through the brown curtain and stepped onto the stage. Security men lined the platform, arms crossed over their chests, their faces hardened like stone. You'd think they were protecting the president of the

137

United States instead of a silly comic book hero. Had the whole world gone mad?

A sea of fans hooted and hollered from the first and second levels of the mall. She'd never heard such a ruckus. With a nervous smile, she waved to the crowd and they cheered even louder. This wasn't so bad.

Suddenly Jack grabbed her wrist, flattened her palm against his chest and stared deep into her eyes. Her fingertips burned where they slipped off his tank top and touched bare skin.

"Gotta give them what they want," he said, his voice low and husky.

"What they want . . ." she repeated, barely able to think. The piercing green of his eyes darkened to the color of a pine forest.

He kissed her. Soft, gentle, smoldering with need she thought would fry her circuits. She dug her gloved hands into his shoulders, pulling him closer, wanting his lips to open.

He broke the kiss abruptly. Dizzy with desire, she glanced into his eyes, waiting for his next command. God, she needed to get away from this man, and fast.

"Chill, kid. It's just a show," he said with a coy smile.

She balled her hand into a fist. "You're enjoying this, aren't you?"

"Aren't you?"

That smile again, that I'm-gonna-eat-you-alive smile. It made her want to snap her whip across his hindside. Instead, she ran it along her open palm and tried to regain her composure. Jack sat down, but she remained standing, whip at the ready. First he punished her with silence, then tortured her with desire.

That's all it was, she reminded herself. Animal attraction, nothing more. It wasn't like she respected this man, thought highly of him as she did her future fiancé.

A middle-aged security guard led the first group of enthusiastic fans onto the stage. Jack handed Frankie a black Sharpie pen.

"I'll sign, then pass it to you to make your mark."

"My mark?"

"A scratch, paw print, whatever."

"Jerk."

"What?" He pinned her with his eyes.

"Your first customer is here, Black Jack." She shot him a forced grin and gritted her teeth. It was going to be a long day. A very long day.

A little boy approached the table with his mom. The kid sported a crew cut and waved a foam hammer that read "Black Jack Banger." The tyke couldn't have been more than six.

"Hey, kiddo, what's your name?" Jack said in a gentle voice.

"Jeffrey."

"Nice to meet you, Jeffrey." He pressed his pen to an eight-by-ten glossy of him twisting the Basher's legs into the shape of a pretzel.

"She's funny," Jeffrey said, pointing to Frankie. "You gonna have kittens?"

The pen slipped, slicing an arc across the Basher's bald scalp.

"No kittens." He slid the photo to Frankie.

"Meow," she purred, arcing a decorative "T" across the bottom of the photo. How could he do it? How could he lie to a little boy, pretending to be this superhero when in fact he was just an average man with an overgrown ego?

"You're gonna have real people babies?" Jeffrey asked.

His mother flushed. "I'm sorry," she said to Jack, then looked at her son. "Jeffrey, honey, that's kind of a personal question."

"Oh." The little boy studied his feet.

"It's okay, kiddo." He patted the boy's tiny fingers and the child's freckled face lit up.

What a joke, Frankie thought, drawing a claw next to

139

her initial. Hundreds of fans crammed the mall, expecting to meet a real live hero, a superstar, a great man. They were really paying homage to a master pretender, a man who dominated the world around him with his body, with brute force.

She slid the photo toward the little boy, whose attention was still riveted to his hero. Frankie tried to tear her gaze from the boy's awed expression, but she couldn't. Something squeezed her heart. Something pure and honest shone out through Jeffrey's hazel eyes.

Something very real.

The mother thanked Jack and Frankie and led the boy away. Frankie must have muttered something, but she didn't know what. She was still feeling a little off balance. She pulled out a metal folding chair and sat down.

The next customer was an animated teenage girl.

"I dropped out last year, but I'm working on my GED." She snapped her gum and shoved her hands into the front pockets of her jeans. "I read what you said in *Wrestler's Wisdom* magazine about getting an education. You made me go back to school."

He capped the pen, leaned back, and considered the girl. "No, kiddo, you did that all by yourself. I'm just glad I said something that inspired you."

"I want to be an astronaut." She jutted out her chin as if expecting him to challenge her.

"Go for it."

"I couldn't have done it without you."

"Give yourself more credit. Something like that comes from inside. Here." He placed an open palm to his chest.

"What's the holdup?" a burly security guard called from the edge of the stage.

"Better keep the line moving," Jack said. "Good luck."

"Thanks." The girl practically floated from the stage.

"Oh, brother," Frankie muttered.

"What?"

"You inspired her? Puhleese."

140

"People find strength wherever they can. But then you wouldn't know about that, would you? I mean, you were born tough as nails, right?"

She wanted to slap him silly, get in his face and shout that he couldn't be more wrong, that she had a soft side, a vulnerable side.

What was happening to her?

"Jack Hudson? I don't suppose you remember me?"

Jack tore his attention from the Franken Niece and glanced up into the familiar, but weathered face of Vicious Vic, an old-time grappler who'd made his name in the Northeast.

"Vic? I can't believe it." Standing, he shook the former champion's hand. "What are you doing in this part of the country?"

"Meryl and I moved back here in '78. Took over her dad's grain business. This is my grandson, Bruce."

Jack smiled at the blond-haired kid, who wore a Black Jack T-shirt. "Hi, Bruce." He shook the boy's hand, but the kid didn't look up.

"Don't mind him. He's shy. Not like his grandpa."

"It's great to see you, Vic. We didn't know what happened to you. You just seemed to disappear."

A twenty-something security guard ran up to them and cleared his throat. "Sir, we really need to keep the line moving."

"Cool it, kid. We'll make sure everyone gets what they came for. Do you know who this man is?"

The guard shook his head, not the least bit interested in Vic's stats.

"Vicious Vic, three-time U.S. Wrestling Champion. His signature move was the Victory Vice. Want a demonstration?"

The guard's eyes widened. "Uh, no."

"Good, then get out of my face and give me a minute with my friend." He turned his attention back to Vic.

"We'd better go."

141

"No, wait. What's been going on? I thought you were going to join the Navy."

"Something dimmed in Vic's eyes.

"Wanted to. But the body was shot. Between the bad knees and ruptured discs, I'd have had to bribe the president himself to pass the physical."

"Your dad was career Navy. That's all you talked about."

"Yup. But things worked out. I took over a nice business, steady work. And I got the best grandkids in the world, don't I, Bruce?"

"Not Dee Dee."

Vic laughed. "Dee Dee is Bruce's little sister. Well, life can't be perfect, now can it?"

Jack's gut knotted. No one wanted perfect. They just wanted normal, healthy, happy lives. Instead, too many of them ended up like Vic, sent out to pasture with their dreams stripped away. Jack was not going to be one of them.

"God, what a life," Vic said. "I'll never forget going three hundred nights a year, fighting with a broken hand, bruised ribs, abdominal tears. Those were the days."

"Yeah." This was one trip down memory lane Jack didn't welcome. Laughing about the pain didn't make it hurt any less.

"Well, we'd better get going. Thanks for the autograph."

"Wait, come here, kiddo." Jack grabbed Bruce and set him on the table. "How about an autograph, right here." He scrawled his name across the boy's shirt.

The kid giggled, and his eyes lit up. Vic lifted him from the table with a grunt. It pained him to lift his own grandkid. What the hell was the matter with all of them?

"Take care," Jack said.

"You too."

Vic ambled across the stage, his grandson jumping up and down, pointing to his shirt. The little boy slipped his fingers into his grampa's palm, and Jack's heart skipped. Well, at least Vic had that. He might have forfeited his dream of serving his country, but you couldn't put a price on love, on family.

"Who was that old guy?" Frankie asked.

He whirled on her, but caught himself before he completely blew.

"That 'old guy' is in his fifties and one of the best wrestlers ever to step into the ring."

He motioned for the security guard to send up the next batch of fans. Anger swelled inside him, anger at the ignorant princess sitting next to him, anger at Vic's lost dream and broken-down body, anger at himself for not seeing this business for what it really was before he got hooked and couldn't wriggle off the line.

He successfully ignored Frankie for the next hour, except when he'd pass her a photo and his arm brushed against hers. Then the electrical current zapped him, making him angrier than a bucking bronc.

A vacation would be nice right about now. It might help clear his head and get his perspective back. He spied the crowd of fans stretched twenty stores deep and took a fortifying breath. They'd be here for another two hours, at least. Sure, the mall manager had scheduled the signing to end in an hour. But it wasn't Jack's policy to walk out on people who'd waited all day to see him.

A pack of gawky-looking teenage boys approached the table, led by a tall redhead in a leather jacket with three earrings in his left ear. He puffed out his chest and jammed his hands into his black jeans pockets. "The guys think wrestling's fake."

"Yeah? I'll send them my chiropractor bills." Jack grinned and signed his name.

"I'm gonna be a wrestler someday."

"Why's that?" He passed the photo to Frankie and glanced at the kid.

"For the babes. I wanna be famous and have them scream at me when I walk into a mall." The kid glanced over his shoulder at the upper level. A crazed group of teenage girls screamed right on cue.

"Seems fun to you, does it? Getting all this attention?"

"Yup. And I'm good at banging heads, right?" he asked his group of hormonally challenged friends. They grunted in confirmation.

"It's not just about banging heads," Jack said. "You've got to be in prime physical condition and know how to execute the moves."

"No problem. I took a kick-boxing class and got an A in advanced tumbling last semester."

Great, another acrobat.

He wanted to tell the kid to chase another fantasy, pursue medical school or become a teacher. But he knew that look. A look he'd seen so many times in the eyes of admiring fans.

Dreams keep you alive, he thought. He couldn't squash this kid's dream, no matter how much he wanted to spare him the pain.

"Good luck, kid," he said with a nod. Frankie passed the photograph to the last of the punks and they strutted off the stage, shoulders squared, chins up. Ah, the power of bravado, the beauty of ignorance.

"Unbelievable," she muttered.

"What?"

"I can't believe you encouraged him to become a part of this . . . this . . . *business.*"

Taking a deep, calming breath, he counted to ten, trying not to let her get to him. She still didn't understand. She probably never would. This woman looked at the world through her own lens, and nothing was going to change her focus. Must be nice to live each day with everything in order, from the number of strokes of your toothbrush to your exact carbohydrate count. Jack, on the other hand, was lucky if he knew which hotel he'd be sleeping in from one night to the next.

"I can think of better careers those boys should pursue."

"Like?" He took a swig of water.

"Law, accounting, politics."

He choked and nearly spit water across the remaining glossies. "Yeah, right, from one circus to the next."

"I'm just trying to make a point. We should be directing our youth into noble professions, not fantasy play."

She cared about the future of the country. He had to give her that. He glanced offstage at the rowdy teens, who were closing in on a pack of giggling girls.

"Nothing I said would have changed his mind." He glanced at her. "Sometimes you just have to find things out for yourself."

She struggled to rip her gaze from his mesmerizing, dark green eyes. She couldn't. There was a lot more to his words than sound and syllable. An incredible feeling of compassion flooded her heart.

A part of her wanted to reach out and touch his cheek, to somehow ease the melancholy she saw there.

"You gonna sign my finger?" A little boy waved a three-foot foam "Number One" finger in Jack's face.

The wrestler turned his attention to the kid and Frankie blinked, struggling to get her bearings. Okay, so she was attracted to the guy. That didn't mean she had to actually empathize with whatever misfortunes he thought he'd endured. He didn't have it so bad. He was a star, admired and loved by thousands, maybe even millions. Surely that must make up for whatever tragedies he thought he'd suffered.

Yet there was something behind his eyes, something in his voice that struck a chord deep inside her chest.

It was time to find a replacement. She couldn't take much more of the grinning and signing, listening to Jack's words of wisdom, tender words that made her sympathize with him way too much.

Pushing her chair away from the table, she stood, and took a step back. He glanced at her questioningly.

"Stretching my muscles," she said.

He nodded and continued to greet his fans. How did he do it? She was exhausted, hungry, and her face hurt. Who would have thought a simple appearance would be such a laborious chore?

But it didn't seem like a chore to Jack. He willingly shared generous smiles and insightful words with those who sought them. If she didn't know better she'd think him a sage, not a barbarian.

Now she *knew* she was suffering from low blood sugar.

What seemed like weeks later, he pushed the last of the photos toward her. She scrawled her mark and summoned a smile.

"That's it." He stood and waved to the lingering crowd.

A security guard led them through the curtain and down the dim hallway. Her stomach growled, and she slapped her hand to her belly to muffle the sound.

"Hungry?" Jack said.

She nodded.

"We'll pick up something on the way home."

She wanted to ask, why wait? Why not stop at a local greasy spoon? Then she studied his broad shoulders and muscular physique, massive compared to the average man. No, they wouldn't exactly blend with the locals, even if they did change into street clothes. And she could use a good blend right about now. Anonymity. No smiling, no nodding, no shaking hands. She just wanted to "be." To fill a bath tub to the brim and sink down, letting the warm water massage away her stress . . . and confusion.

Confusion? Well, of course she was confused. After all, on a regular day she'd be sitting at her desk analyzing numbers, not clinging to the arm of a macho wrestler.

They approached the service entrance to the mall and she picked up her pace, eager to slip into her cotton pants and silk blouse, which hung in the back of the limo. Everything would be fine. She'd change into her comfortable clothes, they'd swing through a McDonalds for a few double cheeseburgers and be home in no time. By seven she'd be settled in the tub, reading *Pride and Prejudice* for the umpteenth time. Then she'd call Bradley and blow him a goodnight kiss.

She glided her tongue across her bottom lip, remembering the taste of Jack—spicy, sweet, male.

God, she needed to get home.

They opened the service door to the back lot. The setting sun glowed orange across the few cars scattered here and there. Jack paced to the curb and she followed. He looked right, then left. She looked right, then left.

"What's wrong?" she asked.

Ignoring her, he marched back to the mall entrance and grabbed the door just before the guard snapped it shut.

"Hang on there," he said. "Where's the car?"

"What car?"

"Our limousine."

"I don't know. I'll check." The middle-aged guard, a short gentleman with a receding hairline and a concerned expression, pulled the radio from his belt and clicked a button. "Central, this is Cooper. Black Jack's limousine isn't here. Any chance it's waiting at another entrance? Roger."

A ball of anxiety formed in Frankie's tummy.

She slipped off her shoes and sat on a wooden bench. More cars pulled out of the lot, and she spied a mall employee locking up the public entrance across the way. In the back of her mind she heard the twang of a banjo.

"About that missing limo . . ." A voice crackled through the guard's radio. "Seems Ray and the driver got to talking about the Grand Dame casino. He says the driver's eyes glazed over, and he started breathin' heavy. Next time Ray made his rounds, the limo was gone."

"Great. Just great," Jack said.

She glanced up at him. "What?"

"We'll need a hotel room," he said to the security guard. "And transportation."

"A hotel room? Why?" She stood and ambled over to Jack.

147

"Our driver won't be coming back anytime soon."

"What do you mean?"

"He abandoned a tag team up north last month. Apparently he's got a thing for quarter slots."

"But that's not acceptable."

She started to panic, a full-blown, I'm-gonna-scream-till-I-fall-over panic. She hadn't had one of those since Kenny Goldman stole her Perfect Patty pencil case in third grade.

"Best just to go with the flow, kid. We'll stay the night. I'm sure Bernie will show up by morning."

"No. I've got to get home. Now, right now." She grabbed the security guard's stiff polyester sleeve. "A car rental agency. Surely you have one or two of those."

"Sorry, ma'am. The whole town's shut down because of the festival."

"How about a cab?"

"Gloria's off duty. Besides, that would be one helluva fare."

"Money's no object. A tractor! I'll buy a tractor!"

"Won't be much help, ma'am. Those only run about twenty-five miles per hour, tops. You'll make it home quicker if you just wait for your driver."

"No, I can't wait. I have to get home." The ringing started in her ears. She was losing control. Her well-planned life was falling apart in twenty-seven different ways. Dressing as a fluff ball, jumping from the catwalk, lying to Bradley, and now being stranded in corn country with a man who tempted her beyond all endurance.

I'm in control, always in control.

Jack placed his hand on her shoulder, and her insides simmered like Mount St. Helens just before it blew.

She'd never make it to tomorrow.

"Francine?"

Her breath caught at his gentle tone. She turned to face him. A slight smile creased his lips.

"It's okay. We'll manage."

"You don't understand." She gripped his bare arm, glad

148

for its rock-solid strength. "I really, really need to get home."

I really, really need to get away from you.

"We'll get home tomorrow," he assured.

"Today, right now! I need to get home right now!"

And then Frankie did something she'd never done in front of any man. She broke down into hysterical tears.

"Shhhh," he consoled, putting his arm around her and rocking her slightly. "You're just tired and hungry. We'll fix that too. You'll be fine. Everything will be fine, honey. You'll see."

Chapter Ten

Jack meant it when he said everything was going to be okay. Unfortunately, he had no control over the timing.

As the security guard, Rich Parker, drove them to the fourth and last hotel in the county, Jack realized they couldn't have picked a worse weekend to be stranded in the quaint farming town. There wasn't a room to be had, and all the stores were closed in honor of the Cornhusker's Festival. They needed food, sleep, and clothes and not necessarily in that order.

He glanced at Frankie, curled into a ball in the backseat. She stared absently out the window as she nibbled on a gloved finger. He'd offered to sit with her, but she'd refused, becoming even more agitated. Hell, he'd never seen someone come apart so quickly. One minute she was in charge, barking orders and making demands; the next, she fell apart, tears streaming down her face, dotting her pale skin below the black mask.

"Let me talk to Pete," Rich said into the radio. He glanced at Jack. "We'll find you someplace to bunk, don't you worry. If nothing else, you can stay in my barn."

A whimper-howl echoed from the backseat.

"But I'm sure we can find a nice room somewhere," Rich amended, glancing at Frankie through the rear-view mirror.

". . . we've got something!" a voice squawked through the radio. "Come by the Lucky Lady. You're all set."

"Thanks, Pete, you're a lifesaver. Ten-four." He grinned at Jack. "No problem."

"The Lucky Lady?"

"Best hotel in Whiteside County. You'll love it. Overlooks Mortimer Park, where they're holding the festival. You should come down. It's a lotta fun. Rides, games, entertainment. Tailspin and the Four-Eyed Iguanas is playing tonight. Last night we had a Liberace impersonator."

"Thanks. But I think we could use the rest." He glanced over his shoulder at Frankie.

"Is she okay?"

"She'll be fine. She's tough, aren't ya, kid?"

She squeaked and buried her face in her gloved hands.

Jack was getting worried. Okay, so he couldn't stand the bossy, arrogant, tough-as-nails niece. But he'd take her any day over the fragile woman trembling in the backseat. It made him want to reach out and comfort her, hold her, make everything okay.

The last time he'd felt that way he'd walked into the biggest mistake of his life. His relationship with Sandra went from comforting to a crazed sexual encounter in less than three minutes. Not something you based a long-lasting relationship on.

Neither was deception, he reminded himself. Which was the Franken Niece's modus operandi. And that scene last night with the bondage? He balled his hand into a fist and tapped it against the window of the mini-van. What was that about? Her way of completely humiliating him?

She hadn't succeeded if that was her goal. She'd only confused him even more about his attraction to two very different women who were actually one and the same.

His head ached. What he wouldn't give for a thick, juicy cheeseburger and a beer, followed by about ten hours of sleep. It wasn't like he'd had any sleep last night, lying in bed, thinking about what had almost happened.

Then he remembered: It was Frankie who'd tied him up, straddled him, ignited his body with need. She never would have gone through with it. It was all a big joke to her.

At least he'd sleep well tonight, in his own hotel room, protected from Frankie by a half inch of drywall. If there was one thing he was good at, it was sleeping in hotel rooms. He sure as hell had enough practice.

"There," the security guard said, pointing to a neon sign of a woman in a full-length evening gown showing considerable cleavage. "It's nice. Hosted the Kiwanis awards banquet there last month."

"As long as they've got beds and room service."

"No problem."

They pulled into the circular drive. Fans crowded the entrance, screaming and waving signs.

"Word must have gotten out you were coming."

Frankie let loose a squawk from the backseat. Jack sucked in his breath. He needed to be alone right now more than he needed food, sleep, or a new life. Scanning the row of grinning faces, he caught sight of a little girl jumping up and down, waving a Black Jack Banger foam hammer.

"Peter Mills, the manager, will be waiting for you," Rich said. "He's got it all set up." He glanced over his shoulder at Frankie, then back at Jack. "Good luck."

"Looks like I'll need it, huh?" Jack got out of the minivan and opened the back door. "Come on, kid."

She clung to the opposite door handle with both paws.

Leaning way into the car, he brought his face to hers. "Well, whadda ya know. I got a coward on my hands. Is that right? You a coward, Frank?"

Something sparked in her eyes.

"Figures. Must run in the blood. Cuz your uncle's the biggest damn coward in the U S of A." He pushed away from the car and greeted the row of fans. A car door slammed behind him.

Out of the corner of his eye he spied Frankie step into place beside him, her chin high, her lips curled into a forced smile.

That's my girl.

"Out of the way! Out of the way!" a voice ordered from the back of the crowd. "This man's here for a good night's sleep, not to be pawed at. You had your chance at the mall."

A tall, skinny guy dressed in a pinstriped suit broke through the crowd. "Sir, it's a pleasure to meet you. I'm Peter Mills, manager of the Lucky Lady."

"Glad to meet you. This is Tatianna."

"It's so good to meet you, ma'am. The whole town watches the show every week. You've really livened it up a bunch."

"Thank you."

She actually spoke. That was a good sign.

"We've got the perfect room all ready for you." Peter pushed through the crowd and led them into the lobby. "I panicked at first when Rich called, but then my assistant reminded me that we had one very special opening." He plucked a brochure from his breast pocket. "The pride of this establishment: The Bridal Suite."

Frankie stumbled, and Jack caught her elbow to keep her upright. Peter hadn't noticed her reaction. A good thing. He was obviously very proud of his special offer.

"It was booked for the Keller wedding, but the kids got fed up with the family bickering and eloped this morning. They were going to get married on the Ferris wheel during the hog races. Anyway, the townsfolk were very disappointed, but Mr. Keller's got a good attitude. He decided to renew his vows with the wife and not cancel the reception. It won't be exactly quiet in the hotel tonight, but the bridal suite was designed with an extra layer of drywall to keep sound out, or keep it in." Peter winked.

Frankie's eyes widened, and she stumbled. Jack steadied her with a firm grip on her arm. She stared at his hand as if it had just sprouted warts.

"The suite is in the west wing, second floor." Peter led them up the stairs. "We have our special theme rooms up there. The Bridal Suite is in the corner for added privacy. I figure you two never did get a proper honeymoon, so we're going to do our best to give you one tonight."

He pushed open the door and Jack froze. People lined both sides of the hallway, applauding, cheering, howling encouragement. Talk about pressure. He wondered if they'd be waiting outside in the morning, expecting a full report.

Frankie dug her heels into the thin industrial carpet.

He leaned close and whispered into her ear. "Come on, sweetheart. Remember what's at the end of this hallway: a soft bed, room service, burgers, champagne, whatever you want. But you gotta walk."

She bit her lower lip and scanned the hall. Just when he thought she was going to make a run for it, she looped her arm through his and lifted her chin.

"You two have fun. And don't worry about the 'Do Not Disturb' sign. We know not to bother you until at least noon."

Peter slapped Jack's shoulder, urging him forward into the mass of fans. The applause grew. He nodded and grinned. Frankie clutched his arm and picked up her pace. Her taste buds must be kicking into overdrive.

The fans waved corn stalks and tossed something akin to rice, as if he and Frankie had just stepped down from the altar. What a mess this was going to be to clean up. Surely they had to know the marriage thing was an angle, that it wasn't real. On the other hand, plenty of wrestlers and their real-life wives acted out the dramas scripted for them. He glanced over his shoulder at Peter. The man's eyes lit up as if he were hosting the president of the United

States in his hotel. And Jack knew he had to keep up the charade, out of respect for the manager and the enthusiastic fans that lined the hall.

They reached the door, he placed his key card in the slot, then glanced back at the crowd. They cheered and whistled. Frankie disappeared into the room, but he hesitated, savoring the moment. Okay, so this he might miss, just a little.

An eardrum-piercing scream from inside the room set his neck hairs on end. He raced inside, the door slamming behind him.

His jaw dropped at the sight of the erotic prints that covered the walls, prints of men and women making love in very unusual ways. A massive, heart-shaped bed, dressed in bright red satin sheets and pink pillow cases filled nearly the entire room. At the foot of the bed lay two white silk robes with the words "Man" and "Wife" monogrammed in bloodred on the breast pockets. A mirror was strategically attached to the ceiling above the bed, and a dozen lit heart-shaped candles filled the room with a warm glow. It smelled of roses and lilacs . . . and sin.

"I can't stay here." She backed up into him.

"It's okay," he said, placing his hands on her shoulders. "We need a room, and this is the only game in town. Food, remember? We can order some food and eat in peace."

"This feels so . . . so . . ."

"Sacrilegious?"

She nodded.

"God will understand."

"But this was set up for a real married couple. We can't do this. It isn't right."

He untied the mask and slipped it from her face.

Mascara dotted her cheeks, deposited by her earlier tears. He brushed at her pale skin with the pads of his thumbs.

"The manager was generous enough to offer us the suite.

155

It's important to him to help us. Our responsibility is to accept graciously."

She glanced down at the red shag carpet.

"Look at me." With a crooked index finger, he guided her gaze to meet his. "We're not doing anything wrong."

Not yet, anyway.

He jerked his hand away and cleared his throat. "I'll call room service. You get changed." He snatched the "Wife" robe from the bed and handed it to her.

She plucked something from her head. "There's corn in my hair," she croaked.

"Go on. Take a bath. It'll make you feel better."

She stared up at him, eyes innocent, like a doe. What he wouldn't give for a complete lack of conscience. Even with makeup smearing her face, the woman was more attractive than a New York model.

I-N-S-A-N-I-T-Y, a voice screeched in his head.

"I'll get us something to eat," he rasped.

Nodding, she stepped across the bathroom threshold, then paused. She turned and shot him a shy, tender smile. His heart skipped a beat.

"Thank you," she said, and closed the door.

Frankie glanced around the spacious bathroom and thanked God for the Jacuzzi-style tub. The designer of the suite probably figured it would be shared by two.

Ambling to the tub, she flipped on the water. A pink bottle of Passionflower bubbles, along with a loofah sponge and massage gloves were conveniently placed tubside. She added bubbles to the water, then went to the sink, gasping at her reflection in the mirror.

"Heavens." She placed her palms on her spotted cheeks and wanted to cry all over again. That would be twice in two days, when she hadn't cried in years.

What was happening to her? Her normally colorful eyes looked gray and bloodshot; her skin was pale and splotched. No wonder Jack was being so nice to her. He thought she'd gone mad. First the temper tantrum, then the personality transformation from Tatianna the Tigress to Wendy the Wimp.

No matter. It wasn't like he was attracted to her. She'd gotten that message loud and clear during last night's blunder.

Her emotions were a tangled mess, her muscles bunched into knots above her shoulder blades and her stomach cried out for food. She could hardly wait to slip into the tub and pretend she was back home. Safe and sound. Far away from Black Jack Hudson. Although she had to admit he wasn't acting his usual hard-assed self tonight.

Good thing she wasn't wearing her contact lenses today. And, strangely enough, she didn't seem to miss them, or her glasses.

She stripped off the skimpy bikini and feathered skirt and hung them on the back of the door. Maxine's efforts to beef up the costume with feathers and fluff had helped Frankie become more comfortable with her role. Or was she just getting used to acting as Tatianna? No, that would never happen, not to conservative Frankie McGee.

Sinking into the cloud of bubbles, she let loose a moan that probably sounded like a woman reaching climax. Not that she would know, being one of the small percentage of women who couldn't have an orgasm. Just as well. Losing control in any way, shape or form completely unnerved her.

Then she remembered the scene outside the mall when she found out she'd been abandoned in corn country with Black Jack Hudson. "God, how embarrassing."

She still couldn't believe she'd completely unraveled in front of him. He must think her a certified flake. Why not? He already knew she was a consummate liar.

"Why do I care?" The steaming water swirled around her shoulder muscles, massaging out the tension. She took a deep breath and submersed herself beneath the fluffy bubbles. In the soundless underwater world she could shut out the nagging voice that scolded her for staying in such a place with a man like Jack Hudson.

Peace. Quiet. The ultimate calm.

A crash penetrated her serenity and Frankie burst through the surface with a shriek.

"Frankie!" Jack's voice boomed.

She shook her head and rubbed at her eyes. The bubbles made them tear.

"What are you doing in here?" She scooped up a thick mass of bubbles to cover her breasts. He couldn't see anything, could he? Her nipples hardened at the thought. "How could you break in on me when I'm . . . I'm . . . taking a bubblebath!"

"I called through the door, but you didn't answer. I thought you were hurt."

"I was submerged." She splashed water at her face to clear the soap from her eyes. "What happened to the door?"

"I broke it down." He crossed his arms over his chest as if expecting criticism.

Something warmed inside. He cared. He was really, truly worried. Either that or he didn't want to add a drowned feline to his list of problems.

"I started to order room service but didn't know what you wanted to drink. I called to you through the door and you didn't answer."

She rubbed her eyes again. Focusing on the sight in front of her, she couldn't help laughing. The satin robe gaped across his chest and exposed his muscular legs all the way to his thighs. Luckily it concealed the more intimate parts of his body.

"What?" He puffed out his chest.

"Nice legs," she chortled, with a lift of her eyebrow.

"It was either this, stay in my trunks and tights, or wear nothing at all."

Her laugh turned into a cough at the thought of Jack's magnificent naked body.

"You okay?" He started toward her, reached out, then snatched his hand back.

"Fine, fine." She scooped up more bubbles for cover.

"Right, sorry." He stepped out of the bathroom, leaving the door open a crack. "How about something to drink?"

"Ginger ale's fine."

"Ginger ale? After a day like today?"

His tone rankled her. "Sorry I'm not as exciting as most of the women you hang out with, but booze and me don't mix."

"How about meat?"

"It doesn't matter as long as it's well done. I like my meat a little tough."

A crash echoed outside the door.

"What happened?"

"Nothing. I'll order us cheeseburgers. Well done."

"Thanks."

He closed the door but it kept popping open thanks to his emergency rescue.

"It won't close all the way, sorry."

"It's okay."

She sensed him walk away. Whew. The air had definitely thinned out in here. She still couldn't believe he'd broken down the door. But then he'd been worried about her.

"That was sweet," she whispered, then caught herself. "Sweet" was not a word one used to describe Black Jack Hudson. Not in a million years.

She rubbed her calves and thighs with the coarse massage gloves until she finally started to relax. It must have been twenty minutes later when she heard a soft tap at the door.

"Food's here," he said.

"Thanks, I'll be right out."

The heavenly bath couldn't compete with the thought of a full tummy. She dried off, ran her fingers through her hair and tied the robe securely around her. Luckily hers was made to fit a healthy-sized woman on the tall side. It draped to her ankles.

She stepped out of the bathroom, her toes sinking into the carpet. Soft music drifted to her from across the room. Her gaze landed on the bed. Jack was sitting on the very edge, a tray next to him. She hadn't noticed until now that the bed was the ONLY piece of furniture besides a chest of drawers.

"I guess we'll have to eat on the bed," he said, eyeing the tray of food.

"Either that or the floor." She hesitated. It felt wrong, naughty.

Her stomach gurgled. She moved to the opposite side of the bed and sat down.

"What have we got?"

"I ordered cheeseburgers, but I guess they had other ideas." He lifted the metal food warmer. A thick, juicy steak filled an eight-inch plate.

"Wow."

"Yeah, they're taking this honeymoon thing pretty seriously." He didn't make eye contact.

"Let's dig in." She snatched a plate, knife and fork and went to work.

"Here's your ginger ale." He popped open the can and filled a glass.

"Thanks." She took a sip and glanced around the room at the erotic prints. Heat flooded her cheeks. She refocused on the meat. She stabbed it with her fork, sliced off a healthy bite and stuck it in her mouth. The tender steak nearly melted on her tongue. She closed her eyes and savored the taste. She'd never realized eating could be such a treat.

The bed shifted and she opened her eyes. He ambled across the room and stared out the window at the festivities below. "Looks like quite a party down there."

"Do you want to go?"

"Dressed like this?" He turned and flicked the neckline of the robe, which gaped in front.

"That's true." She smiled. He did look rather silly. And sexy.

She shoved a piece of steak in her mouth and bit hard.

"I wouldn't be any good to them anyway," he muttered.

"I don't understand."

"I'm tired and cranky. Not what they're used to."

"Surely they wouldn't bother you. You're off duty."

"I'm a celebrity, not a cop. There is no off duty, or haven't you noticed?" He nodded toward the door.

The hallway scene replayed itself in her mind.

"Oh." Sadness washed over her. The man had no privacy, no piece of his life saved just for him. Frankie couldn't imagine living that way. Belonging to everyone, all the time.

"Aren't you going to eat?" she said.

"In a minute." He glanced back out the window.

She finished every last morsel of steak and took a few bites of corn. Now that her tummy was full, she felt much better. Her common sense was firmly back in place.

Jack, on the other hand, ate only half his dinner and nursed one beer. She noticed he'd ordered three.

"You done?" he asked, reaching for the tray.

"Yes, unless you think I'm going to eat the plate, too."

A faint smile creased his lips. "You still hungry?"

Hungry. Yes. But not for steak.

Her pulse pounded in her ears. What the hell happened to her common sense?

"Francine?"

That word again, her full name, spoken from his lips was nearly her undoing.

"No, I'm not hungry." She stood and walked to the window. "You can take the bed, I'll take the floor."

"Don't be ridiculous. That bed's big enough for four adults. There's plenty of room."

"No, really, I insist."

"What, you afraid I'm going to touch you?"

I'm afraid you're not going to touch me.

"I just don't want to make you uncomfortable," she said.

As he placed the tray in the hallway and double locked the door, her heart pounded as if she'd just run a marathon.

"Listen, kid. I'll be uncomfortable if you sleep on the floor and more uncomfortable if I sleep on the floor. So lighten up and let's get into bed."

He untied his robe and she slapped at the light switch. The overhead went out, leaving the room bathed in candlelight. She could still see his body, rippling back muscles and firm buns clad in knit boxer briefs.

She squeezed her eyes shut.

I'll sleep in the Jacuzzi. I'll cushion the tub with towels. No problem.

"It's safe," he said. She opened her eyes. He was stretched out beneath the sheets.

"It's not like I don't trust you or anything," she said.

"Sure." He rolled over, his back to her. "Come on, get in bed. I'll probably be asleep before you climb under the sheets."

Twirling a strand of hair around her finger, she glanced across the room, debating her next course of action. Her gaze landed on a rather colorful print of a man on his knees, his face buried between a woman's thighs. A hand to her forehead, her back arched, the woman had completely surrendered to the obviously amazing sensations.

She gritted her teeth. If sleeping with Jack didn't drive her insane, the prints covering the walls would. Well, it was either stare at the erotic scenes or close her eyes and go to sleep.

Should she blow out the candles? No. Lying in complete darkness beside Black Jack Hudson would be too much for her nerves.

"What's the matter? Afraid you won't be able to resist me?" he mumbled from the bed.

The arrogant, egotistical, insolent jerk.

Marching to the bed, she double knotted the satin belt of her robe and slipped under the sheets. He was right. There was plenty of room. She could go the whole night and then some without noticing she wasn't sleeping alone.

She took a deep breath and stared up at her reflection in the mirror. Never in a million years would she have dreamed up a scenario like this. Herself in bed with Black Jack Hudson. In bed with any man except Bradley. After all, she wasn't one to give her heart or body away to just anyone. No, her heart was meant for the man who met all the qualifications. The man who would provide her with a well-managed, perfect life.

He rolled onto his back, and their eyes connected in the mirror. Her pulse quickened.

"So . . . what's he like?" he said.

"Excuse me?"

"Your fiancé. What's he like?"

Had he read her mind? And how could she talk about Bradley while she was lying in bed with Jack? It seemed wrong, and disloyal, and . . .

Maybe the best thing to do under the circumstances. Talking about Bradley would keep her mind off the all-too-tempting Adonis lying beside her.

"He's not actually my fiancé. When he gets his promotion, he'll propose."

"What does he do?"

"He's one of the top accountants at Lundstrom, Marks, and Beetle. He'll be partner someday. He's smart and hard-working. Bradley knew since he was eight that he wanted to be an accountant. He's so . . . determined. He's a visionary in the field, you know."

He studied her and her body lit on fire. So much for using Bradley as a shield against the sexual awareness between them.

She cleared her throat and searched her brain for all the reasons why she and Bradley were the perfect couple. Talking about Bradley would make him more real. And right now she needed him to be real to keep her sexual hunger at bay. Intense physical attraction was exciting, but it always ended up in a train wreck, as did love. After all, look at what her mother had gone through because she loved Frankie's deadbeat father. Always taking him back, always making excuses. Always crying late at night when she thought Frankie was asleep. And Frankie cried right along with her.

Physical attraction and love be damned. She knew the sensible and forthright Bradley was the man for her. He'd provide her with the security she'd always needed, a sensible life, a perfect life. A life without emotional pain.

Looking into Jack's eyes, she forged ahead.

"We'll take three weeks vacation a year including an educational trip to Europe," she continued, hoping to quell the budding awareness between them. "Then, maybe in six or seven years we'll have a child. If we can work it out with my career. Bradley will make an exceptionally good father. He's already got his eye on the right crib that meets all safety specifications from the American Academy of Pediatrics." She took a breath and studied his eyes in the semi-darkness.

"Kids. I've thought about that," he said.

"You have?"

"Sure. I hope to give it a try someday."

He'd give it a try someday. It sounded like a whim, like trying bungee jumping or riding in a hot air balloon.

"Yes, well, that's our goal. Successful careers, investments, children, if it works into our plan." She glanced at him. "I guess that sounds pretty ho-hum to a man like you."

"No. It doesn't." He rolled onto his side, away from her. "It sounds like you've got it all figured out. That's nice."

An empty feeling settled in the pit of her stomach. "Jack?"

"Good night, kid. We should really get some sleep."

"Oh, okay." But she didn't want the conversation to end.

She wanted to get him talking, ask him about his life, his dreams.

They lay still, bathed in silence for a good five minutes.

"Francine?"

Her heart raced. "Yes?"

"I wouldn't have dropped you. I just wanted you to know that."

Chapter Eleven

The taste of peppermint lingering on his lips, Jack ambled to the bathroom and tapped lightly at the door.

"Who's there?" she called, her voice muffled by the hard spray of the shower.

He pushed open the door. "The big"—he untied his robe—"bad"—he pulled the shower curtain aside—"wolf."

Arms crossed to conceal her voluptuous breasts, Frankie giggled and stuck her fanny out for him to grab. "My, my you have big teeth, Mr. Wolf."

Her rainbow eyes sparkled, her grin widened to a mischievous curl. He stepped inside the shower, gave her a love tap on her round bottom, and nuzzled the nape of her neck. "The better to taste you with, my sweet little thing."

Sliding his hands across the front of her slick, soapy body, he edged them up to cup her breasts, then massaged her nipples.

"Jack," she moaned, locking her fingers around the back of his neck.

"What is it, baby? What do you want?" His fingers trailed

lower, circling her hip bone, then down to graze the sweet nest of curls between her legs.

"Jack." She dug her fingernails into his neck muscles.

"Talk to me, Francine. Tell me what you want." He massaged her inner thigh and she bent her knee to give him better access. "Do you like this, baby? Does it feel good?"

"I need . . ."

"What? What do you need?"

"You know . . . Jack . . . I need . . ." She arched again, and he slid his hand between her legs, cupping the feminine mound with as much tenderness as he could.

Back and forth. Slowly, methodically. Water pounding against his back. He kissed her shoulder, her neck. She tasted of flowers and magic, and he found himself humbled by her surrender.

She arched, opening completely, surrendering to his touch. Trust. Need. She needed him. Not Bradley the accountant. Not anyone but Jack. This was something only Jack could give her.

"Jack!" she cried.

"It's okay," he whispered into her ear, then feathered kisses along the rim. "Let go, baby. Just let go."

"AAAAHHHHHH!" she howled, then fell limp against his chest.

He closed his eyes, savoring the moment, thrilled that he could give her this.

"I need . . ." she whispered.

"What now, baby? What do you need?"

"I need you. Inside me."

Breaking free of his grasp, she turned to face him. His gut clenched at the sight of her, dressed in a leopard-skin bikini, wielding a black whip in her hand. She smiled and fangs gleamed from beneath the black mask.

"Francine?" He spit water from his mouth and took a step back, rubbing at his eyes to clear his vision.

"I want you inside me now. And the name is . . . Tatianna."

She cracked the whip and it sliced open his chest, right above his heart.

"No!" He sucked in air. Had to breathe. Couldn't breathe. Nothing working. Lungs. Had to fill lungs. Had to—

"Jack?"

He glanced over his shoulder at the source of the voice and nearly jumped out of his skin. Frankie clutched the covers to her chest with one hand and reached out to him with the other.

"Argh!" he cried, leaping from the bed. Red satin sheets tangled between his legs, sending him facedown to the floor. He kicked and sputtered, heaving desperate gulps of air to crush the panic. It was no use. The more he struggled, the tighter the sheets bound his legs.

"Aw, hell." He surrendered, turning belly up on the floor. Unbelievable. He could body slam a three-hundred-pound opponent, but succumbed in the first round with a set of linens. He was surely losing his mind.

"Are you okay?" She leaned over the edge of the bed, holding what remained of the sheets all the way to her neck.

What difference did that make? He'd just been naked in the shower with her, touching, stroking her most intimate places.

The mental fog cleared and reality hit him like a Mack truck: He'd been dreaming.

"Did you have a nightmare?" Concern filled her eyes as she pushed a strand of hair behind her ear.

"Yeah. A nightmare."

"You scared me."

Not like you scared me, baby.

"I'm fine. Just embarrassed." He sat up and flailed his arms to detangle himself.

"Here, let me help." She threw the sheets aside. Her

168

white robe parted slightly in front, just enough to expose beautifully curved breasts.

"I'm fine." He sprang to his feet, stumbled to the corner of the room, and clutched the top sheet to his chest.

"Are you sure?" she said, tugging her robe tight in front.

"I'm fine. Sure. Perfect. A-OK."

"It sounded like you couldn't breathe. Do you have allergies?"

"No allergies. I'm fine. Fit as a fiddle, right as rain." And he sounded like a complete idiot. "We'd better get dressed."

"But it's only two A.M."

"Oh." He didn't move, couldn't breathe. Now what? He sure as hell couldn't get back in that bed. Not with her. Not with the dream still fresh in his mind. He put his hand to his chest to rub away the lingering sting.

"I know what you need," she said.

"Wh-hat?" He backed up against the wall.

"A drink of water. Guarantees you won't have another nightmare."

She paced to the bathroom, and he heard the water go on. He took a deep breath and glanced at himself. What a pathetic sight he was, cowering in the corner.

What the hell was happening to him?

Frankie McGee, that's what. He straightened away from the wall and paced to the window. Damn, he had to get a handle on his emotions. She didn't pose a threat to him, not physically, and not emotionally. She was an impossible woman, a stuck up, judgmental, bossy—

"Here, drink up." She walked up beside him, a glass of water in her hand.

"I don't need—"

Shoving the water to his lips, she tipped the glass. He had no choice but to drink it. Either that, gag, or push her away, which would mean he'd have to touch her.

Thank God the water was cold. Very cold.

He finished it in three swallows. There. Now maybe

she'd leave him alone. He swiped the back of his hand across his mouth.

She placed the glass on top of the dresser. "Better?"

"I told you, I'm fine."

"It's okay. Even big, tough wrestlers are allowed to have a nightmare."

He gritted his teeth. She was making fun of him. Wasn't she?

"Should we try to sleep again?" She ambled to her side of the bed and sat on the edge.

He crumpled the top sheet between his fingers. The least he could do was give her back the damn covers.

"Guess you'll need this." He unwrapped himself and flung the sheet across the bed, shoving the edge between the mattress and box spring. He glanced up, long enough to register the look of appreciation in Frankie's eyes. Normally not modest, Jack realized he was parading in front of her in nothing more than tight, knit boxers.

His body tingled in places that were going to embarrass him even further in a minute.

Damn, he had to get his mind off this woman.

Snatching the television controls from the bureau, he sat on the edge of the bed and punched the "on" button.

"I'm going to flip around for a while. It helps me relax."

"Okay."

The bed shifted, then stilled. He surfed the channels, wanting something fascinating to grab his attention and divert his desire.

Why this woman? Why now? She was totally wrong for him. He'd fantasized about finding a laid-back, nurturing woman to share his life with. He knew damn well Frankie McGee was the definition of disaster, married to her career and her perfectly planned life.

The mattress shifted, and he guessed she sought a more comfortable position. He should just leave the room and find a nice quiet spot in the lobby to spend the night.

Wouldn't that look great in next month's issue of *Wres-*

tler's Wisdom magazine? Jack spending his honeymoon night on the couch. Readers wouldn't exactly be writing in for marital advice, that's for sure.

The sound of a woman moaning and groaning drew his attention to the television.

"What the—" he muttered.

A naked woman filled the screen, long blond hair cascading down her back as a naked, semi-hard man sprayed her obviously implanted breasts with whipped cream.

"Hell." Jack clicked the button and landed on a channel featuring two actors dressed as Annie Oakley and Wild Bill Hickok having sex on the bare back of a horse.

He clicked off the tube and tossed the controls to the bureau. Well, it was the honeymoon suite. They probably aired all-night sex shows to get the newlyweds charged up and in the mood.

"Nothing good on?" Frankie mumbled.

"Nope." He started for the bathroom.

"Where are you going?" She propped herself up on her elbows.

His chest ached at the concern in her voice. It sounded like more than concern for the talent. Now he was fooling himself.

"I'll go read or something until I get tired," he said.

"Still spooked by the nightmare, huh?"

"You like rubbing that in, don't you?"

"No—" she hesitated—"I'm sorry if it sounded that way. Actually I think I can help."

I'll bet.

"I'll pass, thanks," he said.

"Okay." She lay back down, but not before he read the emotion in her eyes. He'd hurt her feelings.

Why the hell did he care?

He didn't. Not one bit.

He ambled to his side of the bed and sat on the edge. "What's your idea?"

"Lie down. Get comfortable."

Any requests other than the impossible?

Stretching out on top of the sheets, he interlaced his hands over his chest. His gaze drifted to the mirror. The candles were still burning, and the soft light cast an angelic glow across her face.

He swallowed hard. "I'm ready."

"Close your eyes."

"Why?"

"Just do it. Trust me."

He closed his eyes and felt the bed shift. He peeked through his lids, but she'd just rolled to her side, propping her cheek on an upturned palm.

"Okay, now take a deep breath. In through your nose, out through your mouth . . . okay . . . then another."

Humoring her, he followed orders, planning to feign sleep in the hope of her giving up the psychotherapist act. That wasn't completely true. He was complying with her request because he couldn't stand the thought of hurting her feelings.

Man, he was in trouble. Big time.

"Now pick a focal point. A flower, tree, something that makes you feel good."

A pair of rainbow-colored eyes came to mind.

"You like the mountains," she said. "Picture the Colorado Rockies, the vast, dark green, rolling mountains that take your breath away."

He opened his eyes and looked at her. "You've been there?"

"I've seen pictures."

"Oh."

"Close your eyes."

She placed her fingers on his eyelids, and he thought he'd scream at the gentle touch. The scent of wildflowers tickled his nose. Hell, screw the Rockies.

"Picture yourself hiking up a mountain, forging a new trail, finding hidden lakes and valleys. So beautiful. Keep breathing. In with your nose, out with your mouth. Count to five. Breathe in . . . breathe out. The sun's lighting up the snow-capped peaks. The world is peaceful, quiet. Deep breathing. That's it."

Sure, he'd heard of creative visualization. A lot of the guys used it to cope with the pain. Jack thought it a lot of hooey.

Still, the tension seemed to ease from his shoulders.

"You're walking a narrow trail up the side of a steep mountain. Deep breathing. In . . . and out. You get to the top of the mountain and you feel exhilarated, refreshed. You see a waterfall below you. The sound is so relaxing, the constant, hard sound of water beating against rock. You take off your backpack and lay out a flannel blanket. Breathe. That's it. Picture yourself sprawled out on the ground. Relaxed. Every muscle relaxed. The rush of water drumming in your ears, the sound of birds singing their welcome . . . the feel of sunshine bathing you in warmth. Breathe, that's it . . . in . . . and . . . out. You close your eyes and the sun's heat warms you . . . comforts you . . ."

Not nearly as much as the sound of her voice. He was there, lying on a blanket in the middle of the Rocky Mountains, the sun shining, water pounding.

But he wasn't alone.

Dressed in full hiking gear, Frankie smiled down at him from beneath a floppy tan hat. He squinted to see her through the blinding sun. She knelt beside him and brushed her knuckles across his cheek. Then she touched her fingertips to his lips. He parted them, wanting to taste her, taste every part of her.

He opened his eyes and stared into the mirror, but couldn't make out her expression because she lay on her side. Did she sense his fantasy? Was that why she'd stopped talking?

Jack turned his head to study her. Her eyes were closed, her hands curled, pillowing her head. She looked so peaceful and content.

And asleep.

173

He brushed a strand of copper-streaked hair from her cheek. "At least one of us will get some sleep. Sweet dreams, princess."

Frankie was in the middle of a four-alarm fire. What else could explain the burning of her fingertips and the horrible ringing in her ears?

Flexing her fingers, she thought how soft the blanket was. And how hard. She couldn't help stroking the warm, soft cover. Something vibrated against her palm. She opened her eyes and blinked twice. It wasn't the blanket. It was a man. She started to pull away, then realized it was only Jack. Pressing her cheek against his sinewy back muscles, she squeezed her arm tight around his chest and sighed.

The ringing pierced her eardrums. Content and sleepy, she didn't want to move.

"Phone," he said, his voice thick with sleep.

"Ignore it."

"Okay." He pulled her arm tighter around his chest.

The persistent ring rattled her brain. "All right already." She leaned across him and grabbed the phone off the night stand.

"What!" she said.

"Francine? Is that you?" asked Uncle Joe.

"Yep."

There was a pause, then, "You have to come home. It's an emergency!"

Jack shifted beneath her. "Who is it?"

"My uncle."

"What does that crazy bastard want?"

"What do you want, Uncle Joe?" She pushed a few strands of long black hair from Jack's face.

"Francine . . . it's nearly eleven. And you're just waking up? And is that . . . is that Jack in bed with you?"

"Yeah, Jack's in . . . bed!"

She flung the phone in the air and scrambled to the floor.

"What are you doing?" she accused, standing over him, clutching her robe closed in front.

"What? Who? What happened?" He sat up, his eyes round, his chest heaving in and out.

"You were sleeping with me," she said.

"You told me to."

"I did not."

"You did too. The imagery thing, remember? The Rocky Mountains, the waterfall?" He ran his hand through his hair and blinked. And looked completely innocent.

Of course he was. She was the one who was fondling his chest, hugging and cuddling him. Embarrassment flushed her cheeks.

"I'm sorry. I didn't mean to sound like I was accusing you of . . . anything," she said.

Too bad it was just an accusation. Her gaze locked with his bright green eyes. Her heartbeat pounded in her ears; her pulse raced against her throat.

"Francine? What did he do to you?" Uncle Joe screeched through the phone. "So help me, if he touched you, I'll put him on a card against the Basher in a no-holds-barred match, in a cage, with snow blowers, hedge trimmers and a forty-foot garden hose!"

She snatched the receiver and shoved it against her stomach.

"I'm taking a shower," Jack said, swinging his feet to the floor with a grunt. He hesitated, clenched his jaw and grunted again as he straightened. Pain etched the corners of his eyes. His lips went taut.

Instinct made her want to go to him, help him again, like she did with his nightmare. She couldn't move.

Clutching the sheets as cover, he backed towards the bathroom. "I didn't do . . . you know . . ." He motioned toward the bed with his hand.

"It's okay. I know."

He stumbled into the bathroom and shut the door, five times, the lock not catching.

175

"FRANCINE!" Uncle Joe's muffled cry vibrated against her stomach.

She placed the receiver to her ear. "I'm here. Everything's fine." Shifting onto the edge of the bed, she ran an open palm across Jack's pillow, absorbing his scent into her fingertips.

"That was Jack!" Uncle Joe accused. "You were sleeping with Jack. You're engaged!"

"I'm not engaged, and we weren't *sleeping* together. We just shared a mattress. Our driver disappeared last night and the only room in town was the bridal suite, which, oddly enough, only has one bed."

"What did he do to you?"

"Knock it off, Uncle Joe. I'm a big girl, and he didn't do a thing."

Unfortunately.

She gave herself a mental shake. Time to get back to reality and shove all thoughts of Jack's lips, pecs, and buns out the window.

"But Francine—"

"What's the problem, Uncle Joe?"

He hesitated, no doubt trying to remember his drama of the day.

"You've got to get home!" He started sobbing into the phone, and she couldn't get a coherent word out of him after that. She wondered if Pugsy and the snakes had something to do with his breakdown.

"Are you okay? Is someone threatening you?" she said.

"I'm . . . fine. I can't explain it over the phone. Just p-p-lease come."

"We'll get there as fast as we can."

After listening to another five minutes of moaning and whining, she finally convinced him to hang up so she and Jack could get to work on finding their missing driver. She ran her fingers through her tangled hair and took a deep breath.

Back in the eye of the storm again, she thought. And she

didn't mean her uncle's crisis of the day. She'd awakened with her arm around Jack, caressing his hard pectorals, nibbling at his back like they were a newly married couple, like he belonged to her.

But he didn't belong to her. Jack Hudson didn't belong to anyone.

No, that wasn't quite true either. He belonged to a little boy who needed a hero and an impressionable teenage girl who wanted to be an astronaut. He belonged to a mall full of fans who had lined up hours ahead to meet him and well-wishers who graced the motel corridor, waving corn-stalks and tossing kernels in honor of the newlyweds.

"Sheesh!" She sprang to her feet and paced to the window. None of this was real. She wasn't a bride and Jack wasn't a hero.

Still, the admiration glowing in a little boy's eyes touched her heart. That was definitely real.

But the wrestling itself wasn't. With angles scripted weeks in advance and moves planned just before the talent stepped into the ring, wrestling was make believe, plain and simple. Merely a bunch of overgrown kids play fight-ing.

She spun around and stared at the bed where Jack had struggled to get to his feet. It seemed as if every bone, every muscle in his body screeched in protest.

From real pain.

"What did that old shyster want?" Jack asked, coming out of the bathroom.

He stood in the bathroom doorway, a towel wrapped snugly around his hips as he rubbed at his hair with a second towel.

Electricity crackled and sparked. He looked incredible, droplets of water clinging to his shoulders and chest. Good God, every time she saw the man naked from the waist up, she nearly came apart with wanting. She hated to think what would happen if she saw the rest of him.

He cleared his throat, jarring her from her fantasy.

"My uncle wants us to come home," she said, recovering. "What's today's crisis?"

"He didn't say, just insisted he needs us home ASAP."

"He snaps and we jump."

Someone knocked at the door.

"Now what?" she said.

"I'll get it."

"But you're practically . . . naked."

He eyed her and her skin tingled. "Would you rather answer it in that slinky robe?"

She shook her head.

"Didn't think so." Jack headed for the door. He knew that prim and proper Miss McGee wouldn't be caught dead answering a hotel room door in a robe. No, she'd prefer to be wearing a turtleneck and wool suit. Maybe even a down parka.

He spied their visitor through the peep hole. The manager smiled back at him. Jack eyed the hallway for fans. The coast was clear.

He opened the door.

"Good morning, Mr. Hudson. I hope it isn't too early. We wanted to make sure you got your nourishment before you headed back to the city. By the way, the local police pulled your driver out of the casino this morning. They caught him trying to shove Necco Wafers into the slot machines."

"Great."

"Not to worry. The chief's my cousin. I convinced him to let the man go so you and your wife could get back to Chicago."

"Thanks. I really appreciate that."

"Your car's waiting out front. But first, you should fill up on all our specialties." He lifted the food cover. "Here we have heart-shaped corn cakes, corn-filled crepes, and every newlywed's favorite, fresh strawberries with whipped cream."

He shuddered at the memory of last night's whipped

cream drama, but smiled politely. "Looks great."

"I'd be happy to set it up for you."

"That's okay. The wife's a little shy."

"Right. I gather you . . . slept well?" He grinned expectantly.

They did expect a full report. Wasn't anything sacred?

He bit back his temper. He wasn't usually this testy about fans intruding on his life. It must be the lack of sleep.

"We slept fine, thanks. Could you have our driver bring us our clothes?"

"Right away, sir."

Jack pulled the cart inside and shut the door.

"What have we got?" Frankie said, ambling toward him.

"Don't ask."

"Why?" she laughed.

He loved that sound, that young, refreshing laugh. It made him want to laugh too. Something he rarely did these past few years.

"Let's see what's on today's menu." She lifted the metal dome. "What? No steak?"

She didn't seem nervous or tense, considering they'd slept together . . . touched each other. Hell, he'd just awakened to her delicate fingers grazing his skin, stroking him the way a lover caresses her mate. How could she pretend it hadn't happened?

Denial. That was her trick. Heck, if it worked for her, it could work for him, too.

"No protein. Not good. You need your protein in the morning." She snatched a strawberry and popped it in her mouth. A drop of juice remained at the corner of her lips.

If she reached for the whipped cream, he'd jump out the window.

"These strawberries are delicious." She plucked another one from the plate.

"They found our driver. He's bringing our clothes."

"I can't wait to slip into a fresh pair of pants and a clean blouse." She closed her eyes, savoring the strawberry.

179

He ripped his gaze from her sensuous mouth and snatched a fork, picking at the strange combination of corn, corn, and more corn.

"Eat a strawberry. Balance out your food groups," she ordered.

He wanted to say he'd been feeding himself for the past thirty-seven years, but didn't. He just wanted to eat, get dressed and get the hell out of this room. Even the small confines of the limo would be more comfortable than the lurid bridal suite, which suggested sex everywhere he looked.

"I've got to make a call," he said, grabbing the phone.

"Oh, okay. I'll go wash up and give you some privacy." She ambled toward the bathroom.

Sitting on the edge of the bed, he waited until he heard the water go on in the bathroom, then dialed Butch's number. Jack needed to bring himself back to earth and quick.

"Yellow."

"Hey, coach."

"Well, if it isn't my number-two kid, Jackie Boy."

"Number two?"

"Benson was always quicker at the drop-toe hold."

"Bullshit."

Hearty laughter filled the line. It was good to hear Butch's voice.

"You sure all that fame isn't going to your head?" Butch said.

"Nah. I got it under control." Now if only he could get other things under control.

"They got you swinging from the rafters yet?"

"Not yet. But soon, I'm sure."

"What's the world coming to?"

Jack smiled. Wrestling was everything to Butch. Wrestling and family. A pang of frustration knotted his gut. Would he ever get his chance at having a family?

"How are you doing, kid? Hanging in there? No pun intended."

"Barely. They've got this insane angle—"

"I know, I saw her on TV. How did they get you to take a partner, anyway? You're a solo kinda guy."

"Long story. But I'm getting used to it. I guess that surprises you, huh?"

"Nah. Life's fill of surprises. Besides, your partner looks like a nice girl, if you're into the purring type."

"Very funny. How's Lois?"

"Fine, just fine. When are you going to come by? I've got some things I want to go over with you."

"I'm not sure. Sully's got us running in twenty different directions."

"Yeah, well, stop running long enough to come see me. Looks like you could use a refresher course in mat work. You've been spending way too much time outside the ring."

"Tell me about it."

Frankie padded into the room and swiped another strawberry from the tray.

"Gotta go," Jack said.

"Miss ya, kid."

"Same here. Thanks, bye."

He hung up and glanced at Frankie.

"Who was that?" she said.

"A friend."

"A friend?"

"Yeah, is that so hard to believe?"

"Boy, you're defensive this morning."

Of course he was. He was guarding his heart.

"I'm just tired," he said.

"Understandable, after that long day yesterday and then last night . . ."

Their eyes locked. He struggled to breathe.

Blinking, she broke the spell, then poured a cup of tea. "At least this whole fiasco will make a good story to tell my friends." She paused, the cup to her lips. "Who would I tell?"

"What do you mean?" He walked over to the tray and stabbed a crepe with a fork.

"No one can ever know about my moonlighting as Tatianna. It wouldn't be proper. Although, I have to admit, I kinda liked the attention yesterday." She shifted onto the edge of the bed. "I can't believe I said that."

"Don't worry, it's just me you're talking to."

She smiled and glanced at the strawberry in her hand. He spoke like they were confidants, best buddies, which they weren't. Were they? Hell, he didn't know. But somewhere deep down he knew what he wanted to be.

Another knock interrupted his self-analysis. He welcomed the distraction and cracked open the door to find Bernie on the other side, the knot of his tie halfway down his chest, a smudge of pink lipstick coloring the lapel of his suit. He handed Jack the garment bag.

"Well, look who's here. You take care of business last night?" Jack said.

"I did okay. Heard you didn't do so bad yourself." He strained to peer into the room.

A sudden flash blinded Jack. "What the hell?"

"I'm a freelance photographer for *Wrestling Superstars and Finks*," a voice said.

Jack couldn't make out the face. His eyes were still trying to focus through the haze of white light.

"There's a lot of speculation about Tatianna's real identity," the photographer continued. "Some say she's your ex-wife. We'd like to get a picture of her without the mask."

"Forget it."

"But sir, the fans have a right to know."

The jerk clicked off another shot of Jack, standing half naked in his hotel room door. He shielded his eyes with his hand.

"Get him the hell out of here," he ordered Bernie.

"I'm a driver, not a bouncer."

"You're not going to be a driver much longer."

Bernie shoved at the guy. "Come on. Scram."

"I'll get the story!" the photographer shouted as Bernie dragged him by the collar down the hall. "I'll find out who she really is. Some think it's Monica Moonbeam! Did you know she's already married? That's bigamy, sir. You could go to jail for—"

He slammed the door. "Don't these people have anything better to do?"

"Who was that?"

"Paparazzi. They're trying to figure out who you are."

Her eyes popped wide, and she clutched the material of her robe to her chest.

"Don't worry, I'm not talking. Here are your clothes." He offered her the garment bag.

She stared at it as if he held a hand grenade. Without the pin.

"What? Take it."

"Without my mask and feathers, they'll know who I am."

"Judas Priest, woman, what's the big deal?" He tossed the bag to the bed and unzipped it with a jerk.

"I'll be the laughingstock of the financial industry, I'll lose my job, Mama will never speak to me again, and I can kiss my engagement goodbye."

"Pre-engagement," he corrected.

"My whole life will be over. My well-planned, perfect life."

She gently touched his arm. He struggled to breathe.

"Don't you see? No one can know who I really am. No one."

He wanted to jerk away, tell her to get her damn hands off him. After all, she didn't want to touch him. Jack and this whole business repulsed her. She couldn't stand being part of it. Wasn't that why she was embarrassed and ashamed to let anyone know who she really was?

"Go on and get into costume, then." He snatched his jeans and shirt from the garment bag. "Your secret's safe with me."

Chapter Twelve

They drove home in record time to an awaiting and anxious Uncle Joe. Then they got right down to business: lunacy, as usual.

"I've heard of cage matches, but this one takes the cake," Jack said from across the office.

Frankie stared at Uncle Joe, still shocked by his words. Kidnapping. Blackmail. Escape. All part of next Tuesday night's show, which they hoped to use as a teaser for an upcoming pay per view.

"Look at the figures! Look!" Uncle Joe raced over and dropped a stack of pink message slips in her lap. "The phone hasn't stopped ringing since Tatianna came on the scene. Sponsors are banging down our doors. That means more money for production of action figures, shirts, whips."

"Uncle Joe!" she admonished. "You cannot market whips to children."

"But they love you, Frankie. They worship the ground you walk on. They want to be just like you."

Jack snorted.

She marched to his desk and slapped the message slips dead center. "No whips."

"But Frankie—"

"Where's your sense of decency? You're going too far, and I won't be a part of it."

"I'll find another Tatianna," he said with a pout.

"No, you won't," Jack threatened from the corner.

His nod of support warmed her insides. They were on the same side for once. And it felt good.

"You two are going to be the end of me." Uncle Joe paced to his swivel chair and collapsed. "Fine. No whips. But I'm going ahead with the lawn-mower tattoos. Basher fans will love those."

Frankie rolled her eyes.

"Who's playing Tiger Man?" Jack asked, leaning against the built-in bookshelves. He wore black jeans today, still a size too tight in her opinion. At least the loose-fitting, gray button-down shirt bloused in front, hiding his hard and incredibly touchable chest.

"New talent. Hired him last week," Uncle Joe said. "Hank 'The Hawk' Rogers. Ever hear of him?"

"Nope."

Uncle Joe's eyes gleamed. Something was up. Frankie could feel it. She glanced at Jack. She saw that he didn't think anything was strange. She'd grown used to reading his expressions, guessing his thoughts.

"Hank's been with the Southern Alliance for the last five years. Big guy, six seven, four hundred and ten pounds. Impressive-looking."

"What's the angle?"

"You and Tatianna come out to announce the main event. Tiger Man shows up and challenges you for his woman."

"Jack's still recovering. He's not supposed to fight for another week." Panic swirled in her chest.

"He won't have to fight. Not yet. Tiger Man will challenge him to a match at the Summer Suplex Slammer in two weeks. Jack agrees, but Tiger Man kidnaps Tatianna anyway, to make sure Black Jack will show."

"The whole kidnapping part makes me nervous," she said with a shudder.

"We can play that out ten ways to Sunday. He kidnaps you, holds you for ransom, Jack makes a tear-jerking appeal, real drama."

Uncle Joe leaned back in his chair and tugged on the knot of his tie.

She stared him down. "What aren't you telling us?"

"You like the story, don't you? Those writers you hired are doing a great job coming up with fresh angles. I can't thank you enough for—"

"Stop stalling," she demanded.

"We have to tape it tonight."

"We just got home," she protested. "Couldn't you schedule it for next week?"

"I've got fifteen new sponsors interested in the Summer Suplex Slammer. Fifteen! After Tiger Man's challenge is aired, they'll all lock in, and then some. One of the sponsors is a new candy company that makes licorice in the shape of our very own superstars."

"Great, they can bite off my head when I lose a match," Jack said.

"Doesn't anyone ever get a break around here? You know, down time?" she said.

"Not when the company's on the line," Uncle Joe said.

Not when my life is at risk, she heard.

She searched Jack's eyes. He studied the floor.

"Are you okay with this?" she asked.

"I've got nothing better to do." He glanced up. "What about you? I know you have a date with your fiancé."

"Tomorrow."

"Then there's no problem. Sully's right. It's a good angle."

"But—" she hesitated, remembering the pain creasing

his features as he struggled just to get out of bed. She squared off at Uncle Joe. "Jack won't be fighting?"

"Not tonight."

"I have your word?"

"Yes." He narrowed his eyes at her. "Whose side are you on, anyway?"

"What time is the taping?"

"Seven, St. Louis."

"Great. More travel." She shook her head.

"At least we don't have to worry about our pilot getting waylaid by a pair of snake eyes," Jack offered.

She couldn't help smiling. It had been a helluva night, an interesting night. One she wouldn't forget for a long time.

"You've made our travel arrangements?" Frankie asked.

"Fly out at two, flight back at ten-thirty tonight."

Uncle Joe slapped the tickets on his desk and she picked one up. "Good, I'll be back in time."

Jack walked up behind her, his scent taunting her senses. "In plenty of time for your date."

She closed her eyes, felt his breath against her neck even though she knew he wasn't standing that close.

"Right, in time for my date," she repeated. Heavens, what was she going to tell Bradley? She sure as sunshine wasn't going to tell him about the incendiary burn that raged through her body whenever Black Jack Hudson stepped too close.

"I've got to stop by the apartment. Take a shower," she said.

"I'll pick you up in an hour."

She took a deep breath. "Okay."

"Until then." He snatched his ticket from the desk and left the office.

She shoved her ticket into her purse and glanced at her uncle. "I'm not coming in tomorrow. I'll see you Monday, then?"

He nodded, furiously nibbling on his thumbnail.

"You okay?"

"Fine. Fine." He twirled his tie.

"Uncle Joe, if there's anything you want to tell me, anything at all . . ."

"Now go on." He stood, placed his arm around her shoulder, and guided her to the door.

"You'll be okay?"

"Stop worrying. I've got Maxine to take care of me."

She kissed him on the cheek and stepped into the hallway. Something fluttered in her belly. Call it instinct or panic or just plain exhaustion. She wasn't sure. But something was definitely off-kilter.

A shower. All would be right with the world after a quick, warm shower and a check-in phone call to Bradley.

No, she really didn't have time for that, not right now. She'd call him tomorrow morning, after she returned home and had settled in. After she had a few hours' break from Jack.

She ambled down the hall to the elevators, wondering how it happened, how she'd developed a kinship to a professional wrestler. And not just any wrestler. She'd somehow befriended tough, sexy Black Jack Hudson.

Working closely tended to do that to people. That's how she and Bradley had formed their partnership. They'd bonded during an audit. Yet it took months before she felt as comfortable with Bradley as she did in just days with Jack. Must be the physical nature of the job. Her heart did a flutter at the image of Jack lying beside her in bed. It skipped to a full-blown mariachi beat at the memory of her hands caressing his bare chest.

She dug in her purse for mints.

The elevator doors slid open and Maxine stormed out.

"Hey, Max."

She hugged Frankie, then pushed past her. "Would love to catch up on the wedding night, but I've got a serious bone to pick with that crazy uncle of yours," she said, marching down the hall. "One of these days he's going to go too far. Just too damn far."

"Max, wait—"

The older woman waved her off and disappeared around the corner.

That didn't sound good. Frankie pushed the elevator button again. Oh well, if anyone could keep Uncle Joe in line it was a tough broad like Max.

Jack tapped the knee brace hidden beneath his black stir-rup pants. The joint felt strange today, stranger than usual. Good thing he wasn't fighting. He snapped his Stetson from the locker room bench and fingered the photograph hidden inside the brim. A reminder of what he was working for, his dream, a normal life.

Okay, so his plan for Tatianna to screw up had crumbled to pieces. But something else would present itself. It had to. He hadn't paid his dues for the past twenty years just to have Sully pull the leash tighter around his neck. Sooner or later he would gain his freedom.

At least the flight had been easy. "Easy" being a relative term. Every time his arm brushed against Frankie, his body lit with need. Her scent drove him mad, bringing back the feel of satin sheets, images of a peaceful stroll in the wilderness and the sight of creamy white skin peeking out from beneath mountains of bubbles.

Attraction was one thing, but obsession? He couldn't seem to get her off his mind. It didn't help that he'd been with her nearly every waking moment for the past twenty-four hours. But after today they'd get a good three-day break from each other and Jack could get his perspective back.

He was a grown man with needs. It was only normal to be physically drawn to a woman like Francine. A voluptuous, feisty woman with soft skin and fascinating, iridescent eyes.

"You ready?" Billings said from the door.

"Yeah, sure."

Following Sully's assistant into the hallway, he spotted Frankie sitting on a table, swinging her spiked heels. Even wearing that ridiculous costume, she still set his heart racing double time.

Sex. That was it. He needed to get laid. He'd call Tina. She was always willing and able whenever he came to town. No strings attached.

He walked up to Frankie and she glanced at him, her eyes smiling beneath the mask. He smiled back. He wouldn't be calling Tina tonight, or tomorrow, or any other day.

"Hey," he said.

"Hi." She fingered the row of feathers trimming her skirt.

"You holding up?"

"Sure."

"You guys know the drill," Billings instructed. "I'll signal from the curtain and you come in. Karl will hand you the mike as you approach the ring. I gave Tatianna the script. She's been practicing. Gotta go. They need me out front." He raced off.

"So how does it look?" he asked as Frankie studied the sheet of paper.

"Okay, I guess. I'm not sure I get the part about me and Tiger Man mating in the center of the ring."

"What?" He snatched the script from her hands, and she burst out laughing.

"Very funny." He gently poked her shoulder.

"Hey, watch it or I'll bite your finger off."

"Promises, promises."

She smiled and his heart leaped.

It amazed him how right this felt, how natural. Like long-time friends kidding and joking.

How could that be? He didn't have any long-time friends, with the exception of Butch. Then again, Butch's role was more mentor than friend. Jack had learned early on that being a loner was his calling.

She swung her feet and sighed.

"You okay?" he said.

"Exhausted."

"After tonight we'll get some time off."

"I need it. I haven't see Mom in three weeks."

"You still see your mom?"

She glanced up, a puzzled expression creasing her features. "Sure. Mom expects a visit twice a month and a phone call on Tuesday and Friday. It's in the script," she joked. "What about you? Don't you talk to your parents?"

He looked away. "Nah. I left when I was eighteen. Haven't been back."

"But you call, right?"

He shrugged. "The best day of their life was when I joined the pro circuit."

"That's not true."

She touched his arm, and a ball formed in his chest.

"You're their son. I'm sure they miss you."

He cleared his throat. "Doesn't matter." Glancing at the script, he ached for her to release her hold on his arm, on his heart.

"Looks simple enough. You memorize your lines?" he said.

She didn't answer. He looked up. Compassion filled her eyes.

"I'm sorry," she said.

"For what?"

"Just . . . I'm sorry. That's all." She pulled him close and kissed his cheek.

Something broke inside.

"Come on, you two. We're ready!" Billings called.

Jack helped her off the table and they walked, side-by-side, to the curtain. He noticed a few cameramen buzzing in the hallway. He glanced at Frankie, wondering what she was thinking. Wondering whether she was horrified that he had no family, no ties to anyone.

But her.

Something snapped around his neck, whipping him to the cement floor.

"Jack!" she screamed.

Adrenaline rushed through his veins. What the hell was going on? Camera lights blinded him as he edged his fingers between his skin and the rope that was pressing down on his windpipe. He loosened the suffocating grip but was pinned to the floor, helpless.

"Jack!"

He thrashed and kicked, but it was no use. There were at least three sets of hands holding him down. He caught sight of Frankie being led by a noose down the hall.

He was going to kill Sully. Strangle him with his bare hands. This had to be the part of the angle that the bastard hadn't bothered to share with Jack or Frankie, his own flesh and blood.

"Let me go!" she cried, trying to break away from two hooded men. The look in her eyes set off an inferno deep in Jack's gut. Damn, she didn't get what was happening.

"She doesn't understand," he said to his masked captors. "Frankie, it's okay! It's part of the—"

One of his assailants shoved a rag in his mouth. His eyes watered, his gut split into a million pieces, camera lights blinded him.

This time Sully had gone too far.

"Let me out of here, you overgrown ape!" Frankie demanded from her six-by-six-foot steel cage. "This wasn't in the script."

"I wrote a new script," the four-hundred-pound creature said, adjusting a leather strap across his chest.

"Do you know who I am?" she threatened.

"Shut up and let me think."

"Don't hurt yourself."

He leaped from his chair with such force it flew across the dressing room. Storming to the cage, he glared at her, two sharpened incisors sparkling like fangs.

"Do you know who I am?" he said.

She swallowed hard.

"I'm Tiger Man. Previously known as the Hawk. Last year alone I put seven guys in the hospital. Imagine what I could do to a little thing like you."

With a gleam in his eye, he snapped his teeth and she jumped back. This was no act. This guy was nuts. Kookoo. Psycho.

But he was still the hired help.

"You'd better let me out of here before security comes," she said.

"They're not coming. I've just improved the angle, upped the stakes. Sully's gonna be real pleased with me."

Her head began to spin. "Sully knew about this?"

"The fans are ripe for a good show. And after tonight they'll be all mine. I'll be the hero."

Slinging the rope over his shoulder, he wheeled the cage down the empty hallway.

"You're wrong. Black Jack will rescue me and ruin this angle of yours."

The cage jerked to a halt and she plopped onto her fanny. Tiger Man closed in, hair covering his chest, his shoulders, his face. God, the man was a walking commercial for Rogaine.

With grimy hands, he grabbed the bars and gave them a shake. She could use her whip right about now. Unfortunately, she'd lost it during the abduction.

"I wouldn't count on that husband of yours saving you. He'll be lucky to walk after I get through with him."

Her heart slammed against her chest. "Jack's not fighting tonight."

"Sure he is. He just doesn't know it yet."

His maniacal grin widened to reveal a black abyss where there used to be a couple of teeth. "I've been waiting a long time to take a run at Black Jack Hudson. A very long time."

"But you're supposed to fight him at Summer Suplex in

193

two weeks. That's the plan." She gripped the bars, fear leaving an acidic taste in her mouth.

"I changed the plan."

He laughed, a low, menacing sound. A shiver wracked her body from head to toe and back up again to settle in her throat.

"Jack," she croaked. He wasn't supposed to fight for at least another two weeks. If anything happened to him to-night . . .

She closed her eyes. He wasn't healthy enough to step into the ring. She knew that as sure as she knew she was going to fire this Tiger Man the minute she got back home. Right after she took care of Uncle Joe. She couldn't believe he'd set up Jack like this. Then she remembered Maxine's words: *He's gone too far this time.*

Frankie's heart raced. God help her if anything happened to Jack.

She focused on her breathing. In through the nose, out through the mouth. She'd be no help to Jack if she passed out from a case of nerves. That hadn't happened since she was a kid and Mama was rushed to the hospital in an ambulance. Fear had strangled Frankie's throat that night. Fear that Mama had been seriously hurt.

Like Jack would be if he tangled with this loon.

Tiger Man hoisted the rope over his shoulder and wheeled her toward the screams and cheers of the awaiting fans. They rolled through the Monkey Tunnel and up the aisle. Her mind spun. She had to do something, but what? They approached the ring, the crowd booing and hissing with renewed vehemence. She glared at Tiger Man, panic surging through her veins. Jack would never know what hit him.

With stiff fingers she squeezed the cage bars and let out a blood-curdling scream. The crowd roared back, fully enjoying the show. No. This wasn't right. She had to get Jack's attention, had to—

Jack sprang from beneath the ring and knocked down

Tiger Man. They rolled and punched, but Jack landed on top, nailing his opponent with five quick jabs. He pushed off the momentarily dazed wrestler, grabbed the keys and raced to free Frankie.

"Jack, it's real. This is real." She started sobbing and he cocked his head to one side in question.

"Frankie?"

"He's going to—"

Tiger Man nailed him in the shoulders with a two-by-four. The keys dropped from his hand, and he went down.

"Somebody stop this!" she cried, her protest swallowed by the roar of excited fans.

"Black Jack Attack! Black Jack Attack!"

Tiger Man swung Jack to the metal ring steps with a crash.

She had to stop this.

"You!" She flagged a photographer. "Let me out and I'll give you a picture." She gripped the lining of her bikini top as if offering to expose her breasts.

"Lucious Leeza flashed hers last week." He turned his attention back to the fight.

Tiger Man rammed Jack, shoulder first, into the ring post. The crowd screamed in horror.

Jack curled into a ball, gripped his shoulder with his other hand, and kicked at the mat in pain.

"I'll take off the mask!" she cried to the photographer.

His eyes lit up. "Deal!"

She glanced through the bars. Tiger Man picked up Jack and applied some kind of painful hold, one arm behind his back, the other pulling his neck in the opposite direction. He gritted his teeth in pain, completely helpless against the unexpected and genuine assault.

"Let me out!" she ordered the photographer.

"Take off the mask first."

"You won't get a good shot through the bars."

He nodded and released her.

She whipped open the door and raced for Mulligan,

WHAK's head security manager. He knew who she was; he'd listen to her. The photographer gripped her arm and spun her around.

"A deal's a deal!"

"Hands off me, you stupid ingrate!" She kicked him in the shin and he went down. More flashes nearly blinded her.

Out of the corner of her eye she spied Tiger Man toss Jack into the ring, then whip a steel door under the bottom rope. Jack got to his knees, clinging to the ropes, unable to stand.

"Mulligan!" she cried, running up to the security expert. "Stop the match."

He eyed her, then snorted. "Yeah right."

"Tiger Man's out to hurt Jack, for real. I said stop the match."

"The only person who can stop the match is Sully."

"Sully isn't here, but I am."

"Yeah, so?"

She ripped off the mask, squinting against the onslaught of flashing bulbs.

"Holy shit, Miss McGee. I had no idea."

"Stop this match or I'll have your job."

"Yes, ma'am." He sprinted toward the ring, barking orders into his walkie-talkie.

Jeers suddenly punctured her ear drums. She spun around and her heart stopped cold.

With great pomp and circumstance, Tiger Man swung Jack head first on top of the steel door.

A collective gasp echoed in the arena. Jack lay motionless. Tiger Man grinned and beat at his chest, then went back to work, stomping on Jack's chest.

He didn't move. Not even to defend himself.

She scanned the area. Security men huddled in a corner, planning their approach. They weren't fast enough. Grabbing a metal folding chair, she flew under the bottom rope and stalked Tiger Man from behind. She closed in, wound up and let him have it. Once. Twice. Three times. He wobbled, but didn't go down. His eyes blazed fire when he turned on her.

Roaring, he pounded closed fists against his chest and started toward her. A team of security guards filled the ring and tackled him to the ground. She raced to Jack's side. Sweat covered his still-closed eyes.

"Jack? Open your eyes."

She brushed her fingertips across his cheek. He didn't move. Her heart ached.

"Ambulance!" she cried over her shoulder.

"What . . . what are you doing?"

She whipped her gaze to Jack. His eyelids opened half way; blood dripped down the side of his mouth. She dabbed at it with her finger. He was okay. Everything was going to be okay. Her chest lightened with relief.

"Jack." She kissed him. On the cheek, the eyebrow, the forehead.

"Your mask?" He looked at her with such wonder in his eyes.

"Forget the mask. I was so scared. Tiger Man is crazy. He wanted to hurt you, to prove something. I tried to tell you what was going on. I'm sorry, I'm so sorry."

"But they'll know who you are . . . without the mask."

"How do you feel? Can you tell me how many fingers I have up?" She shoved three fingers in his face. He closed his hand around them and pressed her palm to his chest, above his heart.

"Why did you take it off?" he said.

"I had to stop the match. No one would listen. Mulligan didn't recognize me with the mask on."

"I know the feeling." He smiled and squeezed her hand. She closed her eyes, reveling in his gentle touch, the powerful connection that shot straight to her heart.

"Let's go, Jack. I want to go home."

"Okay. Get the stretcher."

Her eyes shot open. "Dammit, this isn't about the angle,

about building up drama by going out in an ambulance. This is about you being okay. About us walking out of here, together."

" 'Us.' You said 'us,' " he whispered.

"Come on." She started to get up, but he wouldn't let go of her hand. "Jack, please, get up."

"I'd love to, darlin'. But I can't feel my legs."

Chapter Thirteen

"Get your best orthopedic surgeon down here, now!" Frankie ordered the emergency room intern.

Jack tried telling her he was fine, that he could feel his legs again, but she was having none of it. When the doctor said he couldn't keep Jack against his will, Frankie shot Jack a death glare. He'd never seen that one before, and he didn't want to find out what was behind her fiery eyes.

"Are you listening to me?" She got in the doctor's face as he tried to escape the examining area. Jack had to give her credit. When Frankie took charge, she really took charge. There was simply no talking to her.

"I want your orthopedic man down here now, or I'll fly in one of my own!"

She whipped the curtain closed in the doctor's face and turned her attention to Jack. "Why do I get the feeling they're not taking me seriously?"

Her hair flew in twenty-seven directions, her mascara was smudged over her face, and she still sported her Tatianna feathers.

"Gee, I wonder . . ." he teased, eyeing her from head to toe.

"At least you've got your sense of humor back." She rummaged through a drawer and pulled out a hospital gown.

"I told you, I'm fine. Look, Mom, I can even walk." He started to get up, but she jumped to his side and pushed him flat on the stretcher.

"Forget it, mister. You're not going anywhere until you're checked out by a real doctor."

She slipped her arms through the light cotton gown and tied it in front.

"You'd better watch it or they'll admit you."

"I'm fine."

"For being mentally disturbed."

"I'm glad you can joke about this."

"It's all part of the life, kid."

"It's a stupid life if you ask me." She scooted a chair beside the bed and leaned way too close. Her cleavage peeked out from where her hospital gown gapped in front.

"You risk your body, your ability to walk. What is that about?" she said.

"That part wasn't my idea, remember?"

She paled and folded her hands in her lap. "If it's the last thing I do, I'm going to fire that lunatic."

"He was just doing his job."

"No!" She sprang to her feet and paced the cramped examining area. "He wanted to hurt you, to prove to everyone he was the best. I can't believe my uncle knew about this. I just can't."

Jack glanced at the ceiling, her pain hurting him, too. She loved her uncle so much. She couldn't accept that he'd set up Jack to be intentionally hurt.

"I'll take care of my uncle when we get home. Right now we've got to find you a top-notch orthopedic specialist to make sure you can walk out of here on your own two feet."

"I've already told you, I can walk out of here right now."

"Well, you're not going to, not until you get the A-OK

from a doctor. So stop pushing me on this."

"I hate hospitals."

"And I hate wrestling."

Silence fell between them. He closed his eyes. No sense arguing with the woman. She obviously had her mind made up. About a lot of things.

"I'm sorry." She took his hand. The warmth crept up his arm, burning a path straight to his heart. What was it about her touch?

He opened his eyes and glanced at her. "What are you sorry about?"

"About hating wrestling. I know it's your life."

"You have to remember, when I started it was nothing like it is now. Sometimes I don't recognize it at all. A lot of the new guys know five moves, that's it. They aren't traditional wrestlers. They never set foot in a ring before they enrolled in a wrestling school and learned how to fall and get up again a hundred times. And these days, they don't have to know a lot of moves. It's mostly soap-opera drama, a lot of shouting, punching, flying into vats of green Jell-O."

She chuckled, and his heart skipped. He should shut up while he could. But this woman's opinion of him was important. More important than it should be.

"Wrestling, amateur wrestling, saved my life," he said, unable to stop. "I probably would have been dead by the time I was seventeen if Butch hadn't pulled me off the streets and forced me to wrestle. I was a natural. I planned to wrestle in college but didn't have enough money. I figured I'd work the pro circuit for a few years, save some bucks, go back to school."

"But you didn't."

"Nah. I got sucked down so deep, I couldn't even see the surface anymore. Months passed, years passed. You're on the road all the time. You can't remember where you've been or where you're going, much less why you joined this circus in the first place. And you sure as hell don't have time to plan what you'll do once you get out."

She studied her hands, and he wondered if he'd said too much. "Hey, don't feel sorry for me. I chose this life."

"I just can't imagine being so . . . alone."

"Alone? Hell, I'm surrounded by people all the time. The guys become like family. I'm not alone."

And if you believe that, I've got a bridge for sale.

"Well, you won't be alone tonight." Clasping his hand, she brought it to her cheek.

He didn't know how much more of this he could take, her touch, her compassion. If he didn't slam on the brakes, he might as well hand over his soul right here and now.

This could never be. She was Sully's niece, a woman who knew exactly what she wanted and how she was going to get it. And she sure as hell didn't want Jack, a burned-out wrestler with no future, no stellar career to brag about to her mother and business associates.

"Listen, I appreciate your concern, but even Sully would agree you've gone above and beyond the call," he said.

She glanced at him in question, and he steeled himself to the pain he knew he'd read in her eyes next.

"I know it's your job to keep a handle on the talent but—"

"That's what you think this is about? That I'm here because of your contract?"

Pulling his hand away, he interlaced his fingers behind his head. "I can't blame you. With the story line as hot as it is, you can't afford to lose me to a serious injury."

She stood abruptly, metal chair legs screeching against the vinyl floor. He stared at the ceiling, unable to look at her.

"I gotta admit, Sully's getting his money's worth out of you, Frank. Your performance tonight in that cage . . . those tears . . . man, that was Academy Award material."

He glanced at her, and his chest ached. This was the right thing to do, the only thing to do. "You're a natural at this, kid. I never woulda guessed it."

She clenched her jaw and fisted her right hand. One of these days he was going to get a knuckle sandwich right between the eyes.

"And I never would have guessed—"

"Excuse me, sir, ma'am," a nurse interrupted Frankie's threat. "The doctor will be here in a little while. We'd better start the IV."

His stomach clenched at the sight of the hanging bag she wheeled beside her. "I'm fine. I'm really fine."

Sitting up, he pushed himself off the stretcher. His knee gave way.

Luckily, Frankie caught him. Luckily? She looked like she wanted to skin him alive.

"You're not going anywhere," she ground out.

"It's my old knee injury. My legs are fine. I can feel them. See?" He pinched his thigh. "Ouch. See, that hurts, I'm fine. I just need to ice the knee. My legs are fine. There's no spinal injury. I don't need to be here."

The nurse looked at Frankie.

"Needle phobic," she explained.

"Oh." The nurse set up the IV next to his bed.

"Come on, let me go. With Frank's help, I'll hobble my way out of here and you can treat some real sick people."

Frankie stepped away from him.

"Hey, come here. I need your shoulder to lean on."

"Sorry, chief. You're staying here until a doctor checks you out. Like you said, I wouldn't want to take any chances with our prime talent."

He hated the sound of her words, as if she were guarding a choice piece of beef.

"Lie down, Mr. Hudson." The nurse ripped open the plastic-sealed needle. Both his legs wobbled; his vision blurred.

"It would be nice if he could be conscious when the doctor gets here," the nurse said, her voice a faraway echo in a long tunnel.

He felt himself being coaxed onto the stretcher.

"Look at me." Frankie clamped her hands on either side of his face and guided his eyes to meet hers. Train whistles rang in his ears; stars blurred his vision.

"Jack. Look into my eyes. Jack!"

Something pinched his cheek. The discomfort brought him back around. "Huh?"

"My eyes, Jack, look at them."

He blinked and stared through the haze. It cleared and he found himself gazing at the most beautiful colors of the rainbow: blue, green, yellow, even purple.

"You are a sonofabitch, you know that?" she said.

Beautiful eyes, the color of the mountains in springtime, with all the hues blending into one another. He could paint those eyes. It would take a lifetime, but he'd like to try.

"So many colors . . ." he mumbled, the buzz louder in his ears.

"Don't you pass out on me. Look at me. I need your help. My friend's going west this summer, Colorado. Where's a good place to stay? Aspen?"

"Crowded in Aspen. Expensive. Try Breckenridge, maybe Dillon."

"What kinds of things would she do there? Hike? What else?"

"Rafting, horseback riding."

She scrunched up her nose.

"You don't like horses?" he said.

"Never got close enough to find out."

"You've never been on a horse?"

"Have you?"

"Sure. Ride up into the mountains. Nobody around. You're all alone."

"Perfect for you," she muttered. She glanced at the nurse and nodded.

"Why peppermint?" he asked. He had to know.

"What?"

"You always taste like peppermint."

She studied her hands. "I have stomach problems."

"What kind of problems?"

"Nerves. I get all bunched up inside and need something to calm me down."

"Ulcer?"

"Not yet. Maybe another five years."

"What do you have to worry about?"

She narrowed her eyes.

"Before you started helping your uncle, I mean. You have a great job, successful fiancé, loving family. You've got it all together. Your life's planned out for the next twenty years."

"Yeah, well, things don't always go as planned." She stroked his forehead, gently, so gently.

"Like what?"

"You tell me. Surely you've made plans that have fallen apart."

"No. No plans. Just fighting. Save money for retirement."

"And when you retire?"

"I'm going to live."

"Where?"

"Mountains."

"Alone?"

"Always alone."

She blinked, sadness coloring her eyes. The nurse said something and Frankie backed away.

"Francine?"

"I'm not going anywhere, not until I'm sure my talent is on the mend."

She was still mad. He couldn't blame her. But it was for the best. She had to know that. They were growing too close, too comfortable with one another.

She gripped his hand and tucked it under the white cotton sheet. But she still clung to him. She didn't let go.

It felt good.

"Are you feeling better?" she said.

He turned his head to look at her. Concern creased her features. He hated that. Hated making her worry.

"Better," he said.

"What is it with the needles?"

"I don't like them."

"And I don't like peas, but I don't go into hysterics when they end up on my plate."

He licked his lips and took a shallow breath.

"I was ten. Cut my arm. Mom was working. Dad was . . . I don't know where Dad was. The neighbor wrapped my arm and put me on a bus to the hospital. The doctor pulled out this needle . . . it was a foot long. They cornered me. Had to hold me down. I was so scared . . . screaming. I remember screaming. I passed out." He glanced at her but couldn't read her expression. "Pretty dumb, huh?"

"You were all alone? You were ten and all alone at the hospital?"

"I could take care of myself. I always have." He paused. "But you haven't, have you?"

"Nonsense." She fiddled with his blanket, as if it needed straightening.

He fingered her hair, silken waves gone awry, yet still so soft. "You act tough, but you like being taken care of."

She pretended to ignore his touch, but he noticed the flush spread across her cheeks.

"Francine?" He studied her eyes. "That's why you love Sully. He took care of you. I'll bet your fiancé takes care of you."

"Future fiancé," she corrected.

His heart soared with hope. He closed his eyes.

"Jack?"

"I've gotta rest a minute."

Emotion clogged his throat. Of all the pain he'd felt in the last few hours—being whacked with a two-by-four, slammed on a steel door, and jabbed by a four-inch needle—this was the worst. The ache in his chest threatened to break him apart.

He wanted her in his life. He wanted her as more than a wrestling partner or friend. He wanted her as his soul

mate, his lover, his confidante. This was nothing like Sandra. Sure, he wanted to do unspeakable things to Frankie,
erotic things that would drive her wild and make her cry
out in desperation. But he wanted what came after that.
The years together washing dishes and hanging wallpaper.
Sharing, teasing . . . just being.

The worst part was, he knew none of it could happen.
He wasn't right for Frankie. He'd just mess things up, like
he did everything. Hell, if it weren't for Butch, Jack's life
would be messed up beyond repair.

No, if he cared about Frankie, really cared, the best thing
he could do was distance himself. Which was what he'd
tried to do with his crack about her sticking around to
protect the talent. He knew more than work obligation
glued her to his bedside. They'd formed an unexpected
friendship, a unique bond.

A bond neither of them welcomed.

Curtain rings scraped across the metal bar, and he heard
Frankie's soft voice whisper to the doctor.

"Mr. Hudson?"

Jack opened his eyes. Frankie was gone.

"I'm Dr. Latharius, the orthopedic specialist." He extended his hand and Jack shook it.

"Your wife is in the waiting area making a phone call."

Your wife. He sucked in a quick breath of air. His "wife"
was probably calling her fiancé.

"So what's the verdict?" Jack asked.

"Not sure until we take some more pictures." He flipped
through Jack's paperwork. "You're hard on your body."

"Job requirement."

The doctor glanced down at him over the rim of his
reading glasses.

"Professional wrestler," Jack explained.

The doctor nodded and went back to analyzing the
chart. Jack recognized the censure in the doctor's nod. He'd
grown used to the silent and sometimes not-so-silent criticism of his work. But there came a time when you had to

shut out the jokes, the horrified reactions when people found out what you did for a living. You had to believe in yourself enough to know you were happy with your life. And Jack had been happy. To a point.

Then disillusionment took hold, frustration at being paid to act more like a vaudeville clown and less like an athlete. They touted pro wrestling as sports entertainment, and many wanted to drop the word "sports" from the definition all together, as if there was no athleticism involved in a grueling twenty-minute match. He wished somebody would tell that to his body.

". . . at least tonight. Okay?"

He glanced at the doctor.

"What? Sorry, I was thinking about something else."

"I said I'd like you to stay the night for observation."

"Stay? In the hospital? No, I can't, I have to—"

"You have to heal," Frankie said as she slipped through the curtain and pulled it closed behind her. "How long do you plan to keep him?"

"Just tonight. I'd like to confer with his doctor back home if possible."

"Do you have his number?"

"Yes, I think it's here."

Dr. Latharius flipped pages on the chart, and Jack gritted his teeth. They acted like he wasn't even in the room.

"Excuse me, but I have a plane to catch."

They ignored him. He tore off the blanket Frankie had so carefully tucked around his body. He swung his feet to the floor and stood, swaying slightly because of his bad knee.

"I'm leaving now."

Frankie reached out to touch his arm, but missed. She continued to address the doctor.

"You think it's a spinal injury?" she asked.

"Most likely. It would be helpful to know if his doctor has noticed anything between the fourth and fifth vertebrae."

Looking away from his stuck arm, Jack snatched the IV pole and limped out. Pushing through the curtain, he flagged down a nurse.

"I have to sign myself out of here."

"You need a doctor's—"

"Where do you think you're going?" Frankie grabbed his hospital gown from behind.

"Let go of me," he ordered.

"Not until you stop."

"I'm leaving."

"Like hell you are."

He hobbled, she tugged, his knee ached. He really could walk if he put his mind to it. If he didn't have a hundred-and-twenty-six-pound woman hanging on his tail.

"You're making a scene," he said.

She let go and scanned the immediate area. He smiled to himself. Prim and proper Frankie McGee wouldn't be caught dead making a scene.

He wheeled his IV pole to the nurse's station. "I need someone to unhook me."

"Mr. Hudson?" The doctor walked toward him.

"No offense, Doc, but hospitals give me the shakes. I can't stay."

"But your wife, here, said—"

"She's not my wife. Hell, we don't even like each other. Isn't that right, Frank?"

"Well, I see you're back to your completely offensive self." She planted her hands on her hips.

"Thanks, I'll take that as a sure sign of my clean bill of health." He turned to the doctor. "I'm leaving now."

"It will take a few minutes to get your paperwork together."

Frankie touched his arm, her fingers burning his skin through the light hospital gown.

"Jack? I wish you'd stay. Just tonight," she said, her voice a mere hush. "I . . . it would make me feel better."

He glanced into her pleading eyes, and it was all over.

209

The sincerity, the bone-crushing concern. He'd never seen that in a woman's eyes before. Not for him.

"I don't like hospitals," he said, feeling himself slip under her spell.

"I'll stay with you," she promised, her fingers squeezing his arm, tearing at his heart.

"Frankie . . ." He cocked his head to one side. What was she doing to him?

"Please, Jack. Let the doctors take care of you. Just to-night."

Rationally, he knew she was right. Emotionally, he was a basketcase at the thought of spending the night in a hos-pital.

"Frankie, I—"

She placed her fingers to his lips to stop his words. He couldn't breathe. He wondered what she'd do if he kissed them, lightly, delicately.

"Stay. Just this once?" she said.

Captivated by her eyes, the feel of her fingertips against his skin, he could only nod in surrender. He'd never make it through the night. But he couldn't deny her.

She snatched her hand away and flattened it on the counter of the nurse's station. He noticed it trembled.

"Mr. Hudson will stay the night, after all."

"I'll find him a room," the nurse said.

He still couldn't believe what he'd done. In all his years as a pro wrestler, he'd never spent more than a few hours in a hospital. That was all he could take.

But tonight he would face his irrational fear and do the right thing for his body, for once. And he wasn't doing it because he'd finally been struck by common sense after all these years.

No, Jack Hudson was checking himself into hell because of Frankie. Because it would make her feel better.

God, what was happening to him?

Chapter Fourteen

Something awakened her with a start. Frankie didn't know what. Maybe it was the knifing pain that sliced through her neck. A human being was definitely not meant to sleep curled up in a vinyl hospital room chair, she thought, re-adjusting her upper body against Jack's bed.

But she was here for the duration. No matter how much he protested, how many times Jack claimed she didn't need to stick around to keep an eye on the talent.

And that hurt more than anything. The fact he still spouted such ridiculous words. Right. As if she were staying for any reason other than genuine concern over a man who'd become much more to her than an employee.

What he'd become, exactly, she wasn't sure. That would take too much soul searching, something she didn't have the energy for. Her mind and body were spent, thanks to the night's horrific turn of events.

She opened her eyes and glanced at her hand entwined in Jack's. Before, when he'd launched his tirade and de-manded she leave, she'd done so without protest. But not for good. Frankie made her way to the cafeteria, found a warm cup of tea and waited until she thought him asleep. Then she sneaked back into his room where she belonged. Thank goodness the nurse didn't kick her out.

His fingers twitched, and a warm feeling of awareness spread up her arm to her chest. Damn the man for turning her on even when he was unconscious.

"Not again . . ." he mumbled.

Sitting up, she studied his face, shadowed by darkness in the dim room. Sweat trickled across his hairline, and his lips moved as if he were trying to speak.

"Can't . . . not again."

His fingers squeezed her hand, and his legs thrashed beneath the stiff, white linens.

Was it a dream? Brought on by the fact she'd forced him to spend the night in the hospital?

"Jack?" She stood and leaned across the bed, touching his cheek to calm him.

"My legs . . . what happened to my legs?" he moaned.

"Jack, wake up. It's just a dream."

"Not my legs. No life . . . have no life," he moaned.

"Jack." She rubbed his brow with her thumb. Her heart ached to drive away his agony.

"Get away. No more, I can't—"

He jackknifed and flailed his arms. Frankie jumped back to evade his swing and lost her balance. She grabbed for the chair, but missed and tumbled to the floor. So much for being able to comfort him.

"Damn," he rasped.

She sat on the cold floor and listened to the sound of his labored breathing, the sound of a man who'd just run a marathon. She popped her head up to check if it was safe.

"What are you doing here? And why are you on the floor?" He scrunched the bed linens between his fingers.

"I always sleep on the floor. It's good for my back."

"Bull. Why were you hiding down there?"

She pulled herself up and sat on the edge of the bed. "I wasn't hiding. Are you okay? You had some kind of nightmare."

Running his hand through his long, dark hair, he took a deep breath. "He was coming after me. I couldn't see his face. I tried to get away. I swung and—" His gaze drifted to the chair, then up to Frankie.

"I heard this voice, a woman's voice, trying to help me. But he kept coming and . . ." His eyes grew wide. "Did I . . . hit you?"

"Of course not."

"Aw, hell, I hit you." He fell back against the sheets and rolled onto his right side, away from her. "Just go. Get the hell out of here before I hurt you again."

"You didn't hurt me. I fell, okay? You know how clumsy I am."

She stared at his rigid back. This was her fault. No doubt it was the hospital stay that had elicited his nightmares.

She scooted her chair to the far side of the bed in an attempt to talk to him. He rolled onto his other side.

"Come on, don't be a jerk." She lugged the chair back to its original spot.

"Go away." He closed his eyes.

"Stop feeling sorry for yourself." Planting herself in the chair, she leaned forward. "I told you I'd stay with you, and that's what I'm going to do."

"I don't need you here."

His words sliced open her heart.

"Tough. Maybe I need to be here."

His eyes shot open. "I don't need your supervision, boss. I can have nightmares all by myself."

"I'm not here because you're on the payroll. Now relax. I want you to get some sleep. Being up all night won't be good for either of us."

"Can't sleep."

"You're not trying."

"Maybe I don't want to sleep."

213

"Okay, then what do you want to do?"

"Stop the nightmares," he mumbled, sounding like a frightened child.

"Okay, we can do that." She moved closer to him and sandwiched his hand between her own.

He thought he'd go mad.

"No more creative imagery stuff," he said. Hell, he'd completely lose it imagining this woman beside him in bed, touching him, whispering sweet words into his ear. How would he keep his hands off her?

"Then let's talk," she said.

"My second option?"

"Your favorite Christmas," she said.

"I don't remember." He struggled to ignore the gentle touch of her hand, the stroke and caress of soft fingers.

"Okay, I'll start," she said. "I was ten. I got my first make-up kit from Mom, blue eyeshadow, pink lipstick. It made me feel so grown up. I always thought how cool it would be to be grown up, wear makeup, be pretty. That's before I figured out I'm just not the glamorous type."

If she only knew how beautiful she looked right now, hair tumbling over her shoulders, her face scrubbed clean of makeup.

"Your turn," she said, her face lighting with anticipation.

Taking a deep breath, he realized he couldn't deny this woman. He was a goner.

"Christmas, freshman year. Butch gave me an unlimited pass to Singleton's Gym."

"That's your favorite present? Working out?"

"Pretty much."

"What about before that? When you were little. I'll bet you were into GI Joe and Monster trucks." She smiled and his heart skipped.

"I don't recall being a kid."

"Oh, come on, Jack. It's me you're talking to, remember?"

Oh, he remembered all right.

214

"I'll bet you were the big jock at school." She squeezed his hand for encouragement. Warmth shot up his arm and wrapped itself around his heart.

"Just wrestling. That's all. And work. I started when I was thirteen, bussing tables."

"So young?"

"Dad's idea. Almost had to quit wrestling, but Butch wouldn't let me."

"Butch?"

"The guy who ran the youth center where I grew up. He's the one—" He hesitated, trying to figure out how to stop talking. He couldn't. "Butch is the guy who showed me there was more to life than setting off pipe bombs and stealing bikes."

"Oh," she said softly. Would she run now? Abandon "Jack the Loser," as his father used to call him?

She just looked at him, expecting more.

"Butch got me into wrestling," he said, willing to do anything to keep her beside him. "He was the high school coach. But he taught me more than arm bars and headlocks. He taught me to dream high, have confidence in myself."

"Sheesh, I never pegged you for having confidence problems." She chuckled.

He narrowed his eyes.

"Don't take that the wrong way. It's just, you have this presence when you walk into a room, a way about you. I don't know. You just don't seem insecure."

"People aren't always what they seem."

"I . . . I know, I guess."

She studied him with those colorful eyes, and he was lost. Hell, he was insecure whenever she was near him, scared as hell that she'd figure out just how much he cared about her. Then what?

Snap out of it, Hudson.

He marveled at the way the ambient light from the hallway spilled into the room, illuminating her face just enough so he could make out the sweet curve of her cheek, the fullness of her lips.

"What about when you were seven, ten, you know, when you were a kid? Did you collect comic books? Stamps? What?" she pressed.

"No, no collecting. Just . . ."

"What?"

She shifted onto the bed, and he held his breath. Too close. She was too damn close.

"Jack? What did you do as a kid?"

"I painted."

"No kidding?"

"Kid stuff. Never mind." He clenched his jaw.

"No, tell me more."

She squeezed his hand again and everything relaxed.

"Mom got me a paint-by-numbers kit, and I threw out the numbers. It was a great feeling. I used vibrant colors, colors that made me feel alive. It was such a rush."

"Was?"

"Dad put the kibosh on it. Said not to waste my time. Started calling me Van. 'Van, go take out the garbage.' 'Van, go to the store and get me a carton of smokes.' 'Van, go tell your mother I want dinner.' He burst into my room one day—I'd pissed him off about something, who knows what—and he ripped all my pictures down and shoved them into the garbage can. Doused them with paint thinner and set them on fire. That was the end of my illustrious painting career."

"And you never went back to it?"

"Never had a reason to."

Not until you reawakened the desire by casting your spell on my soul.

"That's sad," she said.

"Nah. I found wrestling, or rather it found me. I've had a pretty good life."

"Getting the stuffing kicked out of you for a living," she muttered.

"What's that, boss?"

Her face scrunched in sympathy. "I'm sorry."

"Don't be. I'm a big boy. I made my own decisions."

"I know, it's just—"

"Stop. Back to you. What's your big dream? What did you want to be when you were ten?"

"Besides a cover model?"

He chuckled.

"Hey!" She smacked his thigh.

"Sorry, it's just the thought of you filling out one of those brassieres . . ." His voice cracked. "Never mind."

"Watch it, bub."

"Go on, what did you want to be other than a cover model?"

"No laughing?"

"Cross my heart," he assured.

"I always wanted to be a mom, have lots of kids, make brownies, pies, maybe even learn to knit a sweater or something."

Something snapped in Jack's chest at the image of her kissing a little dark-haired, fair-skinned girl on the cheek and sending her off to school.

"Kinda opposite from the cover model fantasy," he said, recovering.

"I know. Dumb, huh?" She studied their hands.

Slipping his finger under her chin, he raised her gaze to meet his. "Nothing to be ashamed of there, sweetheart."

"It's just a silly fantasy. My career will always come first."

His heart sank. "Why's that?"

"I could never be completely dependent on a man. Not after growing up the way I did."

"What do you mean?"

"My dad was AWOL most of the time. Gambling, philandering, who knows. Sent money home, barely enough to cover things. Uncle Joe helped out a lot." She looked at Jack. "I still can't believe he was behind what happened to you tonight."

"Maybe he wasn't." He couldn't believe the words had come out of his mouth. "You're supposed to take my mind off my injuries, remember?"

"Right." She smiled.

"So? Kismet brought you and your fiancé together to make this perfect union?" Maybe if he kept referring to him as her fiancé, he'd be able to shake himself of her.

"Actually, YAR brought us together. Young Accountants on the Rise. I joined the group to network, make some contacts. And I ended up making the most valuable one of all. Then we worked together on an audit. Bradley and I share the same belief system and moral code. He plans out his activities three weeks in advance, just like me. Can you believe it?"

He shook his head. Why would anyone want to?

"Oh, I have a picture." She snatched her purse from the night table and fumbled through the contents.

Good. That should make it real.

She pulled a small snapshot from her wallet and handed it to him.

"That was taken at the Northeast Accountants' Convention last year."

Jack studied the pair. Frankie wore a serious, business-like smile while her fiancé's nose turned up a hair too much for Jack's taste.

"It's such a good, solid relationship. He's so capable and focused."

He handed her the photograph, and she tucked it away.

"Bradley wants the same things I want. Financial security, career success. Someday, maybe, I'll take a few years off to have a child. We decided one would be financially prudent."

But does he make you laugh? Does he brighten the golden specks in your eyes when he makes love to you?

"We picked out the perfect ring. Pear-shaped, clear, a white diamond in a white gold setting." She extended her hand as if admiring the sparkle of the gem on her finger.

"When he gets his promotion he'll give me the ring, and I'll have everything I've always wanted. A stable, secure life, mothering, budgeting."

"It sounds great." And it did, he thought. What he wouldn't give to have been raised by a mother like Frankie. So giving, caring, and selfless.

Too bad Jack wouldn't be there to see it. Something squeezed his heart.

"Feeling better?" she said.

"Yeah, thanks." He struggled to breathe against the tightness forming in his chest.

"Water?"

"No, I'm—"

"Just to be safe, to keep the nightmares away, remember?"

She released his hand to pour fresh water in a cup. A chill blanketed his knuckles.

"Here, drink." She placed the cup to his lips, and he reached out to steady her hand.

He never wanted to let go.

But he had to.

He downed the water in two swallows, then placed the cup on his nightstand.

"Try to get some sleep." She shifted off the bed.

"Where are you going?" He hoped she didn't hear the desperation in his voice.

"Just getting comfortable in my trusty chair." She settled in the vinyl chair, leaned forward, and stretched her arms across the bed.

"Frankie?" He had to tell her how he felt, how special she was, how much he wanted her in his life.

The words caught in his throat.

She glanced into his eyes. "Don't worry, Jack. I won't leave. Promise."

He closed his eyes, the pain in his chest consuming him. That was one promise he knew she couldn't keep.

Chapter Fifteen

"Thanks for the call, kid, but the worst part of the match was the wounded ego." Jack shifted into a more comfortable position on his couch, his knee resting on a thick pillow. It felt good to be home.

"You actually spent the night in a hospital?" Marco asked.

"Didn't have much choice."

"We thought you were really hurt, I mean for *you* to spend the night."

"Nothing serious. I'm fine."

"Sully's niece didn't look fine when she stormed into his office this afternoon. What the hell did you do to her anyway?"

"I didn't do anything. I told her to fly home. No sense in both of us losing a night's sleep. But she wouldn't budge. Felt responsible for the talent, I guess. I woke up and found her beside my bed."

"No wonder she looked like that."

"Like what?" His fingers tightened around the receiver.

"She was scarier than Tiger Lady. Man, she screamed so loud we could hear her all the way down in the gym. I thought the old man would have a heart attack for sure. She was one crazed puppy. But then I guess lack of sleep will do that to ya."

Lack of sleep and worrying about someone you care about. *Dream on, Hudson.*

"Yeah, well, I'm okay. Taking some time off. Nurse the knee back to working order. What's the word on Tiger Man?"

"Canned."

"No kidding?"

"Right after the niece lit into Sully."

"Interesting."

"Who's running this show, anyway?"

"Fate, kid. Fate."

"Huh?"

"Never mind. I'll see you later this week."

"Gotcha."

He hung up and sank back against the thick cushions.

It was spinning out of control. His whole world was racing at mach speed, and he couldn't do a damn thing about it. Just like always.

It didn't have to be that way. Look at Frankie. She planned things right down to the type of crib to buy for a baby that hadn't even been conceived yet. She didn't wait for chance to step in and point her in one direction or another.

Or nearly cripple her.

He swallowed hard and closed his eyes. During the chaos, the excitement, he hadn't let it sink in—fate nearly took it all last night. Only later, in the middle of the night, did the horror of his temporary paralysis awaken him, snake its tentacles around his throat and squeeze until he thought he would suffocate. He'd gone too far, abused his body once too often, and he would pay the price with his legs. What then? He'd been so scared, he couldn't even see

221

straight. But something had calmed him, chased the madness away.

Frankie.

And what did she get for her trouble? A shove off the bed by a cranky patient. Damn, he'd ordered her to leave, thrown her out of his room.

Yet he hated to think what would have happened if she hadn't come back. With a soothing tone and soft touches she'd eased the panic, slain the demons he couldn't fight himself. When sleep eluded him, she'd shared her hopes, her dreams, and expected Jack to share his deepest desires as well. He'd shared a few, but not all of them, not the ones revolving around Miss Frankie McGee.

It was only normal to have dreams about the woman. She was an angel, a gentle wave in an ocean of turmoil. She'd done more for him last night than she could ever know.

And he hadn't even thanked her. When he'd awakened this morning to find Frankie sprawled across his bed clutching his hand, he didn't know what to say. He could have started with an apology for being such a jerk.

Instead, humbled by her presence, he couldn't speak.

It had been such a long time, maybe even forever, since he'd depended on someone like he did Frankie. She'd helped him dress, made all the arrangements to and from the airport, and babied him all the way home.

The babying part wasn't so bad. She'd fussed over him, repeatedly inquiring about his knee and his back. Could he still feel his toes? she'd ask. No one had ever cared for him like that before and probably never would again.

Jack tapped his knee, still swollen from the Hawk's attack with the two-by-four. "It's almost over," he whispered.

Melancholy settled in his gut. Of course he'd feel some kind of sadness. Wrestling had been his life for nearly twenty years. You don't just walk away from your life, no matter how pathetic, without a little angst.

Angst driven by the fact he hadn't a clue what was coming next.

"Francine. How do you do it?"

She'd probably had her life figured out by age seven. He could picture her as a little girl, ponytail swinging, telling her mother that she wanted to be a financial consultant and marry a successful CPA. Yes, she probably used those very words. At age seven.

And here Jack was, thirty-seven and no clue where to go. He knew he wanted to live in the mountains, but beyond that he drew a blank. Sure, he'd had dreams once, a long time ago. Dreams squashed by an overbearing father.

Jack's frustration grew ugly and self-destructive the night his father trashed his paintings. Thank God Butch stepped in and challenged Jack's anger. Butch believed in the human spirit. He always said if you wanted something badly enough, and worked hard enough, it was yours.

Jack wondered if that translated to people.

"Damn, I've got to let this go," he muttered, covering his face with his forearm. It was clear from "true confessions" last night that Frankie needed stability and security more than anything. Things Jack didn't have to offer.

She made a science out of planning and controlling, whereas Jack sat back and let life take him for a ride. She hated everything he stood for, and he couldn't understand why someone would want to be cooped up in an office crunching numbers five days a week. He knew when he quit wrestling he wouldn't become a suit like Frankie's husband-to-be. No, this time around he would do what he wanted. He'd find happiness and peace traveling and eventually settle in the cabin.

He had enough money to carry him for a while. Who knows, with a little luck, the youth centers might even start to show a profit, although Jack wasn't going to count on it. One thing for sure, it was time to paint again.

Taking a page from Frankie's book, he mapped out a plan for the next ten years. It would feel so good to be in control for once, to take charge and move in the right direction. Even if that direction was away from Frankie.

A loud knock shook him from his thoughts.

"Yeah!" he called out, not eager to use the knee just yet.

"It's Frankie. Open the door."

"Hell," he muttered, rolling off the couch and groping for his crutches. He hated using the things. They made him feel weak and dependent.

"Coming!" he shouted, navigating through the mess of clothes, magazines, and scattered mail. He didn't have it in him to be Mr. Tidy today. It had taken every ounce of energy just to climb the stairs to the second floor this morning when the limo dropped him off.

"Jack, what's wrong? Are you okay?"

"Fine, just give me a minute." He made his way to the door, shoving his overnight bag beside the bookshelves with the tip of his crutch.

Leaning heavily on the crutches, he flipped the dead bolt and opened the door. A brown paper bag stared back at him.

"Frankie?"

She peeked around the bag. "Brought dinner."

He stumbled out of the way as she marched straight to the kitchen as if she lived here. She looked beautiful tonight, her hair pulled back in a braid, her cheeks creamy white with a hint of rose. And her eyes . . . they sparkled more than usual.

Sure they did. Wasn't tonight her date with Mr. Perfect Accountant?

Jack's heart sank. He suddenly wanted her gone.

"You didn't have to do this," he said, hobbling toward the kitchen. He might want her gone for his own reasons, but he wasn't going to be a jerk . . . again.

"Frankie?" He leaned against the breakfast bar.

She buzzed around his galley kitchen, pulling out drawers and slapping utensils on the counter.

"Pots and pans?" she asked.

"There." He pointed to a low cabinet.

"Great." She pulled out a pot, filled it with water, and put it on the stove.

"Listen, Frankie—"

"I talked to my uncle today. He claims he didn't know what Tiger Man was up to last night." She paused and glanced at Jack. "I'd like to believe him, but sometimes I just don't know. There's something he's not telling me. And it has nothing to do with owing people money." She busied herself, cracking eggs, thawing frozen spinach, shredding cheese.

"What are you making?"

"Stuffed shells. Hope you like Italian. Even brought the wine." She plucked a bottle of merlot from the brown grocery bag.

"Stop." He grabbed her wrist, and she released the bottle, letting it clunk on the counter. "Listen to me. I'm trying to talk to you."

Her eyes widened, her pulse beat in her throat, making the sunflower charm she wore dance with each beat.

"What's wrong?" she asked.

"Nothing. I just . . . I want to thank you. That's all."

"Wait until you try it first. I'm not a great cook."

"No, not just for dinner. I want to thank you for last night, today, taking care of me, all of it."

"It's the least I could do considering what my family's done to you."

He squeezed her hand. "You're not a part of that. Don't try to make up for something that wasn't your fault."

"But I feel responsible. You're one of Sully's guys and—"

"I don't want you helping me because it's in my contract. If that's why you're here, then just go."

Stabbing the crutches against the hard wood floor, he hobbled to the couch and collapsed.

Well, Hudson, you've done it again.

He'd started out okay, thanking her as graciously as he could. But the thought of her coming here out of duty

225

infuriated him. He needed her to be here because she genuinely cared, maybe even because she liked him . . . a lot.

"How about some ice for the knee?" she called from the kitchen.

"Whatever."

A few minutes passed. The clank of dishes, running water, and the ticking of the kitchen timer bounced off the cathedral ceiling into the living room. Sounds of home, of a woman taking care of her family.

"Hell." He grabbed a news magazine from the floor and stared at the fine print. Only after a full minute did he realize the article reported statistics about sexual intercourse improving one's mental health.

He tossed it across the room.

"You're testy today." She ambled to the couch and knelt beside him, then propped his knee on an overstuffed plaid pillow.

He held his breath at her gentle touch. His knee felt better already.

"How's this position?" she said.

"Fine." His mind raced with all kinds of positions that had nothing to do with an injured knee.

"Too cold?" She placed the ice bag on his knee.

"It's fine." He crossed his arms over his chest and stared at the entertainment center across the room.

She rocked back on her knees. "I'm not here because of my uncle or WHAK. I was just worried. About a friend."

"I can take care of myself. Have been for over thirty years."

"I know." She brushed a strand of hair off his cheek. Her fingers stilled, and he wondered whether she felt it too, if her body burned in secret, private places like his did right now.

"Everyone needs a little help sometimes," she said. "Even the invincible Black Jack Hudson. It's okay to need someone, Jack."

Not like I need you, babe.

"You okay?"

He cleared his throat. "Yeah, fine."

"You don't look fine."

Her iridescent eyes caught his heart.

"I'll be fine, doc, promise."

"But—"

"Don't worry about me. Marco's stopping by later," he lied.

"I should probably stay until he gets here," she offered.

"No, thanks. I'm okay. Just tired."

"I know the feeling."

Of course she did. She'd been up all night, holding him, soothing him. And what did she get for her trouble? A horny bastard with an attitude. She deserved more than that. Much more.

"Listen, I appreciate the dinner. But I'm fine, really."

She narrowed her eyes. "No, you're not. Something's up. I can tell. I'll stay until Marco gets here."

If she did, they'd both regret it. He couldn't spend another minute with her and expect to keep his hands to himself.

"Go on. Stop babying me. You've got a date, don't you?"

She glanced at her watch. "Oh my gosh! I didn't realize it was so late. I have to be at a restaurant on the north side in half an hour."

"Well, get going then."

"But I wanted to serve you dinner, clean up the dishes, pick up a little," she said, scanning the room.

"That's why I've got a dishwasher. The maid service comes day after tomorrow."

"But—"

"You're driving me crazy, woman. Go on, get out."

She stood, took a deep breath, and ran flattened palms across her hair.

"Do I look okay?"

"Yep." *Good enough to eat.*

"No lipstick on my teeth?" She shot him a full grin.

"You're clean."

"I don't know why I'm so nervous. I guess because I haven't seen him in weeks, and I just want everything to go right. How about my hair?"

"You look great. Any man would be nuts not to fall for you on the spot."

Like I did.

She took a deep breath and stared him down. Hell, he'd been caught.

"Are you sure you'll be okay?"

"Get out of here!" he ordered.

"Okay, okay." She snatched her purse from the breakfast bar and paced to the door. "The shells should ring in thirty-five minutes. If you want bread, pop it in for about ten under the broiler. The salad's tossed and in the fridge."

"Got it."

"I'm sorry I have to abandon you like this."

"You're not abandoning me. Go have a good time."

She pulled open the door, hesitated, and marched back to the couch.

He'd always remember her like this, hands planted on her hips, light brown tendrils wisping across her cheeks where her hair had slipped free from its braid.

"You're sure Marco's coming?"

"Stop worrying about me. I'm not your problem."

But I'd like to be.

"Wish me luck?" she said.

Agonizing pain sliced through the center of his chest.

"Luck." He forced a smile.

She leaned over and kissed him on the forehead. His heart lurched.

"You're a nice guy," she whispered against his skin. "Don't let anyone tell you different."

She whisked out of his condo and closed the door, taking a piece of his heart with her. He'd lose it all if he wasn't careful, ending up with an empty spot the size of the Atlantic in his chest. He had to stop this craziness, focus on getting out of wrestling. On living again.

Only, could he really live without Frankie?

She shouldn't have left him. Frankie paced the lobby of Leo's Fish House, waiting for Bradley to show. She couldn't believe she'd actually beaten him here. But then she'd broken a few traffic laws in the process, to make sure she wouldn't have to explain being late.

"It's not like I was doing anything wrong," she whispered to herself.

No, she'd just been making dinner for another man, icing his injury, tending to his needs. She couldn't remember the last time she'd tended to Bradley. They had such a mature and independent relationship. They worked ten-hour days, met twice a week for a planned outing, and shared a bed on Saturdays. It was a stable, sensible partnership. Nothing like her relationship with Jack.

She chewed her lower lip. She and Jack didn't have a "relationship," not in the technical sense. It was simply a business partnership.

She pulled out her compact and checked her reflection, wanting tonight to be perfect. Her eyes lit with panic. How could she expect perfection when she had to confess her sins, bare all about her exploits with WHAK? Maybe she wouldn't have to tell him everything, not tonight, anyway. Even if the photographers plastered her true identity across the covers of wrestling magazines from coast to coast, they wouldn't come out for another month at least, maybe two. She was safe for now. No one knew she doubled as Tatianna, and Bradley would be the last man to get wind of her escapades. Heck, he probably didn't even know professional wrestling existed.

"Peek-a-boo." Bradley's hazel eyes stared back at her in the compact.

"Bradley!" She turned and wrapped her arms around his neck, giving him a hearty squeeze.

"Hey, take it easy, sweetums."

"Oh, right. Sorry." He never was one for public displays of affection.

"Is our table ready?" He extended his arm to lead them into the restaurant.

"I didn't ask yet. I was waiting for you." She squeezed his arm and grinned. This felt right, normal.

Real.

"You're awfully amorous this evening. Too bad I have a plane to catch first thing, or I'd ask you up to my hotel room."

They strolled through the crowded bar toward the restaurant. Televisions blared, men smoked and laughed. They were having a good time.

She glanced at Bradley. He turned up his nose in disapproval.

The hostess greeted them at the entrance to the Garden Room.

"Dunsmore."

"Actually, McGee," Frankie corrected.

Bradley glanced at her.

"Sorry," she said. She'd forgotten how he liked being in charge, one of the many things she admired about her future fiancé. In complete control at all times, he never left anything to chance. Unlike Jack.

Why was she thinking of Jack? Because she felt responsible and shouldn't have left him to fend for himself. The man could barely walk, much less balance on his own two legs. How was he going to pull dinner from the oven?

It wasn't her responsibility. He was a big boy and, as he pointed out over and over again, he'd been taking care of himself for years. The thought of a ten-year-old going to the hospital alone made her stomach burn.

The hostess led them to a private booth in the corner, trimmed in decorative ivy. Frankie took the seat facing the entrance to the bar, knowing just the sight of it would ruin Bradley's evening.

"What can I get you to drink tonight?" a blond young waitress asked.

"I'll have a glass of chablis and she will have—"

"Brandy, please," Frankie interrupted.

"Francine? That's an after-dinner drink," Bradley admonished.

"I know. But I'm in the mood for it." And she needed a shot of fortitude if she was going to tell all tonight.

"All right then." He nodded at the waitress. "And we'll start with the spinach salad with Italian dressing."

"Actually, I'd like a house salad with blue cheese," Frankie said.

Bradley folded his menu and eyed her carefully. "Blue cheese it is. For both of us."

The waitress nodded and walked away.

"Francine? Is everything okay?"

"Sure. Why?"

"You just seem . . . different."

"It's been a long two weeks."

"Speaking of which, don't you have some confessing to do?"

She bit her lower lip. He knew. He was a closet wrestling fanatic and knew all about her little leopard-skin number. But the show wouldn't air until Tuesday night. There was no way he could—

"Chablis—" the waitress placed a wine glass in front of him—"and brandy."

Frankie curled her fingers around the glass and took a healthy sip. More like a chug.

"It can't be that bad," he said.

She glanced at him, noting his dark brown hair combed back in a perfect wave, hazel eyes that changed color depending on the clothes he wore. Tonight they were brown to match his houndstooth-check suit.

"Bradley, there are things you don't know about me. About my family."

That's it. Blame everything on Uncle Joe.

231

"Your family? You mean your mom? But I love your mom, and I think she likes me. She always makes those lemon tea cakes whenever we visit."

"It's not about Mom. It's about my uncle."

"You mentioned him over the phone. The criminal?"

"He's not a criminal. Just, well, his business is kind of . . . different."

An ear-piercing roar echoed from the bar area.

"Honestly." He snapped his fingers, and the waitress rushed to their table. "Is there any way you can close the doors to the bar?"

"Yes, sir."

"What is it? Basketball playoffs? I wonder if I should have set the VCR," he muttered.

"No, sir. It's Sunday night wrestling."

Frankie choked on her brandy, and fine drops of brown liquid decorated the white tablecloth.

"Wrestling." Bradley's tone was condemning. "Shut the door. Lock it if you can."

"Yes, sir. Your salads will be right out."

"Can you believe that? A bunch of grown men getting paid to jump around like idiots." He snapped open his napkin and placed it in his lap.

"You . . . don't like wrestling?"

He made a face, the same face he made when little kids ran into him in the grocery store, or when Frankie suggested they go miniature golfing.

"Professional wrestling is violent, phony, and completely geared for the lower class. No, I don't like wrestling."

She took a generous swallow of her drink.

"It's all pretend, you know. They don't really fight. No one really gets hurt."

Images of a bedridden Jack Hudson crying out in his sleep invaded her thoughts. He might act the tough guy, but the temporary paralysis had created new emotional scars to rival those from his childhood.

"I read an article about it in *Financiers Magazine* last

232

month. It's a big money maker. I just don't understand it."
He tore off a piece of bread. "It's all scripted, you know."

"Yes, but the athleticism is real."

"What athleticism? One man jumps, and the other
catches him. One man throws a punch, the other pretends
to be hit."

*One man dumps another on his head and the other man's
paralyzed.*

"They're actors, nothing more," he said.

Actors who sacrifice their bodies.

"Your salads," the waitress interrupted, sliding their
plates in front of them.

He opened his menu. "Let's try something different tonight, Francine. We'll have two orders of the fried catfish."

She'd noticed the special price on the menu. Good old
Bradley, always looking for a deal.

"Okay with you, sweetums?"

"Sure." She needed to be agreeable, considering the
bomb she was about to drop.

"Back to wrestling . . ." she said.

He pursed his lips and focused on his salad.

"Sure it's scripted and violent, but what's the difference
between wrestling and that movie you took me to see last
month, remember? *Death Before Danger?*"

"There's a big difference. One is art. The other is car-
toon."

"Some people consider wrestling an art."

Bradley snorted. She hadn't thought him capable of
snorting.

"Okay, so wrestlers are performers. But they really do
sustain physical punishment."

"No, they don't. That's just my point. They've got you
fooled, little girl." He pointed his fork at her.

She gritted her teeth and controlled the urge to bat it
away with her knife.

"Everything's padded to prevent injury," he said, sounding like an expert. "The ring, the mat outside the ring, those pole things that hold up the ropes."

"Turnbuckles," she corrected.

"The floor is like a giant trampoline. There aren't any hard surfaces, so they can't really get hurt."

Except if they're dropped head first on a steel door, tossed out of the ring onto a wooden table, or fall from the top of a fifteen-foot cage.

"Bradley, I don't think you're seeing the whole picture."

"I know what I know."

And that was that. His signal that the conversation was over.

What did it matter? In another month or two she'd be out of the wrestling business and back to her real life. Why make an issue out of it? He'd never change his mind, and it wasn't worth ruining her future engagement.

"Tell me about this uncle of yours." He stabbed a leaf of romaine lettuce.

"He's a businessman who's having some financial trouble with his company."

"What kind of company?"

She hesitated, gripping her fork so tightly she thought it might snap in two. How much should she tell?

"Entertainment," she said.

"Really? Like making movies?"

"Something like that."

"Maybe you can get me a part as an extra."

She stifled a giggle at the image of Bradley dressed in orange tights flexing his kiwi-sized biceps.

He froze in mid-stab of his salad. "It's not porn, is it?"

Was that horror or hope in his voice?

"No, not porn."

Although, according to his diatribe about wrestling, it might as well be.

"How long will you be helping him out?"

"About another month or so. It depends on how things go."

"Why didn't you tell me about him before?"

"He's kind of a character. He's been involved in a lot of businesses, some less respectable than others. It's not something Mom and I are proud of."

"Then why do you associate with him at all?"

"He's my uncle. I love him."

"Well, we can't pick our relatives, that's true."

Something rankled her.

Reaching over, he patted her hand. "You're a good girl, sweets. It's very generous of you to help your uncle."

"You think so?"

"Absolutely. It shows great strength of character, loyalty, and pride."

If he only knew. She couldn't tell him, not now. She'd lost her nerve. And she wanted to enjoy this evening. It had been an insane week, and all she wanted was a nice, quiet dinner with her future fiancé.

"A quarter for your thoughts," he said with a reserved smile.

"I was just thinking about how long it's been since we've had a relaxing dinner like this."

Another roar emanated from the bar. He clenched his jaw.

"I'm not going to let anyone or anything ruin this evening." He took a deep breath, reached into his jacket pocket and pulled out a black velvet box. *The* black velvet box.

Her heart raced triple time. "Bradley?"

"We got word on Friday. Come July first, I'll be the youngest partner at Lundstrom, Marks and Beetle. It's official."

She stared at the box, a million thoughts racing through her mind. This was it. The moment she'd been waiting for since she was seven. Her handsome prince was offering Frankie her dream: a perfect life.

"Bradley, I—"

The bar doors burst open, and a roar blew into the restaurant.

"That's it. We're leaving, and we're not paying for dinner."

He shoved the box back into his pocket and took her hand. As he dragged her through the Garden Room, her thoughts spun and her heart pounded with excitement, nervous energy . . . panic.

Panic?

He marched up to the hostess. "This is a special night and your atmosphere has completely ruined things. I'm not paying for dinner, and I won't be back."

"I'm sorry sir, isn't there anything we can do?"

"No, nothing." He glanced over his shoulder at Frankie. "Let's go, sweetums. We'll find another establishment that has the atmosphere I need to do this properly."

Pushing through the bar doors, he marched toward the exit. Men laughed and screamed at the television. Roared and threw peanut shells.

She couldn't rip her gaze from the back of Bradley's head, studying his expertly combed hair. Her husband. Man and wife. Her very own happily-ever-after.

He stopped so suddenly, Frankie bumped into his back.

"Bradley?" She searched his face. He stared at the television screen above the bar, then turned to Frankie, his eyes wide, his face pale.

"Francine, what are you doing on television? And why are you dressed like that!"

Chapter Sixteen

"So, I guess this means the engagement's off?" she said, leaning against her rental car.

"I don't know, Francine. I don't know what to say or what to think. I'm just . . . perplexed."

It had taken a good half hour to get Bradley to breathe normally and stop pacing. When he finally did, he looked completely defeated.

"I thought I knew everything about you," he said. "You like Heinz catsup, not Delmonte. You never eat red meat for dinner and spend your Sunday evenings reading those fluff romance novels."

"Fluff?" She crossed her arms over her chest.

"I thought we were totally compatible. Completely in sync with one another's wants and needs." He fingered his suit coat where the engagement ring bulged from his pocket. "But this . . . I just don't know what to do with this."

Anger bubbled up in her chest. He was acting as if he was the one to make all the decisions in their relationship.

"You just said you admired me for helping my uncle. It showed loyalty and strength of character. Remember?"

"That's before I knew what kind of business he was in."

"Jumping Jupiter. It's not like I'm selling my body or robbing banks for a living."

"But Francine . . . wrestling?"

She hated that tone, that shaming tone that made her feel like she was four and had just smashed her mother's perfume bottles to smithereens.

This time she'd done nothing wrong. Not in her book.

"I'm sorry this is so offensive to you. I didn't pick my uncle's business. I'm just trying to save it. He's been good to me. I owe him."

"That's another thing." Bradley started up his pacing again. "I never heard about this uncle until today. And now, suddenly, he's the most important male figure in your life?"

He ran his hand through his hair, sending stray waves flopping to one side.

"I'm sorry I hurt your feelings. I'm sorry I lied. I didn't know what to do. It started as a simple financial analysis and ended up—"

"With you taking off your clothes!"

"I didn't take off my clothes. I have a costume. I play a part."

"And that part includes kissing another man, crying over him. You're quite an actress."

No, I'm not. The tears were real, the kisses . . .

"Thank you," she said, recovering.

"I didn't mean it as a compliment." He paced to the restaurant entrance and back.

"My uncle gave me things, remembered my birthday when my own father couldn't be bothered. Uncle Joe asked me for this one thing, to help him save WHAK. I pored over his books and gave advice. Then an opportunity presented itself to draw in thousands of dollars in sponsorship. He needed me to fill in for one of the girls. There was no one else. It was an emergency and I was there."

She didn't dare reveal her uncle's involvement with the mob. One thing at a time.

"And this man you kissed?"

"Jack? He's a twenty-year veteran of wrestling. He's my partner."

Bradley lifted a brow.

"It's a business relationship, Bradley. You should be able to appreciate that."

"Well, I don't. I don't appreciate or understand any of it. I mean, Frankie, professional wrestling of all things."

"Yes, professional wrestling. It's not like I murdered someone, for heaven's sake. It's a job, like any other."

"My God, your job! Francine, you'll be fired."

"That's against the law. What I do with my leave of absence is my own business. No one else's." She swallowed down her own trepidation about her career. Someone had to keep a level head, and it sure as sunshine wasn't going to be Bradley.

"I'll be fired," he croaked.

"What on earth are you talking about?"

"When they find out at work I'll be a laughingstock. I'm engaged to a professional wrestler."

"I'm not a wrestler, I'm a tiger lady."

"Well, that makes it all right, then." He paced to the corner of the lot and back, stopping some five feet from her. That was as close as he'd come since his discovery of her moonlighting as a feline.

"And this man, your partner? What part does he play?"

"He's my husband."

"What!"

"It's part of the script."

"Then there's nothing between you?"

Her fingers burned at the memory of Jack's warm, solid chest. She brushed them against her twill pants.

"Just stop, okay? I'm hungry and tired, and we've been going at this for an hour. Can't we at least get something to eat?" She straightened away from the car and searched her purse for her keys.

"I've lost my appetite," he said, sounding like a six-year-old who'd just had his skateboard taken away, or in Bradley's case, his calculator.

"Okay. So what now?" she challenged.

She'd never done that before. Sure, they'd had their share of "discussions," when she'd plead her case and sometimes even win. Bradley believed in fairness, after all.

She'd been anything but fair to him these past few weeks.

She touched his arm. "Listen, why don't I give you a ride to the hotel and we can order room service."

"I need to think." He pressed his thumb and forefinger to the bridge of his nose.

"You'll think better on a full stomach."

He shoved his hands into his pockets. "I need space, Francine. A little time to figure out what all this means."

Her heart sank as she watched her perfect life swirl down the proverbial toilet before her eyes. "Okay. I'll drop you at the hotel."

"No. I'll catch a cab."

"Bradley—"

"Please, Francine." He sounded pained, or was that irritation in his voice? Irritation that his perfect little woman wasn't so perfect after all?

"You'll call me tomorrow?" she said.

"I've got meetings all day, not that I'll be able to concentrate. I'll try you later in the week," he said, walking toward the restaurant door.

"Bradley?"

He turned.

"I am sorry."

He nodded and disappeared into Leo's.

She ambled to the rented Chevy and slid behind the wheel. Well, that was that. All the months of planning their perfect life together, picking out safe cribs and china pat-

terns, arguing about investments and brands of toothpaste
. . . all for naught.

It was over.

Pulling away from the curb, she headed for the express-
way. It couldn't be over. She couldn't lose it all because of
a misunderstanding.

"Some misunderstanding." She flipped on the radio to a
jazz station, something she wouldn't do in Bradley's company. He preferred traditional classics to uninhibited jazz.

Bradley. A knot formed in her throat. She was going to
lose him because of Uncle Joe. Mama was right. Certain
men always pull you into the eye of the storm. Uncle Joe
was one of them.

Jack was another.

His very essence drew her in, seduced her in a way she
didn't understand. And the jerk didn't have a clue how
attracted she was to him, nor did he care. He struggled to
be civil to her, mostly barking orders and pushing her
away, like last night in the hospital. Pushing her away when
he needed her the most, the fool.

No. He didn't need Frankie. He just needed someone,
anyone who could offer love and compassion against his
protests. Things she needed to save for her life mate, not
give away to a transient, burned-out athlete like Jack. After
all, it wasn't as if there could be anything real between
them. He wasn't stable, focused, or directed. Who knew
what he'd choose to do next. Would he race cars? Climb
mountains? He probably hadn't a clue himself. As a wrestling superstar, his options were limited. With the lack of
respect for wrestling, he'd probably be laughed out of traditional job interviews. Then again, she didn't picture him
dressing in a navy suit and working for a Fortune 500
company.

She didn't picture him fitting into her life, period.

Pushing the car to fifty-five, she merged into the flow of
traffic on the Kennedy and headed west. Her eyes burned
with the threat of unshed tears.

"Oh, grow up," she scolded herself. "If he really loves you he'll forgive you."

Frankie let out a gut-wrenching sigh. She and Bradley never really talked about love. Only commitment, loyalty, and investing in diaper and dental equipment stock.

"He must love me," she whispered, then caught herself. She didn't want love. Not now, not ever. She'd seen what her mother had gone through in the name of love. What else would have compelled Emma McGee to stick to a man who was barely around? If that was love, Frankie wanted no part of it.

At least that was what she'd been telling herself for the past thirty years. She didn't need love and she wouldn't miss it. She'd find happiness instead.

The empty spot in her heart spread across her chest. The temptation of love had never even entered her thoughts until . . .

Jack.

Her breath caught. "This has nothing to do with him."

Yet deep down she knew it had everything to do with Black Jack Hudson, a man who ruled with his heart, not his head. He cared about people, complete strangers, offering compassion and a part of himself every time he shook a hand or told a joke. He was about passion and drive, and going with the flow.

And he'd opened her eyes to a new way of thinking. She actually thought the word "love." She wasn't sure Bradley was aware of the concept. He, too, seemed to lead with his head and avoid those things warm and fuzzy, or the painful ache in your chest that came with a lover's rejection.

An ache similar to the one she felt last night when Jack ordered her out of his hospital room. He didn't want her around, didn't need her help. She thought they'd developed a kind of friendship, but in reality he still saw her as the Franken Niece, the woman most likely to ruin his life with binding contracts and common sense. The woman who didn't understand an ounce of what he went through just to get up in the morning.

He couldn't be more wrong.

"I'm striking out with all the men in my life," she said, spying the exit ramp.

She was being dumped by her perfect fiancé because she'd helped her uncle; her wrestling partner resented her very presence; her uncle had her jumping from catwalks. She was a thousand miles from home and suddenly felt all alone.

Turning onto Golf Road, she headed for the extended stay hotel. She wanted to go home and pretend she'd never heard of WHAK, never offered to help her uncle with his financial troubles.

That's it. She'd pack up and get the hell out tomorrow morning. If Uncle Joe needed any more advice, she'd do it from a thousand miles away. That should be a safe distance.

Who was she kidding? The damage was done. She'd been exposed as a tigress on national television, ruining her engagement, her career, her life.

She aimed for her designated parking spot across the parking lot from the front door. Even the parking lot seemed empty. No one. Anywhere.

Tears welled in her eyes. How did it all come to this? How did everything spin so out of control that she didn't even recognize her life anymore?

"I hate this!" She pounded at the steering wheel.

She hated being out of control, messing up, not being a "good little girl" as her mother used to call her. She hated her uncle, Bradley, and Jack. She hated—

A bang on her window made her jump, and she hit her elbow on the steering wheel.

"Argh!"

"Frankie, open the door," Jack shouted through the window.

"What are you doing here?"

"What's wrong? Are you crying?" He pressed his face to the glass.

"Go away!" She hit the automatic locks three times for emphasis.

"Open the door, Frank. I'm not leaving."

"Then I'll sleep in the car." She flopped down on the seat and buried her face in her hands.

"Frankie, open the door."

Embarrassed at her melodramatic loss of control, she willed him away. Why did he have to show up now? When she was at her weakest?

"Okay, fine. I'll break the window," he said. "I'd hate to see your car rental bill when I get done."

She sat up and stared him down. He balanced on one crutch and wielded the other like a baseball bat.

Gasping, she cracked open the window. "What are you doing?"

He edged up to the car, his lips nearly touching the glass. She couldn't take her eyes off of them, full, moist, tantalizing.

"I'm breaking into your car because you won't open the door," he said seductively.

"You wouldn't do that."

"Wanna bet?"

"Okay, fine." She zipped up the window, snatched her key from the ignition, and flung open the door. "You win. Okay? I'm out."

Marching toward the hotel, she cursed the day she'd returned Uncle Joe's phone message asking for a little help.

"Boss-Frankie-Around day, that's what this is," she muttered.

"Wait up," he called after her.

"I didn't invite you, remember?" She stopped and turned to him. "Why are you here?"

"I have to talk to you." His chest heaved in and out, and he was clearly out of breath from having to peel across the parking lot on crutches. Guilt tickled her insides. The least she could do was listen.

No. She wouldn't let him get to her again. He'd only confuse things, confuse her. She wanted Bradley, the ring, her dream of a perfect life, and thanks to Uncle Joe and Jack, she'd lost it all.

"Business hours are Monday through Friday, nine A.M. to five P.M. If you need to talk to me, make an appointment." She spun on her heel and stormed through the hotel door, burning a path to the elevator.

"First Bradley, now Jack," she muttered. "He probably wants out of his contract. Well, get in line. I could use out of this contract right about now, too."

She punched the elevator button, oblivious to everything but her own frustration.

"Men. All they do is push you around. Jump from a catwalk. Share my bed. Save my company. You're ordering the wrong drink. Don't hug me in public. Marry me. Don't marry me."

The elevator doors opened and she stepped inside, digging in her purse for her key card. She glanced up to press the second-floor button and froze at the sight of Jack, propping the elevator door open with his crutch.

"Don't marry me?" he said, staring at her intently.

"Go away."

"Frankie, he saw it, didn't he? The teaser for the Summer Suplex Slammer?"

"Yes, he saw it. We all saw it. Everyone at work probably saw it. My life is over. Okay? Happy?"

"Honey, I'm sorry."

Pity from Jack Hudson was one thing she could definitely not handle. She didn't want his pity. She wanted . . .

"Get out of my way." She pushed past him and headed for the stairs. She knew he couldn't make the climb, and she needed physical exertion right about now to work off her frustration.

"Frankie."

She ignored the pleading tone in his voice, the compassion. No one could help her now. Not Jack, not Uncle Joe, not even Mama. She'd stepped into this mess all by herself and she'd have to dig her way out.

Heck, she'd waitressed at the Lucky Duck Ice Cream Parlor in college. They said she was a natural. Restaurants were always looking for competent help. It wasn't like she'd be unemployed for long. The thought of using her master's degree to wipe up ice cream spills made her stomach clench.

"Make lemonade," she muttered. So Bradley was having second thoughts. He'd come around. So her boss had probably left a message on her machine about cutbacks. There were plenty of jobs for smart women like Frankie. So Mama would have to move out of her small hometown and change her name. She was getting tired of the small town gossips anyway.

She pushed open the door to the second floor and marched toward her suite. Fortitude was Frankie's middle name. She'd stand tall and walk right through the fire, coming out the other side, a little singed, maybe, but not completely burned to ash.

She wasn't about to let a failed engagement and probable pink slip get to her. Frankie was a strong, independent, and talented woman.

Who at this very moment, couldn't figure out how to make her plastic key card work. She shoved it in the door five different ways. No dice.

"Damn this thing."

"Here, let me," a deep, male voice said.

She'd been so absorbed in her own misery, she hadn't noticed Jack hobble up beside her.

"How did you get here?" She didn't look at him. She couldn't. She hated feeling vulnerable, hated him seeing her this way.

"I took the elevator. There." The green light flashed and he swung open the door.

246

She reached for her key card, and their hands touched. Heat burned a path across her shoulders to the base of her spine. She was tired, that was all. Emotionally exhausted from having her life turned upside down.

Great. Not only had she lied to her future fiancé, but now she was lying to herself as well. The fact was, every time she and Jack touched, accidentally or otherwise, a heat wave of desire spread through her body. And it wasn't caused by exhaustion or stress or nerves.

It was desire, pure and simple. A need so strong it scared the daylights out of her.

"You shouldn't be here," she said.

"I was worried." He hobbled to the sofa.

"You're getting better with the crutches," she said, checking the phone message light. It didn't blink. What was she hoping for? A change-of-heart call from Bradley?

"What happened tonight?" he said.

"Nothing I can't handle. What can't wait until tomorrow?" She settled herself in a chair a good five feet away from him.

"You were crying."

"Nope. But even so, you should be used to that by now." He'd seen her cry at least twice. She'd never cried in front of Bradley.

"You want to talk about it?"

"Not particularly."

Silence fell heavily across the room.

"I came here tonight because . . . I wanted to apologize," he said.

"For what?" She crossed her left leg over her right and interlaced her fingers in her lap.

"For being a jerk. All I've done these past few days is be rude to you. That's not right. You've been so nice. You let me lean on you."

"That's me, the girl with the strong shoulders."

"I'd like to return the favor."

"No need. It's all part of a day's work."

She hoped he'd leave.

She wanted him to stay.

Frankie jumped to her feet and paced to the dresser, where she'd dropped her purse. A peppermint would hit the spot just right. She pulled out the little metal tin. Empty.

"Francine?"

The low and husky timbre of his voice danced across her shoulders.

"What?"

"I brought you something."

She glanced at him.

"Here." He pulled a paper bag from his leather jacket and tossed it to her.

She glanced inside, and her breath caught at the sight of three tins of her favorite peppermint candy.

"I figured you might need them," he said.

He'd remembered her favorite brand. Understood the importance of mints to quell her tummy troubles. She wondered if Bradley even knew she popped the candies.

"Francine?"

That voice, smooth as silk with a slight rumble, skittered across her nerve endings.

"I want to talk. Come over here and sit down," he said.

"I can't."

"Please? The knee's still kinda sore. I'd rather not get up."

Taking a deep breath, she conceded and ambled to the opposite end of the sofa. She might be a liar, but she wasn't completely inconsiderate.

"Do you accept my apology?" He searched her eyes.

She nodded, unable to speak.

"Good. I also came to warn you about the teaser, but I guess I was too late."

She nodded again, fingering the hem of her blue silk jacket.

"You okay?" He touched her shoulder.

"Sure."

"Francine?"

She swallowed hard.

"A friend once told me it's okay to lean on someone. Even a strong, determined woman like you needs to lean on someone once in a while."

"Oh, yeah. I'm real strong." A tear escaped the corner of her eye. He wiped it away with his thumb.

"Hey, come over here."

She shook her head. If she went into his arms, she'd bawl like a baby. Hadn't she embarrassed herself enough in front of this man?

"Francine?" The couch shifted, and she felt his arm slip around her shoulders. With a hand at the back of her head, he coaxed her face against his chest.

She came apart in his arms, sobbing, hiccuping, scrunching the cotton of his T-shirt between her trembling fingers.

"I did . . . everything right. I'm a good girl."

"Yes, sweetheart, you're a good girl." He stroked her hair.

She buried her face against his warm neck. "I always do the right thing . . . make the right choices."

"Shhh. Everything will be okay, honey."

"It's all Uncle Joe's fault. If only he hadn't asked for help." Teary eyed, she sat back and stared into Jack's eyes.

His chest tightened with compassion. How he wished he could wipe away the sadness dulling the rainbow of colors.

"What did I do wrong?" she said.

"Nothing, honey. It's not your fault. You love your uncle. That's all."

"I hate love."

His heart ached. "Don't say that. Love's not a bad thing."

"Well, it sure isn't a good thing. Look at me. I'm a wreck."

He knew the feeling. After she'd left his apartment earlier, the realization hit Jack like a ton of bricks: He'd fallen in love with Frankie McGee.

This feeling was different from anything he'd experienced before. It wasn't just the explosive desire that threatened to eat him alive every time he touched her. No, this was about desire and much more.

"Jack?" She stared into his eyes. "Am I that unlovable that he couldn't overlook this one little thing?"

She sniffed and buried her face against his chest. He rubbed her back. "Shhh. It's okay, honey."

Damn that stupid fiancé of hers. Didn't he know how to hold on to a good thing?

She clutched his shirt like a life preserver, and he gritted his teeth. With every squeak, every whimper, his heart ached in a way he thought would rip him apart inside.

"Frankie?" He gripped her shoulders and gently coaxed her off of him. "Look at me."

Such trust shone in her eyes.

He cradled her chin with his forefinger and thumb. "You are the most lovable person I know. Got that? And I've known a lot of people in my lifetime. You're smart and witty. You're warm and compassionate. And besides all that, you crack a mean whip."

The hitch in her throat sounded like the beginnings of a chuckle. Good, he was on the right track.

"So no more beating yourself up about this. You tried to help and Sully got you into a mess. You're still a good girl. Better than most girls I know, anyway."

"And you're a nice guy."

"So I've been told. But I don't believe it."

"Believe it." She leaned forward to plant a kiss on his cheek.

At least, that's where he thought she planned to kiss him. When her soft lips brushed against his, he broke apart inside, all restraint, all sense completely obliterated.

He wanted her. More than he'd wanted anything in his life.

He closed his eyes and drank in the sensations, the warmth spreading across his limbs, the pounding of his heart. She threaded her fingers through his hair, and he felt his head tip back in response to her gentle touch. He could barely breathe; his thoughts were spinning like a top. What was happening? Should he stop it?

Of course you should, you idiot. She's a woman on the rebound, your complete opposite. You're taking advantage.

He broke the kiss. "Frankie," he breathed heavily against her cheek.

She nuzzled his ear, sending goose bumps across his shoulders.

"Jack . . . hold me." She kissed him again, a little desperately.

He knew desperation. He'd felt it himself . . . whenever he thought of her.

Jack couldn't give her his love. She didn't want it. He couldn't give her the perfect life. He'd never measure up to her idea of the perfect man. Hell, he couldn't even promise her stability. He didn't know what life had planned for him next.

He had nothing to offer.

Except this, right here, right now. She needed him to hold her, touch her, make her feel like the most desirable woman in the world.

Which was exactly what she was in Jack's eyes.

She moaned against his lips, wanting them to part, wanting him to let her inside. He surrendered to her assault, relaxing his entire body, letting her do whatever she needed. His arms fell limp by his sides, and he opened his mouth, savoring the crisp flavor of peppermint. She cradled his face in her hands, and he thought his heart would split in two.

Tenderness. For Jack. Not raw and crude sex as he'd had in the past with a handful of women. No, this was different and wondrous. And probably the closest thing he'd ever get to love.

251

She suddenly sat back and looked into his eyes.

"What . . . what's wrong?" he rasped.

She blinked. "I'm scared."

Relief coursed through him. She knew it, too. Frankie knew they were starting down a path more intense, more meaningful than basic lust.

"You've been with so many other women," she said. "You're so experienced, and I'm just . . . well, a naïve little numbers cruncher."

His heart sank. That's how she saw him. As some kind of male gigolo who took a woman in every town. He started to let her have it, tell her that rumors are not necessarily based in truth.

Then he read the regret in her eyes, the insecurity. They could never be together. But he could give her this. He could make her come alive in his arms and show her just how special she was.

"*You* are the woman I want," he said, trying to mask his own desperation.

Taking the lead then, he gently coaxed her mouth to his and opened immediately, letting her taste his want, his desire. Tonight, he'd give her what she needed most. He'd cherish her and pleasure her in ways she'd never imagined. And when they were done touching, stroking, and loving, he'd step out of the way and let her get on with her normal, real life.

Only, he knew his life would never be the same.

She tugged his shirt from the waistband of his jeans and slid her hands over his skin, her fingers tantalizing his flesh, making him hard with need. He gripped her hips and pulled her close, wanting her to feel the effect she had on his body.

"The bed," she whispered against his lips. She pulled him to his feet, and he leaned on her as he hobbled three feet to the bed.

"I should be carrying you," he said.

"You'll make it up to me."

He glanced into her eyes and was caught there, unable to look away. Yes, he would make it up to her. If it took all night.

Together they fell to the queen-sized bed, Frankie on her back, searching Jack's eyes. Such trepidation filled her rainbow gaze. Trepidation he'd wipe away with gentleness and promise.

"You're a beautiful woman," he whispered, reaching for the top button of her cream-colored blouse. Her chest rose and fell with each shallow breath, with each pop of a button through its hole. The fourth button came free and he spied a delicate lace camisole against her skin. He wanted his hand there, touching her, soaking in her warmth.

He trailed his fingers lower and spread the fabric of her blouse aside, taking in the beauty lying before him. The camisole only enhanced her femininity, making him want to see more, feel more. He skimmed his fingers across her breast, and her nipple peaked beneath his palm.

"Is this real?" she whispered, her eyes lit with desire.

"Does it feel real?"

His hand drifted lower, past her ribs, past her waist. He would do it right their first time, slowly, with painstaking tenderness.

"It feels . . . amazing," she whispered as he unzipped her slacks and slid his hand lower. He stroked the sweet spot between her legs, and she arched against him, a whimper escaping her lips. Reaching down, she helped him peel off her pants and pantyhose.

"Jack," she breathed, letting him touch her, pleasure her.

She sat up and pushed him back against the bed. With trembling hands, she peeled the T-shirt up and over his head, then hesitated. He wondered if she'd changed her mind.

"God, this body." Her eyes wide with appreciation, she ran her hands across his chest, her thumbs grazing his nipples. Then down, unbuckling his belt and stripping his body of the tight jeans and boxers.

In a swift motion, she straddled him, opening to him, while her hands worked magic on his chest. And all he could do was lie there, humbled by her need, willing to give whatever she wanted.

She rocked forward and back. Each time a little harder, a little more desperate, as if she wanted something so bad she would burst into tears if she didn't get it.

He knew that kind of wanting. And he knew just how to give her what she needed most. With his left hand steadying her round bottom, he reached forward with his right and grazed the inside of her thigh. He edged his hand down and found the soft, tender spot, massaging it gently. He watched her gasp for breath, struggle to retain control.

"Let it go, sweetheart," he whispered with another stroke, then another. He could tell she fought it. He knew she would. Frankie wasn't one to give up control.

She bucked forward again, squeezing his chest, claiming him for herself. Need built inside him. The incredible desire turned love that he'd never thought to feel.

The motion, the heat, the sweet moans of a passionate woman as she teetered on the brink of climax did him in. She cried out and arched one last time, and his body released its love inside her.

She collapsed against him, her soft, round breasts warming his chest, one leg wedged between his thighs. Only minutes later did her leg move, brushing against his manhood, awakening his need again.

Would he ever get enough of this woman? Would he ever satisfy his hunger for the woman he could never have?

Chapter Seventeen

She was drunk. Not on liquor or wine or any kind of umbrella concoction.

Frankie was drunk on Black Jack Hudson. How many times had they made love? She'd lost count. Somewhere around three this morning they'd both passed out from exhaustion. She had no clue what time it was. She didn't care.

All she cared about was Jack's arm wrapped around her from behind, their bodies touching from his lips against her hair to their entwined ankles.

This was real, she thought. The warmth, the contentment. He'd been there for her, held her, made a kind of magic she'd never felt before. She'd been shocked by the new sensations at first. Then she welcomed them, losing herself in the beauty of complete and utter surrender. It only made sense that she'd experience this with Jack, an uninhibited man who shared himself freely, without reservation.

But it hadn't always been that way. He'd changed during

the course of their relationship. Then again, so had she.

He stirred, nuzzling her neck. She clutched his hand between her breasts. She couldn't let go, not yet. Once she did, she didn't know what would happen.

Reality would set in, that's what. She'd have to admit that Jack had made love to her out of some kind of obligation or, God forbid, pity. Heavens, she hated that thought. Yet she hadn't cared about motivations last night. All she knew was she needed him inside her, for as long as possible.

And he'd satisfied that need, over and over again.

Opening her eyes, she stared across the room at the basket of silk flowers on the dining table. Fake flowers. Not real. Just like the relationship she had with the man lying beside her. Fake and temporary.

After all, it wasn't as if they could be more than bed mates or wrestling partners. Could they?

He moaned and wrapped himself tighter around her. She placed his hand to her breast, grazing her nipple with his thumb. His hardness pressed against her from behind.

"God, woman," he rasped. "You're going to kill me."

She loved that sound, his voice, thick with need. The power she had over him thrilled her. But thrills were cheap and fleeting. They didn't last forever, nor did they make for a solid future.

Solid, dependable, enduring. The kind of relationship she'd dreamed of her whole life. The exact opposite of her mom and dad's marriage.

Jack brushed his hand across her breast, and her body came alive. Just one touch, one stroke and she fell apart. It might not be a stable relationship, but it definitely had its advantages. Advantages that would disappear the minute they rolled out of bed.

"Francine?" he whispered against her hair.

"Hmmm?" Her eyes teared. Silly girl. Guilt, that was it. Last night she'd almost been proposed to by another man, and yet here she was in bed with Jack.

No, not guilt. Confusion. She'd never been more confused in her life.

"I've been thinking," he said.

"And when did you have time to do that?" she teased. At least she'd enjoy their last moments together.

"I'll admit, you kept me pretty busy last night."

He brushed her hair away from her ear and kissed the rim. She shivered.

"We make quite a team out of the ring, too, don't we?" he said.

She rolled onto her back and gazed into his eyes. Beautiful green eyes shining with desire, flashing with mirth.

"You—" She touched his stubbled jaw with her fingertips. "I don't know what to make of you."

"How about making love to me, again?" His cheeks dimpled with a mischievous grin.

"Don't you have someplace to be today, Black Jack Hudson?"

"Not today, or tomorrow, or the next day." He leaned closer, until their lips nearly touched. "I made a deal with my boss."

"Oh, you did, did you?"

"Yep, only she doesn't know it yet."

A knock at the door interrupted their kiss.

"Frankie? Are you there?" Bradley's voice called.

"Oh, my God!" She sprang from the bed, groping for her clothes. "Quick, pick up, hide, do something."

He just stared at her.

"Don't just lie there!" she whispered, scooping clothes from the floor and tossing them in the corner.

"Sweetums? You okay in there?"

"In a minute, Nipper!" she called back.

"Nipper?" Jack raised a brow.

"Help me! Come on, pick up your clothes, get out of here."

"And just where should I go? He's blocking the only exit."

"The balcony, there's a balcony. I'll keep him in the front room, but just in case, stay out there."

Grabbing his arm, she pulled and he grunted. He finally tumbled out of bed, his manhood ready for action. Her body automatically reacted with a tingling sensation between her legs.

"Don't ruin my life. Please don't ruin my life," she said, coaxing him to the balcony.

He froze and wrenched his arm from her. "Don't ruin your life?"

The fire in his eyes burned straight to her heart. She saw excruciating pain there, tempered with anger.

"I mean—"

"Forget it. I need clothes." He ripped his gaze from her and scanned the floor.

Shoving his shirt at him, she slid open the balcony door. "You'll stay . . . here?"

"No, I'm going to wing it to Aruba," he said, planting his hands on his naked hips.

"Right." She slammed the door and whipped the sheers closed. There. Everything would be fine. Her life was fine. Nothing to worry about.

She glanced at the balcony, regret tearing at her insides for hurting Jack's feelings. That was the last thing she wanted to do. But the comment had just slipped out. Call it panic or fear or just plain stupidity.

Or call it survival. She wasn't ready to give up on her dream of a perfect life. A life with a stable, responsible man like Bradley.

As she passed the bed on her way to the living room, guilt flushed her cheeks. What had she done?

"Francine?" Bradley knocked louder.

"Coming!" She tugged on the sheets, straightening them a bit, but not too much. It didn't matter. He wouldn't get past the living room. She'd make sure of that.

Taking a deep breath, she marched toward the door, catching her reflection in the mirror above the dresser.

"Ah!" she cried at the naked woman staring back at her. Wouldn't that scare Bradley witless? Frankie answering the door in her birthday suit. After all, they might have shared a bed, but they never really looked at each other's complete nakedness.

She snatched her robe from the closet and hurried to the door, tying the garment firmly in place. Running her hands through her hair, she took a deep breath, then flung the door wide.

"Bradley? What are you doing here? I thought you had a plane to catch."

"I rescheduled the flight for later this morning." He paused as he crossed the threshold. "You know, I don't think I've ever done that before."

He gave her the obligatory kiss on the cheek. Well, that was a good sign. He ambled past her to the breakfast bar.

"No coffee yet?" he asked.

"Just got up."

"It's nearly ten."

"I didn't get much sleep." She wandered to the kitchenette and poured coffee grounds into a filter.

"Me either, sweets. I was up all night thinking. Think, think, think." He shifted onto a bar stool and squeezed the bridge of his nose.

She poured water into the coffeemaker. It gurgled and spit.

"I just couldn't believe what you've done to me," Bradley said in a hushed voice.

She stilled. He couldn't know, could he? She glanced toward the bedroom, wondering if the silk flowers had sprouted a hidden camera courtesy of Uncle Joe. She wouldn't put anything past him where ratings were concerned.

"To put our lives in such jeopardy over something like wrestling. I was really angry," Bradley said.

He looked at her as if he expected something. What? A confession? No, he couldn't know about last night. And she still didn't think she had anything to apologize for regarding her wrestling career.

Besides, she couldn't undo what she'd already done, including her all-night aerobics with Jack. Shame strangled her vocal cords as she struggled to carry on a conversation with her ex-pre-fiancé.

Focus, McGee. All's not lost.

"Bradley, I explained to you last night how important it is for me to help my uncle. I don't know what more—"

"Wait." He put up his hand. "Hear me out. I understand your loyalty to your uncle. You haven't had many positive male figures in your life, besides me, of course." He smiled that million-dollar smile. Such bright, clean teeth.

"Anyway, I called a few people at work this morning and happened to mention this whole wrestling business," he said.

"You told them what I was doing?"

"No, of course not. I just mentioned it in passing. It seems I may have been a little unfair. Professional wrestling is a very popular form of entertainment, even with people of our caliber and breeding. As a matter of fact, Lundstrom, Marks and Beetle is trying to get a contract with Doodles Candy, a big sponsor of one of those wrestling groups."

"WHAK, that's my uncle's company."

"No kidding?" His eyes lit up.

"No kidding."

She poured him a cup of coffee, added exactly 1.5 ounces of milk, and passed it to him across the counter.

"Well, hmmm." He scratched his chin. "Maybe this has all worked out for the best."

"How so?" She cradled the mug of coffee in her hands.

"If you could get me front-row tickets for the next show in Chicago, I could bring the executives of Doodles and score some major points. It would be a great boost for my career, sweetums. And where I succeed, we succeed."

It shouldn't bother her that Bradley had gone from

shaming her about wrestling to begging for tickets. But it did.

"I'll talk to my uncle. Is that the only reason you came by this morning?"

"Of course not." He reached for her hand and brushed his thumb across her knuckles. His touch felt unusually cool. "I wanted to talk about us."

She held her breath.

"I was a little hard on you last night. But I didn't know what to think. You lied to me. Imagine, you dancing around naked in front of thousands of people. I didn't think you were that kind of girl."

If he only knew. She cleared her throat.

"I didn't know either," she said, remembering the total abandon of last night, the incredible want, need, possession of Jack's body.

She shoved the memory from her brain and refocused on salvaging the crumbling pieces of her perfect life.

"Bradley—"

"Wait, I'm not finished." He put up his hand. "Relationships have their ups and downs, their good days and bad. But with a little luck, this bad experience may have turned out to be a good one for all of us."

"How's that?"

"It's strengthened our bond and provided a valuable business opportunity, which means more stability for our future." He reached into his pocket. "I guess what I'm saying is, I'd like to try again."

He placed the velvet box on the breakfast bar.

Emotion numbed her throat. This was what she wanted, wasn't it? Images of last night replayed in her mind. Jack's sweet kisses, his gentle, yet arousing touch.

Last night was an anomaly, a fluke. Something she never would have tasted had Bradley not withdrawn his offer.

She stared at the box and thought about all it represented.

Real. This was real. Her dream of security, of happiness, of the perfect life.

She reached for it.

"Wait," Bradley said.

She snatched her hand back as if caught in Mama's cookie jar.

"I'm going to leave the ring with you, but first I'd like to make a few things clear."

She studied his face, his tight-knit brows and pursed lips.

"I expect loyalty and complete honesty," he began. "There will be no secrets between us. Our goal is to devote our lives to one another's professional success, which in turn will lead to personal happiness. That's my offer, Francine."

It sounded more like a business deal than a marriage proposal. She wondered if confessing what she'd done last night would be a deal breaker.

Snap out of it. He's giving you another chance. Besides, you weren't engaged last night when you gave yourself to Jack, loved Jack.

Love. No, it couldn't be. It was just physical desire, the serpent that drew you in and left you writhing in pain.

She sighed, realizing she didn't deserve this ring. Not unless she told all. She watched him deliberately stir his coffee. It would crush him if she confessed what she'd done last night on the rebound from his rejection. In a way it was his fault. She caught herself. She'd made the moves on Jack all by herself, risking her chance at happiness in the process.

He sipped his coffee, then placed the cup on the counter. "What do you think?"

"I'm glad you stopped by."

Talk about feeble.

"Me, too, sweetums. Well, I've got to be going." He headed toward the door. "I heard there's a special wrestling show coming up this Friday in Chicago. I don't suppose you could get tickets for that one? It would score big points for me, for us. Teamwork, that's the key."

She absently followed him to the door.

"Think about my proposal, Frankie." He turned and narrowed his eyes. "Loyalty and honesty. An easy job description for a woman like yourself."

With a hand on the small of her back, he kissed her on the lips. She felt nothing. No electricity, no excitement.

Tell him. Tell him now!

She couldn't ruin everything they'd meant to each other in a matter of seconds. And what about her perfect life?

"Oh, and Frankie, it goes without saying that your wrestling days are over. You won't be prancing around the ring anymore dressed like a Vegas showgirl, right?"

"Tiger lady. I was dressed like a tiger lady."

"You've had your fun. Time to get on with our future." He dropped a perfunctory kiss atop her head. "That's a good girl."

Forcing a smile, she shut the door. A good little girl searching for the perfect, safe life. Her goal since birth. Glancing toward the bedroom, she realized she'd been anything but good last night.

She considered Bradley's offer, a future of well-planned meals and budget vacations. He planned everything down to his thirteen-minute shower in the morning and the hundred-and-two-degree temperature of his milk at bedtime. He calculated every penny spent, picked every movie by how much money it grossed a week after it opened, and lined up his canned peas, kidney beans, and fruit cocktail by expiration date.

Frankie liked being in control, but did she really want this?

Yet Bradley offered stability, security, a nice, normal life. A real life with a handsome prince and new partner at Lundstrom, Marks and Beetle.

But how real was a life without love?

She loved Bradley in her own way. She had to. Why else

would she have invested three years in their relationship?

Yet Bradley's tone had set the hairs bristling at the nape of her neck. Conditions. Everything came with conditions. Whereas Jack acted from his heart and thought later. Lived life to the fullest and rode the wave of uncertainty. A part of Frankie was fascinated by this approach. She wondered what it was like to go with the flow and not micromanage all the time. She'd like to give it a try.

But not with Bradley. That man couldn't go with the flow if he wore two life jackets and sailed in a steel-bottomed boat.

She struggled to make sense of it all, of her perfect, precarious relationship with Bradley. Marry me. Don't marry me. Marry me if you can commit to honesty. But she'd just cheated on him, hadn't she? No, he'd broken their pre-engagement. She wasn't being disloyal. Technically she didn't have to bare her soul about the wonder of last night with another man.

Jack. The man she loved.

"No!" she cried, marching to the breakfast bar and taking a swig of coffee. No denying it: She loved Jack in a totally uninhibited and undefined way. This unstable, transient, fly-by-the-seat-of-your-pants pro wrestler. But how did he feel about her? She thought back on all the things he'd done for her. He protected her, held her, took care of her.

Loved her.

Dishonesty had been her mistake all along. No more. She'd start with Jack. She'd tell him how she felt. Okay, so they were polar opposites and wanted different things out of life. It didn't matter. She had to tell him she loved him, that she would actually entertain the notion of living on the edge and going with the flow, if it meant being with him.

She had to know if they could be more than show biz partners. Frankie would finally do it. She'd stop thinking with her head and start leading with her heart.

* * *

There weren't a lot of women he'd let throw him out of bed or send him half naked onto a public balcony. But then Frankie McGee wasn't a lot of women.

She was *the* woman. Jack's heart and soul, his completely imperfect, aggravating life mate. If only he could convince her of that.

Jack stood in the corner of the cement balcony, out of view of a family getting into their station wagon in the parking lot below. She could have at least given him his pants, for crying out loud. But no, she'd been in a hurry to hide his presence from her fiancé.

Her fiancé? Not for long. Not if Jack had anything to say about it.

Okay, so maybe he and Frankie weren't the most compatible people in the world. But they shared something more important than compatibility. They shared a physical and emotional connection more powerful than anything he'd ever experienced in his life. And he wasn't about to let her go. Not in this lifetime.

Butch always said the best things in life were the ones you had to fight for the hardest. Frankie definitely fell into that category.

She'd accused him of ruining her life? Hell, she didn't have a clue. Her well-planned, anal-retentive life with Mr. Accountant USA was going to ruin her every chance at happiness. And Jack wouldn't let that happen. Frankie had saved him from the loneliness and desperation of the business. She'd not only taught him to take charge of his life, but she'd cared for him in a way no other woman had.

She loved him. Somewhere, deep down in that place she kept locked and under armored guard, Frankie knew she loved Jack. And it scared the hell out of her.

Awake for the better part of the night, he'd plotted how to make it work. Because he loved her, too.

They could have a great life. He'd rediscover painting and make public appearances, continuing his efforts as a positive role model. A lot of retired wrestlers still rallied for good causes and won because of their superstar popularity.

Okay, so maybe it wasn't the life she'd envisioned with bi-weekly paychecks and business socials. But when it came to love, sometimes you had to sacrifice.

Listen to me. Like I'm an expert on love.

No, he wasn't an expert. What he'd had with Sandra wasn't anything like this. And his handful of other flings were just a way to pass the time, a way to take his mind off the discontentment of his life.

Discontentment. One feeling he looked forward to giving up very, very soon. When his contract was flushed he'd move on with his life. He'd more than paid his dues. It was time to reap the rewards . . . with Frankie.

He closed his eyes. The crisp morning air on his half-naked body reminded him of Frankie's delicate hands touching his chest, then working their way down to other, more intimate places. He took a deep, steadying breath. In a minute he was going to break through the sliding glass door with his bare hands. He wouldn't let that pencil-necked geek talk his way back into her life. He'd had his chance and blown it. Now it was time to get out of the way and let Jack make his plea for her love.

He pressed his face to the window, straining to see through the sheers. He spied Frankie amble into the bedroom as if her mind were a million miles away. He tapped on the glass. She glanced up, but he couldn't quite make out the emotion in her eyes. Sadness? Frustration?

He banged on the door. To hell with the audience in the parking lot. Flashing strangers was nothing compared to the thought of losing her.

Desperation drove him to pound again, harder. She opened the door, then turned away and ambled into the living area. He followed her inside, his heart racing.

He could do this. He could tell her he loved her.

"I'll have you know, the people in 115 just reported me to the police for indecent exposure," he joked, wishing she'd turn around so he could read her eyes. He flung the bed sheets to the floor in search of his boxer briefs.

"I'm sorry. I didn't realize I'd just given you a T-shirt," she said, heading into the living room.

"So, what was Prince Charming's story?" He slipped on the briefs, then grabbed his jeans from the floor.

"He came to ask for tickets to Friday's event."

"You're kidding." He limped to the breakfast bar. The knee felt a little better today. Hell, his whole body felt better.

"Jack, listen, about last night."

"I smell coffee," he said, needing sustenance to build his courage.

"I made some for Bradley. Knee still bothering you?"

"Always bothers me."

Like you. Every time I see you, every time I think about you. You bother me by breathing, by smiling.

Time to confess he'd spent the last fifteen minutes going over their lives, dreaming that they could live together and love one another . . . forever.

"Frank, I've gotta tell ya—" He reached for the coffeepot and froze at the sight of a black velvet box. "What's this?"

He opened it and his heart broke into a million pieces.

"Wow," he rasped. All his dreams, all his hopes were washed away in pain.

She snatched the box from him. "Bradley left it."

"He proposed?"

"Kind of." She cradled the box in her palm, a faraway look in her eye.

With a trembling hand, he poured himself coffee and casually leaned against the counter. His eyes burned. Must be lack of sleep. Who the hell was he kidding?

Dammit, Hudson. Don't confuse the woman. The ring, the little box she held, symbolized everything she'd ever wanted, the very things he couldn't give her.

Swallowing hard, he blocked out his fantasy of a life with

Frankie. If he loved her, really loved her, he'd do the right thing.

He'd let her go.

"Anyway," she continued, moving to the couch, "He proposed with conditions. One being that I turn in my mask and whip."

"Ah, doesn't like his woman dressing in leopard skin and feathers." He was surprised he could even speak.

"He also said we need to be honest with one another." She looked at Jack and his heart skipped.

"Honesty's important," he said.

"You think so?"

"Is this a trick question?"

"No, but . . ." She held his gaze with those amazing, iridescent eyes. He had a feeling his dreams would be haunted by those colors for years to come.

". . . about last night, Jack, I have to be honest with you." She sat down on the couch.

This was it. The opening he'd hoped for, his chance to profess his love.

Do the right thing, dammit. You have nothing to offer, no stock options, fiscally sound budgets, no guarantees of any kind.

He took a deep breath. "Don't worry about it, kid. We all make mistakes."

"Mistakes?"

"Well, sure, you screwed me last night and have to face the fiancé this morning? I'd call that a mistake."

"Screwed?" Her eyes grew round.

"We definitely screwed."

Push her away, Hudson. Let her get on with her perfect life.

"Well, of course, I mean, I guess technically—"

"Technically and every other way." He searched the floor for his shoes. "It was a wild ride, though, wasn't it?"

God, he was glad his back was turned to her, so she couldn't read the pain in his eyes. He didn't want to confuse her any more than she already was. He sensed her struggle to process their lovemaking and how it affected her well-planned, perfect life.

Hell, *someone* should be able to live a perfect life filled with food plans, job security, and safe baby cribs.

"Jack?"

He grabbed his shoes and plopped down in a chair.

"It was more than fun, wasn't it?" she said.

"It was great, fantastic, mind-blowing. Glad I could oblige."

"Oblige?"

He heard the hitch in her voice and wanted to kick himself. He knew what had to be done.

"Don't feel guilty about it, kid." He snapped his laces tight on his right shoe. "I took advantage, pure and simple. I knew what I was doing." He tied his other shoe, sucked in a deep breath, and ambled toward her.

"But you . . ." He grazed her cheek with the pad of his thumb. She leaned into his touch and what was left of his heart split in two. "You're just a sweet, naïve kid, aren't you?"

She jerked away from him. Her lips went taut, her face paled. "Is that how I was last night? Naïve?"

"Not completely naïve. You taught me a few things."

Like how to love, and when that kind of love means letting go.

"I taught you something?"

"Sure." Glancing around the room, he searched for misplaced possessions. Nope. Didn't see his heart anywhere.

"You taught me to plan for my future. To set goals and stick to them."

"I did?" Her face lit up.

This was it, his chance to close the door around his heart and lock it for good.

"Sure. I've decided to take up painting again and travel. Can't wait to paint the Alps or the French countryside."

"What about a job? Financial security?" She sat straight, and he sensed the tension coursing through her body.

"It'll work out. Always does." He continued his search of the floor, the sofa, the dresser, stalling, letting her scent seep into his skin. He wanted to remember her scent forever.

"You're going to travel and paint?"

He recognized the horror in her voice, the disbelief.

"Yep. About time I did something for myself," he said.

"What about money?"

"Got enough to last me for a while. After that, I'll go with the flow." He tossed a pillow onto the couch and grabbed his crutches. "Take care, kid. See you at the office."

He pulled open the door and hobbled into the hallway. Only when he'd made it to the elevator did he pause long enough to take a breath. He punched the "down" button and wiped moisture from beneath his eyes. It was hot in here. The hotel air-conditioning must be broken.

Kinda like his heart.

Clearing his throat, he glanced down the hall. His heart wasn't just broken. It lay in pieces back in room 214.

The elevator doors opened.

"Take care, sweetheart," he choked and stepped into the elevator. "I love you, Francine McGee."

Chapter Eighteen

It felt great to be back at Mama's. If only for a few days.

Settled comfortably in the antique rocker, Frankie pushed against the hardwood floor with the balls of her sneaker-clad feet. She closed her eyes and savored the motion that brought back memories of curling up in her mother's arms, feeling safe, secure, and loved.

Love. What an elusive concept. She'd just nearly given her love to a man who thought her nothing more than a one-night stand.

"Here's the tea," Mama said, walking into the living room carrying a small silver tray. "I even made lemon bars. I thought Bradley would be with you."

She studied Mama as she placed a one-inch lemon square on a plate, then poured tea. Her new, cropped hairstyle flattered her round face.

"I like your hair," Frankie said.

"Thank you. Had to find a new hairdresser. Jeannie stopped cutting hair last year. One lump of sugar, right?"

"Two?"

"Francine, too much sugar can ruin your beautiful smile."

"Right, I forgot." No, she hadn't, but she wanted to hear the words again. All of them. She wanted to be nurtured and comforted, and forget that she'd been nurtured by a man who'd just stolen her heart. A man who didn't want her.

"Something's bothering you." Mama settled into the Queen Anne chair, the very place from which she'd read *Anne of Green Gables* to Frankie as a child. Mama always looked impeccable. Today she was dressed in gray slacks and a print blouse, a strand of imitation pearls dipping just below the fold of her collar.

"Sweetie?" she prompted.

"I've had a rough couple of weeks."

"Everything okay at work?"

"So far." No voice-mail messages or pink slips yet, that she knew of anyway. And it suddenly dawned on her that she didn't give a damn about her fancy job.

"It's Bradley, isn't it?" Mama leaned forward.

"How did you know?"

"Just a guess. He's lucky to have such a smart and clever young lady like yourself."

"I haven't been too clever lately."

Mama raised a brow in question.

"I've been helping Uncle Joe."

"Francine, no!"

"He needed me. His business is in trouble. Only, it got away from me."

"Joe Sullivan has no scruples—I've told you that over and over again. We love him, but we don't get involved in his dramas."

"Well, I did get involved, and now everything's a mess." Frankie buried her face in her hands.

The aged floorboards squeaked as Mama walked over and placed a hand on Frankie's shoulder. "Oh, honey. This is all my fault."

"Your fault?" She glanced up.

"All this angst over a man who isn't worth your trouble."

"Jack?"

"Joe Sullivan."

"But Uncle Joe—"

"Isn't really your uncle."

She froze, the wind knocked from her lungs. Staring up at Mama, she felt the room tilt sideways. She couldn't speak.

"I'm sorry," Mama said. "I shouldn't have let him become such an important part of your life. But Joe Sullivan's loved me since the fifth grade."

"What!"

Mama paced to the Queen Anne chair and slowly sat down.

"Joe and I were childhood friends, but he always fancied us as more. Knowing things were bad with your father, Sully took it upon himself to fill in as the loving uncle. He was always such a silly, lighthearted boy. He always made me laugh, but I never considered him husband material. His prospects weren't good. Can you imagine me living out of a suitcase? Packing up and moving every time he got a wild idea about chasing a new angle to make him rich? 'This one's going to make me a millionaire,' he'd say. Always trying to prove that I should have married him instead of Thomas."

"He would have been better than Dad," Frankie muttered. She stood and paced to the fireplace mantel, fingering the pewter picture frame of herself, her mom, and her dad on their one vacation to Florida.

"You loved him, didn't you?" Frankie said.

"Who?"

"Dad."

"No, I wouldn't exactly call it love."

She spun around and studied Mama, who drank tea as if she were discussing the news headlines of the day.

"I don't understand," Frankie said.

"I thought he'd make a fine husband, a good provider. By the time I realized my mistake, it was too late. I couldn't very well get a divorce. That wasn't acceptable in my family, and I had no means to support a child. Besides, your father wasn't a cruel man."

"But he was never around."

"I tried to change him, sweetheart. I really did. We do the best we can." She placed her cup on the glass end table. "But you've got your whole life ahead of you. You can make whatever choice you want."

"And it's an easy one. Bradley is everything I've dreamed of."

Mama studied her fingers, interlaced in her lap. "If he makes you happy, then I'm happy."

"I'm not exactly happy right now. I'm frustrated as hell." Frankie glanced at Mama in apology for the curse. Her mother nodded, encouraging her to go on. "I resent Dad for never being around, I resent Bradley for his expectations, and I resent Uncle Joe for dragging me into this mess."

"What mess?"

"Haven't you heard? I'm his newest star." She flung her arms above her head and wiggled her hips.

"Frankie, you didn't."

She paced to the rocker and collapsed. "It was supposed to be one night. It turned into promotional appearances, being married, and carrying a whip."

"A whip?"

"I'm a tigress who wears a leopard-skin bikini, and my partner is a cowboy named Black Jack Hudson. An impossible, infuriating man. He doesn't plan a thing, just lets life carry him along."

"Planning is good, of course, but—"

"He's an impossible man. I lose all sense of control around him. He picked me up and carried me into the ring. Do you believe that? Against my will!"

"Is that all he did?"

Frankie stared out the living room window at the red begonias blooming on Mama's porch.

"It doesn't matter," she said. "I might be frustrated, but I'm not confused about what I want or who I belong with, not anymore."

"Hmmm. And what do you want?" Mama came up beside her and stroked her hair.

"My perfect, orderly, well-planned life." She glanced into Mama's eyes. "I want to know my husband is coming home at six every night, that he'll take me to dinner on Saturdays, and invest wisely to support his family. Bradley will do all that."

"Then you've decided he's the right choice?"

"He's perfect. He's forthright, dependable, and sturdy. Sturdier than a steel guardrail," she added for good measure.

"And what's Mr. Black Jack?"

"He's just a guy." She paused and fingered the hem of her T-shirt. "A guy who saved me from being splattered into a million pieces. A guy who held me and made me laugh . . . and helped me cry." She sucked in a deep breath. Only then did she realize her face was damp with tears.

"I've always tried to do the right thing, to be a good girl," she whispered. "If I was good I thought Dad would come home. But he didn't. He didn't love me enough to come home. I wondered if I was lovable at all."

But Jack had said as much when he'd made love to her. He'd said she was the most lovable person he knew. Were they just empty words?

She looked into Mama's blue-green eyes. "I sound like a kook."

"No, you sound like you're in love."

"Bradley and I will make the perfect couple."

"We're not talking about Bradley, are we, honey?" Mama's gaze cut right to her heart. Who did she think she was kidding?

"He's a wrestler, Mama, a wrestler who wants to travel

and paint. Can you imagine? He'll probably end up drawing caricatures of people on the street for pocket change. He'll tumble through life doing who knows what."

"And if you're in love, you'll tumble right along with him."

"I can't live like that, not feeling secure, not knowing if my husband will make my child's school play. I'm going to get everything in place and get my happy ending."

Mama put her arm around her. "I followed the rules once and ended up marrying your father. I didn't love him, Frankie. I made that decision with my head, not my heart. Look where I ended up. If you've been lucky enough to find love, think real hard before letting it go. Even if you have to fight for it."

"Jack doesn't love me."

"Nonsense. How could he not love my special little girl? Now come on, let's wash your face. It's all blotchy."

Frankie absently followed her mother into the powder room, where she brushed at Frankie's cheeks with a rose-colored washcloth.

Frankie craved stability down to the marrow of her bones. She needed a man who would be her partner, carry his share of the weight, help her up when she was down.

Jack had held her, comforted her, made love to her. Physical love. A kind of love that led nowhere. And Jack wasn't offering emotional love. She wondered if he had it to give, even knew what it was.

"There, all better," Mama said with a final stroke of the cloth. "That Sullivan. I'd like to take a strap to that silly man."

"When I think of everything I've done for him these past few weeks. I'm going to make Uncle Joe—Sully, pay for this."

"And what about Bradley?"

She glanced into Mama's eyes. "He got me a deal on disposable diaper stock."

"How romantic," Mama said in a sarcastic tone.

"He gave me the engagement ring."

"And you said . . . ?"

"I didn't. Yet. Oh, Mama, I don't know what's real anymore."

"Search your heart, honey. That's where you'll find your answers."

Getting control of her life, Frankie flew back to WHAK headquarters the next day to confront Sully. She secretly made her way through the building, hoping she wouldn't run into Jack. She didn't know if she could handle that today. Or any day.

She hovered outside Sully's door, watching him count a pile of butterscotch candies.

"You impostor!" she accused from Sully's office doorway.

"What? Who? Where?" Sully jumped from his chair and gripped the lapels of his brown polyester suit. His gaze darted around the room. Once he realized he was the only one there, he looked back at Frankie in question.

"When I think of everything I've done for you, and you're not even my uncle." She stormed toward him.

"Oh, well, that." He tugged at his tie.

She pulled the knot free and ripped the tie from his collar. "Why do you bother with this thing? It only gives you away when you're lying."

"Well, yes, gives me away. How is your mother?"

"My mother?"

He nodded, his eyes wide with fear.

"She's fine. But she doesn't want you, Sully. When are you going to get that through your head?"

His eyes dimmed, and he sat back down. "I guess I've always suspected as much."

"Then why? Why did you come around all the time and give me things, take me to ball games, and act like the father I never knew? Because you wanted to endear yourself to Mama?"

"Boy, for a college graduate you sure are stupid," Maxine said from the doorway.

She spun to face the older woman, who was a symphony in red from her tennis shoes, to her spandex pants, topped off by an oversized T-shirt that read, "Mat Men Do It With Submission."

"Just because Sully isn't blood kin, that doesn't mean he doesn't love you," Max said.

"You knew all along and didn't tell me?"

"Wasn't my business to tell."

"Maxine, please, this is a family matter," Sully said.

The older woman backed away.

"Stop right there," Frankie said. She glared at Sully. "In case you haven't figured it out yet, Max is the only family you've got, big guy. So I'd be real nice to her if I were you."

"You're not going to leave me, not now when I need you most?" He reached for the knot of his tie but came up empty handed.

"Why should I care? Why?"

"I hate to interrupt this family squabble, but we've got company." Max slammed the door shut and shouldered the mahogany credenza over to block it.

"Max?" Frankie said.

"Pugsy and the snakes. Quick, help me with this."

Frankie crouched next to Max and gave a hardy push.

"I'll call security!" Uncle Joe said, pulling on his hair.

"What have you done, Sully? Huh?" Frankie cried, giving the heavy piece of furniture one last shove into place.

"I told them to go away. I told them never to come back."

Frankie rolled her eyes. As if a threat from Sully would stave off the mob. Max swiped Sully's putter from the corner of the room.

Frankie supposed she should be scared, terrified even, at the prospect of being attacked by the thugs. In reality, nothing scared her right now. With the explosive anger burning in her gut, she pitied the fool who tried to tangle with her today.

A pounding at the door made Frankie and Max shriek in unison.

"I told them they don't belong here," Sully ranted. "We're a legitimate company. We don't want their kind."

"Like the mob is going to listen to you? What the hell were you thinking, taking money from them?" Frankie swiped a brass bookend from the shelf and weighed it in her hand.

"Mob? What mob?" Sully said.

She glanced at Max, then Sully.

"Max said you borrowed money from the mob and Pugsy and the snakes are bag men coming to collect."

"Bag men?"

"Did you borrow money from the mob or not?" she demanded.

"No! Honest, I haven't done anything illegal since '74 when I opened the midget strip club down in Quincy."

"The what?" Max said, hands on her hips.

"Never mind," Frankie said. "If these guys weren't sent by the mob, who are they?"

A loud thud sounded on the door.

"Dammit, Sully!"

"I liked it better when you called me Uncle Joe. And you shouldn't swear. It's not becoming."

She slammed the book end on his desk and he jumped.

"Okay, okay! They're two wrestlers from OW. They want to sign with us. We've become the preferred wrestling organization since you joined the team." He grinned.

She gripped the bookend with deadly force to keep from hurling it at him.

"They're wrestlers?" she ground out.

He nodded.

"Max?"

Max glared at Sully. "The last time they showed up you were terrified. You said you feared for your life."

"Snakes are poisonous!" he defended.

"Not all snakes."

"Forget the reptile lecture," Frankie said. "I refuse to be intimidated by these idiots."

Another blast busted a two-foot hole in the center of the door.

"I'm ready." Max gripped the putter with firm, bony hands.

"Wait until security comes," Sully cried. "These are violent men. Their snakes are deadly, I know it! And the man with the tuba? He's got knives in there. He throws them at those wiggling creatures."

"Is this a circus or a wrestling company?" Frankie demanded.

They both looked at her. Neither answered.

"Out of my way." She marched toward the door just as a large, hairy head popped through the opening.

"Sully! We want a contract," demanded the beast with one eyebrow growing across his forehead.

"What you're going to get is a concussion if you don't get the hell out of this building," Frankie said, wielding the book end.

"Who the hell are you?"

"I'm the Franken Niece. And you're going to be unconscious in a minute. Now get."

"You won't be singing that tune when we drop our slimy friends in there." He backed out of the hole. "Give me the snakes," he called to his partner.

She scanned the office for a better weapon and her gaze landed on Sully's prized machete. It surprised her none of the wrestlers had used it to slice up their boss before now.

Fine, they wanted to play hard ball? She snatched the machete from its mount.

"Frankie! What are you doing?" Sully said.

"Defending your honor, Sullivan."

"But that's not a toy. I brought it back from the Orient. It's a real weapon."

"Good." She glanced at Max. The woman's blue eyes beamed with pride.

With a two-handed grip Frankie raised the sword over her shoulder.

"Here they come, ready or not." A maniacal voice boomed from the other side of the door. Two burly hands slipped a thick bag through the hole.

"I hear snake is delicious when cooked over an open flame, isn't that right, Sully?" she said.

The burly hands froze. The hairy beast stuck his head through the door. His eyes bulged at the sight of Frankie wielding the ancient weapon.

"What are you gonna do with that?" he said.

"Make mincemeat out of your gift."

His skin paled beneath the mound of facial hair. "You'd really cut up Puffy and Minx?"

"Well, I'm sure as hell not going to use them in our show. I have to draw the line somewhere, and this is it."

"All we want is a contract." His voice softened.

"Contrary to what some people think, we're a wrestling organization, not a circus. Come back when you learn how to fall and get up again fifty times in a row, or when you can show me a proper full nelson, arm bar, or drop-toe hold."

"But—"

"Does the word 'decapitated' mean anything to you?" she said, winding up.

"I'm going, I'm going." He snatched the bag out of the office. "If you ever change your mind—"

"We'll look in the yellow pages under 'reptiles.' "

She heard the scuffle of security men, a few grunts, then silence. A guard poked his head through the door.

"Everyone okay?"

"Fine, thanks." She propped the machete against the wall.

"Let's get this out of the way," Max said. Frankie helped her slide the credenza away from the door.

She brushed off her hands, then picked at the splintered door. What a joke. The whole damn thing.

He wasn't her uncle. There was no real connection between Frankie and Joe Sullivan.

Except the panic in her gut when she'd thought Pugsy and the snakes were sent to crush his kneecaps. Except the memories of presents wrapped with pink bows, including her favorite, the Easy-Bake Oven. Orange cakes were her specialty and sheer torture for Uncle Joe. She'd never forget the pained look on his face as he masticated the horrible concoction. He didn't have to do that. He also didn't have to take her to Red Sox games or the ballet, where he snored in harmony with the strings and woodwinds.

He didn't have to do any of it.

But he did. Because he loved her like his own daughter.

And the thing of it was, she loved him back.

"I can't believe this," she whispered to herself. It hit her like a ton of bricks: It doesn't matter who a person is or what he does. If you love him, you love him.

It didn't matter that Joe Sullivan wasn't her real uncle, that he was a crazy old bat whose scruples were questionable most of the time. She loved him anyway.

And she loved Jack. Even though he was a comic-book hero with no set future, a "phony" wrestler. If people only knew.

She glanced at Sully, who chewed his bottom lip.

"I love you, you big jerk." She crossed the room, wrapped her arms around his neck and squeezed hard. Maybe it wasn't the smartest thing to do, but it was love. And it was real.

"Okay, Uncle Joe. Where do we go from here?"

Pushing away from him, she spied the gleam in Maxine's eyes.

"Come here, Max. You're just as much a part of this as I am, if not more so."

Uncle Joe pressed a handkerchief to his eyes, then his forehead, as if wiping sweat from his brow.

"I don't know what I'd do if you turned your back on me, Francine. I'd be all alone," he said, a hitch in his voice.

"We're quite a pair of blockheads." She put her arm around him. "Look at that lady there. You think she sews costumes and cleans up after you because you're paying her the big bucks?"

"Big bucks?" he said, reaching for his ledger. "But I thought we negotiated only a three-percent raise last year."

Frankie flattened her palm on the paperwork. "Uncle Joe, stop thinking with your head and start seeing with your heart."

He glanced at Frankie and his eyes grew wide. Then he looked at Max. The former Women's Champ actually blushed.

"But Max, you've always been so critical and bossy. You just seemed mad at me all these years."

"That's because you sell yourself short. You're a good man, Joseph Sullivan. It's time you acted like one."

"Joseph. No one's called me Joseph since third grade." His eyes shone with awe and wonder, as if seeing her for the first time.

"Maxine, would you like to go out for dinner tonight?"

"Jumpin' Jupiter, it only took ya thirty years."

He laughed, and Frankie realized she'd rarely heard that sound. Screams, sure. Howls, squawks, even shrieks. But not laughter.

"Now that that's settled, how is WHAK's financial condition? You still need help?" She ambled to his desk.

"Actually, things are looking great. Your three weeks here have really helped, especially this last week with the Tatianna angle."

Her heart ached and she glanced at the floor. It was definitely time to go.

"Francine?" Uncle Joe whispered.

"I'm fine. What about the Tatianna angle?"

"We have advance orders for Black Jack and Tatianna action figures."

"Did I hear my name?"

Her heart caught at the sound of Jack's voice. She hadn't

seen him in days, but her body instantly reacted to that sultry timbre. She closed her eyes, willing herself to be calm. He didn't love her, didn't care about her. It shouldn't matter.

But it did. Her body ached to feel his hands possess her, pleasure her until she couldn't think straight.

"Just talking about merchandising, Jack. Nothing that concerns you," Uncle Joe said.

"I heard there was trouble up here. Everyone okay?"

"I took care of it," Max boasted.

"I'll bet you did." He slid his arm around Max's shoulders.

Only then did Frankie look at him. A spear of pain sliced open her heart. He narrowed his eyes as if trying to read her thoughts, wanting to make sure she was okay.

She broke the connection and studied Joe's ledger.

"Of course, Little Miss Pirate with her machete was a big help," Max said.

"Frankie?" Jack said. "I would have paid money to see that."

"Watch it or I'll do a free reenactment," she shot back.

They all laughed. Except Frankie.

"Well, I've got good news," Jack said to Uncle Joe. "It seems Sumptuous Sally wants back in. Her job as a topless dancer didn't work out."

"Probably knocked out her customers with those double-D kahoonas of hers," Max muttered.

"I told her she'd be perfect to play Tatianna."

Frankie hadn't thought she could hurt any more. She was wrong.

"I figure Frank here is out of the game since she's gonna be walking down the aisle soon. How about it? I can have Sally back for Friday's show here in Chicago."

Uncle Joe glanced at Frankie. "If Frankie thinks it's a good idea."

She felt as if someone had stuck his hand in her chest and was ripping out her heart.

284

This was the way it was supposed to be. Frankie leaving the business to marry Bradley, waking up at 6:37 every morning, flossing exactly seven times per tooth.

No, she knew that no matter what came of all this, she wasn't marrying Bradley. Not next month, next year, or in the next lifetime.

Swallowing the lump in her throat, she grinned at Jack. "Fabulous. The sooner the better."

He didn't care about her. He was happy to send her packing, ready to bring in a new woman to perform with, make love to. She balled her hand into a fist behind her back.

"It's settled then." Uncle Joe rubbed his hands together. "And your contract, Jack?"

"Go ahead and extend it for another two years with a third-year option."

Frankie's heart skipped. "What?"

Jack ignored her.

"Two, maybe three years?" Sully repeated, disbelief in his voice.

"You gonna argue with me or sign me?"

"Sign you, sign you." Uncle Joe searched his desk and dug out a blank contract. He scribbled down the information and shoved it at Jack.

"But I still expect my bonus at the end of this one."

"Of course." Uncle Joe practically salivated as Jack signed his name.

"And set me up in some easy matches for a while. The knee's still not a hundred percent."

"Easy matches." Uncle Joe leafed through a pile of papers. "Right, how about the Basher at The Spring Squash?"

Jack looked at Maxine. "Why do I bother?"

"Beats me."

Frankie studied his face, but he wouldn't look at her. What was happening? His body would never last another six months, much less two years. What about his dream of painting and travel? His plans to live in the mountains?

"Jack?" she said, at least she thought she spoke his name. But he didn't so much as glance her way, and everyone kept talking, as if they were in a movie and Frankie had a nonspeaking role.

"All right then." He tapped on Uncle Joe's desk with his knuckles, then glanced at Frankie. Her breath caught. In slow motion he closed the distance between them, the heat from his body warming her skin.

He leaned forward, his lips nearly grazing her ear. She automatically reached out, digging her fingers into his biceps like he was a lifesaver and she was going down.

"Go live your perfect life, sweetheart. Don't worry, I'll keep an eye on him for you."

And then he kissed her. A gentle kiss that felt suspiciously like goodbye.

By the time she got her wits back and opened her eyes, he was gone.

"Why did he do that?" she whispered, pressing her fingers to her lips.

"Why does a man usually kiss a woman?" Max said.

"No, not that. I mean, the contract. He needs to get out of this business. He won't survive another two years."

"For a girl with two fancy degrees, you don't have much sense."

"Maxine, don't talk that way to my . . . to Francine," Uncle Joe said.

"Max?" She studied the older woman's face, needing answers, feeling completely blindsided.

"He did it for you, Lady Jane. Did anyone bother telling him that Pugsy and the snakes weren't bag men for the mob?"

Frankie looked at Uncle Joe. Uncle Joe looked at Max.

"Didn't think so," Max said. "Jack's putting his life on hold to protect your uncle so you can get your pretty little butt out of here and live your perfect life. That is what's waiting out there for you, isn't it? A perfect life with that pencil-pushing fiancé of yours?"

286

Chapter Nineteen

Two days of introspection and a six-pack of peppermints later, she knew what she had to do. Dressed in faded blue jeans and the Hammerlock Championship T-shirt Maxine had given her, Frankie paced the Lancaster Stadium, Gate Six entrance. Bradley would show any minute, clients in tow. Fanning herself with the ringside tickets, she took consolation in the fact that at least she was helping Bradley sink a lucrative deal before walking out of his life.

"He'll be okay," she whispered. After all, the relationships entangled in love were the hardest to survive. She wouldn't exactly use the word "love" to describe her partnership with Bradley. It had finally dawned on her that partnering with Bradley was the business relationship, and loving Jack was anything but business.

What would Jack do tonight when she climbed into the ring? Would he turn away? She pushed the thought aside. Because if Frankie had learned anything, it was that what's real is what's in your heart. And her heart not only cried out for Jack, every minute of every day, but it also insisted he loved her as well.

She belonged with him, whether that meant holing up in a mountain cabin somewhere, or traveling the country to discover new sights to paint. One thing for sure, she wasn't going to let him continue to abuse himself in the ring, regardless of his contract with Uncle Joe.

What a mess they'd all gotten themselves into. But it was almost over. Time to cut the anchor and sail on life's possibilities for once. She could do it. For Jack. For their love.

The thought of her mother spending an entire lifetime doing the right thing and being unhappy was a wake-up call for Frankie. Who would have thought professional wrestling would be the answer to her unspoken prayers, opening her eyes to what was real and what wasn't? The irony made her chuckle.

A black stretch limo pulled to the curb and a handful of men stepped out. It was an hour before show time, but Bradley always like to be punctual, if not painstakingly early. Good old Bradley. She'd miss him in some ways, and not in others.

"Francine!" he called out, escorting his business associates up the stairs. "These are the executives from Doodles: Bob, Kip, Kent, Phil, and Scott. Tom couldn't come. His wife didn't approve. Said the show was too racy. I told him he couldn't be more wrong."

"I hope she's not too wrong," Kent muttered. They all laughed.

"It's racy enough, don't worry," she said. "Here are the tickets. Bradley, I need a word with you."

"But Francine—"

"He'll be with you in a few minutes," she said to the executives. They ambled toward the gate.

"What's this about?" Bradley said, watching his clients go on without him.

"They'll be fine. I want you to listen carefully to what I'm about to say."

"Can't it wait, sweetums? I hate letting them fend for themselves. This is very important." He stopped in his tracks.

"So is our future."

"These men are part of our future." He gripped her hands. "Now be a good girl and let me do my job so we can invest more money. I have a feeling this is the year for diapers." He winked and pulled her toward the gate. "You'll be sitting with us, of course, won't you, cuddle dud?"

"Actually, no. And Bradley?" She stopped and tugged on his arm until he turned to face her. "You'd better take this."

She placed the velvet box in his hand. "I have to go change for the show."

He stared at the box, then glanced into her eyes. "Francine?"

"I'm sorry, but this isn't going to work. You, me, diaper stock."

He pursed his lips. "Your timing is awful."

"Is that all you can think to say?"

"It's a good thing there's a six-month exchange policy at Smith and Wesson."

She burst out laughing. This wasn't about love or passion. It was about Bradley getting a deal on the bargain of a lifetime: professional, talented, and potentially perfect wife, Frankie McGee.

The old Frankie McGee.

"I honestly don't see what's so funny." He turned up his nose.

"I'm sorry, you're right."

"It's that man, isn't it? That wrestler?"

"Yes and no. It's about knowing the difference between what's real and what's scripted. I've been reading from a script my whole life. It's time to get real."

He scrunched his nose in confusion.

"Don't worry, everything will be fine. You'll impress your clients with front-row seats, and they'll sign on with the newest partner at Lundstrom, Marks and Beetle. Everything

289

will work out just as you planned, professionally. And I have every confidence you'll find yourself a more suitable mate. You're a great catch, Bradley Dunsmore."

She placed a kiss on his cheek.

"I feel like I should say something," he whispered, "or feel sad."

"It's okay. We didn't have that kind of relationship. I hope you do someday. I really do."

"Like you have with your wrestler?"

She smiled. "Go on, get back to your clients. It's going to be quite a show tonight."

He took a few steps away, then hesitated and turned around. "You're sure?"

"I'm sure."

"Remember to check on the Daisy Diaper stock from time to time."

"Thanks, I will."

"And have your wrestler rub cod liver oil on the balls of your feet to keep them soft, just like I showed you." With one last smile of perfect white teeth, Bradley disappeared into Gate Six.

Cod liver oil. She shivered. Now *that* she wouldn't miss.

"Better get ready," she whispered, heading for the talent entrance.

What a joke. She'd never be ready for this performance, especially since it was anything but a performance.

At least he wasn't fighting tonight, Jack thought, squirting his hair with styling gel to keep it under control. Damn, he didn't seem to be able to keep anything under control these days: his hair, his body, his heart.

"Hell," he said to the mirror tacked onto the cement wall of the dressing room. Thinking about it wasn't going to make it hurt any less. He was doing the honorable thing for once, and he should be satisfied.

If only the unbearable ache in his chest would go away.

He suspected it would fade once Frankie was completely out of his life.

Like that would ever really happen. As long as he stayed in this business, worked for Sully, as long as he breathed, he wouldn't be rid of her—the memories of her tight little fist, sweet kisses, tender touches that drove him wild.

At least by staying on he'd made sure she could go on with her life without worrying about her good-for-nothing uncle. The love she felt for Sully was remarkable. If only he could have earned that kind of love from her. A pang throbbed in his chest.

Somebody just shoot me and put me out of my misery.

"Almost ready?" Billings asked from the door.

"Sure. What's the angle?" He grabbed his Stetson.

"Tatianna is going to fight for your honor tonight. You escort her to the ring, then take a seat behind the announcer's table. We figure fans will love to hear you do the mike."

"Sally's okay with this?" They walked toward the Monkey Tunnel.

"She's all set. She's on the card to fight Lucious Leeza."

"That should be interesting." He pictured the petite, large-breasted Sally facing off against the muscle-bound Leeza.

"Oh, I think you'll find tonight's show very interesting. A lot of twists and turns," he said, scribbling on his clipboard.

"I don't like surprises." Jack slowed his pace.

"Hey, all you have to do is talk. Should be easy for a motor mouth like you."

Jack chuckled at the irony. His persona was the epitome of the strong, silent type, but tonight he was expected to add color to the announcer's commentary.

"Who's behind the mike?"

"Prince Priceless."

"This is getting better every minute."

"Just wait," Billings muttered.

"What?"

"Nothing, nothing." His eyes gleamed.

The hair bristled on the back of Jack's neck.

"Bill?"

"There's Sally." He motioned ahead.

She sauntered up to Jack, her breasts spilling over the top of her two-piece costume. All wrong. She was all wrong.

She wasn't Frankie.

"Hey, big guy." She looped her arm through his. "You ready to make some music?"

Leaning forward, she kissed him, but not before he turned his cheek, evading her lips.

"Jack?" she protested.

"When do we go on?" he asked Billings.

"About another fifteen, depending on the heat from the crowd. They're really dead tonight. We might have to call this match early. That's why I want you two ready."

"I'm ready," Sally purred, running her bloodred, fake fingernails across Jack's chest.

Damn, how he missed the feel of Frankie's well-trimmed fingers grazing his skin.

"We're not on yet, sweetheart." He grabbed her wrist and removed her hand.

"You're a real poop, you know that? Here I thought we could have a little fun, like we did in Tulsa that one time. Remember?" Her eyes gleamed.

"Nope." And he didn't. He'd blocked out anything and everything that came before Frankie McGee.

"Jerk!" She shoved at his chest and pranced ahead.

Just as well. Maybe if he aggravated her, he'd be safe from getting mixed up about who he was and what he was doing with Tiger Lady this time around.

"The crowd's falling asleep. They're calling the match early," Billings said, waving Jack over.

He walked up beside a pouting Sally.

"Ready?" He took her arm. She wouldn't look at him.

Good. Safer to have them mad as hell at you than wanting you in their bed.

The music broke, and he led Sally down the aisle. The fans who'd been nearly comatose a second ago, screamed, shouted, and waved signs professing their allegiance to Jack and Tatianna.

But this wasn't Tatianna. The real Tatianna was curled up on a couch back in Boston with her pencil-neck accountant, her perfect man, living her perfect life.

He waved his Stetson at the crowd and forced a smile. Time would fix things. A few weeks from now he wouldn't even remember the fascinating color of Frankie's eyes or the scent of her perfume.

Except every time he saw a rainbow or spied a garden brimming with wildflowers.

He sucked in a quick breath of air. This would pass. It had to.

As directed, he led Sally to the metal stairs, but she didn't let go of his hand.

"Kiss me. After all, we are man and wife."

He complied, hating the feel of her lips, the pinch of those damned fingernails as they dug into his shoulder muscles.

The crowed roared with delight.

He gripped her by the arms and broke the kiss. "Enough," he growled, pushing her away.

Grinning, she acted as if she'd won this round. He was sick of games, manipulation, the whole damn thing.

She climbed the stairs and stepped into the ring, flipping her feathers and wiggling her behind. The men in the audience were practically salivating. Couldn't they see this wasn't the real Tatianna? Didn't they miss the wobbly hitch in her step or the awkward, but determined snap of her whip? Sally didn't even reach for the weapon, tied to a strap around her waist.

Prince Priceless cracked his salesman smile and welcomed Jack to the announcer's table. Jack knew better.

Prince would get in bed with the devil himself if he thought it would earn him a chance at fame.

"Welcome, Black Jack. What a night! What a night!"

"Thanks, Prince." Jack put on the headset.

"So, any predictions about this match? Have you been giving Tatianna some personal pointers?" He raised his eyebrows. Twice.

Jack glared at him.

"Come on, Black Jack. The fans want to know how it's going at the Hudson Homestead, especially in the bedroom."

"Fine and dandy, thanks very much." He directed his attention to Sally's opponent, Lucious Leeza. How the hell did they get Sally to agree to this match? She was outsized by at least six inches and who knew how many pounds of muscle mass. When Sally had left WHAK she said she'd never fight again.

"And here's the delectable, delicious Lucious Leeza. Boy, she looks like she's grown since the last time we've seen her in the ring, wouldn't you say, Black Jack?"

"I'd have to agree with you there, Prince."

"You would? You're actually agreeing with me about something?"

"Don't push it," he threatened. One thing he didn't have patience for tonight was wise cracks from Prince.

Leeza climbed into the ring and the two squared off. Prince rambled about Leeza's stats as former WHAK Women's Champion and Bubble Gum–Blowing Queen for Kentucky. Jack threw in a word here and there, a grunt when necessary, hardly seeing the drama unfold before him.

Bad idea. He shouldn't be here so soon after having his heart broken. Hell, everything reminded him of Frankie. Every time the mat bounced he remembered her uncoordinated falls on her fanny. Every time one of the women threw a punch, Jack remembered her squeak of horror when she thought she'd hurt Marco.

Nothing would ever be the same again. This whole place reeked of Frankie, of the woman he loved so much he had to let her go. Two years? Hell, it might as well be a life sentence.

"Can you believe it?" Prince cried, tugging on Jack's coat.

"Let go of me!"

"How do you explain it, Black Jack? How can you have two wives?"

"What are you talking about?"

"Look! A second Tatianna has just entered the ring. I think someone should be disqualified, but who? Whose side is this new Tatianna on?"

His gaze shot to the ring, where two women dressed like Tatianna faced off. Leeza had disappeared.

"This is incredible! This is the most amazing thing that's ever happened in WHAK, folks. Two Tatiannas! Two! Maybe they're twins. Are they twins, Jack? Did you clone them?"

He couldn't speak. Gripping the table, he struggled to make sense of what he was seeing. He could hardly hear himself think over the crowd's frenzy. Billings hadn't said anything about Frankie being replaced by two Tatiannas, unless one of them . . .

. . . was Frankie.

He studied the second woman and he knew, in his heart, that she wasn't an actress or a twin. It was the woman he loved. Francine McGee.

"Hell," he muttered. How could this be? Her perfect fiancé would break off their engagement for sure, essentially ruining her chance at the perfect life.

Before Jack knew what was happening, he'd scaled the announcer's table and was climbing the ropes. The crowd went nuts. Out of the corner of his eye he spied security form a thick wall to prevent the fans from jumping the guardrails.

Then they were all gone, the sounds, the sights, everything around him disappeared into a mass of nothingness.

He couldn't take his eyes off the woman who stood in the center of the squared circle, a whip in one hand, a leather strap in the other.

A security guard handed Sally a folding chair, which she set up in the center of the ring. That was a first, actually using a folding chair to sit on rather than whack somebody with.

Jack climbed through the second and top ropes and stared at the women. Frankie crooked her finger, beckoning him to come closer. Did he dare? How much more could he take?

He knew one thing, if he got anywhere near her, he'd pull her into his arms and never let go. His heart caught at the color of her eyes, iridescent, tinged with the sparkle of desire.

Please God, don't let me be wrong about what I see in her eyes.

Someone grabbed his wrist. He started to pull away but heard Sally's voice.

"You're gonna have to trust us, Jack. We've got it all worked out."

He froze, staring into Frankie's eyes. So this was part of a new angle?

He wanted out of the ring more than he'd ever wanted anything in his life. Everyone had to read the pain on his face, the heartbreak. Why didn't she just leave?

Sally led Jack to the chair and bound his arms behind his back. He gritted his teeth. He hadn't thought he could hurt any more. Not after letting Frankie go.

With microphone in hand, Sally pranced to the ropes and addressed the crowd. "This woman claims to be the real Tatianna! But we all know that's not true, right?"

The crowd roared.

"So, I say . . . let's fight for him!" She tossed the mike to the mat and they went at it, Frankie charging Sally with Max's winning move, the Ground Hog Grunt.

He couldn't stand sitting there, being the prize they

fought over and yet neither of them wanted. Well, that wasn't completely true. He knew Sally wouldn't turn down a night of crazed sex if he offered it.

But he wouldn't be offering it to Sally or any other woman, for that matter. There was only one woman he belonged with, wrapped skin to skin, beneath the sheets.

Suddenly it all became clear. Sure, he could retire and travel, paint, even move to his cabin in the mountains. But what would it all mean without the woman he loved sharing his new life?

Even when his two- or three-year sentence was up with WHAK, he'd just start another eternal sentence in hell, without love, without Frankie.

Staring straight ahead, he wanted the match to end. His gaze drifted to a group of men in the front row. He recognized one of them, but couldn't place him. The man just stared at Jack, a strange expression on his face. Resignation?

Jack's chair bounced as Frankie went down to the mat and Sally applied a sleeper hold. Frankie went limp. Good, she'd be counted out, and that would be the end of her career as a wrestling queen. So that's what this was about? Closure?

The referee raised her limp arm once, twice, three times and declared Sally the winner. Sally pranced to the corner, straddled the ropes and waved her hands. The crowd cheered.

Until Sally took off her mask. The cheers immediately turned to hisses. They knew their Tatiannas. They'd seen the clip of Frankie being de-masked.

Out of the corner of his eye, he spied Frankie jump to her feet and charge Sally from behind, sending his new partner through the ropes. Frankie raised her hands in victory and ripped of her mask. The crowd cheered, threw peanuts, popcorn, Doodles Candy.

Then Frankie did something he'd never forget: she tossed her mask to the man in the front row.

Her fiancé, Bradley Dunsmore. Jack remembered him from the picture she carried in her wallet.

But Bradley had forbidden her to step into the ring and told her to cut all ties with her uncle or else. Did that mean the engagement was off?

She gripped a microphone. "That Tatianna might have won the match, but *I* won the man."

The crowd let loose an eardrum-piercing cry, which grew into rhythmic chants of "Black Jack Attack."

With a coy smile and sparkling eyes, she sauntered to him and straddled his lap. "Looks like you're mine, Black Jack."

"Sweetheart, I've been yours since that first night you knocked me out."

"No kidding?"

"Nope."

"But I thought you didn't want me, didn't . . . love me."

"I want you to be happy."

"Which only happens when I'm with you." She kissed him, washing away all his pain, all his angst. This was where he belonged, connected to this woman. Forever.

Frankie untied his wrists and he stood, taking her in his arms.

"Francine, I—"

"Ladies and gentlemen," Prince Priceless called over the public-address system. "I'd like to introduce the owner of Wrestling Heroes and Kings, Joe Sullivan, along with former Women's Champion, Maxine the Miraculous."

"What the hell?" Jack muttered, holding Frankie close. He wasn't letting her go this time. Not for anything.

Sully approached the ring with Max hanging on his arm. The pair climbed through the second and top ropes and waved at the cheering crowd. Sully swiped the microphone and motioned for the crowd to settle down. Jack had never seen the man so calm, so . . . normal.

"Ladies and gentleman, boys and girls," Sully began, "it's been a wonderful show tonight in Chicago. Let's hear it for

Black Jack Hudson and Tatianna the Tigress!"

The fans roared.

Sully handed the microphone to Max and shook Jack's hand. Something scratched his palm. He glanced at it. His bonus check.

"What's this?"

Sully grinned.

"Even though I'm sticking around for another two years?"

With a hysterical giggle, Sully pulled the contract from his suit pocket and ripped it into tiny pieces. "You can hang up your boots, son. Although I wouldn't mind you doing some guest commentary now and then."

"What about the mob?"

"A misunderstanding. There's no mob," Sully said.

"You're letting me go?"

"I'm letting you go."

Jack glanced at Frankie. "You did this, didn't you?"

"Yes, I asked him for your freedom."

But Jack didn't want to be free. Not from Frankie.

"Frankie, I—"

"I love you, Jack."

"But your fiancé, your perfect life—you . . . love me?" His chest tightened.

"Without a shadow of a doubt."

"But I'm not a planner. I'm not what you need."

"You're exactly what I need. It's time I trusted my heart. It's new to me, but I'm a quick learner. I've got some money saved up and with your bonus check we should be fine for a while."

"We'll be more than fine." He'd received the news today but had had no one to share it with. "Butch says the fitness centers are finally showing a profit. A healthy profit."

She smiled. "You just fall right into success, don't you, Black Jack Hudson?"

"I'd rather fall into bed with my favorite feline."

"Help! Help! He's lost his mind!" Max screamed, running

circles around the ring. Sully chased after her, trying to pinch her behind. The crowd hollered with delight.

"Get me a minister!" Sully cried. "Where's my friend, Harold Gardner! Quick, before she changes her mind."

Jack smiled to himself. Life was looking pretty good. He wrapped his arms around Frankie's waist and pulled her against his chest, right where she belonged. "Ministers. They're never around when you need them."

Her iridescent eyes sparkled. "Can you marry a person twice?"

"Sweetheart, I'll marry you as many times as it takes." And he kissed her.

CALDER'S ROSE
KATE ANGELL

Dare Calder is the kind of rough-riding, fast-shooting hero who will never let himself be saddled with just one woman. Unfortunately, Shane McNamara has agreed to co-write the next book in his *Texas West* series, and his collaborator is a curvaceous temptress who makes it mighty hard for a man to stick to his guns.

Devin isn't sure which is more dangerous, the Old West or the come-and-get-it look in Shane's eyes. As they corral their characters into courtin', Devin swears she'll leave Shane free to roam the range. But with their face-off more likely to come at midnight than high noon, she realizes no one can prevent a happy ending for their story.

Everyone loves a little ~~meddling~~ help from Mom . . .

A Mother's ~~Day~~ Way
Romance Anthology

♥

Lisa Cach, Susan Grant, Julie Kenner, Lynsay Sands

Is it the king who commands Lord Jonathon to wed, or is it the diabolical scheme of his marriage-minded mama? After escaping her restrictive schooling, Miss Evelina Johnson wants to sow her wild oats. Mrs. Johnson plants different ideas. Andie never expects the man of her dreams to fall from the sky—but when he does, her mother will make sure the earth moves! Jennifer Martin has always wanted to marry the man she loves, but her mom knows the only ones worth having are superheroes. Whether you're a medieval lord or a marketing liaison, whether you're from Bath or Betelgeuse, it never hurts to have some help with your love life. Come see why a little meddling can be a wonderful thing—and why every day should be Mother's way.

___52471-6 $5.99 US/$7.99 CAN

LYNSAY SANDS
THE LOVING DAYLIGHTS

Shy Jane Spyrus loves gadgets. She can build anything B.L.I.S.S. needs in its international fight against crime—although agents aren't exactly queuing up at her door. Some of them think her innovations are too . . . well, innovative. Like her shrink-wrap prophylactic constraints. But they just don't realize that item's potential.

Of course, you can't use wacky inventions to fix all your problems. Jane will have to team up with another *human being*—and Abel Andretti arrives just in time. He will help Jane find her kidnapped neighbor, stop the evil machinations of Dirk Ensecksi, and most of all he will show her how to love the daylights out of something without batteries.

Aphrodite's Passion

JULIE KENNER

Aphrodite's Girdle is missing, and Hale knows the artifact will take all his superpowers to retrieve. The mortal who's found and donned it—one Tracy Tannin, the descendent of a goddess of the silver screen—wasn't exactly popular before the belt. Now everyone wants her. But the golden girdle can only be recovered through honest means, which means there is no chance for Hale to simply become invisible and whisk it away. (Although, watching Tracy, he finds himself imagining other garments he'd like to remove.) Maybe he should convince her she is as desirable as he sees her. Only then will she realize she is worth loving no matter what she is wearing—or what she isn't.

___52474-0 $5.99 US/$7.99 CAN

Baby, Oh Baby!

ROBIN WELLS

The hunk who appears on Annie's doorstep is a looker. The tall attorney's aura is clouded, and she can see that he's been suffering for some time. But all that is going to change, because a new—no, two new people are going to come into his life.

Jake Chastaine knows how things are supposed to be, and that doesn't include fertility clinic mixups or having fathered a child with a woman he'd never met. And looking at the vivid redhead who's the mother, Jake realizes he's missed out on something spectacular. Everyone knows how things are supposed to be—first comes love, then comes marriage, then the baby in the baby carriage. Maybe this time, things are going to happen a little differently.

ROBIN WELLS
OOH, LA LA!

Kate Matthews is the pre-eminent expert on New Orleans's red-light district. It makes sense that she'd be the historical consultant for the new picture being shot on location there. So why is its director being so difficult? His last flick flopped, and he is counting on this one to resurrect his career. Maybe it is because he is so handsome. He's probably used to getting women to do as he wishes. And now he wants her to loosen up. But Kate knows that accuracy is crucial to the story Zack Jackson is filming—and finding love in the Big Easy is anything but. No, there will be no lights, no cameras and certainly no action until he proves her wrong. Then it'll be a blockbuster of a show.

CUPID.COM
Karen Lee

Chloe Phillips has found the killer idea that will save her creative investment firm. Cupid.com, a website that reveals your true love, is sure to be a moneymaker. But soon Chloe wonders if it is more of a cosmic joke. First, the men who view the test product all become bewitched with her, turning her life into a three-ring circus. Then the software pairs her up with AJ Lockhart, the business consultant who's been hired to shut down her company. Worse still, when AJ helps to fend off her unwanted suitors, Chloe finds herself ensnared in a web of desire. Leaving Chloe to consider the scariest option of all: What if her attraction to AJ is no random hookup, but a true love connection?

SPELLBOUND
IN
SEATTLE

GARTHIA ANDERSON

With enchanted blood on her carpet, a house full of Merlin-wannabes unable to clean it up, a petulant cat, and houseguests scheduled to arrive momentarily, Petra Field needs a miracle. She gets a wizard, a whole lot of unwanted sparks, and a man-sized hole in the middle of her living room—a hole into which her feline promptly disappears.

Vorador hasn't felt so incompetent since his days as an untried sorcerer. The girl who leaps after her cat and into his arms causes his simplest spells to backfire—quite literally setting his hair ablaze. And though she claims to be no conjurer, he knows that he's never felt so bewitched, for Petra has a mesmerizing energy of her own: love.

SHOCKING BEHAVIOR
JENNIFER ARCHER

J.T. Drake has always felt he pales in comparison to his father's outrageous inventions. But with the push of a button, one of the professor's madcap gadgets actually renders him *invisible*.

Roselyn Peabody's electrifying caress arouses him from his stupor. The beautiful scientist claims his tingling nerve endings are a result of his unique state, but J. T. knows sparks of attraction when he feels them. And while Rosy promises to help him regain his image, J.T. plots to dazzle her with his sex appeal. Only one question remains: When J.T. finally materializes, will their sizzling chemistry disappear or reveal itself as true love?